GHOST OF A GAMBLE

WICKWOOD CHRONICLES
BOOK ONE

J.E. MCDONALD

Praise for J.E. McDonald

"J.E. McDonald is an exciting new voice
in Sci-Fi Romance."
-Cynthia Sax, USA Today Bestselling Author

"A five-star read about a woman who finds family in
unexpected places, ability she didn't fully understand,
a demon hunter with a score to settle and the small
demon half breed who is, perhaps, the most human of
them all."
-Paranormal Romance Guild

"The intense suspense that kept building was
captivating."
-Stephanie Chapman for Readers' Favorite

"Author J. E. McDonald's debut novel delivers a story
chock full of haunting suspense, humorous dialogue,
scintillating love scenes, and intriguing characters.
The town of Wickwood and its supernatural
happenings are a sure bet to draw in readers, make
them fans, and keep them coming back for more!"
-InD'tale Magazine

"This series starts out strong and just keeps getting better and better. These books are exactly the kind of reading I need: magic, romance, adventure, demons, prophecies, ghosts, and dating apps. Perfection!"
-Lisa Edmonds, bestselling author

"J.E. McDonald weaves the two together so seamlessly that it's difficult to imagine anyone that wouldn't love this steamy and suspenseful story."
-Indies Today

"McDonald's cast of supernatural characters are always impeccably crafted and leave you eager for the next installment of this delightful series."
-Ashley R. King, author

"A fast-paced read with a tension-filled romance and high-stakes plot, Ghost of a Summoning is a paranormal love story you don't want to miss."
-Gabrielle Ash, author of Diamonds & Demons

"A devilishly fun romance."
-Luna Joya, author

More Works by J.E. McDonald

https://books2read.com/jemcdonald

WICKWOOD CHRONICLES

Ghost of a Gamble
Ghost of an Enchantment
Ghost of a Summoning
Edge of a Shadow, Part One
Edge of a Shadow, Part Two
Ghost of a Beginning (Prequel)

GOLDENLACH RIDGE SHIFTERS

Captive Wilderness
Caged Fury
Conquered Betrayal

BLUESHIFT

Star-Crossed Captive
Star-Born Anomaly
Star-Cursed Odyssey (Prequel)

CONTENT NOTES

This novel includes sexual content, some violence, and other material that may be triggering or disturbing to some readers.

A complete list of content notes can be found at www.jemcdonald.net:

To Marcel, the love of my life,
Thank you for your patience, support,
and enduring sense of humour.

CHAPTER ONE

*L*ATE, LATE, LATE. So damn late. Bree picked up her pace as she weaved in and out of the early morning shoppers, her tote bag hitched over her shoulder.

One or two hours she could get away with, but three? Even Theo couldn't be that forgiving. Could he?

The eviction notice she'd found on her door that morning burned a hole in her back pocket, but she tried not to dwell on it while trotting through the bustling morning crowd of old downtown. She skirted around a young family, then bumped into a man with a camera pointed at the clock tower.

"Sorry!" she shouted, dodging between a dog and a bicycle, then breezing past the advertisement board. Her short jog finished in front of Theodore's Bakery.

Bree inhaled the scent of freshly baked bread and thrust open the door. Chimes tinkled overhead. A line of customers snaked through the shop, every table full of coffee-drinking, scone-eating patrons.

"Hey, Fran," she said as she rushed to toss her tote bag on the back counter and grab her apron.

Behind the cash register, a harried Fran, her white hair coming loose from her bun, shook her head, unsmiling. "I tried to call you."

"I turned off my phone." *As usual when I'm sleeping.*

"Theo wants to talk to you."

Bree glanced at the lineup, then back at Fran.

"Go," Fran said, jerking her chin toward the kitchen.

Tying the apron around her waist, Bree pushed through the swinging doors and found her boss taking a batch of buns out of the oven. "Hey, Theo. Sorry I'm late. Fran said you wanted to talk to me?"

Theo's bald head gleamed as he slid the pan into one of the cooling racks before meeting her gaze. "I can't do it anymore, Bree. I'm going to have to let you go." His eyes crinkled with regret.

No. No. No. Not again. This wasn't happening. "I'm sorry. I won't be late again. I promise."

He wiped his brow with his forearm, leaving a smear of flour. "I thought maybe it could work, but you're not made for mornings."

Bree smoothed her apron with shaky hands. "Then I can come later and do the shop work like Fran. I can clear tables and serve people."

He shook his head. "That's what I have Fran for. I hired you for the back and that's the employee I need. I can only hire one other person and I need that person here at six."

From his quiet voice and the hard set of his shoulders, Bree knew he'd already made up his mind. She gave him a small nod and forced her chin not to wobble. "I understand." She stared at the tips of her sneakers. "I'm sorry I didn't do a better job." Being yelled at would have been so much easier than dealing with his disappointment.

A heavy sigh made her head snap up. Maybe he'd changed his mind? The expression in his eyes told her not to get her hopes up.

"Look," he began. "I'll give you a recommendation if you need it. I'll keep an eye out if there are openings anywhere."

Her breath hitched. "You'd give me a recommendation?"

"Hey, when you're here, you're a good worker. It's these early hours that don't suit you."

If it were only the case. Bree's stomach squeezed. Nine o'clock. Ten o'clock. It didn't matter what time her job began. She'd lie awake at night, wanting to fall asleep, *willing* herself to fall asleep, and nothing would happen but her brain playing the haunting sound of the wind whispering through the pine trees in her ears.

Now she'd lost another job because she couldn't wake up in the morning. Her eyes drifted over the pans stacked in the sink, all the dough that hadn't been rolled out yet. Failure made her shoulders slump. She turned to leave, then stopped. "Um, I hate to ask this, but my paycheck?"

Another sigh. "Fran's got it up front."

"Thanks." She pushed the swinging door open and paused. "You were a good boss," she said over her shoulder. The sound of dough smacking the counter followed her into the storefront.

The line in the bakery had diminished, but every table had someone at it. Fran gave her a sympathetic smile. *Guess she knew I was getting fired when I walked in the door.* Bree took off her apron, grabbed her tote bag, and waited until the last person in line had paid. She sidled up to the counter, hip pressed against the glass housing everything from cinnamon buns to focaccia, and gave Fran a half-smile. "I'll get an Americano to go."

While Fran rang her up, Bree scanned the patrons, trying not to let the gloom of being fired set in. She needed a new job or she'd be living on the street in a week. Her eyes darted to the advertisement board full of flyers and posters outside. Maybe she could find something there, something that didn't involve a morning shift.

Fran passed her a coffee and her check. Bree glanced at it and a little of the tension in her chest eased. Just enough to cover what she owed her landlord.

She dug into her pocket for a five to pay for the coffee. She knew she had one. She'd put it there yesterday and hadn't spent it. Or had she? Her front pockets were empty. She quickly checked her back pockets, but only found the eviction notice. Her cheeks heated. Her bank account probably had enough in it for her to use her card, right? It would be a gamble. She swallowed and met Fran's brown eyes.

Fran waved a dismissive hand. "This one's on me. Consider it a going away present."

Bree barked out a laugh. "Like, 'Please go away and never come back' kind of present?"

Fran's hand flew to her chest. "Oh, my, no! I'm just sorry it didn't work out. Now Theo's going to be a person short until he finds someone more suitable."

More suitable. Bree had heard that one before too. The door chimed and a new customer received Fran's attention. Bree lifted her cup. "Thanks for the coffee."

Fran gave her a small smile, then turned her attention to the man in a suit. Bree eyed her check, a hard knot solidifying in her chest. She still needed another full month's rent in three weeks.

The check wrinkled between her fingers as she squeezed it. One option would be to take the money and run. It was enough that if she packed up and left tomorrow, she could settle in a new town and not look back. She'd already paid her last month's rent when she'd signed the rental agreement. No one would miss her here.

Inaya would.

The door chimed behind her as she left the yeasty smells of the bakery. Bree inhaled the crisp air of the street, people-watching as they bustled around her, trying to focus on anything but the unease in her chest. She sipped her coffee, then winced when it burned her tongue.

Rubbing the sting away on the back of her teeth, she strolled the five steps to the advertisement board. Combat boots and black jeans poked from beneath the half-wall where another person stood. Bree scanned the ads. Most were college students searching for roommates. Others were for concerts coming up in the Wickwood area.

The hard knot in Bree's chest mutated into a hot burn. She really needed a job.

Thunk. Thunk. A stapler hit the other side of the board. She straightened. *Thunk. Thunk.* Slowly, she edged to the side and peeked around the board to check out what Mr. Combat Boots had posted. *Probably looking for a roommate.*

She noticed his hair first. Brown with a hint of red, it swept across his forehead to stop below his chin. A dusting of stubble showed through his tawny skin, but nothing you could call a beard. His clothes matched his boots. All black. *He's cute.* Her heart did a double thump. *Really cute.*

Straightening, she stepped around the board to get a better look at his flyer. His golden eyes tracked her, then quickly looked away. He stepped back to admire his handiwork, and she stood beside him, shoulder to shoulder. With her body humming in awareness at their proximity, Bree took a cautious sip of her coffee and read the flyer.

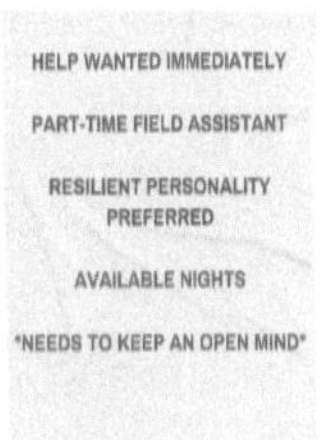

Help wanted immediately. Part-time field assistant. Resilient personality preferred. Available nights. Needs to keep an open mind.

She pursed her lips. "What do you do? Make pornos or something?"

She wouldn't want to star in a porno—not that she didn't have the skills—but taking a leap into adult entertainment wasn't a life goal. But she wasn't a prude and could probably be an assistant.

"What?" He turned so abruptly, he hit her elbow. She managed to hold on to her coffee, but some splashed out of the lid and landed on his jacket with a *splat*.

"Oh my god." Bree set her cup on the ledge of the advertisement board and dug around in her tote for a tissue. "Are you hurt? Are you burnt?"

Eyes wide, he shook his head.

"I'm so sorry." Bree kept digging in her bag. *There must be a napkin or something in here.* "Not that it was my fault, mind you, since you hit my hand. But I am sorry I poured coffee on you." She found a used, crumpled-up tissue, stared at it for a full two seconds, shrugged, and wiped at the front of his jacket. "At least I didn't get your boots wet."

As she turned to reaffirm her coffee was secure on the ledge, she hit the cup with her tote. The cup tipped, tipped... she reached... and it fell to the ground with a dull *thud*. The lid flew off and coffee splattered her sneakers and his boots.

"Oh my god, I can't believe I did it again." *Easy come, easy go.* That's how it was with free pity coffees. She dropped to one knee and swiped at the moisture on his boots. The embarrassment ringing in her ears made it hard for her to hear.

"Please stop," he said, the words finally making it through.

She peered up to see his wonderfully beautiful face twisted in distress. Glaring at the tissue, she grimaced and shoved it into her tote before hopping to her feet.

"Sorry," she muttered. Had she ruined her chances?

Most likely.

She glanced at the flyer. She really needed a job, but if he wanted a fluffer, that was probably a deal breaker.

Probably.

"So, um, you're needing a field assistant? I'm actually looking for a job." Best not to mention she'd been fired five minutes ago.

Instead of saying yes or no, he stared at her with bewildered eyes. She cleared her throat. No change in his expression.

"The porno thing?" She cocked her chin at the flyer. "I haven't worked at a porno shoot before."

"Porno thing?" That snapped him out of it. "What? No." He shook his head. "No porno thing."

From the completely shocked look on his face, she knew he had to be telling the truth. She swallowed hard. Was it something worse? Her mind scrambled to fill in the blanks left by the flyer. Grave digger? Grave *robber*? Neither fit.

No matter what it was, she worried at her bottom lip, believing she might have just ruined her shot at making sure she didn't end up homeless.

CHAPTER TWO

THE FRESH-FACED WOMAN STANDING in front of Zack had him all out of balance. Her pale skin glowed in the bright of the sun. Her forehead furrowed in the most adorable way.

Did she actually seem disappointed by the news that he wasn't shooting a porno movie?

He glanced down at his once-pristine boots. Definitely due for a polish, and his jacket needed another trip to the cleaners. But he couldn't find it in himself to be pissed off. Maybe it had to do with the way her wide gray eyes stared at him. Or the way one corner of her mouth quirked up—like she laughed at herself. Or maybe she was laughing at him. He tensed.

"So, no porno," she said, crouching to pick up the spilled cup and toss it in the nearby trash can. Her honey-colored ponytail swished over her shoulder. "What sort of field assistant are you wanting?"

She gripped the handles of her tote bag with two hands, the words "Bite Me" screaming at him above the pink cupcake decorating the middle.

Zack hesitated. With Amy MIA, he needed someone as quickly as possible, but this didn't look like the girl for the job. "I'm not looking for a field assistant. My sister, Grace, is. It's her company. I'm just putting up the flyers."

His stomach clenched. Grace had said to find someone fast. He hadn't told her it was his fault. He'd spooked Amy with too much of the truth, even though he knew better. Now their former assistant wouldn't answer his texts.

"Okay." The woman in front of him cocked out her hip, hand on her waist. "What kind of field assistant is your sister wanting? I have some experience taking notes and photographs."

How was it that the first flyer he put up found someone who wanted the job? When does that happen?

"I'm not sure you'd find the job suitable," he said instead. She was too cute. Too wholesome. Too everything the opposite of what existed in his world, right down to her boot-cut jeans, pink collared shirt, and the silver bee bracelet on her wrist.

"Well, you already said it's not a porno, so things are looking up." A small frown wrinkled her brow. "Or maybe you don't think I'd be suitable?" A shadow of hurt passed over her features.

"No, that's not it at all," he rushed to say.

"Okay, then."

"Okay," he agreed, getting lost in her eyes and the smile spreading over her face. His chest heated in response. He resisted the urge to rub his sternum to get the sting out.

She rocked on her heels, her eyebrows raised like she waited for an answer. What was the question? *Was* there a question?

She pointed at the flyer. "You forgot something—the name and number of who to contact."

Zack scanned the flyer and swore. Trying to hide his embarrassment, he shoved the stapler into his pocket and took out a marker to scribble his number on the corner of the flyer.

She pulled out her phone and punched in the number. Two seconds later, his phone rang. She smiled. He smiled back.

"Your phone's ringing," she said, pointing to his jacket.

Zack slid out his phone and held it to his ear. He couldn't keep the grin off his face. "Hello?"

"Hi," she said, keeping his gaze. "I'm calling about your help-wanted poster. Could you tell me more about the position and where I can drop off my résumé?"

"Um, yeah, about that." He lowered the phone, feeling like an idiot. If she wanted the job, why stop her from applying?

He'd put up the flyer. *He* should be able to answer legitimate questions about the job—not feel like he was about to scare her off with the truth. Or have her laugh at him. For some reason, he didn't want this woman to laugh at him. Or scorn him. Or sneer. Which was dumb since he didn't even know her name. *Yeah.* He just had to bite the bullet and let her know what it was all about.

He ran a hand through his hair. "We run a ghost hunting business." He got it out as quickly as possible, then braced himself for her laughter.

"Ghost hunting?" Her eyebrows shot up, interest and skepticism entering her gaze. "I've never worked for ghost hunters before."

She said it like it was a shortcoming on her part. *Strange.* But she wasn't laughing. That was a good sign.

"We prefer the term paranormal investigators."

She nodded her understanding. "What sort of fieldwork would I be doing?"

"Well, we have a contract right now with a bed and breakfast, the Granwin House two towns over on the other side of Maybrook. Have you heard of it?" She shook her head. "Our investigation should start this week, and we need someone to take notes and pictures, that sort of thing."

She fumbled around in her big tote bag. "Like I said, I can take notes and pictures." Pen in hand, she opened a small black notebook. One side was full of scribbled sentences, the other blank. She wrote two things on the blank page. He couldn't resist peeking over the edge of the notebook to see. The words "notes" and "photos" topped the page. "What else?" she asked, capturing his gaze.

This close, she smelled like candy apples. He didn't move away. She didn't either. He cleared his throat. "You could be trained on some of the equipment, but probably would mostly be carrying stuff."

She looked down at her list and added "in-house training" and "carrying stuff."

"Anything else?"

"You'd make observations," he said, trying not to stare at her light pink lips. She must be wearing some sort of lip gloss for them to shine like that.

She added "observations" to her list.

"Anything else?"

He shook his head. "Can't think of anything right now." Maybe because he stood so close to her. Her delicious scent made him a little tipsy. He'd always been a sucker for a candy apple.

"What about interviews? Do you interview people?"

"Shit." Zack checked the time on his phone. "Actually, yes. I mean no." He shook his head to clear it. "Yes, we do interviews, but you won't be responsible for those. I have one in an hour and it's a ways out of town, so I have to get going. It was nice meeting you..." He stuck out his hand.

"Bree," she supplied, taking it in a firm grip. "Bree Tisdale."

"Zack Liller."

Her soft hand fit snugly into his. Heat shot from his arm up his whole right side, making his breath hitch. His heart pounded in his chest, and he fought to keep his expression neutral.

Disconcerted, he jerked his hand out of hers. Maybe a little too fast. Her mouth quirked up, and he thought maybe he was flushing.

"Right." Agitated at his complete lack of tact, he ran his hand through his hair. "It was nice meeting you, Bree Tisdale. I hope we meet again." He turned abruptly and jogged toward his car.

"Wait! Zack! Take me with you." Footsteps pounded behind him and he stopped to wait. "I worked for a TV station once," she said, her eyes earnest. "I know how to do interviews. I can take notes, or recordings, or whatever you need."

Was she for real? He hadn't actually thought he'd find someone on such short notice, and he definitely hadn't thought she'd want the job after hearing more details.

"You used to work for a TV station?"

"Yeah. Behind the scenes, but I've seen many interviews up close and personal." She shrugged and nodded at the same time.

People walked on either side of them on the busy street, pinning them in for a few seconds. The sun had risen high enough to warm his face. Though he knew he needed to hurry, he hesitated.

On the one hand, he really needed a field assistant. If he didn't find someone, then he'd be stuck doing twice the work for the entire contract.

On the other hand, if Bree got the job and ended up afraid of him... then what? What was he hoping would happen here? They'd just met and his mind had already gone somewhere it hadn't in ages.

Bree must have seen his indecision, because she stepped closer, met his eyes square on, and said, "Take me with you. You won't regret it." She nodded. "I have a good feeling about this job."

"Really?" Without even touching him, her body heat pressed against his, banishing the chill of the spring morning. He couldn't think of anything else to say.

She stepped back. "I mean it. You won't regret it," she said again, then she crossed her arms over her chest and looked up and down the street.

The self-conscious action had his mouth moving before his brain caught up. "Yeah, come along."

She perked up. "You sure?"

Not in the slightest. "Yep. If you can handle yourself at the interview, I'll let my sister know and she'll probably hire you. No guarantees, though."

"Great!" Her smile could have melted an ice cap. She hitched her tote on her shoulder and clicked her heels together. "Lead the way."

Feeling like this might be the biggest mistake of his life, Zack led her to his car.

CHAPTER THREE

W HAT THE HELL WAS she doing? *I'm about to be murdered.* Bree sat in a car—a really nice car, an Impala, though she wasn't positive of the year, maybe a '68 or '69, all black, with a tan interior she liked digging her nails into—with a complete stranger as he literally drove out of town.

He *had* told her he was going to be driving out of town, but that was beside the point. Her mother might not have given her a lot of love, but what she gave her was good sense with regard to strangers. No hitchhiking ever. And never get into a car with a person who said they had a new litter of puppies.

But here she sat in a stranger's car, on her way to an undisclosed location. Yep. She was going to get murdered.

Bree scooted as far to the right as possible and cleared her throat. "Do you happen to like dogs?"

A slight frown pinched between his eyes when he glanced at her. "Yeah. We always had them at the farm." He refocused on the road.

The muscles across her neck and shoulders tensed.

He cleared his throat. "What about you? You seem like a cat person to me."

"Yes. Cats. Lots and lots of cats."

He looked at her again, a different sort of frown on his face.

"I'm not, like, a cat lady. I'm not even allowed to have cats in my apartment. My friend, Inaya, is allergic to them anyway, and I'd rather she kept coming around, you know?" She couldn't stop the babble spewing from her mouth, and was thankful when he cut in.

"If you don't have cats, why did you say you had lots and lots of them?"

"What I meant was I just like a lot of cats. I like them a lot. As opposed to puppies. Like the ones a serial killer has at his house to lure people to their deaths."

He snorted. When she said nothing further, he flashed her a worried glance. "You think I'm luring you somewhere? Because I can stop the car right now and let you out. I made no mention of puppies, and it was your idea to come in the first place, remember?"

"Yeah, I remember." She squinted at him, searching for any trace of subterfuge. "Why don't you tell me about the person we're interviewing and distract me from my upcoming doom."

He shot her another worried glance. "Okay." He dragged out the word a bit. "Her family lived at Granwin House before it became a bed and breakfast. They owned it for a decade before they sold it."

"Why did they sell it?"

"That's what we're here to find out. She's older and didn't want to talk on the phone. It's been hard to schedule an interview with her. Usually, we have stuff like this done well ahead of time, but she contacted me a few days ago and said it would be okay if I dropped by."

"Does she have a new litter of puppies to show you?"

"What's with you and puppies? Honestly, I have no idea. She didn't mention puppies either." He glanced at her again.

"Good," she said, pointing a finger at him. "That's a very good thing." She wagged her finger at each word for emphasis. "The fewer puppies we have to look at, the better our odds of survival will be."

He shook his head and concentrated on the road.

The further out of town they drove, the more Bree relaxed, which was strange because shouldn't it be the opposite if you were about to be murdered? But Zack seemed as wary of her as she was of him, and it calmed her even if she'd made an incredibly stupid decision to insist on coming along. Bree angled her body a fraction so she could study him without it looking like she did so.

The all-black attire thing worked for him. She could imagine him being full-on emo back in high school, but also wouldn't have put it past him to be a total jock either. He was built under the clothes and had a confident way of carrying himself. His features were defined but not hard, and he had lips to die for. She had to use two different lip pencils to achieve a close equivalent to what came naturally to him. Long lashes too. The jerk.

A fresh rosemary and mint scent wafted toward her whenever he shifted in his seat. Bree inhaled deep.

"You're staring."

She should probably be embarrassed. Instead, she smiled.

He glanced at her quickly, then paid attention to the highway traffic. "Still trying to figure out if I'm a serial killer?"

"Yep." Averting her face, she dug into her tote for more lip gloss and internally insisted the whole serial killer thing was the reason she needed a minute to regain her composure.

Because the truth was much worse. He attracted her. Like, a lot. He had this brooding thing going for him, which was driving her nuts. In a good way. Bree hoped he did something soon to dispel his allure. After all, they were about to be co-workers. She didn't make a habit of messing around with fellow employees. Not often, anyway.

The scenery whizzed by and she took a deep, settling breath. Spring was her favorite time of year. Not the muddy and drab part, but when it morphed into the green and fresh stage, with rain in the air and flowers blooming. It gave her the same "new start" feeling that moving towns always did.

Her phone buzzed. She pulled it out of her tote. Bianca. Her finger hesitated over the green icon, but her stomach clenched. *Not now.* She couldn't handle a guilt trip. Hitting the red button, she dropped it in her bag, then fiddled with the bee bracelet on her wrist.

Zack cleared his throat, and her focus snapped to him. "So your last job was at a TV station?" he asked.

"Um, no, that was a while ago. My last job was at a bakery."

He shot her a glance before returning his attention to the road. "We met in front of a bakery. Theodore's. I saw their logo on your coffee cup. Did you use to work there?"

She slouched in her seat. "Yep." Hopefully that would be the end of the discussion.

"It's cool you go there even though you don't work for them anymore. It says a lot about you."

She straightened. "It does?"

"It says they must have liked you to still be on good terms. They must not have fired you."

Instead of answering, she slouched down again. Silence stretched. She took her time studying the circular instruments and the shiny wooden dashboard.

After a full minute of silence, Zack cleared his throat. "Okay. So they fired you. It must have been amicable anyway."

"Amicable. Totally. The last time I saw Theo we were still talking." Bree smiled, trying to think of some other topic to discuss. "So, working with your sister. That must be dreadful."

Right on cue, her phone buzzed. She dug it out to see the text from Bianca. *We need to talk.* That sounded serious. Too serious for a discussion in front of a guy she had just met.

She tossed the phone into her bag.

Raising his eyebrows, Zack said, "Working with Grace is actually pretty cool. She's a good boss."

Eyes narrowing at him, she waited for him to laugh at the joke. When he didn't, she asked, "How did you guys get into ghost hunting?"

His shoulders tensed.

Neither one of us wants to talk about ourselves. It was going to be a strained car ride then.

Finally he said, "You could say it's a family business."

The tone he used made her think he didn't want to explain any further. Should she ask another question? She felt like pushing. After all, if she was going to work for them, shouldn't she know more?

While Bree contemplated digging further, he slowed the car and flicked on the turn signal. They pulled into a lane on the outskirts of Hewlett. Low rounded bushes and scattered trees surrounded a small farmhouse painted green and beige. Tulips poked up along the edge of a mowed lawn leading up to the house.

Zack parked beside a white sedan, turned off the engine, and gave Bree a pointed look.

"Her name is Selma Rodrigez and I want you to leave the questions to me. I'd like you to observe, take notes, and if you think you have a good question, write it down in your notebook and let me see it before you ask it. It took me long enough to get this interview. I don't want her getting scared off."

"Why would I scare her off? You look much scarier than me."

He startled back a moment, then looked down at himself. "Why do I look scary?" he asked, meeting her eyes.

"I'm not saying you look scary. Just scarier. You're wearing all black and a little old lady might find it intimidating. Out of the two of us, I think I'm the less scary person." Bree opened her door and got out before Zack recovered.

As she strode up the walk, gravel crunched under her sneakers and the spring air grabbed at her ponytail. She heard Zack let out a curse—which made her smile—then hurry to catch up as she hopped up the steps to ring the bell. A gong vibrated inside.

Zack joined her on the awning-covered stoop, muttering under his breath. A lock rattled.

The heavy beige door behind the screened storm door opened a crack, and a head topped with white curls peeked out.

"Yes? Can I help you?" came a strong voice.

"Hi!" Bree stepped forward. "Selma? We're from—" She stopped. *Hell.* She didn't know the name of the business.

Zack took over. "We're from Liller Investigations. I'm Zack Liller. I talked to you on the phone Monday."

"Oh, yes." The woman opened the door wider. "Liller Investigations."

Bree didn't know what she'd been expecting, but the lady wearing go-go boots, hot pants, and a tube top wasn't it.

CHAPTER FOUR

Zack stared at the sight before him and hoped his mouth wasn't hanging open. He let out a grateful breath when Bree took the lead again.

"May we come in?" she asked.

At her baffled tone, he shot her a glance. Yeah, she stood there stunned too, but the twinkle in her eyes and the curve of her mouth spoke of a certain amount of genuine delight. His chest warmed.

"Of course." Selma stepped aside and held the door wide.

The inside of the house came as much of a surprise as the woman who opened the door. Instead of knickknacks, doilies, and floral drapes, the recently renovated house had everything done up in light colors with lime green accents. The furniture in the living room had been pushed from the center, a bright pink yoga mat the focal point. On the TV a twenty-something woman did a shoulder stand. Another quick look at their hostess, and Zack wouldn't have been surprised if Selma had been doing that exact pose right before they arrived.

Selma made her way to the open-concept kitchen on the other side of the living room. "Would you like some lemonade? Some sweet tea? Made some fresh this morning for the girls coming in a bit."

Zack opened his mouth to decline when Bree said, "Oh, I'd love some sweet tea. That sounds about perfect." She stood beside the yoga mat, her head angled sideways to gawk at the woman on the TV doing another convoluted pose.

"She's something else, isn't she?" Selma jerked her chin toward the screen while pouring three glasses of sweet tea on the breakfast bar dividing the kitchen from the dining room. "I don't consider myself advanced, but I'm working on it. The go-go boots make it a little hard, though."

"Why the boots?" Bree asked, spinning around and heading to the kitchen.

"I'm trying to get used to them." Selma shrugged. "Thought if I could do yoga in them, I could do anything." She finished the sentence with jazz hands.

Before Bree could ask another question, Zack cleared his throat. "Thank you for seeing us today."

Selma took a sip of her tea. "I'll be honest," she said as they settled around the breakfast bar, Zack and Bree on stools on one side and Selma on the other. "You only have a short time to ask your questions. I planned it that way just in case you were a serial killer. Obviously *you're* not." She nodded to Bree. "Still not sure about you," she said to Zack.

What was up with the serial killer thing?

"The girls are coming in a bit," Selma added.

"How do you know I'm *not* a serial killer?" Bree asked, genuine concern in her voice.

Selma leaned forward, her eyes intense. "Do you have puppies in your trunk for me to look at?"

Bree shook her head slowly. "No. Just a dead body."

The two stared at each other silently for a moment—then burst out laughing.

Zack didn't know what the hell was going on, but the two women cackling like hyenas—during what he thought was going to be a serious interview—was skewing his equilibrium.

Selma wiped a tear from her eye as the laughter subsided. "I like you."

Bree settled her chin in her hand, pure joy in her eyes, a chuckle on her lips. "Who are the girls?" she asked.

"My dance troupe. We're rehearsing here today. The hall was double-booked and I have the biggest place." She gave her living room a scan, a frown between her brows. "It'll be tight."

"That's what she said," Bree delivered with a straight face.

They broke into gales of laughter again. Zack sat back on his stool and had no clue how to regain control of the situation. If they didn't have much time, he needed to get a handle on things, but the two women were enjoying each other's humor so much, he didn't want to cut in. At least they'd made introductions. If he had to return tomorrow, so be it.

When their laughter had calmed once more, Bree asked, "How long has your troupe been together? What kind of dancing do you do?"

"Oh, we've been together for decades and we've done everything: jazz, tap, ballet, musical theater. A little burlesque." She shimmied her shoulders. "We have a show coming up in a few weeks."

"I need this in my life," Bree breathed, complete rapture on her face.

The warmth in Zack's chest spread further. He cleared his throat one more time. "I have some questions for you about the Granwin House, if you don't mind."

"Right." Selma straightened, and the atmosphere in the room shifted. "Actually, I do mind. I don't want to talk about that house, but you kept calling, so I thought, 'What the hell.' I don't like to rehash the past. Especially about that place."

"Why?" Bree asked.

"Because it was frickin' haunted, that's why. Scared the shit out of me on many occasions."

Zack took out his notepad. So did Bree. When he took out a digital recorder, he waited until Selma gave him a nod before turning it on. "Your family bought the property in 1958, correct?"

"Just after my tenth birthday," Selma agreed, smoothing a stray strand of hair on top of her head. "We weren't from the area, so we hadn't heard any of the stories. My mother always wanted a Victorian, one attached to a lot of land. So when that one came onto the market, and at the right price, she couldn't resist. My father always liked to make her happy." Her face went chalky. "Such a beautiful house. It was supposed to be our forever home." She swallowed. "We didn't last a year."

Zack kept his focus on Selma even though he wanted to look at Bree and see her reaction. "Can you explain some of your experiences?"

"For me it wasn't as bad. I'd heard things, sounds that couldn't be explained away." Selma twisted her lips in thought. "Groaning might be the best way to describe it."

"Like the normal groaning of an old house?" Bree asked.

Zack shot her a glance. She shrugged.

Selma didn't seem to notice, her eyes glazed over in memory. "The house made sounds—the normal sounds a house makes, but not like this. This was above and beyond normal house sounds. Someone might explain it away. I don't know. My sister was affected the most."

She paused and closed her eyes for a moment. When she opened them, she stared into the distance. Zack glanced at Bree, hoping she'd stay quiet. From her expression, he didn't think he had to say anything to her.

Selma continued. "The first night we slept there, Louise had a night terror." She glanced between them. "If you've ever known anyone to have night terrors, you know they're nothing like nightmares. Not even close." Her eyes looked over their shoulders, vacant, lost in the past. "This wasn't bad thoughts flitting through the mind. No. This took her hostage and didn't let go. She lived the experiences. She screamed. They took control of her body and she thrashed, nearly coming off the bed.

Every night they happened, my mother would lie beside her and hold her. Or, I should say, try to hold her. She ended up with a black eye more than once."

Silence descended between them.

Selma still gazed off into the distance when Zack asked. "Where in the house was Louise's bedroom?"

Selma met his eyes, and for a second he knew she'd forgotten they were there.

"On the second floor. We shared. There were enough rooms for us to have our own, but we'd always shared before and I insisted." A shadow of a smile passed over her lips. "Imagine a thirteen-year-old finally being able to get her own room and her little sister making it impossible. I think she was glad to share after that first night, though."

Zack pulled the folded schematic out of his pocket and flattened it on the countertop. "Where was your bedroom?"

After swallowing hard at seeing the paper, she pointed to a corner room on the second floor.

"Did you experience any other unusual activity?"

"Oh, yes. I wouldn't step foot in the attic. Or the basement, for that matter. And I'd often get a feeling of foreboding near the kitchen." She took a sip of her tea and cleared her throat. "Sometimes I thought I saw a woman in a nightgown out of the corner of my eye, but when I looked," she shrugged, "nothing."

Zack noticed Bree writing in her notebook. She showed him the question and when he nodded to her, she asked Selma, "Did the night terrors stay with Louise after you moved?"

Selma shook her head. "They didn't. We had a few hard years after the move. That house took all our money. We moved out, but it didn't sell. We were the suckers who'd bought the property, and anyone who had heard about its history knew enough to stay away. We were stuck with it for years and went almost destitute because of it. As soon as we moved into an apartment in the city, our everyday lives got better, calmer. If we were a close family before we moved, we were extremely close after it."

Bree wrote something else in her notebook and showed it to him. He shook his head.

"Why don't you let her ask her own questions?" Selma asked, some of her initial spunk in her words.

"This is her first interview and—"

"And nothing. A girl's got to learn. She seems to be doing a right good job so far."

So she was. Zack sat back and gave her a nod.

Bree cleared her throat. "I was wondering if it would be possible to talk to your sister directly? Do you think she'd want to share her stories?"

"I'm afraid not, sweetie. Louise died close to ten years ago." Selma placed her hand over her heart. "I miss her every day. Just like Mom and Dad. You never really get over it."

"I'm sorry," Bree said, her face stricken.

"Don't be sorry. Death is a part of life." Selma frowned. "Your boyfriend here already knew she'd passed on. It was one of the things we'd talked about on the phone." She narrowed her eyes at Zack. "Why didn't you tell her before you came?"

With Selma's full censure directed straight at him, Zack was about to answer when Bree did it for him. "Oh! I started today. He probably just forgot to mention it on the drive over here."

"Hmmm." Selma said, keeping him in her sights as she drained the last of her tea. "I'm not sure about this one, sweetie. You could probably do better."

That's what he was thinking. *Wait. What?* "Uh, we're actually not together."

Selma's eyes narrowed. "Since when?"

"Since today," Bree answered with a sigh.

Zack needed to get the questions back on track. "Did your sister ever talk about the content of her terrors?"

"She didn't want to, but my mother pried some out of her. People tortured her in her sleep. Being cut up but unable to move and feeling everything. Absolutely horrible to hear her describe it, and after that, I don't think my mother asked her again. Just held her while she screamed." Selma shivered, rubbing her arm.

Silence hung heavy between the three of them. Bree didn't ask more questions, and for the life of him, Zack couldn't think of any either.

The doorbell rang, making them all jump.

Selma perked up. "The girls are here." She scurried to the front door.

A stampede of go-go boots entered the house. Introductions were made, and before Zack knew it, he held four tickets to their cabaret performance.

CHAPTER FIVE

"SELMA'S AMAZING," BREE BREATHED as the green fields blurred by out the window on their way back to town.

She picked up the tickets where Zack had tossed them on the dashboard of his car and fanned them out in front of her. "I'm so glad you bought four tickets. That Mildred is a bit of a scammer." A cute scammer. Not like she was lying about the scamming. More like she was proud of the scamming, which had been charming in its own way and redeemed her from any wrongdoing.

"Which one was Mildred?" Zack did a double take, his eyes wide. "Wait. I paid money for those?"

Bree laughed. Zack was a delight and he didn't even know it. A frown creased his brow as he concentrated on driving.

"I've never run out of an interview just to get away before," he grumbled and slouched lower in his seat. "I think they were about to give us a free show. Good thing you asked if we could follow up with questions later if we needed to."

"That was rather smart of me, wasn't it?" Bree tucked the four tickets into her tote and turned off the voice recorder on her phone. "But remember, we only have a week to ask questions. She's going on that cruise."

"Right. The cruise." His voice lacked emotion.

Bree crossed her arms over her chest and eyed him up and down. "Are you sulking?"

"No."

"You're probably the sulking type."

"I'm not sulking."

"Brooding then."

"I'm not—" he stopped.

I think I lost the job. Whatever I did at the interview, I did the wrong thing.

Bree went over everything. Selma had liked her. They laughed and joked. They found out good information. They bought tickets to a cabaret. Everything seemed perfectly fine to her.

A long stretch of silence mirrored the long stretch of flat road ahead of them. "I don't get it," she finally said.

"Get what?"

"Why you're mad at me. Why I lost the job. I thought I did well with Selma."

"I'm not mad at you."

Well, if he wasn't mad, he certainly sounded grumpy. *And he didn't deny that I'd lost the job.* Her chest squeezed tight.

Bree didn't think he'd speak again when he said, "That was the best interview I've ever done, and it had nothing to do with me."

She blinked. "Wow."

"I know, right? I've been doing this job for years and apparently I've been doing it wrong. Instead of being polite and trying to make a professional impression, I should ask personal questions and joke about bodies in my trunk. Who knew?"

"You sound upset." *Ah, well. Looks like I'm back to pounding the pavement.*

"I'm not—" He cut himself off again and shook his head. "I'm not upset. I'm just, I don't know, confused?"

"Is that a question?"

"Sure?"

"This conversation is getting weird."

He scoffed at that and shot her another glance. His eyes sparkled like he wanted to laugh when he said, "This is the most normal conversation I've had all morning."

"I'm not sure if I should take offense."

"Nope. Definitely not. Normal is boring."

"You have beautiful eyes."

He looked over at her, eyebrows raised, then refocused on the road. "Thanks."

His startled expression made her ask, "You don't laugh much, do you?"

Shoulders tense, he kept his eyes on the road. "Not in my line of work. I don't find too many things to laugh about."

"Do you live your work?"

"You could say that."

"Don't you ever do anything fun?"

He gave her a quick glance. "Not recently."

"Well, I know about this little cabaret coming up in a few weeks..."

That made him grin.

Bree watched him for a long minute, disappointed the job wasn't going to work out. It would've been fun.

She pulled out her notebook and used her knees as a flat surface to write on. Eyeing the quick shopping list she'd jotted down earlier, she turned to the next empty page: *Why I'm not going to be a ghost hunter.*

It would be a rather melancholy blog post this time, but it couldn't be helped.

When Zack leaned over a little, she angled her body so he couldn't see what she was writing.

Mostly it has to do with the man all dressed in black beside me. Man in black. Not in a Johnny Cash sort of way or that movie with all the aliens in it, (which should really be called People In Black if you think about it.) No. Think Harry Styles when he had longer hair, but a little bit grumpy, and a lot appealing.

She went on to describe, in detail, the color of his hair and the way his fingers gripped the steering wheel. Then his muscular legs and the way his biceps wanted to press out of his leather jacket.

Her cheeks heating, she lifted her head. Houses dotted the horizon as they neared town. Back so soon? She popped her notebook back into her tote. It would have been nice to spend the whole day writing about him. Layers existed in his personality, more buried beneath his reserved exterior. She wanted to dig deeper, find out who he really was—why he did what he did for a living.

"Where do you want me to drop you off?" he asked, straightening in his seat.

Bree resisted the urge to tell him somewhere across town so she could stay in his company longer, and gave herself a mental shake. "Where you found me is great. I have a bunch of stuff to do downtown." *Find a new job. Cry into a glass of Merlot. Eat cupcakes, then take some home and eat more with Inaya.* Again.

He eased into town and slowed for the pedestrians crossing the street. Wickwood was big enough to be called a city, but kept the charm of a small town. The old buildings, which she loved, brought in a lot of tourists. She hadn't grown up here, but Inaya had, and when her best friend moved back for her job at the Wickwood Gazette, Bree jumped at the chance to get out of the town she'd been stuck in.

"Did you grow up here?" she asked as he pulled into a spot near the bakery.

"On a farm past Whitfield Lake." He put the car in park and turned to her.

"I'm sorry it didn't work out," she spoke before he could officially fire her. Twice in one day was a bit much. Not that she'd been officially hired, but still. "It was great meeting you. The interview was fun." She grabbed the door handle to get out.

"Wait," he said, and she turned back to him. "I didn't say you lost the job."

"You didn't have to. I got the picture. No worries. I probably wasn't suitable anyway." She was never suitable.

"I just told you it was the best interview I'd ever had. Why would you think you didn't get the job?"

Bree sat back and crossed her arms over her chest. "Well, you were sulking and brooding, and I thought that meant you didn't want to work with me."

"I wasn't..." He ran a hand through his hair, his eyes troubled. Or maybe they were always like that. "I was thinking, not sulking or brooding."

"Okay. Now that I know what it looks like, I won't get confused."

His features softened with humor.

Bree took a deep breath, knowing she should be honest. "I don't believe in ghosts."

He nodded. "Yeah. I figured that out."

Bree straightened, surprised. "How?"

"I'm pretty good at reading people. I knew you were a skeptic when we first met." He glanced at the advertisement board where his plain white flyer hung in the middle.

They'd only met a couple of hours ago. Why did it feel longer for some reason? A mini road trip was a great way to bring people together. Bree frowned. Or tear them apart.

When she was ten, her mother had insisted on traveling to Grandma's cabin even though her grandma had passed away only months earlier. Bree remembered it being the most painful road trip she'd experienced. She would rather have gone anywhere else than to her grandma's empty cabin. Her mother had said she was being silly. Bree didn't remember too much positive about that road trip.

Zack squared his shoulders toward her. "Tell me this, after listening to Selma's stories, what's your reasoning about her experiences?" All humor left his expression, his face solemn.

Bree squeezed the straps of her tote, going over the interview with Selma, everything she'd said about the Granwin House and her sister, and chose her words carefully. "Well, I believe she and her family went through something horrible during their time at the house, and they believed it was haunted enough to move out and try to sell. But everything must have a reasonable explanation."

"Give me an example."

Bree licked her lips and noticed Zack's eyes dart down, then up. "Just because Louise's dreams happened during the time at the house doesn't mean the house caused it. They'd recently moved, which can be traumatic. They would have had to change schools and everything, leave their friends. All of that can be hard on a young person. She could have gotten nightmares from watching a scary movie. From reading a scary book. Tons of explanations."

If I hadn't lost the job before, I sure as hell have now. But she wouldn't lie. Not for a job. Not so she could hang around an interesting guy with amazing golden eyes.

"Night terrors are completely different from nightmares," he said in a low voice.

Her stomach sank. This was it. This was where she got the boot.

Instead of telling her she wasn't suitable, he met her gaze with a frank expression of his own. "Skepticism can be good in this line of work. It leaves the emotions out so we can concentrate on the data and the evidence."

"Like footprints in flour?"

"Um, no."

Bree tapped her chin with her finger. "I'm not sure where I saw that. Might be handy to bring a small bag just in case."

"We've never used flour in an investigation before."

"You never know, it—"

He cut her off. "No flour."

"Okay. Okay. I get it."

Reluctantly, she brought out her notebook and pen from her tote, turned to her shopping list and crossed off "flour."

Zack tried to peer over the edge of the notebook to read, but she snatched it up to her shoulder and out of his sight. When he slouched in his seat, she asked, "So does this mean I've officially got the job?" She held her breath as she waited for his answer.

"Officially, my sister or her husband, Sam, needs to hire you, but yeah. I'll make sure they hire you."

Bree's whole body tensed. "Are you sure?"

"Yeah. One hundred percent sure."

She gave a squeal and launched herself at him in relief. A job and the ability to pay her rent. She wouldn't be kicked out of her apartment.

Then she realized what she'd done. She was hugging him. In his car. Full-on hugging her co-worker the first day they met and she was frozen in the position. Their bodies were pressed up against each other and she didn't know what to do. For one thing, she enjoyed the feel of him way too much. For another, he wasn't swearing at her or telling her to get lost. For one more thing, his hands had come up behind her and were hesitantly patting her shoulder, and she couldn't get enough of the sweet awkwardness they'd somehow achieved.

After a few more heartbeats of this perfectly amazing, horrid moment of revelation, Zack cleared his throat.

"Oh, my god." Bree shot back into her own seat. "I'm so sorry. That was entirely unprofessional. I was just so excited to get the job." She bit her lip and waited.

A red tinge swathed his neck. "That's okay. I'm totally fine." His voice sounded unnaturally high.

"I'm going to get out of your car before I do something really dumb."

"Okay. That's good. I mean, I'm good. Fine. That's all right."

Bree blinked. Her buffoonery had made him unintelligible. The longer she stayed, the greater the risk she would do something even stupider. Like kissing the stunned expression right off his face. Because, man, he was adorable. Especially when incoherent.

She yanked on the door handle with a little too much aggression and swung it wide. "Okay then. Just, um, call me with the details—where you need me, when, and I'll be there. You have my number from when I called you earlier."

The leather squeaked as she stepped out of the car. She turned back to him, her hand braced against the door frame. "This is probably a weird time to ask, but what does the job pay?" She spoke faster when he opened his mouth. "I mean, I'm totally fine with minimum wage, but what are the hours I'll be working? It said part-time on the poster, but that could be like, three hours in a week or up to thirty-nine, so—" Her words halted when he held up a hand.

"We work on contracts, so you'll get a percentage of the total payment when the work is completed. It's hard to write that on a flyer, so I put part-time. You're guaranteed the money whether or not we find paranormal activity."

"Okay. Sounds fair. When will the job be completed? Is there a set time? Like, by the end of the month?"

"Everything should be concluded long before the end of the month."

Relief poured through her, and she couldn't help but smile. "Great!" She slammed the door and swore at herself internally because of the cringe on his face. "A little too hard?"

He leaned over to roll down the window. "What?"

"Did I slam the door a bit too hard?" she asked.

"Just a little."

"Sorry."

"Didn't break anything."

For once. "Will you call me with the details of my first day?"

"You've already had your first day, but yeah, I'll text you. Should be soon."

"Perfect!" She stepped away from the car. *So much to do, so little time.* Where should she even start?

Giving Zack a final wave, she headed toward the bank to cash her check from Theo.

Zack stared as Bree sashayed down the street. He couldn't look away. The other people on the sidewalk watched her without her noticing. An old couple smiled when she passed by. A kid at a pretzel stand waved to her. She paused to help him count out his change, then turned angry eyes on the stall's operator, waving her finger in his face. The man held up his hands in surrender, then passed the kid his pretzel.

Bree gave them both a wide smile, then continued on her way, skirting around a golden retriever. She spoke to the dog's owner, who smiled, and the man's eyes followed her long after she'd continued on.

Zack frowned.

Then he got mad at himself for frowning. What did it matter if some other guy appreciated her? He'd been doing the exact same thing.

When she walked out of sight, Zack took his phone out and texted his sister.

I've found someone.

The way Bree had asked about the pay made him wonder if she needed money. He was about to tuck his phone into his pocket when it rang.

"I hope you're talking about the job and not your love life," Grace said without letting him say hello.

His stomach jumped at her question. "I was talking about the job."

He wished he could say it was more. Leaning back in his seat, he cranked the window open to rest his elbow on the edge. After their spontaneous hug, he wasn't sure what was going on with him. Or her. He'd had the urge to go all manly and pull her against him and kiss her. Kiss her hard. Not an urge that usually overcame him. Ever.

"That's something at least," Grace said, breaking into his thoughts. "Did Amy call you yet?"

"No. Haven't heard from her since her last text." And she'd been blunt enough that he didn't expect to hear from her anytime soon. *I'm freaked. Need some head space.* Grace had thought that meant something about the Granwin research had spooked her, but Zack knew better.

"What's the new person's name so I can put them on the contract. I happen to be drawing it up right now."

"Bree," he said, and knew his voice sounded weird, but hoped his sister wouldn't notice. He cleared his throat. "Bree Tisdale."

"Are you okay?"

Shit. "Perfectly fine." He shifted in the car's seat and switched his phone from one hand to the other. "Just have a tickle in my throat."

"If you get a cold, I'll kill you. You always get sick at the worst times."

"I do not."

"Sure you do. Conveniently, when there's work to do."

"You're so full of horse shit."

Grace chuckled and he heard a rustle of papers. He could envision her sitting at her desk, equipment stacked neatly and labeled. Everything in its place. All files in their proper folders in the cabinets.

"So the Rivets are ready to do this thing?" he asked.

"Correct. We're starting with the interviews on Friday. Are you coming into the office today?"

"Do you need me?"

"No. Everything's ready, just the contracts left."

"Good." When she would have hung up on him, he added, "And Grace."

"Yes?"

"She negotiated to eighteen percent."

Silence on the other end of the phone. "Well, it's coming out of your cut then."

"Fine." He'd been expecting that.

"You're a terrible negotiator."

"I know."

"Leave it to me next time."

"Will do."

She disconnected the call, and Zack leaned against the headrest and closed his eyes. Visions of honey-brown hair and gray eyes filled his mind. He forced himself to think of something else—to the job ahead, to the last one they'd completed and all the problems they'd had. But no matter how hard he tried, he kept coming back to Bree Tisdale and her smile.

A familiar laugh cut through the air. He opened his eyes and sat up. In front of his car, Bree stood with her hands clutched around her tote's strap and her smile as wide as the store fronts behind her.

"Taking a nap?" she called to him.

"Something like that."

She shook her head and continued on to the bakery. Probably to get a coffee. *A coffee would be great right now.* He'd opened the car door and stepped out before he realized what he was doing.

Sinking into his seat, he slammed the door. He shouldn't follow her. He wasn't a stalker or a pimple-faced teenager with a crush.

He forced himself to start the car and back out into traffic. He had tasks to complete and they didn't include Bree, and he kept repeating that to himself so he wouldn't turn around.

CHAPTER SIX

AFTER DEPOSITING HER PAYCHECK from the bakery, Bree returned to pay Fran back for the coffee, which she refused. She ordered another one to make up for it, would've bought one for Zack too since he still sat in his car, but didn't know if he drank coffee. He seemed the type, but she wasn't positive. She'd only known him a couple of hours, after all.

New coffee in hand, Bree paused outside the door of the bakery. Zack's car was gone. *I'm not disappointed. That would be absurd.* Good thing she hadn't bought him a coffee, though it would have been a nice gesture since she'd spilled it on him right before wiping snot on his jacket and boots.

Bree stood on the sidewalk for a moment, looking anywhere but where his car once sat. She sipped her coffee and watched a fly dance along the curb.

When another car pulled into the parking space, she turned on her heel, strode to the advertisement board and ripped off the flyer he'd stapled there. *No need for that anymore.* With a satisfied smile, she shoved it into her tote.

Happily sipping her coffee, she walked around the corner to her apartment above the pharmacy two doors down from the bakery. Bree jogged upstairs, put her key in the lock, and found it already unbolted.

"Inaya?" she asked, nudging the door open to peek inside.

Her best friend stood beside the stove, her long black hair spilling down her back.

The aromatic scent of the spiced tea filled Bree's lungs as she breezed into the room and shut the door behind her.

"Hey, you." Inaya smiled at her. "Did you get my text?"

A crumpled sandwich wrapper from a nearby deli sat on the counter. Bree set her tote and coffee next to it before digging out her cell. Hunkering down on a barstool, she read her messages.

Taking the afternoon off and going to have lunch at your apartment.

"I got it now," Bree replied.

She'd given Inaya a key to use the place when her friend didn't want to drive all the way home. Or when she just needed some space, since she lived on the edge of town with her parents and three teenage brothers. Some of her clothes were even stored in Bree's closet.

"I'm going to be working late tonight." Inaya's smile fell. "I didn't expect to see you, though. Why aren't you at the bakery?"

"I have some good news and some bad news."

"Oh, Bree. Not again."

"I got fired." She held up her finger to stop Inaya from speaking. "But I found another job already."

"Really." The word came out flat, and her deep brown eyes exuded skepticism.

"Yes, really." Bree yanked the flyer from her bag and tossed it on the counter.

Inaya picked it up, eyebrows raised. "A porno shoot?"

"That's what I thought! But no. They're ghost hunters."

Inaya perked up. "Ghost hunters?"

"Yep. They prefer the term 'paranormal investigators.' And I already helped with an interview and he didn't fire me right away." She leaned forward dramatically. "It's gotta be a scam, right?"

Her friend shifted away, eyes wary. "What sort of plan are you cooking up?"

"If it's a scam, then they should be exposed for who they are."

Inaya pressed her hands against the edge of the counter. "If this is because of your dad—"

Bree cut her off before that line of questioning made her nauseous. "This has nothing to do with my father and everything to do with doing the right thing."

And the right thing would be to stop the Lillers from stealing people's money.

"I was also thinking it might make a great article. You're the real reporter, and this is newspaper-worthy." Way more important than her blog, where she'd gotten into the habit of detailing every disastrous job she'd ever attempted.

Inaya's face softened. "Exposing scammers would make a great story." She hesitated. "You know, I don't believe in ghosts either, but I have seen things and heard stories of the unexplainable."

"Of course. I have too, but there's always a rational explanation if someone takes the time to look for it."

"Hmmm." Inaya didn't say anything else as she turned off the burner, tipped the contents through a sieve, and filled a clear mug with creamy brown liquid. Another aromatic wave washed over Bree, and she inhaled deep.

When Inaya took a sip, she let out a satisfied, lip-smacking, "Ah."

Taking a swallow of her own brew, Bree peered at Inaya over the plastic lid. "So, what do you think?"

"I think," she paused as she took another sip, "if I turn in a story debunking ghost hunters, maybe Brian would stop giving me lifestyle assignments and give me real news stories. Maybe."

Bree straightened. "So you're in?"

She smiled. "I'm totally in. We haven't worked on a project together since college. I'll be sure to give you credit and everything."

Grinning back, Bree ignored the reminder of her failed journalism degree and the stab of regret that followed. Just because her friend worked for an honest-to-goodness newspaper and Bree only blogged, didn't mean she'd hold it against her. Her life choices weren't Inaya's fault.

"I don't really need the credit." Bree set her paper cup on the counter. "I'll just write a companion piece from my point of view on my blog, and I'll be your source. That sounds so cool. I've never been a source before."

"Another one to mark off the checklist."

Bree squinted at her. "I told you, I don't have a 'Every Job In The World' checklist."

"And I still don't believe you."

Taking another sip of her coffee, Bree stared at Inaya, trying her best to be intimidating.

Inaya took a sip of her chai, and stared back with her lips pursed.

The silence in the apartment stretched.

Their straight faces broke at the same time.

"This will be fun," Inaya said with a sigh. "You and I working together on a story."

"You're telling me. You should have been at this interview. It was literally the most amazing thing I've done all week. Actually, wait." Bree dug into her tote bag for her phone. "I recorded the whole thing." She scrolled to her recorder app and pressed the start icon.

"Selma sounds delightful," Inaya said after the recording played for a bit.

"Oh, she is. I have tickets to her cabaret." She slid them out of her tote and fanned them out for Inaya to see.

"We must go."

"We must," Bree agreed with a nod.

They listened to the recording a little more.

"This Zack guy has a sexy voice."

"He does, doesn't he?" Bree set her chin in her hand and listened to Selma's story all over again. Even in this brightly lit kitchen, it sent a chill squirreling down her spine. She shook it off.

"Creepy," Inaya whispered. "She was only ten?"

Bree nodded. Ten. Almost the same as Bree when her Grandma died. For a moment, the heavy sound of the wind rushing through pine trees overrode Selma's voice. That same sound that kept her up at night, even when there were no trees around. If it wasn't the sound that kept her up, it was the memory of her dad's smile, the one so like her own she hadn't seen in over a decade.

She refocused on Selma's voice, not allowing either memory to derail her day. Enough of her nights had been stolen already.

The recording ended with the confusion of Selma's dance troupe entering the house, the sale of the tickets, then silence as they left. She and Zack had only said a couple of things before she'd turned it off in the car.

Inaya's face scrunched with the effort of trying not to laugh. "You stole his tickets."

"Totally." *Sorry not sorry*. She hadn't had any cash on hand.

"Well, this is a great start to a story. I'll open up a shared file online and you can dump everything you learn into it."

"Sounds fair." Bree took another sip of her cooling coffee.

"Maybe don't put anything on your blog about the new job for now? It might be best if we published around the same time?"

Her nose wrinkled as if it had a mind of its own. She'd been really looking forward to sharing her encounter with Zack with her devoted readers, but she also didn't want to clue in the Lillers to her and Inaya's article.

"I guess you're right about that. I can still post my failure at Theodore's, though. Did you know the bakery across town is selling their day-olds for full price? I'll need to warn the good people of Wickwood about it and give Theo some extra business. What about this headline? 'Don't work at a bakery if you like to sleep past six a.m.'" She spread her hands wide like the words were in billboard form.

Brows rising, Inaya tilted her head at her.

Bree dropped her hands and shrugged.

Her lips twitching, Inaya said, "We'll need to do some research."

"Oh!" Bree set her half-empty coffee cup on the counter with a *plop*. "I can do that. I'll look up some stuff online, then go to the library."

Inaya winced, but didn't say anything.

"You don't think I can research well?"

"I'm sure you'll do great research. That wasn't what—" Her lips pursed. "Never mind. I would help, but I have a bunch of stuff to do before heading back to the office. I'll take a look tomorrow."

"Why do you have to work late, anyway?" Bree took another pull of her coffee.

Her friend made a face. "Brian assigned me a collaborative with Melanie and Deanna, and tonight's the only time all three of us can get together."

"A lifestyle collaborative? Sounds sucky."

"Yeah, I thought I was done doing group projects when I graduated from college."

Silence fell as they drank the rest of their drinks.

"Lunch?" Bree asked, eyeing the crumpled sandwich wrapper a foot away.

"I already ate and need to get going." After finishing her chai, Inaya set the mug and pot in the sink. "I'll clean that up later." She scurried to the door and swung her purse over her shoulder. "See ya!"

"Later!"

As soon as the door clicked behind her, Bree scooted over to her laptop at the end of the counter. She might need to research the Granwin House, but the first thing she typed into the search bar was "Liller Investigations."

A website with a black background and white text popped up. *Paranormal Investigators with Unparalleled Experience.* The antique script ran across the top of the page.

Simple and to the point, it detailed services, then highlighted testimonials at the bottom. Not very many, but Bree scrolled through them, each a glowing review of their staff, naming Grace and Samuel in particular. There wasn't anything on specific cases they'd done, or the results of those cases. Or a price list. Just services, the testimonials, and contact information, including an office location in town.

Nothing on Zack, personally.

After hesitating for half a second, she put the name Zack Liller in the search engine. Nothing came up but a social media page. The profile picture had a guy with his back to the camera squatting at the end of a dock, reaching toward the water, fully clothed in all black. *It has to be him.* The man in the image had the same build as Zack.

She clicked on it. The page didn't show much, not even who his friends were, just how long the account had been active. There was one other photo, a landscape shot of a creek at sunset. Nothing confirmed it was his page, but she knew it was him. Her cursor hovered over the friend request button.

She didn't click it. *Don't friend the guy on the first day you meet.* Way too personal.

Clicking on a new tab, Bree typed in "Granwin House." A few search results came up. The first was a link to the bed and breakfast. She clicked on it and was gifted with a color photo of the house. Gray with white trim, a central tower shot three stories high above a small front porch. Triangular peaks flanked either side, one wider than the other. Frilly curtains peeked through the arched bay windows, and delicate moldings framed everything.

"Beautiful," she breathed. No wonder Selma's mother had fallen in love with it. Plus, it had a huge front yard and looked to be backed by a wooded area—a great place for kids to run around.

"Opening Soon" was stamped across the top of the website. There were a couple images of bedrooms done up with four-poster beds and bureaus, and one of a sitting room. It didn't mention anything about ghosts, but had a small write-up saying it was family owned and operated, and the grand opening would be announced soon.

The next item on the search page was an article called "Is The Granwin House Haunted?" Written two years ago, the writer proclaimed himself a skeptic. The man who'd written the article hadn't done much research, only interviewed a half dozen people who lived in the area, none who had ever lived in the actual house. It wasn't very well written, and surmised people would believe what they wanted whether or not the place was haunted.

The next few hits were way out in left field, but one book about local history came up. Maybe she'd find it at the library. Bree didn't bother going to the second page of search results—no one ever went to the second page of search results.

Swigging the last of her now-cold coffee, she typed in "ghost hunter equipment." She wanted to arrive for her first day prepared to make a good impression.

Tons of sites came up. She clicked through a lot of them, jotting items she could afford in her notebook. She had twenty-four dollars and fifty-six cents left in her account after she'd paid Mr. Constable her owed rent and taken forty out for odds and ends she'd need over the next couple of days. Most of the items on the website were expensive, but some she might find at her favorite thrift store.

One thing was missing, though.

Where was that thing I saw about ghosts walking in flour?

CHAPTER SEVEN

THE SCENT OF BOOKS enveloped Bree as she stepped into Wickwood's public library where hushed voices whispered through the air. Her tote bag hung heavily on her arm, full of all the books she needed to return. Several paperbacks slid into the return slot before Larissa, her favorite librarian, looked up from the counter where she helped a high-school student.

"Going to get yourself kicked out again?" Larissa asked, moving toward her after finishing with the teenager, then quickly glanced behind her to the office. The door was closed.

Bree pursed her lips. "That was a total misunderstanding." If Nora Brown, the head librarian, had listened to her, it would have been cleared up in two seconds.

"Of course. So were the other two times."

"Whatever." Bree waved away the comments. "I need to do some research for work and wondered if you could help find some books on the Granwin House."

Larissa's eyebrows shot up. "What does Theo have you doing that for?"

"Um, I'm not working at the bakery anymore."

"Oh, Bree. Not again."

It was both a blessing and a curse that Larissa and Inaya had been friends since they were kids. When Bree moved to town, she made an instant new friend. It also meant Larissa knew about her tragic work history.

A heavy sigh escaped Larissa's lips. "Okay. Let's find you some books." She moved over to the computer station and Bree followed. After some tapping at the keys, Larissa frowned.

"Nothing?" Bree asked.

"Actually, there are quite a few books that have references to the Granwin House in them."

"Great! Let me at them."

"They've been taken out." Larissa glanced at her. "Sorry. They're not due back for a couple of weeks. I can put them on request if you like."

Of course they'd been taken out. The people of Liller Investigations would have them. Bree tapped her fingers on the counter. "What about the books you can't take out? The ones in special collections?"

The mouse under Larissa's hand clicked and she scrolled down. "Yeah, there are a couple." She looked at the closed office door, then back at Bree. "I'm not sure Nora would want me to let you in there."

"Why not? I'm not going to steal the books."

"Of course not, I just—" She shook her head. "Never mind." She took a piece of paper from the notepad beside the keyboard and scribbled two sequences of letters and numbers. "Here are the call numbers. Maybe once you find them, just tuck yourself out of the way." Larissa looked behind her again.

Bree frowned. "Thanks."

Paper in hand, she skipped the general fiction section where she usually spent most of her time and went to the back of the library to the special collections. The fragrance of aged paper and bindings overrode every other scent and she inhaled deep. She set her tote on the far end of the long table, out of sight of the main desk, the entire niche area sectioned off by a row of floor to ceiling bookshelves.

She scanned the books closest to her. They started with 108 and the numbers she held began with 220. She shuffled along, reading their spines until she arrived at the right section, then let out a squeak of delight when she realized the books she wanted were shelved well above her head.

I finally have an excuse to use the rolling ladder.

Maybe that was why Nora disliked her—that one time she'd been in here with no other reason than to climb the ladder and silently sing about books whilst throwing her arm wide in a dramatic fashion. Obviously, Nora had never watched animated features, or she'd be swinging around in here every day.

The bottom rung of the antique ladder squeaked when Bree stepped on it. Tensing, she looked over her shoulder expecting Nora to come barreling around the corner. After a silent and still thirty seconds, she clambered upward, reading numbers as she went.

The books she sought required her to climb to the very top. One was a thick, encyclopedia-type book of houses in the county. The other was a thin, hand-bound book from the thirties that looked like a manual.

Both tucked under her arm, she shuffled down the ladder, then thumped them on the table. She looked behind her again and shook her head. *Larissa is making me paranoid.*

Sitting down, she opened the thick book to the reference page and found the entry for the Granwin House. It had the word "Sheely" beside it in brackets. Turning to page one-hundred–fifteen as instructed, she found a small black-and-white photo of the property sitting in the middle of the page. It didn't do the house justice.

Bree drew her finger over the words as she read the entry. Built by the Sheely family, it went over a brief family history, then who the subsequent owners were until the Granwins bought it in 1891. The article didn't dig any deeper than surface information about the house, but Bree wrote the dates in her notebook.

She tapped her pen on her chin. *Why had they changed the name to Granwin?* She wasn't sure if she was allowed to, but after looking quickly over her shoulder, she snapped a picture of the entry with her phone so she could send it to Inaya, then closed it with a soft thud. The scent of aged paper wafted around her.

Bree turned her attention to the thinner book. It wasn't a manual, but a travel companion for the state. She skimmed the first entry, frowned, and scanned the cover again. *Locations of Import* by C.P. Mullican.

The first entries she read through weren't objective at all. The obviously masculine author noted what the ladies at the hotel looked like, the scents coming off the river, the music playing at the local drinking establishment, poor service at certain restaurants by women who were "hardened with age and strife." Bree cringed at the self-indulgent writing. *The man thinks highly of himself.*

She found his thoughts on the Granwin House in the middle of the book. It wasn't much, but piqued her curiosity:

I'd thought to visit the Granwin House, since it was so close to town. After all, if anyone had read Sheely's Misery *in the well-renowned pulp,* Haunted, *as I had, they knew it as a place of mystery and intrigue. Danger? I had no fear of such. But, alas, my travels did not permit a stop, as I had an interview scheduled the next day with the honorable George T. Shellenberger from the next town over...*

Bree's fingers flexed on the pages. *The ass hat made an excuse to miss the stop.* He'd been scared.

She wrote the words "Sheely's Misery" and *"Haunted"* and "ass hat" in her notebook when someone came up behind her. She spun around, ready to defend herself against Nora. Instead, Zack stood there, eyes lit in surprise.

She sent him her most intimidating expression. "Are you following me?"

He let out a sputtered breath. "No. Of course not. I came to—" His eyes narrowed. "You're messing with me, aren't you?"

"Of course." His chagrined expression relaxed her, but if a guy could get a read on her that quickly, she might be losing her touch. "Came to do some research?"

"Yeah. There were a couple books listed in here with reference to the Granwin House."

"Here they are." Bree pointed to the two in front of her.

His eyebrows shot up. "You're doing research?"

"Sure. I thought I should know more about the place I'm about to investigate." It definitely didn't have anything to do with a debunking article she'd suggested to her best friend. *Nope.*

When he didn't reply, but kept staring at her, she added. "Is that okay, or have I overstepped?"

"What? No! No. That's great. Good initiative."

Warmth spread in her chest. She liked that she might be the reason he couldn't speak more than two-word sentences now and then. To keep from staring at his mouth, she turned to her notes. "Have you ever heard of the 'well-renowned pulp, *Haunted*?'"

He pulled out the chair beside her and sat. His body heat warmed her side as he leaned over to read the passage she pointed to.

"He's referring to a pulp fiction magazine from the twenties, but they only published fiction. Of course, many of them began with 'This is a true story' or something along those lines. I wouldn't use it for research. It was probably submitted by someone from the area, which means it won't be based in any sort of fact, just rumor."

Bree slouched in her seat. Her research hadn't turned up anything useful. Well, except for Zack himself.

"Why did the name change from Sheely to Granwin?" She leaned forward. "Does that usually happen with old houses?"

"No, actually. I've found some other literature on that. By the time the Granwins moved in, the house had such a bad rep, they changed the name when they tried to sell, so it wouldn't scare off potential buyers."

Her gaze kept straying to his lips as he spoke. They were very nice lips.

"Didn't work, though," he continued. "The house stayed empty for many years before it finally sold. Then the next owners experienced the same problem when they tried to offload it."

His eyes lit up as he spoke. Passionate.

Something fluttered in Bree's chest. "That doesn't mean ghosts haunt the place."

"It doesn't." He returned her unflinching gaze.

Lured in by his eyes, she shifted toward him. "Could just mean it was a money pit."

"Could be," he agreed, leaning in as well.

As the space between them shrank, the air crackled with tension, the kind that got a girl into trouble. Big trouble. His eyes flicked down to her lips before meeting her gaze again.

"Hey, Bree," Larissa's voice came from the other side of the bookshelves, making them jump apart. "A hottie just dropped off a bunch of those books you were looking for..." Her voice trailed off as she entered the special collections. She blinked at them. "That's him." She pointed at Zack. "That's the hottie."

A tinge of red engulfed his throat as he gave her a small wave. "Hi."

"Hi." Larissa looked at Bree. "So yeah, do you want me to put them aside for you?"

"Anything interesting in them?" she asked Zack, tilting her chin.

He shook his head. "I took note of all the good stuff."

"Nope. I'm good," Bree said to Larissa.

"Okay. Cool. I'll just leave you to it then." Larissa spun on her heel and walked away.

Bree put her cheek in her hand. "This trip to the library was a total bust. I didn't find anything in this area, and you have all the good stuff. I should probably pick up a couple of paperbacks to make up for it."

"I can also share my good stuff."

Bree perked up. "Really? That would be cool. Where's the good stuff?"

"In my trunk."

"Wait. You keep 'the good stuff' in your trunk?"

"Yeah."

"Oh my god." She looked around even though they were alone. "Don't let anyone hear you say that."

A smile broke across his face. She giggled. Someone shushed her from the other side of the bookshelves which made him chuckle. Without thinking, Bree pressed her finger to his lips.

His laughter died, his eyes wide. She froze. His lips were incredibly soft, and she knew she should move her finger, but she was having a hell of time telling her hand to do it because sizzles ran through her body, and *oh my god* she hadn't moved yet, and it was getting to be a long time and oh shit he started reaching up to—

Zack touched her hand, fingers encircling her wrist, thumb over her pulse. An explosion of tingles erupted through her body. Bree inhaled sharply. The space between them rose in temperature.

Someone sneezed in the main part of the library, and they both leaned back. She swallowed and pulled her wrist from his grasp, keeping his gaze. He let go, breaking eye contact to look down at his hands.

Exhaling a shaky breath, she stood. "I'm going to re-shelve these," she said, picking up the two books, "because I need another excuse to climb that amazing ladder, then we can go check what kind of good stuff you have in your trunk."

When she stepped away from the table, she realized they weren't alone. Nora stood at the entryway, her hawk eyes narrowed on them. How long had she been standing there?

Bree lifted a hand in greeting as Zack stood up. "Hi Nora. This is Zack. He definitely does not have drugs in his trunk. No sirree."

Nora's eyes narrowed further, her paralysis-inducing gaze jumping between her and Zack.

"I'll just put these books back, and we'll get out of your hair," she said, hoping Nora would leave. The librarian didn't.

Her nape prickling with awareness, Bree took small steps backward like a predator had her in their sights, but stopped when Nora held out her hand.

Bree looked at the ladder, then Nora, then the ladder, then Nora's hand. Shoulders sagging in defeat, Bree let out a long sigh and handed over the books. Out of the corner of her eye, Zack swiped her tote off the table and gave it to her as they shuffled past the librarian.

Once out in the open, Zack whispered, "She's intense."

"Yeah," Bree agreed, picking up her pace.

The sensible thing would have been to leave the building straight away, but the paperback racks caught Bree's eye. She veered to the right and headed toward the center of the library.

"I can't go without getting a couple new books," she said over her shoulder, then spun the first rack.

Zack moved closer, the breadth of his chest warming her shoulder. He kept looking behind him as she scanned the titles, adding to the urgency inside her and making her hurry a bit more than she would've liked.

"Oh." Bree snatched up a book with a familiar cover. "I didn't know this one was already in paperback." She tucked it under her arm, then stepped to the next rack to spin it.

In her peripheral vision, Zack tracked someone's movement toward the main counter. But Bree wouldn't turn around and look. *Nope.* She wouldn't give Nora the satisfaction.

"She's picking up the phone," Zack said under his breath. "Why did you say that about the drugs? She's calling the cops."

"That's just your imagination." *She's probably calling the cops.* "This one looks good." She snatched up a sci-fi romance. "If there's blue alien sex, I'm totally in."

"Huh?" Zack spun around so fast his elbow hit the book. Which hit the rack. Which Bree tried to grab for, but she ended up pushing it instead. In the split second it took for her to decide it wasn't going to topple over after all, Zack reached out, tried to stop it, and it leaned past the point of no return.

Bang. Books scattered in every direction, the usual silence of the library replaced by startled shouts from multiple patrons. Bree's arms froze in place where she reached.

A keening sound made her turn and focus on the main counter. Larissa stood with her mouth hanging open, and beside her, Nora's chalky face twisted. Her finger pointed to the door over and over again. Bree finally realized she was shouting, "Out, out, out!"

Larissa mouthed the word "run."

Heart pounding fast, Bree yanked Zack's arm to pull him up from where he'd bent on one knee to clean up the mess. "We gotta go."

He glanced toward Nora, looked conflicted for the space of three seconds, then finally gave in to Bree's urgings. They ran to the exit with her still gripping his arm. The security gate shrieked at them as they dashed through.

The sound of their shoes slapping against the pavement battled with the fading alarm and her heart pounding in her ears. Fresh spring air filled her lungs. They sprinted for a block and a half before Zack stopped in front of his car.

"What the hell was that?" he asked in an almost-whisper, gaze on the pavement in front of him, hands braced on his knees.

With a grimace, Bree said, "Sorry." She gasped for breath. "Nora kind of hates me." *Who knew?* She scowled at the library. *Apparently, everyone else.*

"Kind of?" He looked up at her. "I've never seen such loathing."

"Yeah," she agreed, shaking her head in regret. "I'm going to need to call ahead to make sure she's not working before I go there again. Which totally sucks because I hate planning my life around someone else's shifts, you know?"

His stunned face changed. Small chuckles, then huge guffaws, erupted from his chest. She leaned her hip on his car to wait. He braced his hand on the hood and didn't stop laughing for a full minute. Almost exactly, because the town clock towered in her line of sight, the late afternoon sun behind it making her squint.

Once his onslaught of mirth waned, he stood up and wiped tears from the corners of his eyes. "I don't think I've laughed that hard in my entire life. My insides hurt."

"It's good to let it out."

Zack stared at her, his expression sobering and his forehead puckered. She shifted, uncomfortable with the scrutiny, and crossed her arms over her chest. The book tucked under her armpit almost fell to the ground, but she caught it just in time.

"Shit." Nora was going to kill her.

He flashed her a devilish grin. "I dare you to take it back right now."

That smile did things to her inside she didn't want to examine. "Nope. Don't want to be murdered today." She sighed, staring at the bare-chested alien with forlorn longing. "I'll drop it in the return slot after hours." *Would have been a good read, though.*

Both of them turned when a police cruiser stopped behind Zack's car. Lucas Martinez sat behind the wheel, giving them a measured glare. Bree's heart beat faster.

"Oh, hell," Zack said.

This is going to get awkward. She raised her hand and waved. "Hi, Officer Martinez. How are you?"

"You know him?" Zack asked.

"Yeah. From the last time Nora called the cops." She cleared her throat. "Then after."

The look of curiosity on Zack's face was best ignored, and he didn't get a chance to ask questions because Lucas put his cruiser into park and stepped his long legs out of the vehicle.

"Hello, Bree," he said as he straightened and put on his hat. He didn't smile, but his eyes sparkled with merriment. They'd gone out twice, had fun, and there were no hard feelings. He always said hello whenever they ran into each other around town.

Lucas came up beside them, his gaze raking over Zack, then back to Bree. "We had a call to the station about a possible drug deal."

Bree shook her head. "Nope. No drugs here. Just the good stuff."

"The good stuff," he repeated, looking genuinely perplexed.

"Yep. In his trunk." She ignored Zack as he face-palmed beside her.

Lucas's gaze pierced into Zack. He nodded. "Zack."

"Lucas."

Bree looked from one to the other. "You guys know each other? Great!" She clapped her hands together. "Then let's wrap this up and be on our way."

But Officer Martinez had other ideas. He took out black gloves from his pocket. "I don't have a warrant, but I'd like to ask you to open your trunk." He paused, his gaze never wavering from Zack. "Unless you have something to hide."

With a loud exhale, Zack said, "Nope. Nothing to hide. Knock yourself out." He held out the keys.

"I'd prefer it if you opened your trunk."

"Right. Yeah. No problem," Zack replied, voice flat. He circled the back of his car and popped the trunk. Only after it was fully lifted, did Lucas come to stand behind him.

"That's it?" Lucas asked.

The disbelief in his tone drew Bree to the back of the car. All Zack had in his trunk was a camera, a tripod, and a box of books. "The good stuff!" she shouted and dove for the first hardcover on the stack.

Lucas looked back and forth between them. "Books."

"Yeah," Bree agreed.

"Mrs. Brown overheard the two of you talking about books."

"Yep. In a library," Bree added.

His eyes zeroed in on the book in her hand. "What's that?"

"Collateral damage." She held it out to him. "I don't suppose you'd take it back for me? I kind of forgot I was holding it when we ran."

He took the book, perusing the cover with a tilt of his head. "Ran?" He turned it over to read the back.

"We were kicked out of the library."

Copper eyes flicked upward to meet hers. "Not again, Bree. Seriously?"

She shrugged. "I'm pretty sure if I try to go in there now, I won't be coming out."

Lucas shook his head, took off his hat, and scratched his scalp. "I guess that's that." He tossed the book on his front seat through the open window and peeled off the black gloves.

Bree leaned her hip on the taillight and crossed her arms. "So how do you two know each other?"

"Lucas used to date my sister in high school," Zack said, sliding his thumbs into his front pockets. He shrugged.

"She dumped me," Lucas supplied.

"She dumped everyone," Zack said, then added, "until Sam."

"Yeah. Beautiful women make a habit of dumping me," Lucas said, and Bree shifted as he looked between her and Zack. "How do you two know each other?"

"I'm going to work at Liller Investigations," Bree answered, gauging his reaction. If he knew the Lillers, did he know about their business? Why would a cop be okay with scammers running around his city?

Lucas's eyebrows rose, and silence descended between the three of them. Sucking in a quick breath, she waited for him to call Zack out.

But after a moment, he said to Zack, "Good to see you." He jerked his chin toward Bree. "Be careful of this one." Amusement crinkled the corners of his eyes.

She broke his knowing look to inspect the glossy black paint above the taillight, and released her jittery breath slowly.

"You two stay out of trouble." Lucas stuck out his hand to Zack. "Say hello to Grace for me."

"Will do," Zack replied as he shook it.

Lucas gave them a salute and slid into the front seat of his car.

"This has been an interesting day," Zack said while Bree watched the cruiser roll down the block. It stopped in the "No-Parking" zone in front of the library.

She felt Zack's eyes on her, but kept her gaze toward the library. It seemed like a pretty normal day to her. Except for the fact that she lusted after a guy she just met. She hadn't done that for a while. Well, not since Lucas, actually, and that had been a fairly brief relationship, and nothing close to the heat she'd been feeling for the man beside her since this morning.

It made her question the whole scammers angle. She wouldn't find a con-artist attractive, would she? But what other explanation could there be for a ghost hunting company?

"Why did you get kicked out of the library before?" he asked, breaking the silence.

Bree finally looked at him. "Which time?"

"There's been more than one?"

Like that's unusual. "Well, the first time was because Nora thought I was stealing books. I had two books in my bag—which I'd bought at the bookstore, thank you very much—and the security gate beeped, and she was convinced I'd somehow taken their numbers off or something. She called the cops. I met Lucas that day."

The man in question exited the library, waved at them, and jumped into his cruiser.

She glanced at Zack. His brow crinkled the longer he stared at her. "I had the receipt," she added in case he didn't believe her, since she'd technically just stolen a book from the library.

A strained silence descended between them and Bree took a deep breath, preparing herself for what he'd say next.

"Come out to dinner with me."

Her breath left her like a half-inflated balloon escaping a child. "Come again?" She'd been pretty sure he'd been about to tell her she wasn't suitable for the job anymore, not ask her out.

"Dinner." He nodded once.

She tilted her head and rested both butt cheeks on the bumper of his car. "Like, as in a date?"

"Yeah."

He wouldn't stop looking at her, and she liked it. A lot. It made her all warm and tingly in all the right places. She grinned. "I'd love some dinner."

CHAPTER EIGHT

Z ACK KEPT ASKING HIMSELF what the hell he was doing. He should have gone home. He should have stayed away from Bree and kept it professional. He shouldn't have used any excuse to remain in her company for another hour or two.

The light from her phone brightened her features as she swiped through local restaurants, shaking her head at one, then another.

"You know," he began. Her head snapped up and she met his gaze. "We could go there." He jerked his chin toward the fancy French restaurant across the street called De Bon Gout.

She immediately shook her head. "Nope. No way."

"You don't like French food?"

"I love every kind of food, but that place is way too expensive." Her brows pinched together. "Well, I guess we could, but then we'd have to go Dutch, because I don't want you to think I'll have sex with you if I order the lobster."

His head jerked back. "I wouldn't—" He stopped speaking when she grinned at him. "You're messing with me again."

"You're fun," she sighed, then returned her attention to her phone. She flipped through a couple more places, then straightened. "I've been going about this the wrong way. We don't need a restaurant. We need a truck."

"A truck?" *Call me confused.*

"A food truck. I have an app that tracks them all." She changed from her web browser to the app, and did a little hop when it opened up. "Zulu's is out. Have you ever been?"

He shook his head, but couldn't help but smile at her enthusiasm.

"The best hot dogs on the planet. Guaranteed."

"On the planet? Are you sure?"

"Very."

"Have you tried all the other hot dog food trucks to compare?"

"No. That would be close to impossible. But it says 'Best hot dogs on the planet' on their truck, and why would they lie?"

That made him laugh. "Should we take my car?"

She shook her head. "It's just across the river. Fancy a walk?" She stuck out her elbow like she wanted him to hook his arm in hers. "We can cut across the train bridge."

How could he resist? "I'd love a walk." He stepped close and carefully slid his arm through hers.

For a second, when their sleeves touched, her smile faltered, but then she smiled big again. Arm yanking his, off they went.

They strolled at a leisurely pace, the hum of traffic drifting away, taken over by the more organic sounds of the riverbank: swishing grass, dogs barking, bikes passing them by. Bree steered them to one of the paved paths running parallel to the waterway.

The crisp of the evening settled into the air, the full heat of summer still a long way off. Zack liked spring, the green and newness of it, better than blazing temperatures. While they walked, he kept noticing how their hips would bump every so often, how the sides of their bodies warmed each other.

Their combined silence gave him time to think—and time to watch her out of the corner of his eye. Bree had let her hair down from its ponytail, and the honey-colored tresses moved silkily about her shoulders. Her eyes scanned their surroundings, lips curling into a smile when her eyes snagged on something she seemed to enjoy. He resisted the urge to tug on her elbow, to draw her closer and soak up more of her vivacity.

His mind returned to earlier. Had Bree and Lucas dated? Was there history between them? It wasn't Zack's business to ask, no matter how much she captivated him. He didn't have a claim to her, but it didn't stop him from being curious.

He cleared his throat to break the silence. "I should probably reiterate I would never expect you to sleep with me even if I paid for everything and you got the lobster."

She tilted her head up at him. "Really?"

He sent her one measured nod.

"Well, in that case, we should go back, and I'll get the lobster, and you can pay."

He stopped, their elbows tugging tight which made her stop too. "You want to turn around?"

"Hell, no. I'm totally married to Zulu's at this point." She smiled and marched onward, nudging him along.

Other couples passed them in the opposite direction. A woman jogged with her dog, and a bike whizzed by from behind, heading toward the bridge.

Then Bree said, "Actually, I don't like seafood, so you would've been good either way."

"Why don't you like seafood?" he asked, genuinely interested.

"I worked at a seafood market when I lived on the East Coast. Kind of ruined it for me. If it's in a crab dip or soup, then it's doable, but I can't have it staring at me." She shuddered, and the movement reverberated through his body, igniting his nerve endings.

"When did you live on the coast?"

"After high school. I wanted to see the country, so I got on a bus to visit a friend and ended up staying there for a year." A grin took over her features. "It was an interesting year."

"What else did you do there?"

"What *didn't* I do would be the better question." Her lips pursed in thought. "I was a temp, I bussed tables, that's also when I worked at the TV station." Her shoulders lifted in a shrug. "Lots of things." She tilted her head at him, her eyes narrowed. "Are you trying to get to know me better?"

Hoping he wasn't blushing, he nodded. "Yeah."

"Well, if you're getting to know me better, it's only fair for me to get to know you better, right?"

"I guess so." *This is a bad idea.*

"And since you asked me some questions, it's my turn."

Seeing her brow pinch in thought, Zack braced himself. He knew what her first question was going to be: How did you get into paranormal investigations? He readied himself to give her the roundabout answer he gave everyone. Knowing her this short time, she probably wouldn't stand for it. *This is going to get awkward.*

She leaned forward. "Bungee jumping or skydiving?"

"Um." It took him a moment to clear all the answers he'd had lined up in his head. "You mean which would I rather do?"

"No. I mean which do you prefer? Personally, I like skydiving better. I'm not sure why I put more trust in a parachute than a rubber band, but the whole time I was bungee jumping I kept thinking I would die. It could have had something to do with the jagged rocks at the bottom of the ravine. But when I went skydiving, I just enjoyed the ride, you know? Maybe it was because I was attached to the instructor tandem style, so I kinda knew she wouldn't let me die." She gave his elbow a gentle tug of encouragement. "So which one do you like better?"

He cleared his throat. "I haven't done either."

"We might need to remedy that. Which do you *think* you'd prefer, then?"

"Jumping out of a perfectly good airplane or jumping over jagged rocks. That's a tough choice."

"I know, right?" She brushed a stray hair away from her face. "Give it some thought and we'll do whichever one you pick for our second date."

He slowed their pace and turned to see her better. "Are we having a second date?"

"Honestly, I'm not sure, but if there's skydiving involved, I'd probably tough out the ordeal just to go."

A laugh wanted to erupt from his chest. "Being with me is an ordeal?"

"Not yet, but you never know. We'll have to see how the rest of the night goes."

She truly fascinated him. All he wanted to do was get to know her more. And more. And more.

"I get another one," she declared as she peered up at him. The path branched off, one way heading toward the bridge, the other continuing along the river. "What's your weirdest scar and how did you get it?" They took the path toward the bridge, stepping to the side when a bicycle came their way.

"If I answer this one, you have to answer it too."

She smiled. "For sure. All's fair as the saying goes."

Was this love or war?

After a moment's hesitation, he lifted his hair away from his forehead. They paused on the path and she leaned toward him to get a better look at the crescent shaped scar above his eyebrow. He let his hair drop. "When I was six, I thought I was the best swimmer ever. Like a total idiot, I dove into shallow water and bashed my head on some rocks."

Her hand flew to her mouth. "Oh my god. You could have died. I've definitely heard of people dying from that."

"Yeah. That's basically what my parents kept drilling into me for the next decade." He learned his lesson and then some. "What's yours?" They continued walking, elbows linked as if it were the most natural thing in the world.

She grimaced. "You know those things you put on the ground with the water sprinkler and you run and slide on, but it's just a piece of thin plastic?"

"A Slip and Slide?"

"Right! So my sister and I set one up in our backyard, and we have a bit of a hill, and I slid way too fast and ended up smashing into a tree."

"So where's the scar?"

"On my thigh."

When she didn't say anything else, he gave her the "go on" gesture with his hand. They stopped on the last bit of the path before the stairs up to the bridge, and she put her hands on her hips.

"I showed you mine," he said, managing to keep a straight face.

She angled her chin at him. "Yours was on your forehead. That's a bit different than me dropping my pants right now." Her eyes scanned the area.

People took advantage of the lovely evening before the sun set completely, one family tossing a Frisbee with their dog. Others strolled or jogged.

"I don't see the difference." Zack made sure there was a healthy dose of "I dare you" in his tone.

Her eyes sparkled back at him. When she let go of his arm and reached for the button of her jeans, his heart stopped. Never in a million years did he think she'd actually drop her pants in the street. He should have known better.

"No. Don't." His hand stilled hers, and his fingers brushed the warm, soft skin just above her navel. "I was kidding."

"Are you sure?" Her eyes dared him to take her up on it. "Because I've never been one to back down from a challenge."

He shook his head slowly. "You win." He pulled her hand away from her body, but kept hold of her fingers.

A brilliant smile beamed back at him. "I didn't know it was a contest, but it's cool I've won." Keeping hold of his hand, she turned toward the stairs.

His chest squeezed at the intimacy of the gesture and the electrifying sensation of her skin against his. The wooden stairs creaked beneath their feet and the air cooled the higher they went.

"Tell me more about your time on the coast," he said, his breaths becoming shorter from the way his heart kept leaping into his throat.

"Well, my friend's apartment was smack dab in the middle of a French community," she said, giving his fingers another tug, "so I got a lot of practice. My conversational French improved by going to the corner store." Her brow pinched. "Someone once told me I have an ear for languages."

"How many do you speak?"

Her expression cleared of worry. "I know some Spanish and German. I'd like to learn Japanese. Maybe I'll travel there next." A faraway expression consumed her face.

"You have itchy feet?"

"I don't think so." She stopped and glanced at her shoes. "I use that athlete's foot stuff every day."

He balked. "I didn't mean—" When she grinned, he shook his head at her. "You're laughing at me again."

"Yep." Her fingers entwined with his and they resumed their climb.

He couldn't resist giving her hand a quick squeeze. She cast him a glance, cheeks pink. He wasn't sure if her high color was because they held hands, or because they had climbed four flights of stairs. By the time their feet slapped against the top step, both of them were breathing hard.

"Almost there." A bounce lived in her steps despite the climb. Bree pulled him along the tracks. No train crossed at the moment, but the walkway was full of people either soaking in the view or taking a shortcut.

The breeze off the river had their hair lifting and swirling. Bree's was so long it would sometimes brush his cheeks. He shivered at the sensation.

The narrow walkway forced them to move one in front of the other to let others pass. Made of oak planks and attached to the side of the rails only a handful of feet away from the tracks, the thing was a bit sketchy. Zack had always felt precariously close to the speeding train and avoided being on it at the same time at all costs.

When another couple came toward them, Zack let Bree precede him while still holding her hand. It wasn't until the couple drew closer that recognition hit. Dread settled low in his stomach.

"You!" Douglas Walsh shouted when they made eye contact.

In front of him, Bree twitched, then came to a stop. She sent Zack a glance over her shoulder, eyes wide. He tugged gently on her hand, shielding her behind him.

Douglas stormed toward them, his wife trailing behind. "You owe me five grand, you worthless piece of—"

"Excuse me!" Bree said loudly, coming to stand beside Zack. "How dare you?"

Her shout made Douglas stop and hesitate before the man refocused on Zack. "I'll win the court case, smear your names across the state." His voice was less forceful, but still hostile. "You and your sister. You backstabbing—"

"What's with the name calling, sir?" Bree said loudly, stepping forward, hands on her hips. "Are you eight years old or something?"

The wind whipped at her hair, her cheeks turned bright pink, and her eyes flashed. Zack's heart rate accelerated at the sight. He thought he should probably step in front of her and take over, but he was pretty sure she'd take the lead again.

Straightening, Douglas looked over the crowd that had gathered. The four of them created a bottleneck on the walkway, no one able to pass by. Awkwardly, Douglas moved to the side so a bike and a man with a dachshund could go the one way, and a couple with a stroller could go the other. Everyone gave them cautious glances as they passed.

"We're doing fine here, folks," Bree said when one man hesitated beside them, concern in his eyes. "This gentleman and his lady are going to mosey on their way, aren't they?" She sent Douglas a death glare.

Douglas's eyes narrowed at Zack. "This isn't over," he said. He stormed away, his wife keeping her head down as she followed.

"Yeah, you better keep walking," Bree muttered. She watched them for a full minute before she grabbed Zack's arm. "Let's go."

Zack replayed the scene over in his head as they finished crossing the bridge. He hadn't had to do anything. Bree had taken care of it all—an angel of righteousness holding a fiery blade. Had he ever met anyone like her before? He didn't think so.

Actually, he did know. Without a doubt, he'd never met anyone like her.

Bree's hand on his arm, he took her fingers into his. It grounded him, and the tension in his chest dissipated. He entwined their fingers, holding tight. When Bree looked at him through her eyelashes, he forgot how to breathe.

CHAPTER NINE

I N THE RECEDING LIGHT of the pink and purple sunset, she and Zack waited at the end of a massive line. Zulu's, the most popular food truck in town, topped its hot dogs with the strange and the gourmet. The excited chatter ahead of them underscored the reputation of its iconic menu.

They stood a foot apart. Somewhere on the last leg of the walk, they'd stopped holding hands and Bree tried to find a reason to take hold of Zack's again. Because she really, really, wanted to hold his hand.

"Are you sure you don't want to go anywhere else?" Zack asked as the wind lifted his hair away from his forehead, exposing a bit of his scar. "Might be waiting a while."

"Zulu's dogs are worth the wait."

His eyes twinkled while the sounds of the river drifted to them when the wind shifted directions. The food truck had stopped next to a popular skate park. The *whoosh whoosh* of skateboard wheels mixed in with the conversations of the people waiting for their evening munchies.

A man shouted when someone's order was ready. The line shifted, and they shuffled up a foot.

"So..." Bree began.

"So..." he repeated back to her. "I suppose I owe you an explanation about what just happened."

She opened her mouth to say he didn't have to, then snapped it closed. This was the stuff she needed to find out for her blog and Inaya's article. Part of her believed he couldn't possibly be part of a scamming operation. She liked him. A lot. The man oozed sweet and genuine like a cinnamon bun.

But despite her knee-jerk defense of Zack, the situation on the bridge had created a nauseous swirl in the pit of stomach and supported her original assumption.

He cleared his throat. "We had a contract with Douglas and his historic hotel a few months ago. He wasn't happy with our results."

What did that mean? Bree held her breath, wanting him to tell her more, but scared that if she asked, he might clam up. The handle of her tote bunched between her fingers.

Zack stared over the heads of the people in line toward the food truck. He didn't meet her eyes until a minute later when he said, "Sometimes clients expect outcomes from us we aren't willing to give. We have a reputation for being fair and honest, and sometimes it means people aren't happy at the end of a contract."

Fair and honest? Those weren't words she would attribute to ghost hunting. Bree searched his gaze for the lie. Wasn't it all smoke and mirrors? Didn't they feed into people's fears and "rid" the house of spirits so the clients could get on with their lives? If that were the case, why would anyone be mad at them? Unless, of course, they thought the "ghostly occurrence" continued.

His expression changed, like he debated whether or not he should go on, but then said, "Douglas wanted his hotel to be certified haunted to attract more customers, but when we got there, nothing we investigated came up paranormal. On top of that, he..." Zack hesitated. "...did some things to convince us there were spirits at work. We found him out, and he got mad—demanded we give him a full refund. It's become a legal matter, but our court date isn't for a while yet."

Bree's brain stalled at the first part of that explanation. "What do you mean by 'certified haunted'?"

Another name was called out from the food truck. They shuffled forward.

"That's what we do. We confirm if there's true paranormal activity, and if there is, we issue a certificate. It's also why we have to be absolutely certain it *is* haunted. Our reputation is on the line every time we award one."

Bree blinked. Then blinked again. "People want their properties to be haunted." Her words came out flat.

"Yeah." A slow smile quirked at the corner of his mouth. "You appear to have a problem processing that."

Ya think? "What makes you say that?"

"You're not talking very much."

She narrowed her eyes and gave him a playful slap on the shoulder.

"Ouch," he said, rubbing where she'd hit him, but his eyes brimmed with mirth.

They shuffled forward.

"So, this bed and breakfast we're investigating," Bree said after a minute, "they want it to be haunted? They want this certificate thing?"

"Yeah."

"That's just..." She searched for the right word. "That's just weird."

His smile fell. "Not in my world," he muttered, turning away from her to stare at the food truck.

She could tell she'd hit a sore spot and rushed to add, "I can't figure out why someone would want to live with ghosts—if they *are* real. I mean, wouldn't it be better to get rid of them?"

"Sometimes people want them gone." He didn't look at her when he answered, and they took another step forward. "We don't do it often. We need to call in colleagues of ours, specialists, if that happens."

"What kind of specialists?"

He didn't answer right away, and she hated that she kept putting a wedge between them with her words. But this was new territory for her, and she couldn't help but be curious.

Yesterday, she would have said with one hundred percent certainty there were no such thing as ghosts. After meeting Zack, and experiencing his belief in his job, she would say she was ninety-nine percent sure there were no such thing as ghosts. That one percent grew stronger with every moment she spent with him. It didn't want him to be a scam artist, and neither did she.

"We know mediums, priests, a demonologist." He hesitated again. "A witch—they're from all over the country so it depends where we are and what the problem is."

"A witch?" She tried not to sound too skeptical. Ghosts were one thing...

"She's a good witch."

"Of course. I wouldn't think you the type to associate with bad ones."

He cocked an eyebrow at her—probably wondering if she was about to laugh her head off at him or not. She wasn't. She could tell he believed in what he told her. Whether or not it was true, his certainty of it meant something to her.

"So..." she said, trying to think of a change of topic.

"So..." He took a breath. "You have a sister too. Just the one?"

She tensed, then forced her shoulders to relax. "Yep. Just the one sister. A twin, actually." She touched her bracelet, giving it a twirl.

His eyebrows shot up. "Cool. Do you look alike?"

She laughed, but knew it didn't come out genuine. "Not at all. We're fraternal. She's blonde and takes after our mother. I take after our father." She shrugged. *Please let that be the end of that line of questioning.*

A strained silence descended between them. Zack didn't ask any follow-up questions, and eventually her breathing evened out.

They shuffled forward, nearly at the front of the line. She noticed how tense he grew after mentioning the guy who had shouted at them on the bridge. The tension lingered, even after discussing her sister, likely his attempt to change the subject. The least she could do was try to recapture their earlier light mood.

"I have a challenge," she said, bouncing on her toes.

He squinted at her, his gaze wary. "What sort of challenge?"

"I'll order your hot dog and you order mine. We'll try to see if we get each other's orders right just from knowing each other for one day."

"What if we order something the other hates?"

Bree shrugged.

He stared.

"What are you?" she taunted. "Chicken?"

His shoulders straightened. "You're on."

"Great!" She jumped and clapped her hands together. "I only have one addendum."

"What's that?"

"You have to order me the biggest dog. I'm hungry."

"Not a problem."

There was only one couple ahead of them in line now, making the menu easy to read. Zack kept looking at her, then looking at the menu, then back at her.

She grinned, already gleeful at how this would turn out. Whether good or bad, at least it would be interesting.

The couple stepped to the side and Zack moved up to the window. "Name on the order?" the woman asked, her eyes fixed on the notepad in front of her.

"Bree," Zack answered.

The woman raised an eyebrow, and wrote the name down. "What'll you have?"

Bree sneaked up behind him, wondering what he'd pick with so much to choose from. Hot dogs with pickles, chips, chili, coleslaw, Caesar salad—the choices were endless. Or there was always a plain dog. *Boring.*

Zack cleared his throat. "Large chili cheese fries, extra cheese please."

Nice. Bree kept her face blank when he turned to look at her, not wanting to let on to her internal happiness. He paid then stepped to the side.

She sidled up to the window.

"Name?" the lady asked.

"Zack."

No eyebrow rose this time. Instead, a smirk pulled up one corner of the woman's lips. "What'll you have?"

"Large Sauerbraten, please."

Turning quickly to him, she tried to gauge his reaction. Those beautiful golden eyes remained blank with not so much as a hint of a smile dimpling his cheeks.

She narrowed her eyes. Had she made a mistake? He came across as a meat and potatoes kind of guy. The German-inspired dog felt like a good choice. Maybe he was a plain old mustard kind of guy. Both kind of fit.

Bree paid the lady, only lamenting the loss of eight dollars for a moment before they shuffled to the pickup window. The dent to her minuscule budget was worth it if she got to spend more time with Zack. She'd just need to be extra thrifty with her shopping tomorrow.

They both stayed quiet as they waited for their orders with the people who'd ordered before them, watching the skateboarders grind and catch air. Bree fiddled with the strap of her tote. Maybe he was a vegetarian? Nah. Maybe he was deathly allergic to a food in her choice? He would have said something. Wouldn't he?

A name was called, then another, and people who'd been behind them in line joined the crowd waiting for their orders.

Was he worrying about his choice as much as she was? It didn't look like it. He leaned against the side of the food truck, his arms crossed over his chest, his eyes—he was staring at her again. He'd been doing that a lot. And she liked it. It made her throat dry up.

A disturbance in the skate park caught her eye. A petite girl recoiled from another's harsh words. Bree, realizing what was happening, stepped toward them, intent on helping. She didn't know what skateboard etiquette had been broken, but there was no need for intimidation. After only two steps, others intervened, forcing the bigger kid to back off.

The small group soon dispersed, and they resumed rolling down the ramps. Bree returned to her place by the pickup window, eyes narrowed in their direction until she was sure there would be no further altercation.

The back of her neck tingled, and she realized Zack watched her, eyebrows raised and head tilted. Heat rushed to her face. She would never apologize for stepping in when someone was threatened. Ignoring it went against her nature. It would be easier to jump off the train bridge than let a bully prey on the underdog.

She rocked back on her heels and watched the people around them, hoping Zack's attention would be grabbed by someone else for a moment. It wasn't. He kept his eyes on her and her belly warmed. Fidgety, she tucked a piece of hair behind her ear.

"Bree, your order's up!" the guy at the window yelled.

Exhaling a long breath, she reached and grabbed the paper boat nestling her massive hot dog. Topped with French fries, chili, extra cheese, and garnished with green onions, it was a work of art. *And* it smelled amazing. Her stomach rumbled in anticipation.

Zack's eyes crinkled. Had she given away how good his choice had been? The drool dribbling out of her mouth was probably his first clue. She tried to remove the grin from her face.

An expectant expression raised his eyebrows, making her think he wanted her to bite into it right away so he could win the challenge.

"We're going to do this together," she said, keeping the hot dog away from her face so she wouldn't accidentally shove it in her mouth.

"Zack, your order's up!"

He took his paper boat, the dog topped with slices of beef, sauerkraut, and a dark gravy with raisins, then garnished with expertly drizzled mustard.

She watched his face, trying to figure out if he deemed it a masterpiece or a travesty. She'd thought she had him figured out, but now couldn't read him. She frowned. *Not a good sign.*

Wordlessly, they both moved away from the truck, the crowd, and the skateboarders, and ambled toward the river. They stopped short of the walking paths, the grassy embankment the perfect picnic place. Bree sat, crossing her legs under her, juggling her hot dog so none of its perfection tumbled onto the grass. Zack sat beside her, his long legs stretched out in front of him.

They looked at each other.

"On three?" she asked.

He nodded.

"One. Two. Three." They bit into their dogs. Bree groaned and closed her eyes. It may have lost some of its initial heat, but it tasted like heaven. Cheese. So much cheese. And perfectly cooked French fries. The light spice of the chili pulled it all together.

Involved in her own hot dog, it took her a minute to realize Zack wasn't groaning at his. Her eyes popped open. He was chewing. He wasn't grimacing, but he didn't look ecstatic either.

"Oh no!" she said, but with her mouth full it came out more like, "Waaaoooh." She chewed and swallowed. "You don't like it."

"I do like it," he said, though she wasn't entirely convinced. "I've never tasted anything like it."

"You don't like sauerkraut."

"Actually, I do."

"You don't like mustard."

"I'm okay with mustard."

She frowned, trying to figure him out. Something was definitely off. He took another bite and smiled as he chewed.

"It's really good," he said after he swallowed. "You just surprised me. I wouldn't have picked it, but it's tasty."

She squinted at him in the light of the setting sun, watching him closely. He wouldn't keep eating if he hated it, right? He'd make fun of her for getting it wrong, right? Most of the guys she'd dated in the past would have gloated like toads if she'd come up with the idea then gotten it wrong.

Deciding not to worry, Bree dug back into her hot dog and treasured every bite. Nothing could beat fries and cheese on a hot dog when a girl had an appetite.

The last of their hot dogs eaten, the napkins all used up, they sat side by side, shoulders almost touching, and gazed across the water to the twinkling lights of the businesses on the other side of the river. With a sigh, she patted her satisfied belly.

"So..." she said, breaking the silence, even though the silence was quite nice.

"So..." he echoed.

"You have all that good stuff in your trunk just going to waste."

A breath huffed out of his nose, and he turned toward her. "I honestly never know what's going to come out of your mouth. You know that, right?"

"I might've heard that one before." She pulled up her knees and rested her head on her arms. If he'd said it a different way, she might have taken offense, but his eyes still held their delicious twinkle.

"You went to the library to look for books on Granwin House, couldn't find any, and you honestly want to see what I've got in my trunk?"

"Yeah. Why not?" Why wouldn't she take an interest in her job? It only had a little to do with writing an article with Inaya.

She tried to push down the guilt, genuine interest for him infusing every part of her. But what if he turned out to be a scam artist? *Please, no.*

Swallowing around the sudden tightness in her throat, she said, "Or at least tell me all the cool stuff you've found out so far."

"Most of my notes are in my trunk with the books."

"You found some cool stuff, though, didn't you?" She could tell from the way his eyes lit up.

"It has an interesting history. There's still some to read and go through."

She slapped his knee. "I could help! I can read, you know."

"I suspected as much."

The quick grin accompanying the statement made her full stomach flutter. He appealed to her on so many levels: his relaxed air, his brooding mannerisms, his moody style and shaggy hair. Every time they were close, like they were *right now*, her whole body gravitated toward him. She leaned closer, her eyes on his mouth.

But even with everything appealing about him, part of her mind kept screaming, "He could be a scammer! Just like your dad!" And her dad had bamboozled way more people than just her mom with his good looks and smooth words.

No matter how hard that voice screamed, when she was like this next to him, her body humming, she didn't want to listen. He was hot, and yummy, and introspective, and all the good stuff a man should be. If she wasn't careful, they'd end up in bed together. She didn't want that on the first day they met. *Don't I?*

Bree shut down that hopeful question real fast. She had standards—and her twenty-four-hour rule.

Muting all the screaming voices in her head—the ones telling her to stay away, the ones reminding her they'd just met—she focused on his eyes. "I have one more question to ask," she said, her face only inches away from his.

"What's that?"

Shivers broke across her skin at the way his voice roughened. She exhaled, her breath touching his lips, and lost herself in his eyes. "Your place or mine?"

CHAPTER TEN

H ER PLACE WAS CLOSER.

Zack wouldn't have said no even if he'd wanted to. She'd been too excited to get a look at his books. Did he know anyone who got that enthusiastic about research? Well, maybe him, but he wasn't as outwardly exuberant about it.

He'd thrown his jacket on the back of the couch, and now they sat cross-legged on the rug in her living room, the box of books between them. She'd made them tea, some kind of herbal blend smelling like earth and flowers. His cup sat beside him on the floor, too hot to drink, but the steam created fragrant aromatherapy.

He didn't think she was aware he was in the same room. Totally engrossed, she hadn't turned those big eyes his way in minutes. It gave him time to study her apartment—and her—at his leisure.

One lamp at the end of the couch illuminated the area where they sat. The wood floors around the rug were polished to a shiny gloss. White trim framed butter-colored walls, and the kitchen opened up to the living room, a half-wall and breakfast bar separating the two spaces. Potted plants took up most of the front bay window, healthy and green.

There was only one bedroom. The door had been ajar when they'd come in, revealing an unmade bed and laundry on the floor. He'd seen worse.

When they'd arrived, she'd changed into yoga pants and a T-shirt that said "Baking is cheaper than therapy" and made sure to close the bedroom door behind her. Music played from the speaker in the kitchen, its soft beat and mellow lyrics wrapping around the apartment.

His gaze settled on Bree. She'd tied her hair back again, revealing her long neck, her throat exposed by the V-neck of her shirt. The material hugged her body more than the button-up shirt she'd been wearing all day. She had lovely curves, full hips, not bony at all. When she'd spontaneously hugged him in the car, he'd felt all that softness pressed up against him. He'd liked it. Maybe too much.

The memory made him shift where he sat, trying to relieve the tightness growing in his jeans.

He forced himself to concentrate on the book she had in front of her, a detailed history of the more prominent historical sites in the county. Granwin House was listed along with dry details of the Sheely family, the architect, and the techniques used during construction. Zack watched as she thumbed through the pages, reading, scanning the black and white photographs that accompanied the entry. The slow drag of the pages across her fingertips sent shivers of awareness down his spine. He couldn't look away.

"You're staring," she said, her gaze fixed on the pages and her voice calm.

He twitched. How could she tell? He hadn't made a sound. Maybe it was like when she'd studied him in the car this morning. He'd felt the perusal without having to look.

He was about to apologize, then stopped himself. "Yeah," he agreed.

She glanced up from the thick book nestled in her lap, her smoky gaze capturing his and warming him from the inside out. The moment lengthened. Her lips parted. And he couldn't stop his eyes from dropping to fixate on them.

With a flick of her lashes, she returned her focus to the book. "It says here it took the Sheelys almost two years to complete the house. Seems like a long time."

He cleared his tight throat and nodded. "They had a few problems during construction that set them back."

"Supplier problems, flooding, a tradesman fell and broke his neck," she read from the book, then met his eyes. "Was the site haunted before they began building?"

He tensed and waited for her laughter, but it never came. Instead, interest raised her eyebrows.

"It's possible," he said. "I've seen it before where a house was built on a sacred burial site, but none of my research points in that direction for this case."

She stared at him a moment, nodded, then dove back into her book.

It wasn't a new story, though. He couldn't pinpoint why the Wickwood area attracted so much paranormal activity, but it kept them in business, so he had no reason to complain.

Bree cleared her throat. "It says Matthew Sheely was a doctor, but it doesn't say much else about him."

"Yeah, he ended up opening a practice in the house after his wife and son died, taking on clients who wouldn't be able to pay. He was a pillar of the community."

Bree met his eyes. "How did his wife and son die?"

"They both died of tuberculosis a few years after the house was built. If I remember correctly, I think the boy was about seven or so."

"So sad." Her forehead puckered as closed the book, then picked up another. "Especially hard because he was a doctor and couldn't save them. Probably wouldn't have forgiven himself."

Zack hadn't thought of it that way before, but she was likely right. He watched Bree leaf through the next book, a history of the area during the early 1900s, a little after the Granwins purchased the property. Brow furrowed, she skimmed through the mundane happenings of the area.

Clasping his hands behind his head, he stretched his legs out and leaned against the couch. Minutes ticked by while he memorized her shape, from the way she touched the ends of her hair without thinking, to the way the sides of her feet flexed against the carpet.

"You're staring again," she said without looking up.

"Yeah," he agreed, continuing his perusal.

She lifted her head slowly, and when her eyes met his, they held heat and a shadowed promise.

Electricity licked up his spine. Her tongue moistened her bottom lip, and the lower half of his body tightened.

"We're supposed to be doing research," she said, but her voice came out rough and not much louder than a whisper.

Maybe he affected her the same way she affected him.

"Are we?" Research hadn't been on his plans for the evening, but if it made her happy, he'd continue. Usually, he'd finish after the investigation. He wanted to get a feel for the place first and follow up after the property owners' interviews. He'd completed all his preliminary research, but it didn't matter. Watching Bree pore over books was pure joy.

Silence and tension crackled, neither of them looking away. He kept waiting for her to do something, anything, to break the spell, to bring them back to the research.

When she closed the book with a quiet *thud*, his heart thumped an echoing response. When she set the book aside and rolled onto her hands and knees, he swallowed, his throat suddenly dry.

Bree crawled towards him, her neckline falling away from her body, exposing cleavage and a hint of white lace. His heart beat hard in his chest. He remained frozen, mesmerized by the intensity in her eyes, a deer in headlights. Closer and closer she got until her face filled his vision. Her arching eyebrows, high cheekbones, and wide lips—just plain beautiful. But no, nothing was plain about her. He dropped his hands to his sides.

"I'm going to kiss you." She bit her lower lip.

"Yeah, cool. That's fine. Good. That's good."

She smiled, turned serious again, and grazed his lips with hers.

So soft. His entire body hummed at the contact. Her mouth tasted of sweets, her breath minty, and the combination hit him low in the stomach. The warmth that had started earlier turned into an inferno. His fingers dug into the rug beside his thighs, willpower the only thing stopping him from touching her.

Bree's tongue darted out, licking his bottom lip. His cock not only twitched, but stood at attention. Her mouth moved over his, touching and tasting, heat building between them.

She pulled away, examining his face. A quick breath filled his lungs with her scent. Then she brushed his lips again, and he hung onto the rug for dear life, letting her lead this exploration—to figure out where they were headed. One of her hands crept up to touch his cheek while she exerted more pressure against his mouth. His skin, his scalp, *everything* tingled.

Her heated eyes kept him captured as her tongue swept out to taste him, and he couldn't look away. The light from the lamp made her look like she glowed. And when her tongue stroked his, he couldn't hold back any longer.

His hands flew up to cradle her delicate jaw, keeping her close, holding her still. He devoured her, needing more, wanting it all, and the temperature rose between them. She groaned encouragement, her eyes closing. No other kiss he'd experienced had gotten this hot this fast, and Zack closed his eyes and gave himself over to the moment.

Shifting positions, she broke contact, and he almost groaned aloud at the loss. Then she was there, sitting closer, practically in his lap, her mouth finding his again. Her hands gripped his shoulders tightly, drawing him near, then traveled up his throat through his hair, her fingernails digging into his scalp.

Their mouths turned frenzied. His hands found her waist, and he pulled her closer. Their chests fused together. The sensation of her soft breasts against him stole his breath. He broke the kiss, gasping, to inhale her throat, and she tipped her head to give him better access. The scent of her skin intoxicated him. He wouldn't be able to walk a straight line if his life depended on it.

She shifted, then lifted her leg. Her knees straddled his hips with her hot core pressed against his fly. Yoga pants did nothing to conceal her softness as she settled herself fully.

Their labored breaths mixed with the mellow beat of her music. His fingers skimmed up her spine and she gasped. How he liked that sound. Hands on her hips, he urged her closer, unable to get enough of her, and his cock strained against the material between them. The way her tongue stroked his over and over, mimicking the thrust of her hips, made him fear he would come in his jeans.

Holy shit. He didn't want to stop and needed more.

The thought caused him to break their kiss. "How far do you want to go with this?" He gasped a lungful of air. "I need to know now before we go any further."

"Australia," she panted.

His head jerked back, not sure if he had heard her correctly. "What?"

"Far. Really far." Her fingers dug into his scalp. "The 'all the way' kind of far." She squeezed his thighs with her knees.

His heart beating fast in his throat, he held her gaze. "Are you sure?"

"God, yes. Stop talking and kiss me." Hand on his nape, she pulled him in for more.

Her lips and tongue explored and his answered. *Drowning.* He submerged himself in her taste and touch, and didn't want to ever resurface.

Had he wanted a woman this bad, this fast, before? He couldn't remember, couldn't think as her fingers tore at his shirt, jerking it from the waist of his jeans. Those fingers skimmed his abdomen and chest, creating shivers that shot to his toes.

"Touch me," she whispered against his mouth.

His heart rate accelerated at the heat in her eyes, the rasp of her voice. Skimming his fingers around her waist, he reached under the elastic of her pants. His palms filled with the warm flesh of her bottom, and he squeezed. She gasped and ground herself harder against him.

"Yes," she breathed against his mouth, and his fingers flexed against her skin.

He lifted her slightly, bringing her closer, settling her heat higher on him. They were wearing too much clothing, had too many barriers between them. One hand on her ass, the other traveled up her spine to her neck, her skin smooth and soft.

Hot. The room had become impossibly hot, his insides burning up. Her thighs squeezed his hips and a tremor reverberated through his entire body.

A loud *thump* echoed from the apartment next to hers. Bree jerked and ripped her lips away. They both froze in time. Little patches of reality squeezed between them: the music, the scent of tea, another thump from next door.

Panting, Bree closed her eyes and pressed her forehead against his. "Pittsburgh," she groaned.

His ragged breathing caught in surprise. "Pittsburgh?"

"Yeah, my brain's going a mile a minute. I'd really, really like to go to Australia. I think it would be great with you, but we're about to be co-workers, so probably Pittsburgh is best."

"Pittsburgh. Got it." What the hell was he allowed to do? Her analogies were too ambiguous.

She smiled and gave him a light kiss, then moaned, "But I really want to go to Australia." She ground her hips into his and his cock ached.

Grabbing a fistful of his shirt, she jerked him toward her for another brutal kiss. It was so savage, he wasn't sure if she was angry with him or not—or if she'd drawn blood. When she let go, his shoulder blades thwacked against the couch. *Oomph.* He touched his lips, liking the ache.

"I'm not going to want to stop if we go any further." Without waiting for him to respond, she rolled off him and hovered in a squat two feet away.

"I can agree with that." He dropped his hand and dug his fingers into the carpet so he wouldn't grab her.

"And I don't want to start the job off this way." A frown puckered her brow.

"Okay." His chest rose and fell in an attempt to catch his breath.

"You're okay with it?" She brushed loose hair out of her eyes.

"Yeah, of course." He cleared his throat, trying not to sound like he'd just run a marathon. "I respect your decision. I didn't come here expecting anything other than spending time with you and doing some research."

Her face flushed even more. "That's hot."

He really wanted to grab her and hold her close.

The song changed to one more up tempo. Bree rose to her feet. "I don't think I'm going to be able to concentrate on any more research tonight." She began tossing all the books into the box.

He stood too and set the last book on the top and stared at her a long moment. "You can keep those until I see you next if you like," he said, gesturing to the box with his chin.

"You're going?" Her eyes widened in a plea.

He swallowed. "Um, I thought you were kicking me out."

"Nope." The corner of her mouth kicked upward. "I just needed some distance before I shucked off my pants."

His cock twitched. It was nice to know he could make a woman want to shuck off her pants.

When he said nothing, she picked up her mug from the floor. "How about we finish our tea, which has cooled off way too much, and watch a movie? I can make popcorn."

He laughed. "I can't believe you can eat after those hot dogs."

"I have a healthy appetite."

"I've noticed."

Her expression fell a little.

"And I like it," he added.

That quirk of her mouth kicked upward again as she moseyed to the kitchen. "Check what movies are streaming," she called over her shoulder. "The remote's on the side table."

Tearing his gaze away from her swaying hips, Zack picked up the remote and flopped onto the couch. The sounds of her rummaging through cupboards echoed back to him. Within moments, the microwave hummed.

"Watched anything new recently?" he asked as he scanned through the menu of trending movies.

"Not really," she called from the kitchen over the noise of the microwave and popping corn. "But I'm pretty easy to please, just no horror."

A half-laugh escaped him before he could smother it.

She straightened from getting a bowl underneath the cupboard, her eyes wide. "I didn't make a connection between horror movies and the work you do until this second."

"It's okay," he said, shaking his head. "I didn't take offense. Not all horror is about ghosts or dead people."

"I can't deal with the gore. If it's not gory, I'm usually okay, but I get nightmares if I watch any sort of scary and gross combination."

"Which is kind of funny since you're a skeptic."

"Just because I'm a skeptic doesn't mean my brain doesn't remember disturbing images."

The microwave dinged. Breaking their prolonged stare, she took out the steaming red and white bag, opened it carefully, and dumped the contents into a big blue bowl.

The scent of popcorn and butter wafted toward him long before she sat down next to him. She placed the bowl between their hips, and when she crossed her legs under her lotus-style, their knees touched. Zack didn't move away. She didn't either.

She dug into the bowl for a fistful of popcorn. "Do *you* like horror movies?" she asked before jamming a huge amount of popcorn into her mouth.

CHAPTER ELEVEN

*C*LICK. BREE TENSED WHEN the loud sound of the deadbolt reverberated through the kitchen.

The masculine body beneath hers tensed too.

Zack's eyes flew open, only inches away from her face. From toe to shoulder, she could feel every part of him. Through his jeans, his cock twitched to life when she shifted. His throat reddened.

They didn't end up watching a movie. One question had led to another. They'd talked for hours, eating popcorn until the bowl lay empty between them. If they'd both purposefully steered clear of talking about their families, neither of them mentioned it, but they'd talked about everything else under the sun.

When she'd told him about her first job scooping ice cream, it had felt like the most natural thing in the world to hold hands. To press the side of her thigh against his. To lay her head on his shoulder. By the time he'd told her all the lifeguarding stories he'd thought interesting, she'd fallen asleep, her ear over his heart, the steady rhythm lulling her. It had been the fastest she'd fallen asleep in a long time, and couldn't remember when, if ever, she'd slept so soundly.

Now, morning sunlight stabbed Bree in the eye as she listened to her best friend let herself into the apartment. Zack's wide eyes remained glued to hers. She couldn't move. The door shut with a click, followed by the thud of a purse dropping on the table by the door.

"Hey, Bree, you home? Did you get a new jacket?" Inaya's soft footfalls came toward the couch, then stopped. "Oh, my, I've interrupted something. I'm so sorry."

Both of them flew off the couch. "No, you haven't interrupted anything," Bree said at the same time Zack said there was nothing going on to interrupt.

Standing side by side, four feet of respectful space yawned between them.

When they both stopped blubbering, Inaya crossed her arms over her chest. "Uh huh." After a second, she smiled at Zack. "Hi."

"Hi." He smoothed the front of his shirt, then ran his hand through his hair.

"I'm Inaya. You must be Zack." Inaya swiveled her head to Bree, her eyes wide and saying, *as soon as we're alone you're giving me* all *the dirt.*

Crossing her arms over her chest, Bree thrust her jaw forward, not wanting to go on the defensive. "You're here early. Did you perchance not make it home last night?"

Inaya's cheeks tinted to a dark pink. "I should go. I can see you're busy."

At the same Bree said, "Yes, you should probably go," Zack sputtered, "No, no. That's not necessary."

Inaya narrowed her eyes at both of them, then she spun on her heel, saying over her shoulder, "I'm going to use the bathroom."

Once the door shut behind her, Bree turned to Zack. "Sorry about that."

Zack cleared his throat. "Uh. Yeah. No worries. Nothing to apologize for."

Their eyes met and all the feelings she'd had inside of her last night bubbled up to the surface. It didn't help that the look he sent her way held as much heat as when she'd been straddling his lap. She shivered.

A big part of her regretted that she hadn't followed through with her desires the night before, that she hadn't lured him to her bed and had her way with him. She'd walked a fine line between holding herself back and giving into temptation. He'd been sitting in her living room, looking delicious, and she couldn't stop herself from kissing him. She'd had to have a taste. Had to touch.

But if they had gone all the way, she definitely would've regretted it. She hadn't even met her new boss yet. Her previous experience sleeping with a co-worker hadn't ended well.

What she and Zack had already done crossed the line. Her usual quick, no-strings-attached hookup wasn't on the table here. They were going to work together. She needed to regain control, needed to keep it professional.

Bree took a deep breath and shattered the awkward silence that had descended between them. "I'm totally fine with forgetting last night ever happened."

His head snapped back like he'd been hit. "Huh?" Rapid emotions played across his face.

Not the reaction she thought he would have. She flexed her fingers at her sides, trying to rid herself of her unreasonable but growing panic. "It's not a big deal," she asserted.

"Not a big deal." A frown wrinkled his brow.

"Yeah, it's fine." Her stomach clenched at his sobering expression, but she couldn't stop her lips from moving. "Just cuddling. We're consenting adults and all that." She pressed her lips together.

"Right. Just cuddling. Cool." His words didn't ring quite true, and a strained silence surrounded them for a few seconds. Then he took a breath. "I don't think—"

The door to the bathroom opened, cutting off whatever he was going to say.

Inaya squinted at them as she walked around the peninsula to the kitchen. "Are you guys going to stand there and stare at each other all day?"

Zack swiped a hand over his face, then squeezed the back of his neck. "What time is it?"

Crossing her arms over her chest, Bree flicked her gaze to the clock on the microwave. "Eight-thirty."

"Shit. I've got to go." He ran his hand through his hair. "I'll get cleaned up and then—" He snapped his mouth shut, spun on his heel, and scampered to the bathroom.

Bree tried to ignore the sting of disappointment in her breastbone. So he was going to do the whole "I'm late for an appointment" schtick. She'd thought he was different but shouldn't be surprised. When a guy stayed for breakfast—that's when you knew he wanted more than just... cuddling.

Why should she want more? If a girl went in with any expectations other than cuddling, she was bound to get hurt. She knew better. The easy lessons were always the most painful to learn. "No strings attached" kept everything simple.

Inaya banged around the kitchen, getting out the pot she used to make chai. "Want some?" she asked.

"Sure," Bree said as she shuffled to the breakfast bar and hitched her butt cheek on the stool. Inaya made the best chai she'd ever tasted. Her friend would never buy it from coffee places because she said they didn't make it right.

As she watched Inaya get out all the ingredients and start the burner, Bree set her chin in her hand. All of yesterday had been amazing, and now he was going to rush out of here like they'd done more than fall asleep in each other's arms. Her emotions wouldn't settle on whether that was a good thing or a bad thing.

They'd kissed. It had been a fantastic kiss. Maybe the best ever. She'd loved the softness of his lips, the roughness of his facial hair. And the way it had made her feel—well, she'd tingled everywhere. That tingle had morphed into an all-out burn in about three seconds flat. She'd wanted to keep both of them burning all night long.

Had he felt the same way? Maybe he cuddled with every new employee. If the scamper to the bathroom was any indication, he wanted to get out of here fast.

Well, if he was going to scamper, then the least she could do was optimize the awkwardness. Maybe if she made breakfast, he'd change his mind.

No. She was definitely not going to tempt him back into the apartment with food so he wouldn't break one of her unwritten cardinal rules.

That's why, not a minute later, Bree moved around to the other side of the counter and took out the pancake batter bowl.

Inaya raised her eyebrows as she stirred the chai. Bree resisted the urge to shrug.

When Zack came out of the bathroom and stopped between the living room and the kitchen, she had the grill warming and the whisk in her hand twirling the goopy batter. She smiled.

He smiled back for a second before he glanced at the phone in his hand, then tucked it into his pocket. He frowned at her, opened his mouth, then closed it. When he took his jacket off the couch and slung it over his shoulders to head to the door, Bree whisked a bit more furiously. Inaya's eyebrows went up so far they hid under her bangs.

Zack paused in front of the door. Bree stopped whisking.

"Grace says the job starts tomorrow. I'll text you the particulars." He didn't look at her when he said it.

Bree set down the bowl of batter. "Sure." She tried to keep her voice light as she played the good hostess and moved toward the door to see him out. "Thanks."

He met her eyes. "She wondered if you could stop by the office today so she could meet you." He must have noticed her unease. "It's not an interview or anything. You still have the job, don't worry. She wanted to give you a quick rundown before the client interviews and get you to sign the contract. I'll text you the address of the office."

She already knew it from doing her research earlier, but nodded. "Okay. I can do that."

Out of the corner of her eye, Inaya watched them with avid interest. Zack's eyes darted to her friend, then back to her.

He didn't make a move to open the door, clearing his throat instead. "I need to go and... go. I just need to go."

"Yeah. I get it. No worries."

"No. Crap." He turned to her fully. "I'm making a mess of this. Last night, I know we didn't—that's to say, we weren't—I mean, it might not have been. Shit." He huffed a breath. "Look, this isn't not a big deal. I mean it's a big deal. Like not a *big* deal but... I don't know. It's at least a deal."

"A deal?"

"Yeah. This is a deal. Don't make it less than it is." Without warning, he leaned forward and gave her a quick, hard kiss, looked like he was about to say something else, but snapped his lips closed instead. Then he left.

The closed door captivated her until Inaya clucked her tongue. "That was interesting." The sound of liquid pouring into a glass mug filled a beat of silence. "And kind of sweet."

Bree turned around with a heavy sigh and touched her lips with her fingertips. When she realized what she was doing, she dropped her hand to glare at her friend. "You could have made it easier by not staring at us like we were a bad soap opera."

"Since when do you want me to take it easy on guys?" She sipped her chai and slid a second mug close to the batter bowl.

Bree pursed her lips and walked back to the counter. *Good question.* Why should she want Inaya to take it easy on Zack when with any other guy she'd brought home, she'd be sticking it to him with gusto? What made Zack different? Why wouldn't she enlist her friend to see what kind of grit he had?

The need to make pancakes had fled, but Bree picked up the bowl of batter to stare at it as hard as a fortune teller to tea leaves.

"He didn't stay for breakfast," Inaya said, stating the obvious.

"No." Bree returned her attention to the closed door, wondering if he really had some place to be this early.

"But he said it was a deal."

"Uh huh."

What was a "deal" anyway? Probably something she didn't want, that's for sure. She should be happy he didn't want breakfast. She should be glad he brushed her off. If they weren't working together, she'd probably never see him again. That's how she liked her relationships. Quick and painless. *Right?*

"Are you going to stare at the door all morning?" Inaya asked, breaking into her thoughts. "Or let all the batter fall on the counter?"

Bree started, not realizing the bowl had been tipping. A glob of batter splooshed up on her.

"Ugh." Laughing at herself, she managed to get most of it off her T-shirt with a dish cloth. "What a mess."

Inaya hummed in agreement. "What's a mess is that you've slept with the guy you're going to help me do an exposé on."

Bree's heart lurched at the thought. "We didn't actually sleep, *sleep* together." But the clarification didn't matter when she thought of everything they'd talked about the night before. "It's gotta be a scam. Right?"

"He doesn't seem like the scamming sort."

"No. He doesn't." She knew firsthand that looks could be deceiving. Her dad had always been considered handsome and charming—just tools to get what he wanted. But she'd already decided Zack was nothing like her dad.

"So are we going through with it?" Inaya rinsed the empty chai pot and set it in the bottom of the sink. "Because I've got to tell you, I already ran it by Brian and he's all in."

Bree glared at the bowl of batter. "If they're scammers, then they need to be exposed, no matter what happened last night." It hurt her to say those words, but she wouldn't dwell on it. *This is important.* One less scammy business meant people everywhere were safer.

With her chest feeling like someone had sat on it, she set the bowl in the sink to deal with later. "I'm going to take a shower."

"I'll be gone when you get out." Leaning a hip on the counter, Inaya took another sip of her chai. "I'm going to do some research on this haunted house."

"I'll type up everything I've learned so far and put it in that shared file. There's a box of books there too," Bree said, gesturing in front of the couch.

"Cool. Do you want to meet for lunch?"

"Maybe," Bree said over her shoulder as she peeled off her batter-infused T-shirt. "I need to go shopping and get ready for the job tomorrow. Lots to do. I'll text you." Deep in her room already, she shouted the last bit as she finished undressing.

"Okay," Inaya called from the kitchen. "Let me know."

Bree heard the front door close as she stepped into the shower. With the water spraying her, she went through everything that had happened with Zack over the past day.

He'd been kind. He'd been interested. He'd been tender and sweet, and respected her boundaries. She'd thought she could read him, but then he'd given her a lame excuse this morning. Of course, there was the slight chance he had somewhere to be. Then why didn't he say what it was about?

Maybe because it's none of your business, since you've only known him for less than twenty-four hours.

There was that. Bree massaged apple-scented shampoo into her head. She'd have to buy a new kind when she went shopping today, something mysterious and cheap. What did mystery and ghosts smell like, anyway?

She thought about the food truck game and how she wasn't sure if she had read him correctly. He hadn't been one hundred percent into her choice. Why not? It had meat, sauerkraut, onions, mustard, that German-style gravy—

Her eyes flew open. The gravy! It had raisins in it. She could definitely see him not liking raisins. And he hadn't said a word about them, just kept eating, pretending he loved it. He should've been honest with her. Then he would've won the game and she wouldn't have been second-guessing herself for the past day.

Finishing her shower, she patted herself dry, her mind moving to her blog. She needed to finish writing about her experience at the bakery and post it today. A couple of her readers had asked in the comments section when her next post would be, and she didn't like to disappoint them.

Before she did that, she had a bunch of places to stop: the grocery store, the thrift store, the drugstore. Keeping her spending under control would present a challenge. The other tricky bit would be to keep her emotions in check.

She must stay focused. Besides making her next month's rent, the point of taking this job was to expose scammers. People who cheated others out of money just because they could—those were the kinds of people who needed to pay. Just like her dad. He would scam money off a child if he could. She'd seen it happen. If the Lillers were doing the same thing, they needed to be stopped.

Helping those people, the ones who'd been wronged, there was no better feeling. From Jimmy and his lemonade stand, to the bakery patrons who'd find out about the underhanded dealings of the place across town, she lived for that feeling of vindication, the satisfaction of helping someone in need.

Her attraction to Zack was secondary. Because no matter what Zack said, whatever had transpired between them, it wasn't a big deal.

CHAPTER TWELVE

ZACK PARKED IN HIS spot at Liller Investigations, right beside his mother's beat-up white pickup truck, surprised to see it there.

He turned off the ignition and sat there a moment, thinking, trying to get the feelings Bree created in him settled, so he could deal with the emotions he knew would surface conversing with his mother.

One more deep breath and he climbed out of the car, took the metal steps on the outside of the building two at a time, and pushed open the door to the second floor where they shared office space with two other businesses. He strode across the empty common space and through the door marked Liller Investigations.

His mother sat on the scuffed black leather couch in the foyer, a mug of tea in her hands. With her wire-rimmed glasses propped on the top of her head and her white hair swept into a bun at the base of her neck, she wore her usual uniform of jeans and a blouse.

"Zack." Her gentle voice drifted toward him as she set the mug on the side table, then stood to hug him. "I think you've grown taller."

"I don't think I've grown since high school, Mom." He returned her squeeze and gave her a kiss on her weathered cheek. The scent of Earl Gray filled his head. "How are you?"

"Just a bit tired, but good, sweetie." She patted his arm and sat down, grabbing her tea. "Your father's been asking about you."

Zack tensed. It never took her long to go there.

"You should come for a visit," she added.

"I know. I will. Soon."

"How soon?" she asked, her eyes vulnerable.

Realizing he'd fisted his hands, he forced himself to relax and met her gaze. "As soon as I can. When this job is done." When her eyes continued to plead with him, he caved. "How about this weekend?"

Relief lived in her resulting smile. She opened her mouth to respond, but the rustle of Grace leaving her office with a manila folder in her hands interrupted them.

"I think everything is in order," she declared, then took a spot on the couch where Mom sat too. "All we have to do is sign in three places." She opened the folder.

"What's this?" Zack asked, dread settling in his chest.

Grace blinked at him like he'd lost a few too many marbles. "The mortgage transfer. I told you about it two weeks ago."

He remembered the conversation. He also recalled saying he didn't like the idea. "I'm not signing that."

Grace, who had been in the process of passing the first page and a pen to their mother, let her hands slump in her lap. "You're serious."

"Hell, yes."

"Don't curse," his mother said over top of his next words.

"I'm not going to take the farm away from Mom."

A heavy sigh expelled from Grace's chest. "We're not taking the house away from Mom. It was her idea."

"It was your father's idea," their mother interjected.

"Whatever." Grace pressed her lips together in a thin line. "Either way, it wasn't *my* idea, and these papers take nothing away from her. It means if she dies, the title gets split between the two of us—"

"Stop." The word was almost a whisper, and for once, his sister listened. He didn't want to talk about his mother dying. Working around death every day was bad enough. He didn't need to have his mind go there with his mom.

"Look." Grace set the folder aside. "We're not here to gang up on you or anything. This was Mom's—and Dad's," she added when their mother opened her mouth to interject again, "idea. We can let it sit if you're not feeling it, but I let you know the papers were drawn up yesterday."

"Yeah." He ran a hand over his face. "I didn't know you were talking about those papers."

"What papers did you think I was talking about?"

"Contract papers."

"Oh. Well, I have those too. Sorry for the confusion."

All three of them stared at each other.

Their mother huffed out a puff of impatient air. "Well, I didn't come all this way not to sign something. So give them to me. You two can sign them at your leisure." She wiggled her fingers toward the folder.

Grace passed it to her, but kept Zack's gaze as she did so, then frowned.

Their mother took her glasses from the top of her head, balanced them on the end of her nose, and shuffled through all the papers until she found the spots to sign. Once done, she stacked them neatly in the folder and handed it to Grace before popping her glasses on her head.

"Now," she said to Zack. "I'd love some help doing errands if you're free."

He could do about a hundred other things, starting with heading home to change out of the clothes he'd worn since yesterday and take a shower. "I'm free."

"We'll take your car. I like how it vibrates."

Grace snorted as she got up from the couch and headed down the hallway. "Is the new girl stopping by today?" The clack of her heels echoed off the walls along with her voice.

"Bree. Her name is Bree. And I think so."

Grace paused and peered at him over her shoulder, an expression of suspicion narrowing her eyes. *Like a bloodhound that caught the scent.* It must have been his tone that betrayed him. Zack resisted the urge to squirm and tried his best not to look like he spent the night on the couch with their newest employee.

After a moment, his sister continued on to her office, but not before casting one last shrewd glance over her shoulder.

"A new girl?" His mother took his arm and bumped her hip against his playfully. "Is she cute?"

CHAPTER THIRTEEN

THE ADDRESS ZACK TEXTED her led to a historic red brick building, its cracked masonry and narrow windows adding to its charm.

Bree squinted at the hastily made paper sign pointing to the back staircase. With a shrug, she trudged up the metal stairs—more of a fire escape than anything—to Liller Investigations. Strange they didn't have a street-front entrance, but what did she know? Maybe that was how all paranormal investigators did it, like ghost *feng shui* or something.

A brick held the door slightly ajar. Bree pushed it open and found herself in a cramped hallway. Three doors greeted her. She headed to the one with Liller Investigations written across it.

Her phone buzzed. She dug it out of her tote and read the text from Bianca. *Call me. Please. It's important.*

Her fingers gripped the phone tightly. She didn't want to hear what their dad had done this time—that he'd finally been caught and incarcerated. *Or worse.* No, she couldn't take that call. Not now.

Tucking the phone into her tote, she knocked on the door and waited. And waited.

Nothing happened. No one answered. No noise came from the other side. She knocked louder, then pressed her ear to the door.

A muffled curse was followed by a deep voice shouting, "Come in!"

Bree opened the door and stepped inside an empty foyer. A black leather couch sat on one side, with two large, framed photos of English castles hanging above. On the windowsill opposite it, a wilting fern blazed bright green, with hints of brown on the tips of its fronds.

A Black man with hair cut close to the scalp poked his head out of one of the four rooms down the hallway. "Hey. I know you." His British accent lilted toward her.

Bree smiled. "I know you too." He'd been working at the soup kitchen when she'd volunteered there. Well, not volunteered exactly. "Sam, right?"

He pushed a rolling chair through the door until he sat in the middle of the hallway. He'd always cut a handsome profile, but now even more so in dress pants and a button-up shirt.

"That's right," he said. "Good memory." A strained expression passed over his features.

He doesn't remember my name. Well, she would not make it easy for him. Bree put her hand on her hip. "I also remember you used to make up names for people, like 'Red Hat Randy,' and 'Sighs A Lot.' What did you make up for me?"

Embarrassment flashed in his brown eyes. "I promise to never make up another name for another person ever again."

"Too late. You've gotta share now."

He stood and put his hands up in mock surrender. "Don't hate me."

"Never."

"I used to call you Lady Come Lately because you were—"

"Always late. Yeah. I get it." With a smile, she shook her head, both at herself and him.

"So you're the new girl."

"I think I like the other name better, but if you have to call me anything, Bree is just fine."

"Bree!" He threw his hands up in the air. "I knew that." His charming accent made up for his faulty memory.

Movement behind him made Bree stiffen. A woman with tawny skin like Zack's leaned against one door further down the hall. Dressed in a power suit, her hair slicked back in a twist, she straightened away from the wall and walked toward them with purposeful strides.

Bree stuck out her hand. "Bree Tisdale."

The woman took it, appraisal in her eyes. "Grace Liller. Thanks for coming onto the project last minute."

"My pleasure." Bree hesitated. "Actually, I'd been looking for a job, so it was perfect timing." She wondered how much she'd overheard of her and Sam's conversation. Probably a hell of a lot. The office wasn't big. Bree took a cursory look around. Was Zack hiding somewhere?

"Would you like anything?" Grace asked. "Coffee? A glass of water?"

"Water would be wonderful, thank you."

Further down the hallway, an alcove housed a cupboard and a water cooler. Grace returned with a glass full to the brim. Bree took it, careful not to spill, but didn't drink it.

They both stared at her for a moment, waiting. Bree smiled.

After a beat, Grace asked, "Did you have questions at all about what's going to happen tomorrow?"

"Oh, yeah, about a million of them, but I thought I'd go with the flow. You know, learn as I go."

Unblinking, Grace stared at her.

If her new boss wanted questions, Bree would go with the one weighing on her mind since she'd met Zack. "I was wondering about the wage? Zack didn't tell me much about it."

A peculiar glint entered Grace's eyes. "Oh, he didn't, did he?"

"Um, yeah. He said it was a contract, but nothing else."

"Hmmm."

When Grace didn't say anything more, Bree glanced at Sam, slightly worried. He shrugged, his eyebrows raised as if he didn't understand his wife's reaction either.

Needing to focus on something other than Grace's discerning gaze, Bree studied the office. Sparsely decorated, a few more photos of castles peppered the walls of the hallway. It didn't scream "We hunt ghosts!" and it didn't scream money. It didn't scream much of anything, except maybe they liked things on the modern side. Her gaze snapped to Grace. A resigned expression crossed her new boss' face.

Grace turned on her heel and strode to the office she'd come out of. "This way," she said over her shoulder.

With one last glance at Sam, who grinned at her, Bree followed. The other woman sat at her desk, shuffled papers, looking quite official. And intimidating.

"The contract is here. Your cut is eighteen percent. It's not usually that high for the assistant position, but for some reason this time around it is. So—" She held out a pen to Bree. "If you will sign, I'll give you some details about tomorrow."

Bree hesitated a moment, then walked forward. Setting the full glass of water on the edge of the desk, she took the pen.

A quick glance at the numbers, and she inhaled sharply. Eighteen percent of the contract was more than she would have earned at the bakery in a month. Trying to keep her chill, she picked up the stapled pages and skimmed through the rest of it. The professor from her accounting class in college had said to read a contract before she signed. Truth be told, she was having a hard time allowing anything to sink in. The numbers on the first page kept swirling in her head.

The other thing running through her mind was that the people who hired them were getting swindled. Who could afford to pay so much money to get some fake ghost hunters to come to their house and get rid of fake ghosts? Oh yeah, Liller Investigations was definitely going down. They'd built a business on taking money from scared people.

Bree glanced at Grace over the top of the papers. Problem was, Zack—and now Grace and Sam—didn't appear to be the swindling types. They seemed like normal, everyday sort of people. Especially Sam. She'd gotten to know him at the soup kitchen. He'd come off as being honest and straightforward, making people relax in the presence of his easy-going manner. He wasn't a criminal. Or, at least Bree didn't think so. What was going on here?

She also knew the best scammers had pretty faces and smooth words. Being told stories of her dad's exploits over and over again taught her that. Seeing him in action as a child had taught her that. Were the Lillers the same?

Only one way to find out. Bree flipped to the last page, set the paper on the desk, and signed then dated her name on the line beside Grace's.

With deft fingers, Grace took the papers and stacked them on some others to her right before motioning to the chair. After Bree sat, Grace said, "Tomorrow is the interview. I'd like you to mainly observe and see how we interact with clients. I want you to write down anything you find interesting in a notebook, and I'll also give you a recording device. If questions occur to you, run them by me separately before you ask."

So that's where Zack got it from.

Under the intense pressure of the woman's unyielding gaze, Bree felt compelled to respond and gave a small nod

Grace's brow twitched like she wanted to raise it again, forcing Bree to stifle a smile.

As if to qualify her last statement, Grace added, "We've done many of these investigations. I want you to follow our lead and please don't feel the need to get creative. Understand?"

"Zack told you about the interview." Of course Zack told his sister, *his boss,* about the interview with Selma. Bree's cheeks burned.

"What interview?" Grace asked, a frown pinching her brow.

Oh god. Zack hadn't told her. How to get out of this one? Grace didn't seem like the kind of lady one joked with about having dead bodies in the trunk. If Bree told her about the interview and how unorthodox it had been, given Zack's reaction, Grace's would probably be worse. Liller Investigations was *her* company. Clearly she wanted everything to be professional—something Bree could never be. Though there was the time she'd been a temp at a big law firm. She thought she'd pulled off professional pretty well there. Of course, they *had* fired her, but it wasn't for anything related to professionalism.

Her mind scrambled for something, anything, to distract her. "I got a bunch of speeding tickets and worked them off at the soup kitchen downtown." The words exploded from Bree's mouth.

Eyes wide, Grace stared at her, her limbs still.

"Community service," Bree added, her voice pitched higher than normal.

Grace blinked, let out a puff of a laugh, then sobered quickly. "You're not the first one to work off some tickets, but I'm not your priest. It's unnecessary to tell me all your sins. I just need you to show up to work on time and do your job."

The bang of a door closing in the foyer echoed down the hall. Bree pursed her lips. "Right. On time. About that..."

Grace's eyes widened. "That's why you got all the speeding tickets, isn't it? And Sam called you 'Lady Come Lately.' Holy shit. I should look into investigating as a job." Her lips curled into a small, secretive smile.

Zack came rushing into the office, then stopped dead. A wave of awareness washed over Bree, making her skin tingle.

Only this morning his body had been pressed against hers.

"Hi," Zack said, his throat bobbing in a swallow.

"Hi," Bree replied, eyes skimming over him.

He looked really good. He'd showered and changed, and she leaned forward to inhale the scent of rosemary and mint coming off him. She resisted the urge to lick her lips, wanting to bury her face in his throat and breathe deep.

When his skin turned pink under the black collar of his T-shirt, Bree realized she'd stared a bit too long

Her gaze flew to Grace. Her boss's earlier smile was replaced with narrowed eyes darting between the two of them.

Bree's body heated in an entirely different way. She'd never been one to embarrass easily, but this was her boss's brother. She hadn't seen him as her boss's brother until now. She'd seen him as a guy she liked, someone who she might work with, and tried to keep her involuntary reaction to him under wraps by keeping her face blank.

Grace's eyes narrowed more.

"Did you need anything else from me?" Bree asked, needing to get out of there.

After another beat of silence, Grace passed her some papers. "Here's your copy of the contract, the interview times, and the address for tomorrow. Don't be late."

Bree took the bundle, stood, and slid it into her tote before picking up her glass of water.

"And talk to Sam about getting a digital recorder," Grace added as she stepped over the threshold to the office.

Then Zack followed her out, saying, "I'll see you to the door."

Bree would have turned to see Grace's reaction to that statement, but Sam poked his head out of his office and offered her a rectangular digital recorder. She crossed to him to take it. "Thanks."

"My pleasure." Sam paused dramatically. "Bree."

With a smile, Bree tucked the recorder into her tote. Sam gave her a salute before ducking into his office.

She and Zack continued out, and she paused at the window next to the fern. Zack followed suit, turning to her.

"You didn't tell your sister about the interview."

He didn't react. "I gave her my notes. Like I usually do."

"You didn't tell her I was there."

He shrugged, sliding his hands into his pockets. "It wasn't pertinent to the information obtained."

"What if she wants to go to Selma's cabaret?"

His head jerked back. "Excuse me?"

"Well, you bought four tickets, so how will she know about it if you don't tell her?"

He leaned against the window frame and crossed his arms. "You stole the tickets."

"So?"

His eyes narrowed and his lips formed an accusatory purse. Then he jerked his chin at her hand. "Are you going to drink that water?"

"Nope."

"Okay. Then I'll drink it." He extended one hand.

She dumped it on the wilting fern before he could make contact. His eyes widened.

Bree grinned. "It was thirstier."

CHAPTER FOURTEEN

S HE WAS LATE.

Zack checked his phone for the twentieth time, hoping somehow the satellite that always kept the clock precise to the second was wrong.

He glanced behind him again, waiting for Grace to come out of the Victorian house and give him shit. The door remained closed. He looked back at the road, and his chest eased when a plume of dust traveled up the drive. A car appeared over the rise.

As it drew near, his heart seized. It wasn't her. The woman's hair was the wrong color. But as the light blue hatchback rumbled closer—it needed a new muffler—it was Bree's same high cheekbones, same wide lips. But she had black hair.

She parked in line with the rest of the cars on the property, opened the door, and stepped out.

He sucked in a sharp breath.

The day he met her, Bree had been pretty. He'd been attracted. He'd wanted to get to know her better. He'd wanted to kiss her. Now he couldn't even find words to speak.

She'd not only changed her hair color, she'd changed her whole look. Gone were the jeans and collared shirt. Now she wore a goth power suit, burgundy with high heels to match, and a huge carpet bag slung over her shoulder. One white streak at her temple stood out against the black of her hair.

When she stopped in front of him, her scent washed over him, some sort of flower he couldn't name but made his mouth water. So different from the candied apple fragrance the day he met her.

"I think I'm late," she said after a minute of him just staring at her.

He couldn't respond.

"Should we go in?" she asked with a frown.

"Your hair is black." That didn't come out the way he'd wanted it to at all. Her frown deepened. "It's a nice black," he added.

Her frown softened a bit, but her hand reached up to touch the ends tentatively. "I needed a change."

"You're pretty. It's pretty. The hair. *Your* hair. I'm an idiot."

When she gave him the big smile he'd gotten used to, he relaxed.

She leaned forward. "I love it when you're incoherent."

"What—?" He wasn't able to ask what she meant by that, because the front door to the house squealed open.

He turned to find his sister jogging down the steps. The stiffness of her movements made it clear she was going to chew out their new recruit. He moved in front of Bree, but she stepped ahead of him in the next moment.

"You're late," Grace said, her suit jacket open to reveal the pinstriped shirt underneath.

"I apologize." Bree's tone was assertive, calm. "There was an accident on the highway and it backed up traffic."

Grace's frown eased, concern seeping into her eyes. "Anyone hurt?"

Bree shook her head. "Not that I saw. A semi fishtailed and the front end went into the ditch. There was an ambulance there, but it didn't speed away with anyone. Once they got the truck off the road, traffic was at a crawl for a while."

Grace nodded, appeased. "The Rivets are waiting." She jogged back to the house ahead of them.

Zack turned his head in time to see Bree open her carpet bag. He stopped dead in his tracks. "What is that?"

"What?" Bree asked, snapping the bag closed.

"Was that a Ouija board in there?"

She opened the top wide. "I did some research on ghost hunting equipment, and this was one thing I could afford." She reached in. "I got it at the thrift store."

He stopped her, his palm pressing against her arm. "Don't. Don't take it out. Seriously. Don't let my sister know you have it. Ever."

Brows drawing together, she let the edge of the board game go. "Fine. Just trying to help."

"That's definitely not helping."

As she settled the game back into the bag, he noticed something else. "Is that a bag of flour?"

"Um, no?"

"I told you we didn't use flour."

"I did some research and found a couple of instances where it was helpful."

"Not for us." He ran a hand through his hair, trying to control his temper. "We use science and hard evidence. We don't rely on guesswork and games."

Red stained her cheeks. "I didn't say you did."

"The stuff in your bag says it." Shaking his head, he walked toward the house, then turned back. "Just keep it all in there, okay?"

"Okay," she muttered, hitching the bag over her shoulder.

If his sister saw any of that stuff... Zack pushed down his gnawing unease and led the way up the old plank stairs into the house that had been considered haunted for over a hundred years, Bree trailing behind him.

The squeak of the hardwood floor and the scent of polished oak greeted Bree as she stepped into the foyer of the Victorian mansion. Her stomach fluttered. She'd already made a mess of things and she'd just arrived.

Four suitcases of varying sizes were lined up on the right side of the door. The left side of the foyer opened into a sitting room. Flowered settees, Persian rugs, plants in every corner—it had a quaint feel, not stuffy despite the antique furnishings.

A man, a woman, and a little girl took up the slender couch. Another woman tended to the tea on the coffee table in the middle of the room. Sam and Grace sat opposite the family in two armchairs upholstered in the same floral pattern as the couch.

"I've explained about the semi-truck," Grace said as she gestured for Bree and Zack to take the love seat in front of the bay window.

"We hope no one was hurt," said the man sitting on the couch.

"It didn't look like it." Parked on the highway, she'd watched the semi being pulled from the ditch, feeling every minute drag by. Without the delay, she would have arrived with plenty of time to spare. She'd woken up extra early just to make sure. Having the interview scheduled for the afternoon helped.

The man stood and offered Bree his hand. "Fletcher. This is my wife Adeline, and our daughter Rory."

The little girl with frizzy blond hair tucked into a ponytail hid her face further under her mother's armpit.

"And this is Merle. She's in control of the kitchen and almost everything else, too." Fletcher let out a laugh while Merle gave her a nod, no smile, setting the teapot down on the tray atop the coffee table.

"Nice to meet you." Bree returned the nod, then joined Zack on the love seat.

Tight fit. But there was nowhere else except the chair Merle took on the other side of the room. The entire length of Bree's thigh squished against Zack's.

Heated by his proximity, she clutched her carpet bag in front of her, but it was so big, half of it crossed over into his lap. She shifted, trying to get some space between them. It didn't help. Instead, she opened up the bag, dug out her notebook—which took some doing because she'd fit a ton of stuff in there since she hadn't known what she needed today—then set the carpet bag beside the love seat and prepared to take notes.

Everyone stared at her.

Bree cleared her throat. "Sorry. I'm ready now. One hundred percent."

Shooting her a tight smile, Grace turned her attention to the family. "Let's start with why you called us."

"Dammit," Bree muttered before Fletcher could say a word.

Seven pairs of eyes swung toward her.

"I forgot to get out the recorder," Bree whispered in embarrassment, cheeks flaming. She reached down and dug around in the bag for thirty seconds. Not finding what she was searching for, she turned her full attention to the contents of the bag, found the recorder at the bottom, placed it on her lap, and tried to exhale quietly, which came out like a hiss instead.

Everyone still stared at her. She smiled, trying to keep her cool while her whole side heated from being so close to Zack. Sam gave her a thumbs-up sign. Bree turned her attention to Fletcher, hoping everyone else would follow suit.

Eventually they did, and Fletcher gave her a half-smile. "We'd always wanted to open our own business, so this was a dream opportunity." He refocused on Grace. "It's a beautiful house and we bought it for a song. We hadn't heard the stories before we moved in." He glanced at his wife. "After we realized it had some activity, we thought it would be a compelling feature for the bed and breakfast. We've put a lot of money into this house and don't have the means to move again so soon."

"Tell us about some of your first incidents," Grace encouraged.

Fletcher looked at his wife.

"They began the day we moved in," Adeline said with a shrug. "Things going missing. Ending up in places they shouldn't be. Honestly, we've been pleased about the activity." She hesitated, shooting a glance at Merle, then at her daughter. "Two of us, anyway."

Bree's gaze strayed to the girl, wondering if she had anything to do with missing items. Seemed like something a little kid would do. One eye peeked at her from behind the sleeve of her mother's blouse.

"Then there were strange sounds," Adeline continued. "Ones that couldn't be explained."

"Like an old house shifting?" Bree suggested.

Adeline blinked at her. "Well, that would be explainable, wouldn't it?"

Heat flared to Bree's cheeks again, and she avoided looking at Grace, knowing her boss would be glaring at her right now.

"This was more like moaning," Adeline said as she looked at her husband.

"Screaming," Merle muttered.

Everyone turned their attention to her.

She nodded her gray head. "I've heard screaming. I know I haven't been here as long as the Rivets, but I've heard a great many things. And one of them is screaming."

Rory shot to her feet, making Bree jump. The girl scurried out of the room and up the stairs, her thumping steps echoing through the foyer.

Fletcher turned to them. "She's always been a sensitive kid."

"Kids are often more receptive to supernatural things," Grace agreed, then flicked her eyes toward Zack.

Bree felt Zack nod, or something like a nod, but so small someone else might have missed it. Except she was plastered to his side, so how could she miss anything? She'd probably notice if his body temperature dropped a degree.

"With your permission," Grace said, returning her attention to the parents, "I'd like Zack to talk to your daughter. He's had some experience in this area."

The couple looked at each other, then Adeline nodded. "Sure. You can try. She often doesn't open up to strangers."

"I'll give her a few minutes," Zack said, his voice rumbling through Bree. He leaned forward, resting his elbows on his knees, his leg fusing to hers even more. "Where do you experience the most activity in the house?" he asked.

Fletcher pursed his lips. "Personally, I'd say on the main staircase. I've seen things out of the corner of my eye, but when I turn, there's nothing there."

That happens to me all the time. It's called dust. Bree resisted the urge to say the words out loud.

Everyone focused on Adeline. "I've seen a figure in white on the stairs. When I blinked she was gone, but it definitely looked like a woman. Maybe wearing a nightgown." She turned to Merle.

The woman smoothed the pleats in her skirt. "Near the kitchen I sometimes feel this heaviness in my chest." She raised her hand to her breastbone.

"If you had to put an emotion to the feeling in your chest, what would it be?" Sam asked.

"Dread." She exhaled. "Definitely dread. It's also where I hear the screams. Near the kitchen."

"Well, it can't be because of your cooking," Fletcher said, laughing, then coughing over the laugh. No one else joined in and he put up his hands in surrender. "Her cooking is magnificent. Truly. We're lucky to have her. Just thought we were getting a bit too serious there for a minute." He coughed again.

Grace gave him a smile, then said, "Sam has some blueprints. We'll go over the entire house and I want everyone to say what they've seen or heard in each area." The Rivets and Merle nodded as Sam took out large, rectangular sheets of paper from a tube and spread them out on the coffee table.

When Bree leaned forward to get a better look, Zack got up and made his way out of the room. Bree looked at the blueprints, then the doorway where Zack had gone, then back at the blueprints.

With a sweep of his hand, Sam gestured to the basement. "What can you tell me about this area?"

"There used to be a lot of water down there. I had to do maintenance on the old water heater all the time. Since we got a new one, I don't go down there as much. Ended up putting a whole new floor over the old one to get rid of the stains."

"Did the water problems disappear with the old water heater?" Sam asked.

"Definitely less," Fletcher replied. "But I'll find the occasional puddle. Don't like going down there, to be honest. It's a bit creepy. We only use parts of it for storage."

After staring at the door again, Bree noticed Grace watching her. Her boss gave her a small nod.

While Sam asked the family about the main floor, Bree got up, notebook and recorder in hand, and made her way to the foyer. With one last glance at everyone poring over the blueprints, Bree walked over the creaky floorboards to the staircase. Hand trailing up the banister, she made her way to the second floor and paused on the landing. Voices led her to the right. When she saw the light on in the first room, she stayed out of sight from the doorway, not wanting to interrupt.

"What's your favorite thing to do in the summer?" Zack asked.

"I dunno." A moment of silence followed the girl's answer, accompanied by rustling movement.

Bree crept closer to see what they were doing, glad the floor didn't squeak like it had downstairs. She peeked around the doorframe. The pair sat on the floor, their backs to the door, a dollhouse in front of them. Zack dressed a Barbie doll while Rory undressed another.

"I guess I like to swim," Rory said after a minute.

"No way. I like to swim too."

Rory paused in her task. "Really?"

"Yep." Zack nodded. "I always tried to be the fastest swimmer out of anyone in my school."

"Did you do it?"

Zack held up the fully clad doll, wearing an off-the-shoulder neon pink prom dress. "Yeah. I was the fastest once upon a time. Then someone faster beat me." He shrugged and handed her the doll.

"Now this one. Their fingers always get caught in the sleeves."

Zack hummed in agreement, taking the naked doll and the bright blue prom dress from Rory. "I can see why you needed my help. They're a bit tricky."

Bree leaned against the hallway wall, almost out of sight. She was pretty sure Zack knew she hovered there, but she didn't want to startle the girl.

After another minute, Zack spoke. "So tell me about living here. Do you like it?"

Rory shook her head. "I don't like it at all. I want to move back to our other house with my old friends."

"Why don't you like it?"

Rory shrugged. "Like Merle said. The noises. It's scary. Sometimes the screaming is so loud I have to cover my ears."

The words made Bree's heart squeeze tight. No kid should have to endure something like that. Did her parents fight? Scream at each other until Rory couldn't take it anymore? Bree swallowed, remembering when she and Bianca would hide in the closet together, holding each other tight when their parents argued. This little girl didn't have a sister to hug, making Bree want to envelop her in warmth.

More silence between Zack and Rory, then he asked, "Is it just at night?"

"It's loudest at night," Rory whispered.

Another twitch of pain shot through Bree. Parents usually argued worse at night, believing their sleeping children wouldn't hear.

Zack held up the Barbie now clad in blue satin. "How does she look?"

"Beautiful. Now this one." Rory handed him another naked doll and a green prom dress.

"What's your favorite place in the house?"

"I dunno. Here I guess. Or outside. Or the kitchen if Merle is making dessert."

"What's your least favorite part of the house?"

Dainty shoulders slumped forward. "I don't go to the attic anymore."

Struggling with a dress sleeve, Zack tilted his head. "Do you want to talk about it?"

She shook her head. Quiet descended between them, then Rory said, "Mom and Dad said we get to stay at a hotel while you guys are here, so that's good."

"You're right. That is good. Okay. Let's not talk about this silly house anymore. We've got a prom to get to."

Something did a flip-flop in Bree's stomach at the tender scene. Dress situated, Zack handed Rory the doll in the green dress and she handed him another.

"Didn't I do this one already?" he asked holding up a blue satin dress.

"It was a different Barbie. They shopped at the same store, and when they show up at the prom there's gonna be *drama*." Rory elongated the word.

Wanting to leave them to their play, Bree took a step back, but the floor squeaked. Both their heads whipped in her direction.

"Hi guys," she said. "Whatcha playing?"

"Dolls," Rory said dismissively, returning to the row of dressed Barbies in front of her. Zack grinned at her as he dressed the last doll, appearing unashamed to play with Barbies. Bree's stomach did another flip.

"Wanna play?" he asked.

She raised her eyebrows when Rory piped up, "If she plays then she has to be the bad girl no one likes and tries to ruin everything and then goes to jail because she's so bad."

Zack's eyes challenged Bree as he pressed his twitching lips together.

Never one to back down from a challenge, Bree said, "I'm definitely in."

This had suddenly become more than exposing scammers. She needed to debunk this whole haunted house thing and help this little girl on the road to a better environment.

And if Zack was a part of supporting the whole "ghost" story to make a buck instead of exposing what was really going on here, then he had to go down too.

CHAPTER FIFTEEN

"Rory," Adeline called from the main floor. "It's time to go."

The girl jumped to her feet, dropping her two dolls on the floor. She hesitated, looking around the room.

"What is it?" Zack asked, knowing she was excited to spend a couple nights in a hotel.

Rory bit her lip. "You'll, you know, take care of everything, right? Nothing bad's going to happen to my dolls and bed and other toys, right?"

"We'll take care of everything," Bree said, but Rory stared at Zack and waited.

He wasn't sure why Rory didn't trust Bree's answer, but he gave the little girl a nod. "We'll make sure nothing happens to your stuff." After a moment of staring him down—gauging his reliability?—she ran out of the room, the thumping of steps echoing a second later.

Clutching the "bad girl" Barbie, Bree stood. "That was a close one. I almost got sent to jail on a misdemeanor."

A chuckle escaped him. "I don't even know how she knows the word. She can't be older than six."

Bree shrugged as she set the doll on the top floor of the dollhouse with a handful of others. "She's pretty smart for her age."

"Yeah," he agreed. A little too smart. A little too perceptive. And what she'd seen or heard in the house had definitely scared her.

He stared at Bree for a moment, taking her in. She'd been good with Rory even though the girl had resisted. She knew how to fit into a tough situation—a good skill for a paranormal investigator.

Bree's eyes met his. A question burned in her gaze, but when they heard the others in the foyer, she picked up her notebook and recorder and led the way out of the bedroom. At the bottom of the wide carpeted staircase, the Rivets stood beside Grace and Sam.

"It seems strange to just leave you guys here," Fletcher said, a valise in one hand, and the other holding a suitcase covered in Disney princesses.

"We've done this many times before," Grace said. "It's best to have the occupants leave so we're not influenced."

Merle came out of the kitchen and joined them, an overnight bag over her shoulder. The frown hadn't left her face.

Fletcher hesitated, then smiled. "It's for the best." His eyes strayed to his daughter. "Like a mini-vacation, right Rory?"

Holding her mother's hand, Rory only nodded, staring at the floor. At the last moment, before everyone left, she peeked up under her lashes at Zack and smiled. The door closed behind them.

"Looks like someone has a crush on you," Bree whispered behind him, so close he could feel her breath on his neck. A shiver broke across his skin.

He turned his head so that he could see her better. Her red lips were so close. He had the urge to run his fingers through her long, black hair. Had the new color changed the feel of it? Resisting the urge to bury his face and find out, he inhaled her new flowery scent deep into his lungs and exhaled slowly. "She's too young for me."

Her mouth quirked up. "Ya think?"

At the sound of Grace clearing her throat, both their gazes shot away. His sister stood with her arms crossed, staring at them, her head cocked to the side. Beside her, Sam wore a huge grin.

"I hope you brought some better shoes," Grace said, wrinkling her nose at Bree's high heels. "You and Zack are starting with the perimeter."

"Sure did," Bree said, stepping away from him. "Brought my glass slippers."

For two blinks Grace stared at her, then turned on her heel and went out the front door.

Why did Bree insist on antagonizing his sister? Or were their personalities so different that they were bound to clash?

Bree shrugged at Sam. "I don't think she gets my sense of humor, Sammy."

A dry laugh huffed out of him. "Yeah. She'll eventually warm up to you. Just don't be calling me Sammy in front of her." Shaking his head, he followed Grace out the door.

"They'll be getting the equipment," Zack said when she raised her eyebrows at him. "You might as well change into your glass slippers. The perimeter means a lot of walking."

With a nod, she disappeared into the sitting room, probably to retrieve her carpet bag, while he went outside to help with the equipment.

The Rivets were already gone, not even a plume of dust left to mark their departure. Several cases of equipment sat beside the van, Grace and Sam taking inventory of them. Zack scooped up three tripods and the case holding EMF meters.

"Please tell me you didn't sleep with the new girl," Grace demanded without looking at him, intent on taking everything out of the van.

Zack's throat heated. Technically he had slept with her, but not in the way Grace meant. Thank god Bree had enough sense to stop them before it could go too far. He kept telling himself it had been the smart thing to do, even though being so close to her in the sitting room had brought all his desires to the forefront. It had taken a huge amount of willpower to concentrate on the Rivets' interview.

When he didn't answer, Grace faced him fully, her eyebrows up near her hairline. "You had sex with the new girl? Dammit, Zack. What the hell were you thinking?"

"I did not have sex with the new girl—I mean Bree." He lowered his voice and glanced behind him. "I did not have sex with Bree." He followed the statement with the look he knew Grace would understand meant "back off."

"Are you going to be able to remain professional here? I have you two paired up. The only other way would be for her and me to be paired, and I'm not sure we'll both make it out alive if we do that."

"I can stay professional. It's not going to be a problem."

She stared at him a moment, eyes disbelieving, then turned to slide the last case out of the van. "Where is she, anyway?" Grace asked. "Trying to shove her feet into those glass slippers?"

In that moment, Bree stepped outside. She had changed into black skinny jeans, and a tight death metal T-shirt from the eighties, emphasizing her curves. The best part about the whole outfit were the black combat boots. Something did a somersault in his chest at how hot she looked. How was she able to change her style like that? The woman he'd met yesterday wouldn't have worn combat boots, but this woman looked right at home in them.

Bree left her carpet bag on the landing and jogged out to them. "What can I do?"

Grace gave her the side-eye. "You can start by helping us bring the equipment into the house."

Bree reached for two of the cases.

"Let me take those ones," Grace said, grabbing them from her, ones that held thousands of dollars of equipment. "You can take those over there." She pointed with her chin, indicating the cases holding more tripods.

Frowning, Bree reached for them as Grace strode to the house. Their eyes met and she had questions there, but he wasn't going to explain Grace's lack of trust.

He tilted his head toward the house when he noticed Grace had stopped on the top step, her gaze locked on Bree's carpet bag. An icy ball of dread settled in the pit Zack's stomach.

Bree's eyes went wide. The carpet bag had opened where she'd dropped it, revealing its contents.

Grace continued to stare at it for a full thirty seconds before she turned around and trapped Bree with a murderous gaze. "What the hell is this?"

She didn't yell the question, which for her meant a lot worse than if she'd been screaming.

Bright pink stained Bree's cheeks. "Um. It's not what you think."

Zack might have found the stare-down comical if it hadn't been so serious.

With a noise of utter frustration, Grace turned her gaze to Zack. "Keep her away from me." Then she spun on her heel and entered the house without looking back.

Sam blinked at the two of them with his eyebrow raised. "What was that all about?"

Bree stared at her scuffed combat boots. "I have a Ouija board in there."

A strangled guffaw-snort exploded out of his face. "You what?"

"And flour," she added.

"I hope you brought it along because you planned to bake," Sam said, his tone filled with disbelief.

"A deck of tarot cards."

Silence descended between the three of them. Zack held his breath.

"A few crystals."

He couldn't help himself and started to laugh. Like, in a weird way because he was trying not to laugh. He didn't want to hurt her feelings, and nothing about the situation was actually funny.

Sam tried not to laugh too, his hand covering his face. "What else is in there?" he asked through his fingers. "And if you say a lamp, I'll probably believe you, because I haven't seen a carpet bag like that since Mary Poppins." The way he changed his Oxford accent to cockney had Bree finally lifting her head.

"Carrot cake."

That took the laughter right out of both him and Sam. "Why the carrot cake?" Zack asked.

"I thought we might need a snack at some point and I make a mean carrot cake." She leaned toward him. "It has a secret ingredient I'm sure you'll love." She waggled her eyebrows.

Oh no. "It's raisins, isn't it?"

She shook her head. "Nope. Definitely not raisins."

He let out a sigh of relief. Bree tilted her head, her eyes narrowed.

"Well, right." He needed to change the subject. "We should probably get the rest of this inside."

When Bree started toward the front door with her two cases, he jogged ahead and set his load on the landing. "Let me," he said, reaching toward her. "I'll take those in."

Her expression fell. "She really meant for you to keep me away from her, didn't she?" She handed them over, her defeated tone breaking something inside him.

Zack didn't know how to respond. He set the cases behind him while Sam carried the last of the equipment inside. He took a breath. "I'll just be a minute, then we'll start the perimeter walk."

Bree nodded, her eyes downcast. Zack's chest constricted. He hated seeing her so dejected. He'd thought Grace had been warming up to her, but now he didn't think it possible. With one last encouraging smile, he went inside to see how pissed his sister really was. It was a miracle she hadn't fired Bree already.

Their newest employee's hours at Liller Investigations were numbered if he couldn't calm the storm, and fast.

CHAPTER SIXTEEN

B LADES OF TALL GRASS swished against Bree and Zack's legs, the chirping of birds and the buzzing of insects the only sounds between them. Grasshoppers jumped left and right to get out of their way.

Walking parallel to the highway, a black duffel bag slung over his shoulder, Zack had made a beeline for the wheat field south of the property. She'd followed, her notebook in hand and her combat boots sinking into the soft earth.

She swallowed. How had she made such a mess of her first day on the job? So far it had been a spectacular fail. She hadn't impressed her boss, the family probably thought she was a flake, and Sam had a good laugh. She wouldn't be surprised if Grace asked her to leave before the night investigation.

Deep down, the failure hurt more than she wanted to admit. She was supposed to be here to expose them as scammers, but she found herself liking them, wanting to impress them—Zack in particular. It was irrational, she knew, but that didn't take away the sting.

Well, she wouldn't do another thing for Grace to hate her. She would embody the epitome of professionalism for the rest of her time at Liller

Investigations, however short that might be, even if it killed her. To expose them as scammers—or not—she needed to stay employed a while longer.

Did she dare let her mind go there? Accepting the alternative meant believing ghosts were real, and they were not. Which left only one option.

She steeled her spine. What did she care if they all hated her, anyway? She was pretty sure they wouldn't want to be chummy once Inaya printed her story.

Pressure squeezed her ribs tight. The thought of Zack hating her didn't sit well, but if Liller Investigations took people's money in bad faith... she had to stop it. *Right?* She'd always made it her mission to help the underdog, to help those who couldn't help themselves. Her mind flashed to her friend, Jimmy, in kindergarten and the tears in his eyes behind that lemonade stand.

She'd told Inaya she wasn't doing this because of her dad. Was it the truth? *It's for every person the Lillers would steal money from in the future if I don't stop them.*

But the Rivets wanted ghosts in their house and the certificate that proved it. In that case, who was getting hurt here? That little girl, that's who. Their arguments happened at night. Using ghosts as an excuse was horrible and wrong in so many ways.

Bree exhaled slowly to relieve the stress in her chest. To distract herself, she wrote what she could remember of their interview with the Rivets in her notebook, thoughts that wouldn't be recorded by the digital recorder. She'd put it in Inaya's shared file when she got home.

That done, she took in the countryside, the warm breeze on her cheeks, the faint sound of cars traveling the highway on the other side of the hill, the wooded area they headed toward. She stepped carefully between the stalks of wheat and tried to enjoy the walk and the company—the very preoccupied company.

She glanced at Zack, then away, noting how his hair fell forward, how he ran his fingers through it to get it off his forehead. She remembered his hair as they'd snuggled together on her couch, how soft it had felt, how she'd wanted to bury her face in his scent.

Her body warmed at the memory of her straddling him, wanting to go so much further than they had. When she'd driven up to the house earlier, she'd felt the heat in his eyes. If they had been alone, she would have taken hold of his jacket and brought him in for the kiss she'd been fantasizing about since yesterday. She needed more of his taste on her lips.

Every part of her hummed at the thought and she stole another glance. Zack's head was bent, his eyes fixed on the device he held, an EMF meter, trying to pick up electromagnetic fields. The digital numbers constantly changed, but he didn't appear concerned.

When she couldn't take the silence anymore, she asked, "Can I try?"

Zack lifted his head. "Yeah. Sure. Okay."

"Wow. Three affirmatives. You must have been somewhere far away."

He blinked, then shook his head like a cat with ear mites. "Just thinking."

Probably about where he'll bury my body if Grace ends up killing me.

He stretched the meter toward her. Bree tucked her notebook under her armpit before taking it. "So what am I looking for?" She tried to concentrate on the job at hand and not the way his nearness made her body react. "This thing hasn't stayed still since we got out here. Am I surrounded by ghosts?"

"Probably not." His features relaxed, his mouth quirking up in the corner—which did nothing to help her infatuation. "There are electromagnetic fields everywhere. We're searching for the strong ones so we can set a baseline for the night investigation."

"Are we coming out here at night?" she asked, glancing around. The vastness of the open area pressed in on her. She could only imagine how unnerving it would be at night.

"No, but sometimes EM fields come from unexpected things." He nodded toward the highway. "Like power lines and such." He squinted at the meter in her hand. "Right now everything is low, and that's to be expected in an open field, but as we work our way closer to the house, we should expect a change because of the appliances and other gadgets using electricity. If anything were to spike this far out, we'd need to investigate because it could affect our readings in the house."

It all sounded rather scientific and not...scammy? Bree frowned. From Grace's reaction to the stuff in her bag, to Zack and Sam's reactions, and now all this scientific talk—her stomach clenched at the idea of posting a blog and painting them as liars, even to her small group of dedicated readers. Not to mention Inaya's debunking article that would circulate all over the city.

Her unease didn't lessen as the ground shifted from the soft, tilled earth to loose stones and hard-packed dirt. They left the wheat field and skirted the edge of the woods.

"Do we need to check anything out there?" she asked, pointing the meter at the poplars and bushes, sunlight streaking through the branches. A rustling sound told her critters were nearby, but nothing big enough for concern. Probably squirrels. The numbers on the meter didn't change.

"No," Zack said, stopping. "But this is where we'll put up the first stationary cameras." Setting the duffel on the ground, he bent on one knee, pulling out nylon straps, two tripods, and two cameras.

He attached the first camera to one tripod, then placed it against the tree trunk. About ten feet up, the camera pointed toward the house.

"Hold this," he said.

Bree held the tripod securely to the trunk and glanced at the house about a football field away. Using straps, he cinched the tripod to the tree in three different places, then took out a hammer and nailed the top and bottom strap for added measure. When she let go, the thing didn't move an inch. He repeated the process with the second camera, this one facing away from the house, and intertwined the straps to secure it to the first camera.

"Why two cameras?" she asked when they both stepped away to admire his handiwork. Standing side by side, she was entirely too aware of him.

"I like to be thorough." He gave her a nod and picked up the duffel.

They continued their walk. About a hundred yards further, he repeated the process, securing two more cameras to a tree. That completed, they walked again, skirting the house in a huge arc.

Zack stopped abruptly and frowned over his shoulder.

"What is it?" she asked, searching for movement.

He didn't answer for a full minute. His head turned in the direction of the woods, his gaze distant. Maybe he heard something? Bree focused her attention in that direction. All she could hear was the gentle rustling of leaves in the breeze. Not even the noises from the highway made it this far.

Zack focused back on her. "What does the meter say?"

Bree had forgotten that she held the thing. "Um. Right." She pointed it in the direction they'd been walking. "Nothing unusual."

"What about over there?" He gestured in the direction where the poplars changed to aspens.

Bree pointed the meter in that direction. The numbers spiked. Her heart rate sped up. "There is something that way." She showed him the numbers on the panel.

He nodded once. "Then let's go."

Tall grass swished around their legs. More grasshoppers jumped. Bree waved her hand in front of her face, the gossamer touch of unseen cobwebs brushing her cheeks.

Zack glanced over at her. "We'll have to check each other for ticks when we're done."

"Ticks?" Bree shuddered and knew she sounded horrified.

He shrugged. "Comes with the territory, but it isn't a big deal. Haven't you ever gotten a tick on you before?"

She shook her head. "Nope. Not even once and I'm pretty sure I'm not sad about it."

He flashed her a smile.

With ticks in mind, Bree kept checking the legs of her jeans, brushing at her arms while trying to keep hold of the EMF meter. She glanced at Zack, pretty sure he was laughing at her. His eyes twinkled while the rest of his face remained impassive.

When she felt a tickle on the back of her neck, she gave a yelp and spun around, whacking at her nape. The heel of her boot caught on a ridge and she went flying. She landed on her ass with a *thud*.

"Bree!" Zack bent on one knee to help her. "Are you okay?"

"Fine," she said, her butt smarting. "I'm not usually so clumsy."

He held out his hand for the EMF meter, took it, and with a firm grip on her wrist, pulled her to her feet. Bree dusted off her bottom. "Did I trip on a rock?"

"Not quite."

Bree looked down. Underneath a layer of dirt and hidden within the tall grass sat a flat, rectangular stone, too perfect to be naturally formed. Hunching down, she brushed off the grime and found an inscription.

"This is a headstone."

"Yeah," Zack replied.

"Isabelle Sheely. Wife. Mother. 1845 to 1873," she read aloud. Bree peered up at him. He didn't look as shocked as she felt. "Are there more?"

"I wouldn't be surprised." He backed away a few feet, in line with the first headstone. "Here's another one." He bent on one knee. "Richard Sheely. Taken too soon. 1866 to 1873." He stood, his eyes sad.

Bree's heart lurched. After exchanging a long, solemn look with Zack, they fanned out and searched for more.

They found a total of three gravestones.

"I recognize these names," she said, coming up beside him.

He nodded. "Matthew, Isabelle, and Richard Sheely."

Tucked under his armpit, Bree noticed the numbers on the EMF meter spiking erratically. She took it from him while he finished his notes. He pulled out two more cameras from the duffel on his shoulder, and together they secured one pointing toward the cemetery from the front of the wooded area. The other they walked about fifty feet and pointed it across the cemetery toward the house.

"What gives off electromagnetic fields at a grave site?" She scanned the area for nearby power lines, but there were none. Nothing around but the poplar wood on one side, and the aspens on the other. They couldn't see the house from here, the aspens blocking the view.

Zack didn't answer. She turned to him, wondering if he'd heard the question.

But he was staring at her. He'd heard her.

She needed to get to the bottom of this. "Paranormal investigators use EMF meters because they believe ghosts mess with electromagnetic fields, right?"

"Something like that."

She studied the grave markers, then the sporadic meter readings. Was he trying to say there were ghosts, *right now*, making the thing go bonkers? She couldn't let herself believe it. There had to be a more plausible explanation, like underground power lines. That was a thing, right?

The wind picked up for a moment, the sound eerily familiar, and for a second, she was transported to another place. A place where pine trees dominated instead of aspens, where trout lilies covered the ground, and bees danced from bloom to bloom.

Bree shivered, then shook herself out of it, surprised to see goosebumps covering her arms when it was far from cold out. She refocused on Zack. "How did you know this was here?"

"I didn't." He returned her gaze with an unnervingly level one.

"But you..." She paused, processing everything. "You told me to scan in this direction before the meter acted up."

"Like I said, I like to be thorough." He turned away, stopping her next question.

How *had* he known about the cemetery? "Have you been here before?"

"No." He walked away, the duffel bag secure over his shoulder.

She followed. "Did you find out about this cemetery in your research?"

"This is the first I've seen or heard of it." He picked up his pace and Bree had to jog to catch up.

"But?" She drew the one-word question out.

The look he shot her should have stopped her questions, but she wasn't easily scared off. "How did you know about the cemetery?"

He didn't answer.

"Zack."

He spun around to her. "It was just a hunch, okay? That's it. I get hunches."

"Hunches?" With everything that sounded scientific earlier, this really did not, and she couldn't keep the skepticism from her voice.

He'd known something was in this direction before the meter had, and if it wasn't a "hunch" then what could it be? The only other explanation was if he'd come out here earlier and made this happen, but she couldn't believe that he'd do that to her. Would he? The thought stung.

He turned away and walked along the edge of the aspens, making a soft curve toward the house. She jogged to catch up and noticed the EMF meter stabilized the farther they moved away from the cemetery.

They stopped one more time to set up a last pair of cameras. Zack said nothing as they secured the equipment to the tree. Now that Bree was familiar with the process, she stayed silent while holding the tripods steady.

She knew she'd said something wrong, but wasn't sure how to fix it. Every time she opened her mouth to try and bring back their earlier camaraderie, she shut it again, not wanting to make it worse.

The quiet and strain between them remained until they circled all the way to the house.

CHAPTER SEVENTEEN

Zack knew he was being an ass but couldn't help it. He wanted to be honest with Bree right now, knew he'd hurt her feelings with his curt answers, but the panic in his chest had grown too acute to ignore.

The tall grasses abruptly changing to short where the Rivets mowed the property. Bree marched up beside him, shoulders squared and chin jutted forward. He wanted to erase this new tension between them, to take her fingers in his like they'd done when they'd walked to the food truck. Holding hands had made him feel on top of the world, like all the regular bullshit in life didn't matter.

Instead, he curled his fingers inward, making fists. He needed to focus on the job, not Bree and how she made him feel. There were still cameras to mount at the front of the house, but he could do it later. He needed some space, a place to clear his head, some time to figure out how he should approach Bree's questions. She was a skeptic, after all, and skeptics never took the news of his abilities well.

As they walked around the side of the house, Grace came out to stand on the porch, watching their approach. He could tell from her posture she'd lost the animosity she'd had before their walk.

A long breath eased from him. Grace glanced between the two of them, then looked him square in the face, her eyebrow raised in question.

He forced himself to focus on his sister's face and not the carpet bag beside her on the landing. "We've got eight cameras mounted across the back of the property," he began. "Might be a good idea to mount a few further into the woods too."

"I can get Sam to do that next," Grace answered with a nod.

"We found a cemetery," Bree piped up from beside him. "It's so overgrown you can't see it until you're on top of it."

After a glance in Bree's direction, Grace gave him a pointed stare. He knew what she was asking.

"There was some activity."

"Yeah, the meter went super active there for a while," Bree added.

Another glance at Bree, then Grace raised both eyebrows at him. He nodded. "Yeah, it seems legit."

"Like, legit ghosts?" Bree turned to face him fully.

He didn't want to answer. Hell, that's why they were here and why he was good at his job. But with Bree, he kept stopping himself from telling her the truth right before he spit it out.

"I mean," Bree went on, "I know we're here to find ghosts, or spirits, or whatever, but couldn't there be another explanation why the meter went berserk?"

Zack watched his sister, gauging her reaction. Her mouth quirked up at the corner. "Of course there could be other explanations, but I trust Zack's—"

"Hunches," he cut her off.

Grace frowned at him, her head tilted, then nodded once. "I trust Zack's hunches." She refocused on Bree. "Look, I was a little harsh earlier. Sam got me realizing you're trying to help, even if it's misguided. Just leave the equipment management to us and keep your carpet bag at home." She nudged the bag in question with her foot.

"Okay. No problem." Bree took a deep breath. "Do you have something against the bag itself or just its contents? Because I've gotta tell you, it's a pretty amazing bag. I got it for five bucks at the thrift store yesterday, and I can fit a lot of shit in there. So if you don't have anything against it, I'll dump all the contents into the garbage and call it a day. Except for the carrot cake. I wouldn't put that in the garbage. It's delicious. But I want to see if I could fit a lamp in there, so I'd rather not get rid of it altogether." When his sister blinked at Bree, she added, "It was Sam's suggestion. About the lamp, I mean. You could probably fit a small child in it. Or a large one, actually."

Zack couldn't tell if his sister was amused or not. Personally, he was trying very hard not to laugh, and failing miserably. Good thing Bree couldn't see his expression. His sister remained intent on ignoring his mirth.

"Either you get rid of it or I will." The stare she sent Bree held absolute promise.

Bree stared back, lips pressed together.

Grace exhaled loudly, looked down at the carpet bag, and bent to pick it up. Bree scrambled up the steps—whether she thought his sister was going to do it harm or not, he'd never know—and lunged for it before Grace could make contact.

Startled, Grace jerked away, and the heel of her boot got caught on the strap as Bree pulled it to her chest. The combined momentum of Grace wrenching her boot free, and Bree jerking the bag away, had them both stumbling.

Seeing Bree topple backward down the steps, Zack leaped forward, trying to break her fall. Her spine hit his face. *Thwack*. Pain shot through his sinuses. His heel slipped, and what should have been a save ended up being both of them tumbling down the last three steps and landing in a heap, dust tickling his face.

When he opened his eyes, he realized it wasn't dust, but flour. He and Bree were covered in it from head to toe.

His head and ass ached from the fall, pain throbbing up his spine. Footsteps thumped down the stairs toward them. Through the flour coating his lashes he saw both Grace and Sam trying to help Bree off him.

"Are you okay?" Zack asked, holding onto her hips and not wanting to let go.

"Am I okay? Are *you* okay?" She disentangled her limbs and allowed Sam to lift her to her feet. "I just crushed you." She inspected her jeans and tried to rub off some of the flour. It wasn't helping.

Sam stuck out a hand and Zack grabbed his wrist. With a yank, he jumped on his feet, then looked down at himself. His clothes weren't black anymore.

His gaze returned to Bree. If she'd had any wrinkles, she would've appeared eighty, since her hair was now coated in the stuff.

"Streaks suit you," Bree said, her face grave. Then her lips twitched.

The laughter began deep in his belly and couldn't be stopped. It rippled through his body, exploding out of his face in huge guffaws. It actually hurt his abdomen. He braced his hands on his knees to stay upright.

Bree wasn't doing any better than him. Her silent giggles turned into full-blown laughter to match his. Tears ran through the flour on her face, creating streaks, and her arms were wrapped around her stomach.

Grace threw up her hands and marched into the house. Sam took up residence against the banister at the bottom of the stairs. Arms crossed, he chuckled along with them.

It took a long while before Zack could stop laughing. They looked ridiculous, and every time he tried to get the flour off him, it made it worse.

When their laughter finally subsided, Bree placed her hands on her hips and took a good look around.

"What a mess," she breathed.

Zack followed her gaze. Her carpet bag had exploded in the fall, everything tossed out, the broken bag of flour open on its side. The spray pattern from where it hit made an almost perfect oval, except for the void their bodies created.

Sam pushed away from the banister and bent on one knee to pick up the items closest to him, crystals, which had come out of their wooden box.

Zack did the same where he stood, starting with the Ouija board at his feet. He picked up the board and the planchette and placed them in their box.

As he and Sam picked up items and dusted off the flour, Bree remained frozen in place. They worked their way toward her. When she still hadn't moved, he stood up beside her, arms full of her stuff.

"What a mess," she whispered again, staring at the house.

When Sam opened the carpet bag, Zack dumped everything inside. He gave her arm a comforting squeeze. "It'll be okay."

She snapped her head toward him and blinked before giving him a watery smile. Her chin quivered a little when she nodded. His chest tightened in sympathy.

Bree scanned the ground around her. Squealing, she bent on one knee to pick up the square baking pan covered in plastic wrap, white frosting only slightly squished under the thin barrier.

"I can't believe this landed right side up." She sent him a big grin.

He smiled back. "Carrot cake?"

"Yes!" She took the carpet bag from Sam and ushered them both over to the picnic table at the side of the house. "Carrot cake makes everything better, so we must have some." She smacked both the pan and the carpet bag on the table, then dug around inside. "Did you happen to put a cake knife in here?" she asked no one in particular.

"Yeah," Sam answered. "I put a funny-looking knife in there."

"Then where is it?" She rooted around some more, but came up empty-handed. Hefting out a defeated sigh, she turned the bag upside down and dumped its entire contents on the picnic table. Everything clattered and rolled. Sam winced. Zack tried to keep his laughter under wraps.

"There it is!" she declared, waving the shiny blade about before peeling the plastic wrap off the pan. "This was prettier before the fall."

"Are you sure?" Zack asked. "Because it lived in a carpet bag all day."

She narrowed her eyes at him, but didn't respond as she sank the knife deep into the soft baking. Flour fell from her shoulders onto the table as she cut the piece.

Zack broke eye contact and asked Sam, "How's everything going inside?"

"Cameras are all mounted," he said, leaning a hip on the edge of the table. "We were finishing up the microphones when Grace saw you two returning. She's probably done by now."

Sam watched Bree's movements, appreciation glinting in his eyes as she lifted a square of golden-brown cake from the pan and placed it on a napkin. Zack didn't know where the napkin had come from, because it wasn't covered in flour like everything else.

"Is that from scratch?" Sam asked.

"It sure is." Bree picked up the napkin and passed to Sam. "Since you seem so excited, I'll let you have the first piece." She dug out a plastic fork from the side pocket in the carpet bag, and Zack realized it must have been where the napkins came from.

Sam took a bite and groaned. "Wow. Just wow. That's amazing," he said around his mouthful.

Bree beamed as she passed a napkin full of cake to Zack.

He squinted at the piece, not entirely sold on Sam's reaction. The man liked marmite for god's sake. He took the fork Bree offered. Her eyes were round and hopeful as she watched him.

Wondering at her fixation, he took a forkful and shoved it into his mouth and chewed. *Delicious.* But as soon as a raisin rolled over his tongue, he had the urge to spit out the whole bite.

"You said there weren't any raisins in here," he managed to say around the cake in his mouth, trying to keep it in.

"No. I said the secret ingredient wasn't raisins." She leaned forward, her face so close to his, he could close the distance and kiss her. "It's pineapple." When she leaned back into her own space, her eyes twinkled.

He forced himself to swallow. "You did that on purpose."

"You lied to me."

"I did not."

"You lied by omission."

"Okay. Yes. I hate raisins, and I didn't want to hurt your feelings on our first date." As soon as he'd realized there were raisins in that gravy, he'd wanted to stop eating, but she'd worn such a worried expression while he ate his hot dog, he hadn't wanted to be truthful.

"Was it a first date?" she asked. "Because I'm not even sure. It was really nice. The walk. The hot dogs. Then my place. I keep telling myself it's no big deal, but you said it *was* a deal and I don't know what that means. And now we're working together and your sister hates me and I have no idea what to do about anything." She lifted her hands in a shrug.

Zack couldn't take his eyes off her. Not from the way her face flushed or the way her eyes heated. Or the way she'd crossed her arms over her chest and tapped her toes against the ground in agitation as she waited for his response. Everything about her made him want to kiss her.

The sound of metal hitting metal snapped them both out of the staring contest. Sam shoved the knife into the cake again, cutting himself a second piece.

He paused in his task to raise his eyebrows at them. "What? If you don't like the cake," he said, pointing at Zack with the icing-covered knife, "shouldn't someone eat it?" He lifted his napkin to his face and took a huge bite. "Because I'll be honest," he added, the words muffled by the enormous amount of cake in his mouth, "I could definitely eat this whole pan."

Bree beamed at Sam, then swung her gaze to Zack and her eyes turned into narrow slits. "Next time, you'll tell me the truth."

"Next time we play a hot dog game?" Zack scratched his chin, trying not to laugh at her perturbed expression.

Sam snorted, almost choking on his cake. "Last time I played a hot dog game," he said after finishing his mouthful, "I ended up married." He pointed the knife back and forth between the two of them. "Be careful of that." He cut another piece of cake, put it on a clean napkin, saluted both of them before heading to the house.

"Do you think he's taking the cake to Grace?" she asked, her gaze following him up the steps.

"Yeah. He's good that way, and she doesn't have a hate on raisins." When Bree swung her gaze to him, he gave her a small smile. "Do you forgive me?"

"I'm thinking about it." She inched closer to him.

"How long do you think it will take?" He took a step closer to her.

"Not sure." She licked her bottom lip, and flour fell from her hair onto her shoulders.

"Guys!" Grace called from the top step. They broke apart as if they were on fire. Zack resisted the urge to whistle like he hadn't been caught misbehaving. "Go get yourselves cleaned up and be back here by sunset."

"Yes, coach!" Bree yelled back.

Grace froze for an instant, shook her head, and disappeared inside.

"I think she's warming up to me," Bree said with a smile.

"Yeah, totally," Zack agreed.

"You lied to me again, didn't you?"

"Yeah, but it's just so your feelings don't get hurt."

"I have pretty tough feelings. Usually." She crossed her arms over her chest, but leaned closer. "I haven't decided if I think it's sweet or if I should smack you."

"You could do both."

Her eyes flared. "You like to get smacked?"

"By you? Undoubtedly."

"Careful now. Talk like that can go to a girl's head."

Their elbows were touching. If he leaned forward, he could kiss those bright red lips dusted with flour.

Footsteps jogged toward them, making them step apart. Sam sidled up to the table. "So Grace sent me out here to stop you guys from doing the dirty on the picnic table. We can feel the heat from the house, so yeah, you'll have to play your hot dog game when the investigation is over. Yeah?" He picked up the knife and cut himself another piece of carrot cake.

Bree cleared her throat and went back to cleaning up all the items she'd dumped out of her bag. Zack was about to help when he caught Sam's pointed stare right before he lifted the cake to his mouth.

Hands up in surrender, Zack stepped away from the picnic table. He knew his brother-in-law was watching out for him, but it kind of sucked too. If they weren't on an investigation right now, he'd take Bree somewhere beautiful and secluded, somewhere they could get to know each other better without work getting in the way. That thought led to another...

Sam was still giving him a strange look.

"Right." Zack dropped his hands and cleared his throat. "Okay. So I'm going to head to my place for a change of clothes. And stuff. Right."

Bree paused her tidying to blink at him. "Hey, Sam?"

"Uh huh?" He took another bite.

"Isn't Zack adorable when he's incoherent?"

CHAPTER EIGHTEEN

Despite shaking herself out before getting into her car, Bree created flour tracks as she jogged up the steps to her apartment. The door was unlocked, and she found Inaya making herself a sandwich.

"How chaotic is it at your house if you're basically living here now?" Bree asked as she closed the door and dropped her carpet bag next to the coat stand.

Inaya lifted her head to respond. When she saw Bree's state, her jaw went slack. "What happened? Did a ghost sit on you?"

"I thought I'd gotten most of it out." Bree flicked her hair over her shoulder.

"I like your new hair, by the way. It suits." Inaya cut her sandwich in two. "How was your first day?"

Bree sat on the stool, her shoulders slumping forward. "My boss hates me."

"Zack's sister?"

Bree nodded and grabbed half of Inaya's sandwich, shoving it into her mouth before Inaya could snatch it back.

"Hey!"

Bree chewed. "I insulted her by bringing a Ouija board," she said around her mouthful.

Inaya's eyes went round. "Oh, Bree, you didn't."

Waiting until after she swallowed, Bree said, "Some other stuff too, like flour." She blew a strand of hair out of her eyes and set down the sandwich. "I dunno. I thought I was being helpful? I'd read all about ghost hunting and thought I was bringing things they could use, but Grace got soooooo angry. She told Zack to keep me away from her."

"Oh, dear. Did she fire you?"

Bree straightened. "No." Hope bloomed in her chest. "She told me to get cleaned up and return for the night investigation."

"Well, hey, then we can go forward with the article. I have to say, from the research I've been doing, it's super interesting."

Her stomach sank. "Right. The article." *Then Grace will* really *hate me.* "What if they're not scammers?"

Inaya blinked at her. "Do you believe in ghosts?"

The roar of wind rushing through pine needles filled her head, followed by an image of a bee buzzing along a curving line of yellow lilies. Bree shook off the faint memory and said, "No. I don't believe in ghosts."

"Neither do I. So how can they run a business getting rid of an imaginary thing?"

"Right. Exactly." Even as she agreed, her heart told her something different.

"What time do you have to be back there?"

"At dusk," Bree replied, shoving another bite of sandwich in her mouth and jumping up to hurry to her room.

All of her clothes were on her bed from where she'd left them that morning. She's been conflicted because she'd wanted to look professional for the interview with the family, but also knew she might be doing manual work. It had taken her forever to decide. She packed an extra set of clothes just in case. Good thing, too. Who knew it would be necessary for two extra pairs of clothes?

Bree took a quick shower, glad to get the gritty feel of flour out of her hair and off her skin. When she stepped out of the bathroom, a towel wrapped around her middle, she heard Inaya holler that she was leaving.

"Okay!" Bree shouted through her closed door. A worn-out graphic tee adorned with a sugar skull and a pair of black skinny jeans called her name. She'd bought both at the thrift store yesterday for two bucks each. After getting dressed, she hurried out to the kitchen, wanting to get to the Granwin House early this time around.

She glared at the carpet bag on the floor. It was a great bag, but entirely covered in flour. She grabbed a cloth hanging on the faucet and tried to dust off the white haze.

From within the bag, her phone buzzed. Bree's heart leaped into her throat. Maybe it was Zack checking in on her? Maybe offering her a ride? She quickly dug it out and looked at the screen. Bianca again.

Her thumb hovered over the red icon. She couldn't keep brushing off her sister, but with everything going on, she didn't want to take the emotional journey that talking to her would entail. She declined the call, but sent her a text. *Can't talk right now. Working. Will call you later.*

There. That should tide her sister over. If Bianca was anything, she was responsible and would want Bree to focus on her job.

Bree kept brushing at the flour on her bag. It took her a good twenty minutes to clean it to her satisfaction. When she was finished, she made sure to leave the Ouija board and crystals at home.

Two hours later, the sun dipped below the horizon, casting the Granwin House's kitchen in a red-orange hue that poured in through the wide window above the enamel sink. Bree tucked a lock of hair behind her ear and tried to ignore the fact that Zack stood beside her, their shoulders touching. Tried to disregard his freshly washed scent.

She'd thought the couple of hours apart would have dulled her attraction, but it hadn't. The desire to get him alone so she could eat him up had only grown. Hot dog games, indeed. Part of her brain screamed at her to be careful, to not trust him. But that part grew quieter in his presence.

Sam spread the blueprints across the kitchen counter, and the four of them leaned over to get a better look.

"One group needs to start in the attic and work their way down," Grace said, pointing to the rectangle at the far end of the one page. "The other starts in the basement." She pointed to the opposite end.

"We'll take the attic," Zack said, his tone confident.

She shivered from the memory of what Rory had said about the attic, resisting the urge to rub her arms. The girl hadn't elaborated on what had made her so scared. It was a childish fear, Bree knew, irrational. Still... she wanted to ask Zack if he was sure he wanted to start there, but then told herself to stop being juvenile.

There's no such thing as ghosts. Whatever had frightened Rory was most likely conjured from a child's imagination. And boy, did Rory ever have an active imagination. After ten minutes of playing with the girl, Bree knew that.

Or, the fear could have come from her parents fighting in the attic or something along those lines. If that were the case, Bree might be able to find some proof of the arguments up there.

"What did you find out from Rory?" Grace asked Zack.

"She likes to play Barbies and this house scares the shit out of her. Especially the attic."

Bree's stomach clenched.

Grace lifted an eyebrow at him, but didn't comment.

"You know," Sam began, "Rarely Smiles didn't really—"

Bree cut in. "I thought you said you weren't going to make up names for people anymore."

"Ah. Right you are." Sam grimaced. "*Merle* wasn't as thrilled to have ghosts in the house as the Rivets."

"To them, it's a business angle. To her it's a constant feeling of dread." Grace paused. "Not the most appealing job description, but some people don't have the luxury of being choosy about their jobs."

Her boss's genuine empathy made Bree's throat tighten with misgivings.

"So we'll start in the basement," Grace said, spreading the papers flat where they curled up at the edges. "You two move down, we'll move up, and we'll meet back here."

Sam nodded before rolling up the blueprints.

With a look of determination, Zack picked up one of the black satchels at the end of the counter and slung it over his shoulder. Bree had brought her carpet bag, but also a smaller shoulder bag, knowing she wouldn't want to lug the larger one all over the house. And not wanting to anger Grace any further, she'd left the carpet bag by the front door and slung the smaller bag across her body.

After a moment of digging in his duffel, Zack pulled out a digital camera. "I'm going to put you in charge of this," he said, passing her the camera. "The batteries are new, so you're good to go. Did you bring your notebook and recorder?"

"Yep." She tapped the small bag at her hip, then slung the strap of the camera over her neck.

Nodding in farewell, Grace and Sam headed down the steps at the side of the kitchen to access the basement. Their footsteps echoed up the narrow passageway.

Bree followed Zack out into the foyer and asked, "What kind of shots should I take?" She let out a nervous laugh. "I mean, I understand if a ghost jumps out at me I should probably snap a picture, but what else should I keep my eyes open for?"

He side-eyed her as they trekked up the carpeted steps to the second floor. "If a ghost jumps out at us," he said, taking the EMF meter out of the bag, "we can call it a night and go out for a late dinner."

"That sounds nice." She smiled when he raised his eyebrow at her, very much like his sister. "Not the ghost jumping out at us, but the dinner."

Once on the landing of the second floor, they headed left to the end of the hall and climbed the narrower staircase to the top floor. There was no carpet, and their footsteps creaked more than they had on the first flight of stairs, the sound reverberating through the walls. *Definitely going to scare off the ghosts before we get there.*

The stairwell darkened as they reached the top. The last of the sunlight had faded a while ago, so the small window on the landing didn't help. A single, closed door greeted them, its wood stained dark with age.

Giving her one last long look, Zack opened the door to the attic. The lights were off inside, and he reached in to flick them on. Four table lamps with Tiffany-inspired shades turned on. Oak rafters angled toward them, and furniture and rugs were grouped everywhere. The Rivets had tried to make the attic cozy, not what she expected of people who wanted to market their B&B as haunted.

Zack stepped in ahead of her, and they each walked around, exploring the space. A dollhouse stood prominently in one nook. When Bree moved closer, she saw that the arms and legs of all the naked dolls had been pulled off and scattered on the floor. *Weird.*

She turned her attention to the rest of the room. One particular grouping of chairs and side tables in the bay window was especially charming, a stark contrast to the creepy dolls.

Despite the fact they'd made an effort to make it inviting, Bree wanted to leave. *And that's just silly.* She forced her feet forward, feigning indifference.

"Note the time we've entered the area in your notebook," Zack said, lifting the EMF meter and scanning the room, "and any conversations we have, and the time of any noises we hear in case we need to cross reference with the other team. Start your recorder as well, noting the time when you turn it on. You can clip it to the outside of your bag or your pants so you don't have to carry it."

Bree dug out the recorder, turned it on, and clipped it to her bag. She glanced at the time on the camera before writing it in her notebook.

"Take lots of pictures. You never know what will turn up once we look them over."

"Does film or digital make a difference?"

"Honestly? Yes. Many people will only use film because they get better results. In my experience, those results are false positives. That's why I prefer digital. It skips the developing process, and possible human error, altogether."

Bree cocked her head at him. "Have you ever captured the image of a ghost before?"

Zack hesitated, glanced at the darkened window in the corner of the room, then back at her. "Yeah. A few times."

It was the first time he'd ever outright admitted something like that since she'd met him. She faced him fully. "What do they look like? Orbs of light?"

"No." He ran his hand through his hair. "Those orbs investigators usually attribute to ghosts are most likely specks of dust in the air or mistakes during developing."

When he didn't explain further, she asked, "So what do they look like then?"

"People." He gazed at the bay window.

Bree shivered. It hadn't been cold in the room when they first stepped in. "Can you show me sometime?"

His head snapped to her, the corner of his mouth turning upward. "Yeah. I can show you sometime."

They walked further into the room. The temperature rose, then went cold again. *Drafty attic.* The lights flickered.

"What was that?" she asked, spinning around in a large circle.

"It can happen with strong paranormal activity."

Swallowing, she jotted down the time of the flicker in her notebook. "You know, I watched some ghost hunting videos, and a lot of the investigators would shout out questions, hoping the ghosts would answer and their recorders would pick it up. Do you do that?"

"No. If there are ghosts here, they'll let us know. We don't need to shout."

More flickering.

"Like that?"

"Something like that." He stared at the window.

"Are you getting one of your hunches now?"

His eyes captured hers. "Yeah." After considering her a moment, his gaze returned to the window.

Before Bree could give in to the urge to run downstairs, she picked up the digital camera and snapped pictures where he stared. As he took a few steps in that direction, she clicked the shutter button, and didn't stop. It couldn't hurt to be thorough. The more pictures she took, the more evidence there would be, one way or another.

His toes bumped into the chair in front of the window, and the lights flickered one more time before going out completely.

A gasp trapped in Bree's throat and she gripped the camera.

"Keep taking pictures." Zack's voice made her jump. "There's a light sensor and it'll capture night vision shots in the dark."

Bree did as he said, even though she couldn't see a thing. As she fought the panic clawing at her throat, she kept taking pictures. She wasn't afraid of the dark. She didn't know why dread filled her. It had nothing to do with ghosts. Nope. Because ghosts weren't real.

The floor creaked in front of her.

"Please tell me that's you," Bree whispered, her death grip on the camera making her knuckles ache.

"It's me," Zack said, surprisingly close. "Turn in a circle and get as many shots as you can in every direction."

She did as he said, her hands shaking. It wasn't because she thought there were ghosts in the attic with them. *It's adrenaline, that's all.*

"Okay," she said after a minute, glad for Zack's presence in the pitch black. "I've finished."

A shaft of light stabbed the darkness. She squinted against the glare. Zack held a small flashlight. "Why didn't you turn it on earlier?" she asked, heart pounding. "I couldn't see a thing."

In the light's beam, he wore a pained expression, his brow furrowed. "It messes with the night vision shots."

"Are you okay?"

"Just a headache," he said, his voice calm and measured.

The reassuring tone settled her racing heart, her grip on the camera loosening.

The door to the attic slammed shut. Bree spun around. There was no one there. She dropped the camera to hang around her neck and scurried to open the door. *There's no way I feel safe with the door closed.* She tugged on the handle, but it wouldn't budge. *This has to be a joke, right?*

"Did Grace or Sam do this?" she asked, trying the keep the edge out of her tone. "Are they messing with us?"

He didn't answer. She braced her foot against the wall and rattled and turned the knob as hard as she could. The door wouldn't move a fraction. "Help me with this," she pleaded over her shoulder.

Zack remained in the center of the room, unmoving.

"Zack?" she asked, letting go of the door.

"Come here."

The way he said it made her look at the door, examine it like it might hold a grudge. Dread circled in her belly, but it was just a door. She obeyed his instruction anyway. Following the beam of the flashlight, she stopped in front of him.

"The door won't open until they want it to," he said, but now that she stood in front of him, his tone had calmed.

"They?" The light from the flashlight cast his features in dramatic shadows.

"Whoever is here with us. It's fine. They don't seem malevolent."

Her heart leaped into her throat. "How do you know?"

He shrugged.

"One of your hunches?"

"Yeah."

No laughter lived in his guarded expression. No stress either. She reached for his hand. For a moment he hesitated, then intertwined his fingers in hers. Slowly, her heart rate lowered.

"Zack, what's going on?"

His lips twitched. "Just a normal day at the office."

A dot of dark beneath his right nostril caught her eye. "Your nose," she whispered.

His free hand flew to his face, touching it. Blood dotted his fingertips. Quickly, he yanked a tissue from his pocket and wiped his nose clean.

"That happens sometimes. Nothing to worry about." He tucked the tissue away.

Yet, worry gnawed at her.

Her fingers in his, she tugged him closer. Leaning forward, he kissed her forehead. Minute fireworks spread across her skin, comforting.

Thud. Bree jumped, turning, searching for the source of the sound. The lights flickered, then turned on fully, making her squint against the brightness. They were alone.

"Looks like they're done playing with us." Zack smiled fully then. Fingers entwined, he tugged her to the door. It opened easily.

"What the hell?" She barely managed not to shout the question. "That had to be Grace and Sam's doing, right?"

"They're in the basement."

"Yeah, but—" Bree stopped her rationalization. *What the hell?* The whole thing was beyond weird.

It wasn't until they'd passed through the door completely she noticed it didn't have a lock.

CHAPTER NINETEEN

THEY CLIMBED DOWN THE stairs together, Zack a little ahead because of the narrow steps. Bree didn't let go of his hand, and he didn't let go of hers. After experiencing activity upstairs, he clung to the casual comfort of it, needing the contact to erase the unsettling sensations rioting through him.

Except for the occasional board creaking underfoot, silence covered the second floor like a heavy quilt, melting the tense energy following them from the attic.

Bree remained quiet as Zack flicked the light switch on in the first room, illuminating a bedroom decorated in blues and grays, a four-poster bed against the wall between two windows.

He lifted the EMF meter, feeling bereft when Bree let go of his hand to dig her notebook out of her bag. He noticed she wrote the time at the top of the page. Muted clicks filled the room as she took pictures, circling the room. The shaking in her limbs dissipated, her hands steadied as she took her last shots.

She pointed the camera at him. *Click.*

"Hey," he said, sticking his hand out.

She jerked the camera out of his reach. "What?"

"You're not supposed to take pictures of me."

"Why not?"

He didn't have a ready answer.

At his silence, she sent him a small smile. His unease of what had happened upstairs dissipated, comforted that she'd bounced back from it. A less resilient person would have been tearing down the driveway already.

Keeping his gaze, Bree let the camera hang from her neck, and slid her notebook from her bag. That smile still in place, she scribbled something inside. When he leaned over to see, she didn't turn the page away. It was the time, along with a note about him being camera-shy and whining about it.

"I'm not part of the house, that's why."

She shrugged, tucked the notebook away and lifted the camera toward his face again. He gently angled it downward.

"You're quite photogenic, you know," she said.

"No. I didn't know." He walked the outer edge of the room, monitoring the EMF meter. Nothing spiked.

"Well, you are."

He heard another click of the shutter and snapped his head toward her. She was taking a picture inside the bureau. *Thorough. I like it.*

Once he'd gone through the entire room, he stopped by the door. "Ready for the next one?"

"I am if you are," she replied, but she didn't have the enthusiasm she had a couple of hours ago.

Yeah, paranormal investigating can do that to a person.

They walked through the next two rooms, both with four-poster beds done in different colors. They repeated the process of Bree taking pictures and Zack monitoring the EMF meter for each. Again, nothing spectacular happened except he was pretty sure Bree had taken a few shots of him while he wasn't looking. He didn't know why he thought that, because every time he turned to her, she pointed the camera elsewhere. *Just a hunch.*

By the time they'd made their way to Rory's bedroom on the family's side of the house, they'd gotten into a relaxed groove with each other. They didn't have to speak as they took pictures and readings, and made a patterned grid through the bedroom.

That's why Zack jumped a bit when Bree asked, "Do you think someone came in here after the Rivets left?" Her voice shook.

Zack lowered the EMF meter and took a good look at her face. "Sam and Grace set up cameras in here. We do that for every room. Why?"

"The dolls. When we left this afternoon, they weren't like that."

The dollhouse was where it had been earlier, but instead of the dolls being dressed for prom, they were naked and disassembled, their body parts strewn about on the bottom floor. Blonde heads without their bodies stared vacantly at them.

A fissure of apprehension trickled down his spine. "Grace or Sam wouldn't do that."

"We should ask them though, you know, to be thorough and because I'd rather think about them playing jokes on us than—" She stopped mid-sentence and tore her eyes away from the scene. "I'd rather it be them playing jokes on us."

He tried to give her an encouraging smile, but knew he failed from the stricken expression on her face. "Of course, if it makes you feel better, but..."

For once, he wanted to allow her the skepticism that seemed shaken to its core, but neither his sister nor Sam would stoop so low. They didn't need to. The look in Bree's eyes told him she knew that.

She nodded and took pictures of the dolls.

Affection swelled in Zack's chest. *She has resilience, all right.*

When she was done with the dollhouse, she continued to take pictures of the rest of the room until she came to stand beside him at the door.

"So where are the cameras?"

Zack scanned the walls. "There," he said, pointing to the one corner, a cylindrical camera mounted where the ceiling met the wall.

"Who goes through the recordings?"

"We divvy up the work. It takes many hours to go through the footage. It's the longest part of the investigation, really."

"Do the cameras record sound too?"

"No, but there are sensitive microphones connected to recorders everywhere too."

"Okay. Since there are cameras, we'll be able to review the footage and find out who moved the dolls."

He gave her one nod. "Yeah. Definitely."

"How come you're saying it like it's not actually 'definitely'?"

"I didn't know I was."

"You definitely were."

He raised an eyebrow at her.

"Are we done in this room?"

"I think so."

The next room was the master bedroom, Fletcher and Adeline's. Nothing unusual happened in it except Bree took some more surreptitious shots of him as he scanned for EMF spikes. Without much fanfare, they moved onto the last room on the level.

He turned on the light. Bree stepped in, then stopped so abruptly it was like she walked into a wall.

"What is it?" he asked, moving closer.

"This was the room Selma and her sister slept in."

"Yeah, it is."

Bree kept walking in, then paused again. "It's seriously cold in here."

Zack pointed the EMF meter where she stood. The numbers blinked and rose at a fast pace. He checked the thermometer attached to the meter and noted that the temperature dropped just as fast. Bree remained rooted in place, her gaze frozen on the area directly in front of her, but there was nothing there. Nothing visible to the naked eye, anyway.

"Take your pictures."

The words snapped her out of her trance and she took shots in rapid succession, starting with the area right in front of her, then fanning out to the rest of the room. She was almost frantic about it, the clicking nonstop. Prickles of concern stabbed at him, and he moved in front of her. She paused, but her eyes kept staring over his shoulder, agitated.

He laid his hands over hers on the camera. "Bree," he said when she wouldn't meet his gaze.

Her eyes snapped to his. "Why do I feel so weird?"

"What do you feel?"

"I don't know. Itchy? Annoyed? Confused? I feel like I should run out of this room and out of the house and maybe not stop moving until I get home. Is that ridiculous?"

She'd let the camera drop and grabbed his hands like a lifeline, her fingers gripping his with more strength than she ought to possess.

"Have you ever worked as a physiotherapist?" he asked, glad she was focusing on him.

She blinked. "Um, no?"

"Is that a question? Are you unsure?"

"No?"

He smiled. "What about a massage therapist?"

Her eyes lost some of their panic. "Actually, I trained as a massage therapist for almost a whole semester, then dropped out because I realized I wanted to get the massages all the time, not give them. It was the last time my mother gave me money for school. After that, I had to pay my own way."

The distraction worked, her death grip loosening, the blood returning to his fingertips. Her eyes losing some of their panic, Bree stepped back and squared her shoulders before lifting the camera in front of her face to take more shots. She stopped to check the screen, then resumed taking shots.

He admired her resolve. She had grit, and that was what this job took.

That thought led him to another. He'd believed their former assistant had grit too. Then he'd been honest with her and Amy had left with barely a word.

He rubbed the back of his neck and noticed Bree shiver.

"Another cold spot?"

"Yeah. It's about the third I've walked through." Bree rubbed her arm.

The EMF meter kept spiking, then dropping to nothing. They hadn't discovered anything in their walk resembling this kind of movement except the cemetery itself. He'd need to check with Sam if they'd had anything similar happen while sweeping the house.

They circled the rest of the room and came to stand by the door. Bree looked down at the camera, thumbing through her last few images on the digital display. She hesitated. "What's that?"

"What?" He came up beside her to take a peek.

The image was fogged, a smear of white covering a quarter of the screen. He took the camera from her and made sure she had a clean lens. There was nothing visible on it that would cause such a mark. He examined the image, then the one before and the one after. The white haze only showed up on the one.

"You might have taken your first picture of a ghost."

"What?" She grabbed the camera from him and brought it close to her face. "There's no way to know that."

"We'll need to take a closer look at the office, enhance the image, examine the layers, but there's a pretty good chance it is."

Hours ago, he might've kept those thoughts to himself. Maybe their experience in the attic gave him the courage to express them. He hoped she was starting to open her mind to the paranormal. But as her frown persisted, he worried he'd gone too far.

The door behind him slammed shut. Bree yelped. He spun around, then stepped forward and gripped the doorknob. The knob wouldn't turn. He pulled. The door stayed stuck.

"Not again," Bree muttered, her words filled with apprehension.

Pain sliced through his forehead. Zack winced. Trying to cover his reaction, he inhaled deeply and tried the door one last time. *Totally stuck.*

When he stepped away, Bree took his spot, yanking so hard her arm should have popped right out of its socket. Her breath rasped in short bursts. She braced her foot against the jamb and pulled, her knuckles white.

The pain in his head receded, allowing Zack to step behind her and place a hand on her shoulder. "Bree," he said softly. His words drowned in the panic of her breathing.

She didn't stop yanking.

He leaned closer. "Bree." He was so close, a lock of her hair moved from his words.

She let her hands drop to her sides, but her breaths remained ragged.

He touched her other shoulder and turned her to face him. Her wide eyes darted everywhere in the room. The temperature continued to lower around them, so cold he wouldn't have been surprised if their exhales turned foggy.

Whatever manifested in the house, it appeared to focus on Bree at this moment. The more she let it take hold of her emotions, the stronger it could become. He needed to distract her. A simple question wasn't going to work. They needed to change the whole energy of the room.

Zack gently laid his hand against her icy cheek. "May I kiss you, Bree?"

Her eyes shifted and focused on him. *Good.* That's what he needed.

She gave him a tiny nod.

Cradling her jaw, he leaned forward and laid a chaste kiss on her other cheek. Some color returned to her face. He nibbled at the corner of her mouth. Her lips parted, sweet breath warming his skin.

When he pulled away, she wore a ghost of a smile. His hand brushed over her shoulder to circle her body.

Determination glinting in her eyes, Bree grabbed the lapels of his jacket and yanked him toward her. Their bodies slammed against the door. Her lips smashed into his with a fervor he didn't expect but had no arguments over. As her mouth plundered his, he ran his hands up her body, burying his fingers in her hair.

She broke apart for a moment, her chest heaving. "I've been wanting to do that all day."

"Yeah?"

"Yeah."

Their chests collided again, her camera pressing into his stomach. They each tried to take ownership of the other's mouth. The kiss was a little bit frantic and a lot hot, tongues giving and taking.

Zack's cock strained against the fly of his jeans like it wanted to be a front-row spectator. Movement against his outer thigh urged his hand downward. His palm connected with Bree's leg as it wrapped around him to squeeze him close and his cock twitched its enthusiasm. Delicate fingers skimmed around his waist and up his spine. She dug her nails into his shoulder blades. Shivers skated through the muscles of his back.

When she bit his bottom lip, sucking it into her mouth, he moaned, broke the kiss, and braced his hands against the door to catch his breath. Then he gave in to the temptation of nuzzling her neck.

She rolled her hips in response.

He mimicked the action and inhaled deeply. "You smell so good."

Her hands traveled up the front of his shirt, fingers skimming over his nipples through his T-shirt, then circling his neck. "You don't smell too bad yourself. Minty. I like it." She pressed her lips to his throat and took a nip.

He told himself to stop. The kiss had served its purpose—to distract her. The energy in the room had definitely shifted, but that one nip had him holding her face in his hands and reclaiming her lips. *So sweet.* He wanted to take his time and she responded in kind, their tongues exploring.

With every second that ticked by, Zack got more turned on. He couldn't get enough of her. He wanted to taste everything. Wanted it all.

Muffled voices drew his attention, and he reluctantly broke away from her lips. Inhaling her scent deep into his lungs, he pressed his forehead against hers. "Sounds like Sam and Grace are coming this way."

"Maybe they can let us out," she suggested softly, then bit her bottom lip, her eyes traveling to his lips, then to his eyes. "Or not."

"Zack?" Grace's muted voice came through the door.

With heavy limbs, he pushed away from the door, Bree following. "In here," he said loud enough to be heard through the door and down the hallway.

Bree stepped away from him, smoothed the front of her shirt, and tucked a lock of hair behind her ear. He wanted to grab her hand and hold it, but she picked up the camera and held it tight in front of her, fiddling with the controls and studying the last pictures she took, like she wanted to avoid meeting his eyes.

Movement in the hallway broke the light coming from under the door. The next moment, the door swung open, no hesitation in its movement to show it had been stuck.

Grace stood in the doorway, her brows crunched in a frown, Sam not far behind her. "Why was the door closed?" she asked, looking between the two of them

"We've been having problems with some of the doors," Zack replied blandly.

"Really?" Her question wasn't steeped in skepticism, but excitement.

He knew the feeling. They hadn't had a house this active in a long while.

"We've been hearing the noises Merle talked about," she said, eyes alive. "We can't place them, but we're still digging around on the main floor. When you didn't check in, and didn't answer my texts, we thought it best to search for you." She stared at Bree as she made the last statement.

Zack took his phone out of his pocket and tried to turn it on. Nothing. The red light that showed it needed charging wasn't even on. "Dead," he said, tossing it to her.

She tried to turn it on too, then looked at Bree. "What about yours?"

Bree shook herself like her mind had been somewhere else and slipped her phone from her back pocket. She pressed the button on the side. "It won't turn on." She frowned at him. "I have a portable charger in my bag downstairs."

Grinning, Grace glanced at Sam over her shoulder. The smile stayed in place when she met Zack's gaze. "I knew this was going to be a good one."

He'd thought so too.

"A good what?" Bree asked, looking genuinely confused.

"A good haunting," Sam supplied when no one else answered. "They're always after a good haunting." He shrugged, then bit into the red apple he held. "You have any carrot cake left?" he asked around his mouthful. "Paranormal activity always makes me hungry."

CHAPTER TWENTY

B REE BLINKED AT THE comment, not sure if she'd heard right. Hungry? She'd lost her appetite long ago, somewhere between the doors locking and Zack believing she'd snapped a picture of a ghost. The only thing helping her keep it together at this point was Zack's steady presence beside her and their make-out session.

As Grace and Sam jogged down the steps ahead of them, Bree's head still spun from the kiss. It had driven her to forget where she stood and what she'd been doing. She'd just wanted to ride the waves crashing over them.

Bree paused on the bottom step, a hand on Zack's arm. He stopped too, his head tilted in question.

She stared at his lips for a moment, those lips that could make her feel all kinds of tingly, then asked, "Do ghosts make you horny?"

"What?" His brows shot up.

"That kiss back there was weirdly timed."

His face relaxed. "It had its purpose."

"Which was?"

After a silent beat, he said, "Well, we were let out of the room, weren't we?"

She stared at him, disbelief ricocheting through her body. "You gave a ghost a peep show? On purpose?"

He shrugged. "Not exactly." He opened his mouth to say more, then shut it. Pursing his lips, he said, "It had its purpose."

That's weak. "Ulterior motives?" she asked, more than a little incredulous and a lot insulted. "You kissed me because of ulterior motives?"

He stepped toward her, their chests almost touching, and looked her right in the eye. "I kissed you because I wanted to."

Zack leaned closer, like he was about to kiss her again, when Grace and Sam's voices carried from the kitchen. He sighed instead.

Bree exhaled a breath of disappointment while they continued on to the kitchen.

Had Grace and Sam been holding the door? They couldn't have been. She'd heard them come up the stairs, their voices becoming louder as they neared. And that wouldn't explain the severe cold spots in the room, or how being in it had jacked up her emotions in a bad way.

The kitchen door clacked closed behind her, and she focused on the blueprints spread out on the countertop in front of Grace and Sam. The carrot cake she'd put in the fridge sat beside the large pieces of paper, and Sam ate it straight out of the pan with a fork.

The huge smile he sent her wiped away any of her suspicions about him. Down to his core, he was a nice guy, one incapable of scaring a woman by holding doors shut and tearing limbs off dolls.

"Doesn't anyone ever feed you?" Bree asked as she leaned against the counter beside him. She didn't want to look at Grace because she was pretty sure Grace would know about the kissing thing if she did. Instead, Bree stared at the blueprints like they were the most interesting things in the world. Spoiler alert: they were not.

"They feed me once in a while, but I haven't been able to stop thinking about this cake all evening. It's getting to be the witching hour, so I need to keep nourished."

The glow of the microwave clock drew Bree's gaze. "There's no way it's midnight."

Across from her, Zack shook his head. "Yeah, I agree with her. That clock has to be wrong."

Grace looked down at the watch on her wrist, the only one of them who wore one. "It's five to midnight. That's why I was getting worried about you guys."

Bree's gaze locked with Zack's. A shiver sizzled up her spine. They'd been walking around upstairs for an hour, maybe an hour and a half at the most. Not three. Three wasn't possible.

"We've lost time," Zack said quietly.

Grace hit him in the arm, breaking his gaze. "No way," she said, smiling. "The Rivets are going to love this."

"This is freaky ass shit," Bree said, exceedingly unexcited that she had lost more than an hour of her life without knowing it. What had happened during that time?

Zack had said there were cameras everywhere, so they'd be able to track their movements and—

Bree froze. *Oh shit.* She licked her lips. "Are there cameras in every room?" she asked, keeping her voice light.

"Yep," Sam said after placing the empty baking pan to the side. "We'll be able to find out what you two have been up to."

"What?" She swung around to confront him. "What do you mean by that?"

He put his hands up, surrender-style. "We'll be able to find out where your missing time went. What did you think I meant?" His gaze swung to Zack, then back to her, then to Grace, then back to her.

"Oh. Right. That's what I thought," Bree said, forcing an awkward chuckle. "I definitely didn't think you were referring to the kiss Zack and I shared in the middle of a haunted room. Or was it haunted? I don't know, but we were stuck there, and I was scared, and he kissed me, and it was seriously hot, and I don't know why I'm telling you this except that apparently we were recorded, so you guys would've found out anyway, and it probably wasn't appropriate at all, but it made me feel a lot less scared, so I guess it worked." She took a breath like she'd been underwater for a minute.

Sam's eyes went round as she finished her speech vomit. Bree cut a glance at Grace, whose eyes were glued on Zack, his expression both horrified and amused. Bree thought him very talented because she'd never seen an expression like that before.

"Um," Zack began, then cleared his throat. "Because we have hours of recordings to go through, we split it up, and you and I probably would have been the ones to watch the video. The likelihood Sam or Grace would have seen any of it was quite low."

"Oh." Bree felt like an idiot. Actually, she knew she was an idiot. "Well, just forget I said all that." She glanced at Grace.

Her eyebrow was raised, intrigue in her eyes, not anger like Bree would have expected.

"You don't keep secrets very well, do you?" Grace asked.

"I don't know about that," Bree responded truthfully. "I think I've kept a good many secrets in my life." She'd kept Bianca's secrets, and any of her friends' secrets.

She even kept some of her dad's secrets.

"But not about yourself," Grace prodded.

Bree hadn't thought about it that way before. "I guess so. If it's about myself, I tend to blab it. If it's about others, I can keep it." She shrugged, uncertain why it mattered.

"Hmmm," Grace responded.

"What does 'hmmm' mean?"

"Nothing. Just, hmmm."

"I don't think there's been a 'just hmmm' in the history of the world." Bree looked at Zack and Sam for confirmation.

"She's probably right about that, love," Sam agreed.

Grace raised an eyebrow at him.

"Or not. I'm going to wash this pan out." He turned and froze. "Um, guys." They all looked to see where he stared.

The cabinet doors were wide open. They'd been closed when they'd come into the kitchen, and now they were all open. A small sound escaped Bree as she gripped the countertop. *There's no explanation for this.*

"We've been looking in that direction and didn't notice it until now," Zack said.

Grace nodded her agreement.

Bree's fingers tightened. *Creepy.*

Whistling a happy tune, Sam proceeded to the large farm-style sink and set down the pan. When he lifted his hand to close the nearest cupboard, a can of beans fell out. *Bang.* Everyone jumped. More cans fell like they were being pushed. One by one.

Sam backed away. *Thud. Thud. Thud. Roll.* The countertop quickly became covered in cans. A few rolled to the floor, the sound echoing through the kitchen.

Then everything stopped.

Bree's heart pounded hard in her chest.

Sam cleared his throat, then stooped to pick up a can.

Zack moved to help.

Bree remained frozen to her spot. Even when all the goods were put back and they closed the cupboards one by one, she couldn't tear her gaze away. Sam washed the pan. Zack returned to the kitchen island like nothing was wrong, while Bree had the urge to scream.

The cupboards opened on their own. Things flew out of the cupboards. The cupboards opened on their own. Her breathing grew shallow. *Not enough air in here.*

A warm hand covered hers and she twitched. *Zack.* She exhaled a slow, thin breath. He stood beside her, and she couldn't stop herself from leaning into him. Grace's eyes were on them, but Bree ignored her, not caring what his sister thought at that moment, and continued to watch Sam's movements.

One question kept bouncing around in her brain, accompanied by the roaring of wind through pine trees. *Do I believe in ghosts?*

The roar of the wind, a buzzing bee, a path of lilies. Why did she keep remembering that? Where had she seen that before?

"Okay," Grace said, grabbing her attention when Sam rejoined them, "let's recap."

Bree inhaled deeply and focused on the blueprints, her fingers curling into Zack's. He stayed close.

Grace moved the blueprint of the basement to the middle of the counter. "We started here, but didn't unearth much. I felt," she hesitated, "weird about the space, but can't form any specifics about it. We didn't find any of the water Fletcher had talked about."

"Pretty unsettling down there," Sam agreed.

"Creaky wood floors," Grace continued. "Dirt and concrete walls. It hasn't been used for anything other than storage, besides the furnace and the water heater. I can see why. I didn't want to spend more time than needed down there. I wouldn't have been surprised to find more water either."

"Is water significant?" Bree asked.

"Some people believe it can act as a conduit to the paranormal," Zack explained, squeezing her fingers.

"A conduit?"

"One way they can make their presence known on our plane of existence."

A shiver rippled over her skin from head to toe. "Do you believe it?"

Zack hesitated, his eyes flicking to his sister, then back to her. "I've witnessed situations where no other explanation fit, except for it acting as a conduit, but I'm also not going to assume every puddle I come across has something to do with the paranormal."

Why does he have to make so much sense? Why am I questioning everything I used to believe? Why can't I look away from his eyes? Bree licked her lips and his eyes flared.

The clearing of a throat snapped their attention back to Grace. She spread out the blueprint of the main floor. "We toured each of these areas. Our EMF meters went off the charts here," she pointed to the room next to the kitchen, "which is actually right here."

She pointed to a single door Bree hadn't paid much attention to. She'd assumed it was a closet or pantry.

"It may have been used as a formal dining room when the building was first constructed, which makes sense with the kitchen access," Grace finished.

"They could have used it for the clinic too," Zack added.

Bree looked at him. "What clinic?"

"Remember, Matthew Sheely was a surgeon?"

"Right. I remember reading he was a doctor. I don't remember the book saying he was a surgeon. But if they used the dining room as a clinic space, they'd have quick access to boiling water."

Grace nodded. "Makes sense to me. It's also where Merle said she heard the moans."

Bree gripped the edge of the counter with her free hand. "Merle heard moans where people were probably operated on? Is this what we're saying right now?"

The three of them stared at her and said nothing.

The door they'd been talking about swung open, hitting the chair beside it with a bang. Bree yelped and squeezed Zack's fingers hard. The force of bouncing off the chair swung it back, closing it with a snap. Silence followed. Bree stared at the door, her heart racing, and waited for something else to happen. When nothing did, she turned to Grace.

Grace didn't appear one hundred percent composed either, her face pale, her eyes wary. She cleared her throat. "We also had a spike near the stairs, both at the top and the bottom, when we came to find you guys."

Her voice was way calmer than it should have been, but Bree decided to forgive her for it. Could someone have rigged the door to open? *Maybe*. But the cans falling out of the cupboards? *Unlikely*. Things were getting harder and harder to explain away.

"What did you two discover in the attic?" Grace asked looking at them.

Bree glanced at Zack, he tilted his head to her, giving her the lead.

"Um, well," she began, "it's spooky up there. They've tried to make it cozy, but I can see why Rory doesn't want to spend any time up there. While we were there, the lights went out." She looked between Grace and Sam, remembering she'd initially thought they'd been behind it. "Did you guys have a power outage too?"

Sam shook his head. "What time was that?"

Bree checked her notes. "Looks like a little after nine twenty-three. The next notation is at nine forty-five. I didn't note the specific time. Sorry." She frowned, waiting to be reprimanded.

"It's kind of hard to take notes in the dark and be freaked out at the same time," Grace said with a small smile.

"Yes." Bree straightened, setting her notebook on the counter. "Yes, it is."

Sam examined his own notes. "We were in the basement and didn't have any abnormal activity during that time frame."

Bree believed him. They weren't responsible for what happened in the attic, and that freaked her out even more. She'd rather it had been them so she could blame someone other than... what?

After the attic, the dolls in Rory's room, being locked in Selma's room, then the cupboard doors, Bree didn't know what to think anymore.

That led her down another path. "All my times could be wrong, couldn't they? I was using the time from the digital camera."

"What does it say now?" Grace asked.

Reluctantly releasing Zack's hand, Bree turned it on and read the screen. "Ten forty-seven." She met Zack's gaze. "It lost time with us."

"Then we can't trust your noted times," Grace said. "Worse things can happen, like losing all the pictures or videos."

An icy ball settled in Bree's stomach. She let the camera hang around her neck and grabbed Zack's hand again.

"Why don't you tell us what happened next?" Sam asked.

Bree nodded. "Right before that, Zack had a hunch directed at the window. Would you like to explain?"

"A hunch?" Sam asked, looking between the two of them.

Zack ran a hand through his hair. "I've been calling them hunches, but yeah, I was hunching pretty hard next to the window. There was a rocking chair there—" He stopped for a moment, glanced at Bree, then at his sister. "I focused for a long time on the chair. Bree will have images of it in her photos."

After a moment of silence, Grace asked, "Anything else in the attic?"

"After the lights went back on, the door slammed shut and locked us in." Bree turned to Zack. "I wanted to ask you about that, because I'm pretty sure there wasn't a lock on the door. How exactly were we locked in?"

"It was definitely stuck. I have no explanation for you."

Bree could tell he was keeping things from her, but she didn't know exactly what. "That makes no sense."

"You'll find many things make little sense in this line of work."

"Well, how can you work at a job if nothing ever makes sense?"

"We have ways."

"It must be very fulfilling."

"Not in the least."

"That's illogical."

His eyebrows shot up. "How is that illogical?"

"So what happened on the second floor?" Grace cut in when Bree was about to respond with another juvenile comment.

Zack went through their investigation of the second floor, highlighting the dolls in Rory's room and getting locked in Selma's room. He didn't mention their kiss, but Bree's cheeks burned anyway. While they went through the evidence, a frightening certainty settled over her.

When he finished his explanation, Grace straightened away from the counter. "This is looking very good for the Rivets."

"You'll certify their house?" Bree asked, though she knew the answer.

"Yes." Grace nodded. "They'll be happy."

"If the stuff going on in this house happens to them every day, I'm not sure I'd want to live here. Even if it attracted people who wanted to experience it."

Grace shrugged. "Scary sells. If it didn't, we'd be out of a job."

Bree tensed, her mind going to Inaya's article. It was so wrong. Liller Investigations wasn't trying to scam people. They were doing a very weird and often unexplainable job. They weren't con-artists.

The truth of it sank in, deep. *Undeniable.*

Zack let out a quiet hiss, and she realized she strangled his fingers. Bree loosened her grip and found him watching her, a pucker between his brows and a question in his eyes.

She patted his hand in apology. "So what's next?" she asked the room in general.

"That's it for tonight," Grace said, rolling up the blueprints. "We'll leave the cameras up. Sam and Zack will come get them in the morning, and we'll begin data analysis tomorrow."

Sam retrieved her carrot cake pan from beside the sink. "Squeaky clean."

A noisy creak from the other side of the haunted door had them all turning their heads. A low sound wrapped around the kitchen, almost like distant thunder, but then it morphed into the cry of a wounded animal keening its displeasure. Then nothing.

Bree cleared her throat, her dry tongue sticking to the roof of her mouth. "We're the only ones in the house, right?"

Silence answered her, then Zack added, "In corporeal form, sure." He looked her in the eye, "Do you want me to walk you to your car?"

"That would be great," she said in a rush. Bree picked up shoulder bag, hands shaking, and kept her eyes on the side door while she speed-walked out of the kitchen.

CHAPTER TWENTY-ONE

Z ACK RESISTED THE URGE to put his arm around Bree. Her shoulders were tense, eyes wide, and she had a death grip on the strap of her satchel. Every time the floor creaked underfoot, she glanced over her shoulder like they were being followed.

He couldn't blame her for being jumpy. Hell, everything that happened tonight made *him* jumpy, and he did this for a living. The strange occurrences from their night investigation would affect anyone.

On the way out, Bree grabbed her carpet bag where she'd left it near the front door. Once they stepped onto the porch, she let out a long breath. The night had cooled considerably. Fresh air and brisk wind slapped at them. Moisture hung in the air. Zack inhaled deeply into his chest.

Bree paused on the top step, opened the massive bag and pulled out a portable charger. Shaky hands shoved the cord into her phone before she dropped both back inside, then she retrieved a short, black jacket out of its depths. She shrugged it on quickly before jogging down the steps. Zack followed, wanting to stay close.

A few yard lights illuminated the front of the house and the driveway. Their feet hit hard-packed dirt, and Bree hesitated, looking back. She worried at her bottom lip, wide-eyed gaze moving upward and settling on the attic.

"What is it?" he asked, when she remained frozen in place.

She didn't answer for a beat, then a scowl overtook her features. "I hate that house."

He snorted. "Well, I don't think you'll need to return, so once you drive down the lane, you're done with it."

"That's the problem." She rubbed the side of her one arm like she was chilled despite the jacket she wore. "I keep thinking about Rory living here. If I got freaked out the most I've ever gotten freaked out in my life, except for the time in grade school when Tommy Harding filled my lunch bag with slugs, then how can a little girl live here and be happy? I mean, the Rivets seem like good people. I wasn't sure at first, but they are. So why do they want to put her through that? How could anyone in their right mind let their kid grow up in a haunted house?"

The question hit him in the gut. Zack shoved his hands into his front pockets. "Trying to make the most of a hard situation, I guess."

"I guess." A gust of wind lifted a strand of her hair and she tucked it behind her ear. Her gaze bounced between him and the house. "I don't understand what happened in there. If you go through the same thing every time you investigate a house, no wonder you brood a lot."

The bark of laughter burst from him unbidden. "It's not like that every time. It was an extremely active house. More than we usually experience." Another strand of hair lifted in the wind. Zack's fingers twitched to grab hold and tuck it where she'd put the other one.

Absently, she brushed it out of her way. A heavy breath passed her lips, then she turned and continued the walk to where everyone was parked. Zack fell into step beside her.

"It's going to take me a long time to fall asleep," she said, gazing up at the stars when she stopped beside her car. "What a pretty night."

There weren't any clouds, even though Zack could smell the rain. *Must be raining somewhere.* His mother always said that when the unmistakable damp scent blew their way.

"Do you have someone who can stay with you? Your friend I met the other day or—" He stopped speaking when he realized they hadn't covered this territory in any of their previous conversations.

"Or what?" She tipped her chin at him, the overhead yard light reflecting in her irises.

"I never asked if you had a boyfriend. Or girlfriend. Or anything." He ran his hand through his hair. *Why do I always have to sound like an ass when I talk to her?*

Her eyes crinkled at the corners as she stepped closer, their boots touching. "I don't have a girlfriend. Or boyfriend. Or anything." She leaned forward, gripped the lapels of his jacket, and kissed his cheek, her breath hot on his skin.

Zack swallowed. She stepped back, her eyes hooded in the dim light. He wanted to reach out and pull her close, to make the kiss less platonic, but he kept his hands firmly tucked into his pockets. "Did you want to call someone to stay with you?"

After some maneuvering and muttering under her breath, Bree dug her phone out of her carpet bag and looked at the home screen. "It's almost one a.m. I can't call Inaya right now. I mean, I could call her and she'd come, but I don't want to call her, because I'm a grown-ass person, and I'll leave the lights on, or something equally brave." She nodded when she finished the statement, eyed the house, then him. "It's called adulting."

"Sometimes it's okay not to do the adulting stuff on your own, you know."

"It is?"

"Yeah." This time he couldn't stop his hand from grabbing the strand of hair caught against her cheek. He let the silky, black lock whisper through his fingertips for a moment, then tucked it with the others behind her ear.

She snatched his hand before he could lower it. Shivers ran through his veins as she opened up his fingers and pressed his palm against the flat of her cheek. Her air-chilled skin warmed quickly under the heat of his hand. She leaned into him and closed her eyes. He couldn't look away.

When she turned her face and kissed the center of his palm, his mouth went dry. Her eyes opened slowly, and she let his hand drop but kept contact, entwining their fingers and holding him close, not letting him escape.

"What about me?" he asked, engrossed in the sensations shooting all over his body from the simple act of holding her hand.

"What about you?" Her eyebrows puckered.

"What if you call me? I can stay with you and keep you company tonight. If you want. If you needed someone. Or not. There's no pressure. Or anything. At all." *I'm useless.*

"Do I have to call, or could I just ask you since you're standing right here?" A smirk hovered at the corner of her mouth.

"You don't have to call. That would be unnecessary. Sorry. I'm not sure why I don't make sense around you." He resisted the urge to bang his head repeatedly against the roof of her car at how asinine he sounded, but just barely.

A full smile broke across her face. "Zack, would you like to come to my place and make sure there aren't any monsters hiding under my bed? Then maybe stay the night to make sure they stay away?"

"Yeah. I'd like that." He tugged on her fingers, then let her go. "I need to check in with Sam and Grace before we leave. How about you get in your car? I'll be about five minutes, then I can follow you to your place. Does that sound okay?"

She nodded. "I can do that."

He waited until she'd gotten in and locked her door before jogging to the house. Grace and Sam were finishing with the last of the equipment.

"That took a while," Grace said, rising to her feet from where she crouched by one of the EMF meter cases. "Did you walk around the house five times before taking her to her car?" Her voice didn't carry any of the snark he'd usually expect with a statement like that. Instead, she sounded amused.

He picked up two of the cases. "She's a bit freaked out. You can understand why."

"Which is why I'm not mad about it." Grace slung her laptop bag over her shoulder and picked up two tripods.

"I'm going to follow her home and make sure she's okay."

Opening her mouth, Grace paused, then nodded. "Understandable. I don't think I'll be falling asleep quickly tonight." She gave Sam a wry smile. "So, you know what that means."

A shudder ran through Zack. "Yuck, guys. I don't want to hear about your sex life."

Laughter erupted from Sam. "It's not what you think, mate. She's going to make me rub her feet. Works like a charm every time."

Zack stared between the two of them. They both nodded.

"Huh." With a shake of his head, he walked to the front of the house, then out to the van.

Illuminated by the overhead yard lamp, Bree waited in her car, hands tight on the steering wheel like she was about to race in the Formula 500. Once he set down the cases at the rear of the van, he gave her a wave. She lifted her fingers in response, her shoulders tense.

Maybe she needs a foot rub?

The thought made his mind wander to places it probably shouldn't, massages, oils, Bree without her clothes on...

"You're staring."

"What?" Zack's head whipped around to his sister.

She stood with her arms crossed, her one eyebrow raised. All the equipment was already packed into the van. "You've got it bad, don't you?"

He slid his keys out of his pocket. "Not sure what you're referring to."

"Right." She shook her head and headed to the front of the van to climb into the passenger seat. "Drive safe."

"Always," Zack replied over his shoulder, sliding into his car.

The van's engine rumbled. Grace gave him a salute as they pulled away from the house. He started the Impala, turned on his lights, and followed Bree once she drove down the lane.

The highway was mostly empty this late at night, the drive to town uneventful. His mind kept replaying everything they'd experienced in Granwin House. How Bree had faced each challenge with strength and perseverance—a sight to behold with fear gripping her, but not letting it bring her down.

Ever-present in front of him, Bree's taillights lit the way. She kept to the speed limit, mostly, making it easy for him to follow. Three times over the hour he saw critters at the side of the road, but none darted onto the highway.

Wickwood glowed in the distance, an orb of yellow hovering around the city to light the way. Bree slowed as they neared the edge of town. She kept to the main highway bisecting the city until she turned off near the center of town. Old downtown was quiet for a Friday night. They rolled past the library, the bakery, and parked behind the pharmacy.

When Bree got out of her car, she appeared uncertain, pink staining her cheeks in the dim light of the single street lamp in the alley.

"You okay?" he asked, coming to stand beside her and take her hand.

She shook her head. "It's silly. I was freaked out the entire trip. Kept looking in the back seat like someone sat behind me. Kept thinking some apparition would jump out in front of the car. I'm glad you stayed close.

It made me feel a lot better. But I was serious before. I don't think I'll be getting any sleep tonight."

He pulled Bree closer and her arms came around him. The squeeze she gave him constricted his breathing, but he didn't shy away.

He closed his eyes and let himself get a feel for the space they took up. He listened. Nothing in her backseat. No one was with them in the alley.

Then she said, "I need to use the bathroom."

He chuckled. "Let's get inside." She stepped away and he hesitated. "Unless you don't want me to come in? It's totally fine if you've changed your mind. I wouldn't want you to have me over if you didn't want to anymore or—"

He stopped talking when she took his hand and led him to the entrance of her apartment. They climbed the stairs together in silence, and she balanced her carpet bag on her hip to unlock the door. Once in the foyer, she dropped his hand and everything she held, and made a beeline for the bathroom. Zack stood uncertainly for a moment, took off his jacket, and hung it up on a hook by the door.

His eyes scanned the apartment. A few dishes sat in the sink and he had the urge to do them for her. Would she be insulted? He had the idea she'd give him grief about it. He continued on to the living room. The door to the bathroom opened right before he was about to sit down.

"Did you do it yet?" Bree asked.

"Do what?" he asked, glancing at the dishes.

"Check for monsters."

He knew he stared at her too long when she crossed her arms over her chest and lifted her chin. "You said you would check for monsters under my bed, so you damn well better do it. Don't stop there either. There's all the closets and cupboards too. I'm not going to assume non-corporeal forms stick to human-sized spaces at this point."

Was she losing some of her skepticism? He didn't know how she wouldn't after experiencing such an active house, but had assumed she'd find ways to explain it away. Most hard-core skeptics would.

A chance existed she was "taking the piss," as Sam would put it. Was she making fun of him right now? His gut told him no. She was scared and wanted reassurance.

Bree looked over her shoulder toward her bedroom, then over his shoulder to the kitchen. "Are you getting one of your hunches now?" She glanced at the front window. "Do you think there's anything paranormal in my apartment?"

He hadn't gotten one of his hunches when he'd been here before, but with her wearing such an earnest expression, he wouldn't half-ass it. If he was going to look for monsters, then he better do it right.

Zack shook his head. "Not right now, but I'll do a walk through just to be sure."

Her shoulders sagged a bit, like weight and tension eased from her spine. He needed to do this for her. Shifting his focus, he walked the perimeter of the living room, then into her bedroom. Bree followed close behind.

Nothing tickled at the back of his brain, or pressed against his chest. Nothing made his skin crawl, or shot pain through his forehead. He let his eyes scan over every object: the unmade bed, the laundry on the floor, the few dozen outfits splayed across the end of the bed like she'd tried on a hundred things this morning.

"Just ignore that," she said from behind him, her hands tugging on his jacket.

Instead of responding, he refocused and moved to her closet. It was half empty—everything else on her bed—except for the *Lord of the Rings* poster hanging on the back wall, Legolas front and center.

"Ignore that too."

Hard to, but he didn't comment on it. "Nothing inside the closet."

She gave his jacket a tug of encouragement.

They left the bedroom and moved on to the bathroom. He dutifully opened every cupboard and did the same in the kitchen. When he'd completed the whole inspection, he turned to face her. "We're completely alone. No—" He paused. "Hunches."

She narrowed her eyes at him. "Someday you're going to have to tell me what you were really going to say."

Maybe someday. Not today. But he was glad to see her normal sass replaced the pensive expression she'd been wearing since the Granwin House.

"Are you okay on the couch?" she asked when he didn't respond.

"Of course." He glanced at it, smirking a bit. "It's a very comfortable couch."

"I know, right?" she said over her shoulder as she made her way to her bedroom. "Inaya gave it to me and I fall asleep on it all the time." She left the door slightly open, and he heard her rustling around inside, the sound of hangers running along the rod in the closet echoing to him.

Zack took out his phone—he'd charged it in his car on the way—and saw he had one message from his sister saying they'd made it home okay. He wrote a quick text back, and when he was done, Bree came out of her room holding a pillow and a puffy comforter, her cheeks pink. In yoga pants and a snug-fitting tank top, she looked downright delicious. His mouth went dry.

"Is this okay? Do you think you'll be warm enough?"

"It's fine. Great. It's great. Perfect. I'll be hot. No. Not too hot. I'll be perfect. You're perfect." *Dammit.*

She stopped in the middle of the room, eyes wide. "I have no idea why it turns me on when you speak gibberish, but it definitely does."

"That's nice."

She chuckled.

"I mean, that's good. You're nice. Better than nice. Shit."

"Don't stop now. You've successfully distracted me from my unreasonable bout of fear." Her smile fell. "Now I've put myself right back there." She shook her head and tossed the pillow and blanket onto the couch. A heavy sigh followed. "Anyway, it's almost three, so I'm going to see if I can get a couple hours." She frowned at him. "You should too if you have to be at the house in the morning."

"I'm used to sleepless nights."

Her frown deepened. "I guess we all have sleepless nights."

Hers probably weren't like his. They stared at each other. Bree fidgeted with the edge of her tank top. For a second he thought she would yank it right over her head, but then she turned on her heel and marched to her bedroom.

She stopped at the door and turned to meet his gaze over her shoulder. "Thanks. For staying here. I—" She looked him square in the eye. "I really appreciate it."

"No problem." As responses go, he knew it was a weak one, but she sent him one of her stellar smiles before disappearing into her room, the door remaining slightly ajar.

Zack glanced around. He usually slept nude, but didn't think she'd appreciate his bare ass on her couch. Instead, he took off his shirt and boots, but kept his socks and jeans on. Not the most comfortable way to sleep, but he could handle it. After turning off the lamp, he tucked himself into the comforter, plumped up the pillow, stacked his hands behind his head, and stared at the ceiling.

And stared. And stared.

He kept listening for Bree, heard the springs in the mattress squeak when she shifted, heard the rustle of her blankets. Then silence. More squeaking, more rustling. Finally silence again. Zack relaxed into the plushness of the couch a little more. He knew he wouldn't be getting any sleep tonight. He never did after having such a heightened paranormal experience.

It was why he rarely visited his mother.

The soft shush of bare feet on carpet prompted Zack to sit up. Bree stood in her doorway. The streetlight coming in through her front window highlighted the way she bit her bottom lip.

"I can't sleep."

He lifted the edge of the comforter.

She scampered across the room and dove in beside him. The touch of her arms and hands and fingers on his bare skin felt amazing. She tucked her head under his chin, her hand over his sternum. His heart rate sped up. Instinctively, he covered her fingers with his own and stroked her back with his free hand.

"I can't seem to relax," she whispered.

"Do you want me to rub your feet?"

She pushed off him, separating their chests. "Good god, no." Her eyes widened comically. "I'm so ticklish there I can't stand when anyone touches me below my ankles. It's not the cute kind of laughing thing either. One touch, and it turns into a scream-fest-slash-ugly-cry like you wouldn't believe."

"No pedicures for you then." He pressed his lips together in an attempt not to laugh.

She shuddered.

"Okay. No foot rubs." When she didn't move, he added, "I promise."

Her eyes remained narrowed on him for two more heartbeats, then she curled back into him.

Loving the feel of her head tucked beneath his chin, he rubbed circles on her back. "Is this all right?"

She nodded. "It's just my feet," she murmured, and her body relaxed into his, limbs melting. The air under the comforter warmed considerably with her presence. Every so often her fingers would twitch against his sternum, and electricity shot to all corners of his body.

A few minutes later, she spoke again. "My brain won't shut off."

Without thinking twice about it, he kissed her temple. "Tell me more about this Tommy Harding and the wrongs he did to you in grade school."

"Ha!" she said against his skin, her breath making him shiver. "That's not as interesting as you might think. Not as interesting as you, anyway." She looked up at him through her lashes. "Tell me about your childhood. Something you're okay sharing with me."

So she understood he didn't enjoy talking about his childhood. He shouldn't be surprised; she was perceptive. But he didn't consider all of it taboo. "When I was five years old, we moved to the farm. It had always been my dad's dream to own and work the land, and that's when he could afford it. He'd been saving up for a down payment as soon as they got married. Most farmers are born into it, and they take it over from their parents. My dad was the opposite. He'd been born in the city, but longed for something different."

Bree yawned. "It is a bit unusual. Do you remember living in the city?"

"Before that? Not really. Most of my childhood memories start with the move. The house was run down, so it took a while to renovate it to my mother's liking. Three years I think. There was always something else to fix, something to paint. Grace and I helped out as much as we could. We weren't allowed to just sit around. We didn't have a TV to use as an out. If we wanted to escape the renovations, we had to go to a friend's house. Every time I'm there now, I need to fix one thing or another."

Bree made the *umm hmm* sound of agreement.

"I don't mind, though. I like to tinker around with repairs."

The soft snore issuing from her made him stop talking. He leaned his head back and snuggled down deeper.

She shifted. "Don't stop. That was totally working. Your voice is so nice." She patted his chest.

Zack smiled, gazed at the ceiling, and recounted every repair he'd done on the house, listing them one by one. Whenever he paused, Bree would wake up. So he kept going. He didn't stop until he'd mentioned everything up to the shingles he'd replaced last year.

When her soft snore turned into a moderate one, he allowed himself to close his eyes.

CHAPTER TWENTY-TWO

BREE WOKE UP ALONE.

Twisting to squint over the back of the couch, she saw the clock on the kitchen wall said ten twenty. She must have been dead to the world, because she hadn't felt Zack move, hadn't heard him get up or leave.

Despite their haunted experience the night before, she hadn't slept that well in ages. Well, except for that first night when he'd slept on her couch.

What was it about him that had her mind calming and her heart relaxing? Why did it eradicate the haunting roar of the wind like a distant memory? Why did it eliminate the fear that the next call from her sister was going to be about her dad? When she lay next to Zack, snug in his arms, all her worries faded away.

She let her head fall on the pillow and inhaled. His scent remained, rosemary and mint and a little bit of man sweat—a heady combination.

If she hadn't been so tired and freaked out last night, he wouldn't have stood a chance. Not with his gentle ways, and not with his cut body. He pleased her on so many levels without even trying. He hadn't pushed.

He hadn't presumed. And that was so hot, if he'd been there right now, she'd have their clothes off in ten seconds flat.

Bree sat up and stretched, trying to rid herself of the disappointment his absence created when a note on the side table caught her eye. She snatched it like a pickpocket would a hundred-dollar bill.

Sorry I had to leave. Didn't want to wake you. Actually, I tried to wake you but you kind of punched me so I thought I better let you sleep. I should be at the office after lunch if you'd like to join me and go over the recordings.

He'd signed his name and had drawn a remarkably realistic image of a lily. She tilted her head at it. Had she mentioned lilies were her favorite flower? She didn't think so. Under the lily in brackets he wrote: *If you think this is cheesy, ignore it.*

Bree had the urge to press the note to her chest. *That's foolish. Stop it.* Instead, she got up, walked to the kitchen, and fastened it to the middle of the fridge—on top of all the takeout menus, and beside the help-wanted flyer Zack had posted the day they'd met.

A knock at the door made her heart race. When she heard the jingle of keys, she knew it was Inaya before the door opened.

"Hey, you," Inaya said as she tossed her keys on the side table and took off her cardigan. "I texted, but you didn't get back to me."

Bree rubbed a hand over her face. "Just got up and haven't turned on my phone yet. Shouldn't you be at work?"

"You make it sound like you don't want me around. Plus, it's Saturday." Inaya surveyed the apartment. "Do you have company?"

"No."

Inaya's gaze went to the comforter and pillow on the couch. "But you did." She smirked at Bree and slumped onto a stool at the kitchen island, setting her chin in her hand. "I don't suppose you'd tell me all about it."

"I don't suppose I would."

"Hmmm."

"What?"

"Usually, you would. Usually, you'd dish all the details without batting an eye. But the other day I got a sense this one was different."

Bree crossed her arms over her chest. "What do you mean different?"

"You know," Inaya waved her hand in front of her, "different. Special. Important." She shrugged.

"I don't know what you're talking about." But even she could tell that her words didn't sound truthful. She mimicked Inaya's shrug. "I don't know what it is."

"How did your investigation go last night?"

"Oh my god, Inaya." She slapped her palms on the countertop. "It scared the shit out of me."

"What do you mean?" she asked, eyes wide.

Bree walked around the peninsula. "I mean, these people are *not* scammers." She slid onto the stool next to Inaya's. "I saw shit that couldn't be explained. We were all standing together, and the cupboards opened, and shit flew out of the cupboards. I'm not joking. There will be a video of it. I'm not shitting you."

"That's a lot of shit."

"You're telling me," Bree finished on a long breath, then let out a nervous laugh. "We can't write that article. I'm sorry." She hung her head.

"Too late. Brian is so excited about it, he wants to print it as soon as possible."

Bree's head snapped up. "No. You can't. I've told you, they're not scammers."

"And I'm telling you it already has a place. We have to write it. Boss Dude was adamant this is happening. I have to produce, or I'll lose my new position."

Bree straightened, searching her friend's excited brown eyes. "What new position?"

"The one I got yesterday. The one I came here to tell you about." She squeezed Bree's knee. "I get to do real news articles now."

"Oh, Inaya. That's great! I'm so happy for you." Bree's smile melted into a frown, the urge to cry overwhelming her. "What are we going to do?"

Inaya scratched the middle of her forehead. "I *need* to submit an article. We'll just make it different from the one I originally proposed. If you said scary shit happened, we'll write about the scary shit. As long as it's good, I can't see there being a problem."

"Thank you!" Bree gave her friend a tight squeeze. "You're the best."

"I know, I know. Now make me lunch and dish out all the gory details."

"I told you, I wasn't going to talk about Zack."

"I meant the haunted house."

"Right. I knew that."

It didn't take long for Bree to whip up some soup and sandwiches, all the while giving a play-by-play of the investigation. Inaya took notes, asked questions, and used the voice recorder on her phone to record everything.

"This is great," Inaya said after finishing her last bite. "It's going to be a fabulous article." She dusted the crumbs off the counter and onto her plate. "It's basically free advertising for the Rivet family too."

"I hadn't thought of that, but yeah, it will be great publicity for them. A win-win." Bree frowned, not feeling right about the whole thing. "Do you think the Lillers will be pissed because I helped you write this?"

"I don't see why." She held the plate aloft, her expression contemplative. "I mean, if we'd done the exposé, then yeah, I'm sure they would've been pissed, but how could legitimizing their business be bad?"

"You're right, of course." But the feeling of dread in Bree's stomach wouldn't go away. "I'm supposed to go in and help with the data analysis today. I'll let Zack know about it." It would ease her conscience.

"Do what you need to do," Inaya said, putting her plate in the sink and grabbing her purse from the table. "I was going to ask if you wanted to go shopping with me. I need new shoes, but it sounds like you'll be otherwise occupied."

"Yeah, I'll be busy." The thought of seeing Zack again so soon sent a rush of awareness through her. Not only that, the chance to go through the recordings from last night energized her. "I need to shower and get ready." She turned on her phone where she'd left it plugged in on the counter last night. He might have called or texted.

"I'll talk to you tonight," Inaya said, opening the door.

"Happy shoe shopping!" Bree yelled over her shoulder as she raced to the bathroom to grab a shower.

Afterward, she dressed in blue jeans and a red T-shirt as fast as possible. Intent on leaving right away, she grabbed her tote off the kitchen counter. Beside it, her phone buzzed. She snatched it up, hoping it was Zack.

The screen showed a picture of Bianca. *Is this a good time to call? I really need to talk to you.*

Bree sat down on the kitchen stool and stared at her phone for a good minute. If she didn't talk to her sister, the problem wouldn't go away—whatever Bianca's problem happened to be.

It's probably about Dad.

Maybe the law had finally caught up with him. Maybe he would spend the next ten years in prison for fraud, identity theft, or any of the other hundred things he'd done to steal people's money.

Straightening her spine, Bree texted back. *I'm free.*

Her phone rang a second later. Bree took a deep breath and touched the green button. "Hey."

"Bree. Wow. I was starting to think you'd fallen into a hole."

Her eyes closed. Bianca's familiar voice comforted her despite the criticism. "No holes. Just been busy." Now for the moment of truth. "What's up?"

"Okay, so this might come as a shock..."

She gripped the countertop with her free hand.

"...but Mom is getting married."

Bree's eyes flew open. "What?" She blinked at the refrigerator, trying to understand. "To who?"

"Jessica, of course."

Of course? "That was quick."

"They've been together for two years."

Had it been that long? She'd only met Jessica the one time when they'd first started dating. Bree had made the mistake of going home for her mother's forty-fifth birthday. The visit ended as usual, her mother comparing Bree to her sister, pointing out all her flaws, and saying how she'd never measure up. How she was *just like her dad.*

Bree had left feeling shittier than when she'd arrived and vowed it would really be the last time. She'd been wandering from town to town, searching for her place ever since.

"Look," Bianca said into the silence. "I know you stay away for reasons, but Mom wants us to stand with her at the wedding."

"I'm sure you can do well enough for us both."

"It wouldn't be the same."

"Why isn't she asking me this?"

Bianca's exhale came through the phone. "She didn't think you'd answer if she called."

With a grimace, her eyes slid closed. She probably wouldn't have.

"She's changed, Bree," Bianca continued. "Jessica is good for her. She's a better person. She's happy." Bianca took a deep breath. "They're going to get married at Grandma's cabin and she wants you there."

Wind roared through pines. Bree opened her eyes. Grandma's cabin. Bree hadn't been there since she was ten. Since the last time after her grandma died.

After a long silence, her sister said, "I'm sorry I didn't believe you, Little Bee," using the nickname their grandma had given her.

Icy tendrils spread through the hand that held the phone. "Believe me about what?"

"About Grandma being there at the cabin with us even though she was dead."

The roar of the wind through pines became so loud she wasn't sure if Bianca said more. With the wind circling around her, she'd followed that plump bumblebee along a path of yellow trout lilies. She'd followed the bee knowing it was special, knowing it wanted her to follow. She'd been so sad about her grandma's death, and that bee had been the first thing to bring her joy. She walked deeper and deeper into the woods, chasing the bee until she came to a clearing, butterflies dancing in a beam of light.

Bree's heart raced. She hadn't felt alone in that clearing. She'd known someone was there with her. *Grandma.*

The wind, the roar. Memories crashed over her one by one.

Bianca's voice broke through. "Will you come for the wedding?"

Why hadn't she remembered the butterflies before now? *Because there's no such thing as ghosts.* Bianca and her mom hadn't believed her. They'd said she was making up stories like her dad. *A liar.*

What had happened at the Granwin House last night shook the doubt that had been drilled into her head as a child. Her mother had been wrong, and she had been right, a little girl with no power to resist the logic of the adults around her. But she wasn't a little girl anymore, and adults weren't disputing what she'd seen. The Lillers knew it had been real. *Believed* in it.

Bree stared at the help-wanted flyer on the fridge, knowing Bianca waited for a response. A ragged exhale passed between her lips. "I'll think about it."

Bianca said nothing for a moment, then asked, "Have you heard from Dad?"

"No. You?"

"No."

Probably for the best. No news was good news. Or she could say, no news meant no really, *really* bad news.

After a stretch of silence, Bianca sighed. "I miss you, Bree. I still wear the bracelet you gave me every day."

Bree's hand went to her own, twirling it, her throat so tight she couldn't say anything.

"I'd like to see you soon," Bianca went on. "Maybe we could go on a trip together if you don't want to come here."

Thinking about rent and the empty refrigerator, Bree swallowed around the lump in her throat. "I can't afford it."

"I could pay for us both."

"I don't want you to do that."

More silence.

"Look, I gotta go," Bianca said after a while. "I'd like to have a full conversation with you, you know, to find out what you've been up to. Answer your phone more often, okay?"

"Sure." She knew she didn't sound at all sure, but couldn't help it.

A sigh echoed over the line. "Talk to you later."

"Bye, Big Bee." Bianca's nickname slipped out of her mouth right before Bree hung up.

She sat there, staring at her phone for long moments, realizing she hadn't used the endearment since their grandma passed away.

And her mom was getting married. She shouldn't have been so surprised. Her mom had been single for over twenty years. She deserved to be happy, no matter how crappy she'd been to Bree in the past.

Why had she forgotten about the bumblebee that had led her along a path of trout lilies? How had she not made the connection between the imagined sound of wind keeping her awake at night all these years? She had no answers, but remembering it now brought a swell of emotions she didn't really want to deal with.

It took her a long time to stand, to focus on anything but the phone in front of her and the hard lump in her throat. Giving herself a shake, Bree tucked her phone into her tote and headed out the door.

Liller Investigations was on the north end of town, but with Wickwood being a small city, it didn't take long to get there. Glad to focus on something other than the conversation with her sister and the odd memory of the bumblebee, Bree's heart raced as she climbed the metal steps to their office space. The opportunity to see Zack lightened her steps.

With the door unlocked, Bree let herself in, passed through the foyer, and halted in the Liller Investigations common space. The fern looked a lot better than the last time she'd been there.

She poked her head around the doorjamb of Sam's office. No one there. Grace's was empty too. Voices led her farther down the hall.

"It wasn't that at all." An unfamiliar woman spoke from the last door on the right. "I knew you might think so, but I didn't leave because of anything you told me. I'm sorry. I shouldn't have bailed without an explanation."

Silence met her declaration. Bree paused two feet away, hesitating. "Hello?"

Zack's head popped out. "Hi," he said, his serious expression replaced by a lopsided smile when their eyes connected. He stepped fully into the hallway.

"Hi." His smile made her grin, and she knew it was a goofy one by the way her stomach fluttered for just being near him.

A second later, a blonde with pale skin poked her head out of the room. With her long hair and square black glasses perched on her nose, she had a natural, effortless beauty.

"Oh, hey," the blonde said. She strode into the hallway wearing leather pants that fit like a second skin and a short leather jacket. "You must be the new girl."

A feeling of inadequacy swept over Bree, probably amplified by her chat with her sister, and she clenched the strap of her tote bag.

"Bree," she supplied, then compared Zack's all-black attire with the other woman's. *Did I miss the memo?*

"Right. Bree." The blonde stuck out her hand, and Bree took it automatically. "I'm Amy."

"Amy worked with us on three projects," Zack said. A frown creased his brow, his eyes troubled. "Then left suddenly."

"Yeah," Amy agreed, her chuckle strained. "I kind of scared myself and had to get away to clear my head. Feel pretty bad about it, leaving without a good explanation." She gave Zack a rueful side glance.

She'd been apologizing when I arrived. "You want your job back," Bree guessed, her stomach rolling.

"Hell, no." This time Amy's laugh sounded genuine. "I am *not* the right person for this job." She shook her head. "It allowed me to do some soul searching, and I think I'm going to go back to school. I was telling Zack about it when you arrived. Hey, have you seen Grace? I need to apologize to her. Sam too."

Bree shook her head. "I just got here."

She glanced at Zack, trying to keep her face neutral, but she couldn't help her concern. Something weighed on his mind. He avoided looking directly at Amy and his expression resettled into something more solemn.

The urge to step between them, to protect him, washed over Bree, but she didn't understand why.

"Well, I'll text her and track her down." Amy peered up and down the hallway like Grace would come out of the shadows. "Anyway, I feel bad for leaving you guys in the lurch," she said to Zack. "So if you want help to go through recordings, let me know. As long as I'm off site, I think I can handle it."

Amy reached into the room to grab a black motorcycle helmet and tucked it under her arm. *That explains the leathers.*

"You call me if you need anything," Amy said to Zack.

After a hesitation, he said, "Sure."

Amy strode down the hall.

"What was it?" Bree called before she could get too far.

Amy stopped and frowned at her. "What was what?"

"What scared you so much that you had to leave?"

Zack stiffened beside her.

"Oh." Amy gave a dainty shudder as she tossed her hair over her shoulder. "I read the story called *Sheely's Misery.* Scared the crap out of me. There was no way I'd set foot in that house after reading it." Her eyes shifted to Zack. "It wasn't the other thing. I promise." She gave him an apologetic smile, then continued on her way.

"Keep in touch, Amy," Zack said as she neared the door.

"I will," she said over her shoulder. "And I'm sorry I cut you guys off. It wasn't a cool move on my part." She turned and disappeared through the exit.

"Did you find that story yet?" Bree asked into the resulting silence.

"No. You?"

She shook her head. "We should probably read it."

"Yeah."

When the rumble of a motorbike shot through the building, Bree moved to the window at the end of the hall and looked onto the street.

Amy backed away from the curb, the ends of her blonde hair sticking out from her helmet, the low-rider planted firmly between her thighs. Another rumble, and she cruised down the street.

"I think I need to get myself a motorbike." Bree rocked back on her heels. "That's hot."

Zack snorted. "Don't let her boyfriend hear you say that."

She raised her eyebrow at him. "Nothing wrong with appreciating someone from afar."

"No." He reached up and touched the ends of her hair. "But it's nice to appreciate someone up close too." His eyes held hers.

Was he going to kiss her? Bree licked her lips, her pulse racing from how his eyes heated.

The outer door to the office clicked open. They both tensed. Zack dropped her hair and stepped away.

Grace and Sam exploded inward, laden with black equipment cases and duffel bags. "Did I see Amy driving down the street, or was it another paranormal event?" Grace asked, piling everything into the corner, her eyes scanning between the two of them.

Heat scorched Bree's cheeks, like she'd been caught with her hand in the cookie jar.

"It was her." Zack ambled toward his sister, reaching for the equipment bags. "She said she would text you and also apologized a lot."

With a surprised "Huh," Grace pursed her lips. "Did she say why she left?" Grace passed Zack two cases.

"Yeah, she said she beat Sam at poker, but he wouldn't pay up." Zack delivered the statement in a deadpan tone. "Something about seeing someone she knew who could make debt payments happen faster."

"It was only twenty bucks!" Sam shouted, his throat flushing. "I hardly think it's any—" he stopped talking when Grace snickered. He shook his head. "Taking the piss. Again." He set his load of duffel bags on the floor and strode to his office. "Just for that, you lot can put all the equipment away. And clean it. And—" he closed the door to his office with a slam.

Bree moved forward to help and raised her eyebrows at Grace. "A little sensitive about his debts?"

Grace chuckled. "A little." Her face sobered. "So what was the real reason she disappeared?"

"She'll probably tell you herself," Zack answered, "but she read something that scared her. She didn't give us much more."

One nod and Grace said, "I'll let you two get to work."

Her tone held a hint of censure, like she thought she'd caught them being naughty, but other than one last pointed stare, Grace didn't comment.

It wasn't like she and Zack had been kissing or anything. Or about to. Or maybe they had been about to. Bree didn't know.

Trying not to obsess over it, she asked, "So, have you looked at the picture of my ghost yet?"

CHAPTER TWENTY-THREE

S ITTING DOWN IN THE office chair, Zack connected the camera to one laptop in the editing suite and waited for the pictures to download.

His mind wouldn't stop processing what Amy had told him. Could he believe her? He wanted to, but the unease he felt since she'd turned up at the office hadn't gone away.

The day after he'd told her the truth about himself she'd run, only leaving the one text. She'd said it wasn't that, but what was he supposed to think? He glanced at Bree. He didn't know if he'd ever be able to open up to her. Not after Amy's reaction, and definitely not considering how skeptical Bree had been in the beginning.

Sure, the experience at the Granwin House might have shaken her, but he knew most people had a knack for believing what they wanted to believe. Testing how open-minded Bree had become wasn't on the table for him, at least not yet.

Bree sat quietly beside him, her hands in her lap, and stared straight ahead. Not really at the laptop screen either, more like above it.

She was uncomfortable about something, but he wasn't sure what. Analyzing the recordings? Or Amy's appearance? Or being alone in this room with him? Or that he'd been about to kiss her when Grace and Sam had walked in?

He'd promised himself to keep it professional while at work, but she'd been entirely focused on him, eyes warm and concerned.

Holding her all night had been magical. She'd snuggled into him like she belonged there. Like she felt safe in his arms and accepted him. Like she wanted him to chase her nightmares away every night.

In this room, stiffness had overtaken her posture, her fingers twisted together. He didn't want her on edge.

"I'm sorry I had to leave so early this morning." She jumped a little when he spoke, turning to focus on him. He continued, "I didn't want to, and I wasn't sure if you'd want me to wake you up. You looked so peaceful and were snoring so loud, I—"

"Excuse me, I do not snore." She flipped her hair over her shoulder, eyebrows raised.

That was the reaction he'd been hoping for. "Says who?"

"Says—" She squinted at him. "Okay, it's me who says so, and I guess I can't know since I'm the one sleeping—"

"You could always record yourself."

Her eyes narrowed further. "That's sort of weird."

"Recording yourself? How so?"

"I don't know. It just is."

The computer dinged and the completed download grabbed their attention. Thumbnails of images popped up on the screen one by one. Bree leaned forward, studying them, then pointed her finger at the screen. "That one."

Zack clicked on the image. He kept his thoughts to himself, but it looked likely that Bree caught something otherworldly in her photograph. Mostly, the image was of the bedroom, the door and bureau taking half of the frame, but one quarter of the image resembled the smoky reflection an oil slick would make in a mirror.

"What are you doing?" Bree asked when he brought up the menu.

"Saving it, then importing it into an editing program."

"What are you going to do to it?" Her tone held distrust.

He turned his head to look her in the eye. "We're going to use the tools in the editing program to enhance what's already there. We'll always have a copy of the original. In fact, while we're playing with the copy, I'm going to save all the photos and videos to two external hard drives."

"Seems sensible."

"I'm a sensible sort of guy."

She snorted.

The reaction caught him off guard. "What have you learned of me in the past few days to make you believe I'm not sensible?" he asked, genuinely curious.

She bit her lip and his eyes wandered to her mouth. Such a beautiful mouth. Made for kissing. And laughs. And jokes. His heart sped up.

"Well," Bree said, answering his question. "You work for a ghost-hunting company. Most people might not think that's very sensible."

He raised his eyebrow at her, hoping he delivered it as well as his sister. "That's all you've got? My job?"

She stared at him for a full ten seconds. "Yep." She blew upward at the stray bit of hair hanging in her eyes. "That's all I've got. Guess you're mostly sensible after all." She turned to the laptop screen.

With a small smirk, he brought up the image in the editor. "Ever used this program before?"

She shook her head.

"I'm going to walk you through this so you can work on other photos after this one."

"Got it."

First came the curves and masks, then the dodging and burning tools. He mentioned a couple of other techniques too, including going over the entire photo with a magnification lens, but didn't want to bog her down with too much information when the photograph would need simple processes. As he explained the program, she leaned in closer, inch by inch, until they were shoulder to shoulder, their heads almost pressed together.

"So dodge the white areas and burn the dark ones, and we'll see what happens." He didn't know why he whispered.

Intent on the task, she barely nodded as she moved the cursor over the image. "How do we know this isn't dust or a light flare or something like that?" she whispered after working on the photo for a couple of minutes.

"We don't right now. Hopefully enhancing it will give us answers."

As she continued to dodge ten percent at a time, then burn the darker areas to increase the contrast, lines inside the smoky area became more defined. A definite shape emerged, but he wouldn't call it. He'd wait for her to decide.

Five minutes later she stopped and let go of the mouse. "It's a face," she said, voice flat. "There's a face in the image."

"Yeah," he agreed, waiting for her to come to terms with it.

An outline of a head took up the right corner, a woman by the looks of it, hair streaking over a portion of her cheek. The cheekbones and chin really defined it as a face, everything else mostly non-existent.

Except the eyes. When Bree had taken the picture, they stared right at her.

"There's a freaking face in the photo." The statement wasn't one hundred percent steady. "Not my face. Not your face. We were the only ones in the room."

"Yeah," he said again.

She pressed her fingers to the bridge of her nose. "Could it be a double exposure?"

"The camera does have the ability to do double exposures," Zack said, and she perked up. "But who is it? How could we have double exposed someone who wasn't in the house with us?"

"Right. How could we?" she asked, her voice thin with a half-finished thought.

Zack leaned across her and took the mouse, saving the image, then printing a copy. The image emerged from their cutting-edge printer on an eight by ten matte photo paper. He slid it from the tray and held it out to her.

"You can take it home and frame it. Your first official ghost."

She stared, not touching it, then shook her head. "I'm not sure I can do that."

"Why not?"

"I've seen some horror movies, and they've had haunted pictures and videos where an evil thing comes out of the inanimate object and kills everyone but the main character in some gruesome way. Why in the world would I want to put something like that up on my wall?"

He turned it to face him, regarded the faint image of a woman, then held it out to her. "It's just a picture, not cursed. Those are movies. They're not real."

"What I thought was real and what was not has been turned upside down in the last twenty-four hours. How am I supposed to know anymore? What am I supposed to believe?" She took the picture anyway and held it tight between her fingers, her gaze fixed on it like it might disappear.

She had the right to be freaked out. He'd only been in a handful of houses—for the job, anyway—as blatantly haunted as the one they'd investigated last night. Zack wanted to reach out and touch her, but he held himself back, not sure his touch would be welcome. Sure, he'd held her all night, but that was then and this was now.

"Do you want to take a break? Grab a coffee? Clear your head?"

Bree set the photo on a clear spot on the desk, and for a moment he thought she'd take him up on his offer, then she slouched in her chair. "I'm good. I'd like to keep going."

"Okay." He respected her fortitude. "You keep going through the photos. I'm going to line up the videos and prioritize before we divvy them up with Grace and Sam."

"Make sure to give one of us Selma's room," she said without looking at him, her concentration focused on the laptop in front of her.

He tried not to smile at her self-deprecating tone.

Quiet entombed them as they both concentrated on the work. Occasionally, he'd glance over to her and admire the pucker of concentration between her brows, or the way she set her chin on her fist.

When he had each of the recordings organized into the appropriate folders, he sat back in his chair and swiveled toward her. "I meant what I said earlier. I'm sorry I had to leave you alone this morning."

Sitting back, she rested her elbows on the arms of her chair. "I'm a big girl. I only cried for a minute or two."

He leaned forward. "I'm so sorry. I should have—"

The wide smile she gave him stopped his words. "Dude. I'm messing with you. It's fine. Really. I was cozy and glad to sleep in." Her smile shifted into a frown. "Did you get any sleep?"

He shrugged. "I got enough."

Her eyes narrowed. "That's not an answer."

Should he tell her the truth? He searched her eyes. He wanted to, he really did, but he was... nervous about revealing too much of himself. Even admitting that said a lot. Bree was special. He wanted to be around her all the time. She mesmerized him. She intrigued him. But if she couldn't accept him for who he was, then they weren't meant to be together.

The thought sent a lance of pain through his gut.

"I don't sleep when I've been in an active house." After saying it, a portion of the weight he'd been carrying around since he met Bree lifted.

She blinked. "You don't sleep well, or you don't sleep, like, at all?"

"One hundred percent insomnia. It'll last for a couple days, then I'll be back to normal." Whatever normal was. He wasn't sure.

"You laid on my couch, held me all night, and you didn't sleep at all."

"Yeah." He waited for her to call him weird. Or a freak.

Her chin quivered. "I'm so sorry. I can't believe I took advantage of you like that."

He shook his head, not following.

"I used you to get some sleep, one of the best sleeps I've had in ages, and you couldn't sleep at all?" She leaned forward and grabbed both his hands. "I feel like a total ass. The least I could've done was stay up with you and commiserate. Why didn't you tell me? I could have gotten out the gin and we could have played strip poker."

"Don't say that."

She pulled back a little. "Why?"

"I'm really good at poker."

After a long blink, she burst out laughing, but sobered quickly. "Will you ever forgive me?"

He squeezed her hands, thankful she was connecting with him again. "I can tell you honestly, holding you all night was the best way I've spent one of my sleepless nights. Seriously," he affirmed when it looked like she'd deny it. "I can't think of a place I would've rather been." He gave her a cocky smile. "Though the strip poker thing is pretty tempting."

She tipped her head to the side. "Well, if you're having another sleepless night tonight, you let me know."

"Chances are good."

Laughing lightly, she let go of his hands and leaned back in her chair. "So tell me about this here," she said, jerking her chin toward the laptop's screen.

Zack froze, his limbs turning icy. An image of him in the attic took up the whole screen. One where he stood focusing toward the window. One where he was having one of his "hunches."

An aura glowed around his entire body, a golden halo of light. Grace had told him when they were kids his aura was gold, then told him when they were teenagers it glowed brighter when his dad was around, but he'd never seen it with his own eyes. *How had Bree captured it?*

"Um..." He stopped speaking, not knowing what to say. He didn't want to lie to her. He wanted to tell her the truth, but the words died on his tongue.

"The funny thing is," she said, leaning forward to grab the mouse and click to the next image. "I took a boatload of pictures in a short period of time. With the first one, I thought maybe it was the glare from the window, but it was dark outside, not sunny. Maybe from the lamp? But the angle is wrong." She kept clicking through the pictures and all of them had the same ethereal glow around his body. "It doesn't go away. Not even later when I took your picture in another room. It couldn't have been the lamp. It couldn't have been glare." She looked him in the eye. "So what is it?"

He stood and left the room.

I'm a chickenshit. He stopped halfway down the hallway. Why was he so freaked out? Why couldn't he tell her the truth?

He expected her to follow and resume her questions, but she didn't. He let out a breath, not sure how he felt about it. She was only a few feet away. He could return, explain why he left. Or he could continue to avoid her questions, avoid her.

Not something I want to do. But telling her the truth? The thought scared the shit out of him. Hell, it had taken him a full minute to admit he was an insomniac. But this? This was next-level.

Zack inhaled through his nose, trying to get the tension in his spine to ease. He leaned back against the wall and pressed his head against the hard surface.

If his sister saw him right now, he knew she'd be worried. He knew it should make him move, to go back inside the editing suite, but his feet remained glued to the floor. Maybe he needed his big sister right now.

Or maybe he needed to get his act together and face the woman he was coming to care about.

Another deep breath, and Zack pushed away from the wall. He paced one way, then the other, before turning on his heel and striding into the little office. He froze at the sight before him.

Bree held a photo in her hand, one of him. It was a side angle, his chin in profile, revealing half his face. The rocking chair sat in the corner beyond him. Maybe he'd been turning his head at the time.

Her cheeks bright pink, Bree met his eyes briefly, then looked away. "If I'm going to hang anything on my wall, it's going to be this."

The chair caught him when his legs went weak. "Why?"

"Because I like it. It's beautiful, this light around you." She lifted her eyes to his. "About the other stuff, the hunches or whatever you actually call it—when you want to tell me more, you will. Or not. That's your choice. I'm not going to pressure you."

At her words, the tension left his shoulders like he'd taken the strongest muscle relaxant in the world. She stared at him, eyes searching his face. He knew he should say something, but didn't.

She nodded once, set the photo aside with the other, and got back to work.

CHAPTER TWENTY-FOUR

A MILLION QUESTIONS LIVED on the tip of her tongue, but Bree bit them all back. She could tell Zack struggled internally—maybe with trusting her. The thought hurt.

The embarrassment of having been caught printing his picture overwhelmed her. She told herself she didn't care what he thought, that she'd only wanted a keepsake.

The mortified part of her knew the truth—the image of him surrounded with golden light did something to her she didn't want to examine. It was an image she would always want to take with her, no matter where she landed next.

She felt his eyes as she clicked through the photos one by one, searching for abnormalities, using the enhancing tools when she thought it might clean up the image. A long time passed before he turned in his chair and focused on the laptop in front of him.

The editing suite wasn't what she'd been expecting. She'd thought there would be more computers and equipment, but it was three laptops, the same amount of hard drives, three chairs, and a flat-screen TV mounted to the wall in an eight by eight-foot room.

The work helped distract her from the earlier phone conversation with her sister, but her mind still wandered back to it occasionally. The more she thought about her grandma's cabin, the clearer the sound of the wind rushing through the pine trees became.

And her mom was going to get married there. Bree didn't know what to think about that.

She kept going through the images, absorbing the comforting warmth of the man beside her. After what seemed like a hundred pictures, her eyes shifted to Zack's screen. "Can I see the video with everyone standing in the kitchen at the end of the night?"

She needed to see it, the one where things fell out of the cupboards, to watch with her own eyes that no one pulled strings, that it had actually happened. She wanted the distance of the video to analyze it with an objective eye instead of having her heart in her throat the entire time.

He queued up the recording, changing it to full screen. There were a lot of hours of footage, and he fast-forwarded through the bulk of it. Bree watched as the four of them stood around the kitchen island, the blueprint between them. Fixing her gaze on the cabinets behind her and Sam, she avoided looking at Zack to stay focused. She didn't blink, not wanting to miss a single second.

One of the cupboard doors opened a fraction.

"There," she said, pointing. "Can we magnify the cupboard?"

"It'll make the image blurrier."

The video continued on. None of them had noticed the cupboard move, and none of them turned when another door opened a smidgen. Bree held her breath, her heart pounding. Then, all the cupboards gradually swung open in unison. Sam turned, then everyone else looked too.

Bree gripped the edge of the desk as the canned goods tumbled out. She kept waiting for her rational brain to take over and give her an explanation. The only thing that came out of her mouth was, "Can we see it again?"

He started the video near the same spot. She knew she must be leaving fingernail impressions on the underside of the desk from her grip. The doors opened. The cans came spilling out.

"I—" she said, then stopped. She didn't know what to say. How could anyone explain this? How could there be any explanation except the house was haunted? "I don't understand any of this. You know that, right?"

"Yeah," he said, pausing the video where Sam washed her cake pan in the sink. "Sometimes—"

She turned to him, her throat dry, and he began again. "Sometimes there are no rational explanations for the things that happen. It's not our job to understand them. It's our job to keep an open mind. No one is making you believe anything you don't want to believe."

The sentiment appealed to her. No rational explanation existed, and that was all there was to it. She didn't need to believe in ghosts. Or spirits. Or the paranormal. He wasn't expecting that of her and it meant a lot.

She nodded once to let him know she appreciated his outlook. "What about the time loss? Have you found an explanation?"

"Unfortunately, no." He gestured to his laptop. "I've been going over the span we spent in the attic, and it looks like we've lost some time there, but it doesn't account for all of it."

Bree leaned forward. "What did you find?"

"When the door locked on us, and we were standing together, how long do you think that was?"

"I don't know, maybe five minutes?"

"On the video, we stood together for nearly twenty minutes." He rewound the video and showed her. They stood together, not moving, their fingers entwined. He fast-forwarded until the lights came on—almost twenty minutes later.

"We were frozen." Her heart pounded hard in her chest.

"Something like that."

"Has that happened to you before?"

"Not for that length of time. No."

"It hadn't felt like we were frozen."

"No," he agreed.

"That's when your nose was bleeding too."

He didn't comment on that.

Bree swallowed, trying to wrap her mind around it. "What about the rest of the time? We'd lost over an hour."

"I skimmed through other videos, but haven't found anything else. I was about to review Selma's room. I have a feeling I'll track some of the time there too."

"One of your hunches?"

"No." The corner of his lip twitched. "Just a feeling."

"So you've watched the footage of Rory's room already?"

"Only the part while we were in there."

"What about the dolls?" She shivered remembering how creepy they'd been.

"Haven't gotten there yet."

Her heart jumped. "Can we do it now?"

"Sure."

He cued up the video to the beginning. Rory's dolls were left where they'd abandoned them after playing together. Zack pressed fast-forward, and in a blink, the dolls were dismembered on the bottom floor of the dollhouse.

"There!" Bree said, pointing. "Slow that part down."

Zack rewound it to before the event and played the video in real time. Again, the dolls were how they'd left them, then in an impossible second, they lay haphazardly on the bottom floor of the dollhouse, their clothes taken off.

"What the hell?" Bree whispered, her brain unable to accept what she saw.

Rewinding it one more time, Zack played the video in slow motion. Right before the dolls moved, a streak of white shimmered across the screen. She watched the clock counting in the corner of the screen. Two seconds. That's all it took for the dolls to be unclothed, disassembled, and moved. And yet, it didn't look like the recording had been tampered with, or that Grace and Sam had been involved. No, the streak of white had torn the dolls apart in the space it took to inhale a breath.

Blood pounded in her ears.

"I'll take still images so we can enhance them in the editing program," Zack murmured, but she could barely hear him.

A ghost had moved the dolls. Not Sam. Not Grace. A ghost. Because nothing else could have moved so fast. Nothing else was invisible save for the slightest hint of white. *I don't believe in ghosts.* She kept telling herself that, but wasn't sure she could fall back on it anymore.

When Zack finished taking his still shots and sent them to his computer, Bree cleared her throat. "Maybe I can analyze one of the more benign videos? You know, to clear my head for a bit? Something boring."

"Yeah, no problem. I'll let you watch one of the outside cameras. They should be pretty uninteresting."

He sent the files to her computer.

The footage came from one camera they'd set up on the edge of the property by the aspen trees. He set up two video feeds beside each other, one facing toward the house and one away. The timestamp at the bottom of the video showed a total of twelve hours of footage.

"You don't need to watch it in real time," Zack said, turning back to his own laptop. "It would take too long. Put it on fast speed and stop the video if you see any blips. Otherwise, it should be the leaves blowing in the wind, which looks like a shimmer or a jiggle depending on how blustery it got last night."

"I don't remember there being much wind until we were leaving."

"Yeah, I think it should be a fairly boring video."

"Perfect." She needed boring right now.

Bree watched the leaves wiggle for an hour before she had to get up and use the bathroom. When she returned, Zack hadn't moved from his spot. He watched the video of them in Selma's room and her stomach did a somersault. Bree looked away, sat in her chair, and resumed the video of the trees.

Half an hour later, a streak of white across the screen made her jump out of her skin with a yelp.

"Holy shit," she breathed, her heart racing.

"What is it?" Zack asked, leaning toward her.

"I don't know." She hadn't stopped the video, and did so now, putting it in reverse by toggling with the mouse until the streak of white went in the opposite direction.

She pressed play, and they both watched the side-by-side recordings in real time.

The blur was a large, white blob ambling its way across the frame, well away from the house. It took thirty seconds before it left the frame.

Bree's mind raced. "What the hell was that?"

Zack remained silent as he got up and moved to the chair on the other side of her so he could take control of the mouse, then muttered, "We're going to find out."

He rewound the image until the blob was at its closest to the camera, right in the middle of the screen, then took a still shot. He saved the image, then sent it to his computer.

When he went back to his laptop and opened the image in the photo editor, Bree leaned in close. He cropped in underneath the white blob, and when he hit enter, the shadows beneath the blob enlarged.

Legs. There were legs, clad in black, underneath what had to be a sheet. Someone had run around the forest with a sheet over their body, pretending to be a ghost. Bree's heart sped up to the same tempo as when she'd first seen the streak of white.

"What's going on?" Her eyes hopped between Zack and the screen. "What are you trying to pull? Who is that?"

She stood abruptly, the chair careening across the floor to hit the wall with a soft *thump*. "Why have you lied to me about all this stuff? I can't believe you've been lying to me." She'd been so close to believing, then this happened—what she assumed Liller Investigations was all about from the beginning: one big hoax.

He stood too, his arms by his sides. "I haven't been lying to you."

"Then *who* the hell is that?" She gestured to the laptop.

"I don't know, but we'll find out. We'll get answers. I promise. That's what we do."

The gravity of his expression gave her pause. What was going on in his head? At first he'd appeared as angry as she'd felt when the legs under the sheet became clear. Now he looked conflicted. Could she trust him? She wanted to, but...

Her eyes strayed to the legs on the laptop screen, but returned to Zack when he ran a hand through his hair.

"This happens sometimes." He swallowed hard. "People want so badly to get certified that they pull stunts like this. We'll investigate and find out the truth. We don't give out certifications until all doubts are cleared. You've met Grace. You know how seriously she takes herself and our business."

Bree couldn't argue with that. Maybe she would have thought that Liller Investigations could fake a haunting a couple of days ago, but not now. The Rivets were the ones who wanted the house haunted. Could these legs belong to one of them? It was the only thing that made sense. She and the Lillers had been in the house when this happened according to the timestamp.

Everything has a rational explanation. That was what she believed only a few days ago. Why would she doubt that now?

Her stomach twisted. So many doubts came from her personal experiences in that house last night, things she wouldn't have believed unless she'd been there. Not to mention the old memories that had resurfaced after her chat with her sister. Bree had arrived at the office with a newly opened mind, and now she didn't know what to believe.

"What are you doing tonight?" Zack asked suddenly.

Her eyes whipped to him. "What do you mean?"

"Do you have plans?"

She crossed her arms over her chest. "Are you asking me out? This hardly seems like an appropriate time." Her eyes darted back to the image.

"Yes. No." He rubbed his hand along the stubble of his jaw, the sound making her shiver. "Sort of?"

His confusion intrigued her. "What did you have in mind?"

"I promised my mom I would visit her out at the farm, but I also have the very insistent need to spend more time with you."

Her chest did a little jump at his earnest expression.

"Would you like to come?" His next words came out in a rush, like he tried to get it all out before she told him to stop. "I think we both need some distance from this. I'm not exactly sure what *this*—" he waved at the image of the legs, "—is, but we'll find out. I'll tell Sam and Grace about it." He exhaled loudly. "It's a nice farm. There's a lot of space. A guest room. A creek. Right."

She didn't know what to say. His incoherence was sounding like her logic. "You want me to meet your mother?"

"Yeah, and see the farm and enjoy the fresh air..." He lifted his hands, then let them drop. "And spend time with me."

A strange ball of emotion settled in her stomach. Zack oozed vulnerability. She didn't understand why, but her instincts made her want to ease his conflict. And she didn't want to examine those instincts at the moment. She just wanted to go with it. Even though doubts plagued her, she didn't want to give up on him. If seeing where he grew up would give her deeper insight into who he was as a person, who the Lillers were, then she shouldn't pass up the opportunity.

"Okay." Her fingers stilled against her thighs, shocked that she'd agreed to meet his mother.

But when his face lit up at her agreement, she couldn't take it back. He looked too happy, too relieved.

"Right. Okay. I'll call my mom and let her know to expect a guest."

"She doesn't need to make a fuss." Already Bree regretted the decision. How often had she met a guy's mother? *Like, never.* And she'd only known Zack for a handful of days. She didn't want him to make too much of this.

Besides walking around the Granwin property, she hadn't visited anyone out in the country in a long time. Breathing more fresh air appealed to her. She'd been cooped up in apartments in one town after another for a long while.

But meet his mother?

She'd have to stop thinking about it that way. Going to the farm would also allow her to see Zack in his element. Last night, she'd listened to him recount renovation after renovation. Warmth spread through her chest at the memory. Now she'd have a firsthand look at his craftsmanship.

"Fussing is my mom's middle name." Zack grimaced. "Sorry. I hope that doesn't scare you off."

Of course it does. "Nope. Never," she said with a smile.

He gave her a relieved grin in return. "Great. I'll call her and let her know we're coming, and to not make a fuss if possible." He turned, then hesitated. "You're sure you're cool with this?"

His uncertainty endeared her.

"Of course." She also needed to be clear with him. "We're going as friends, right?"

"Right. Friends. Absolutely." With one last smile, he dashed out of the room. He returned in three seconds, snatching his cell phone from the desk, then wiggled it at her. "Need this."

"You sure do."

He chuckled and strode down the hallway, his boots echoing off the walls.

What the hell am I doing?

It wasn't the first time she asked herself that question, and it sure wouldn't be the last.

Her eyes wandered to the computer screen, then to the printed pictures lying beside the keyboard. Her throat clicked in a dry swallow.

The work here had freaked her out. She questioned a lot of things, including what Zack meant to her. If stepping out of the city for a while would clear her head and allow for some answers, maybe that's what she needed to do.

And she never shied away from an adventure.

Bree rushed into the apartment, a mixture of anticipation and nervousness bubbling in her stomach. She wasn't surprised to find Inaya in her kitchen, laptop in front of her, a shoebox open on the counter revealing red and white sneakers.

"Nice shoes," Bree said to her as she streaked past, grabbing her carpet bag by the door and tucking it under her arm. Before tossing it on the bed, she took out the photo of Zack and her ghost, and slid them into the top drawer of her nightstand. Zack's photo lay on top, drawing her eyes to his golden aura. After a quiet moment, she carefully closed the drawer.

What would she need for an overnight at the farm? She crossed the room, opened the closet, and yanked out a bunch of shirts.

Inaya came to the door and leaned against the jamb. "What are you doing? Going back to the haunted house?"

Shooting her friend a quick glance, Bree shoved jeans into her bag. "No. Zack invited me out to his family farm. Which, now that I think about it, is almost as scary."

A beat of silence. "Holy crap, you're going to meet his family?"

"His mother." Bree didn't know why she'd agreed to it. She'd thought by now she'd have convinced herself to call it off, but she wanted to see where Zack had grown up. She wanted to meet his mother—see if she was as cold as her own. For some reason, she didn't think his mom would be like hers.

She eyed a yellow knit top on the bed, then on impulse swapped it for the T-shirt she wore.

"This sounds super serious."

Pulling the top over her head, she shrugged. "I don't think it is. We haven't known each other long."

"Yeah, but..."

When Inaya didn't finish her sentence, Bree turned toward her. "What?"

"Have you ever met any of your boyfriends' mothers before?"

Bree turned away, jamming some socks into the bag. "No, but I don't see how that's significant."

"You don't see how that's significant?" Inaya's tone held a heavy dose of disbelief.

Bree brushed past her to the bathroom to grab some toiletries. "I don't want to psychoanalyze the thing," she said as she dumped everything from the back of the sink into the bag. "I just want to enjoy some fresh country air for a change, free of ghosts and cemeteries. That's all." She crossed to the bedroom, grabbed a book off her nightstand, and tossed it in too.

"Uh huh." Inaya lifted her brows at her. "That's an amazing bag. You could probably fit a person in there."

"Probably." Bree zipped it up, slung it over her shoulder, and headed toward the door.

Inaya followed. "How did your analysis stuff go?"

"It was strange, and eye-opening, and confusing." *So confusing.* She paused next to the kitchen counter, her carpet bag heavy on her shoulder, and turned to meet Inaya's gaze. "I met one of their former employees today, and she'd gotten so freaked out, she left. Remember the *Sheely's Misery* story I noted in the shared file?"

"Ah, yes. The library fiasco you wrote about so elegantly, the shenanigans more suited to your blog than the article."

"Right! Well, it scared her so much that she left town and wouldn't answer their texts for days."

"I looked it up and downloaded a PDF of all the *Haunted* issues. I haven't had the time to read them yet. Could do it tonight."

"I wish I had time to go through them with you. I'd like to talk to you more about what happened today, get your opinion about everything." Bree glanced at the time. "But Zack is going to pick me up right away. He wanted to try and make it there for a late supper. Can you drop the PDF in the folder so I can read it later?"

"Can do." Inaya stared at her with concerned eyes. "You've got a lot going on. Are you sure this trip is a good idea?"

No. Of course she wasn't, but she was going to do it anyway. She gave Inaya a big smile. "I think it's exactly what I need."

For a moment, she debated whether to tell Inaya about the person running around with a sheet over their head, but she didn't want the exposé back on the table. The idea made her clammy all over.

I need to figure things out on my own. She would fill Inaya in on the details when she returned. Waiting a day wouldn't matter in the long run.

Inaya came in for a hug. "Take care of yourself."

"Of course." Bree returned the squeeze, then stepped away. "Feel free to stay the night if you want."

Inaya followed her to the door. "I'll probably order a keg and have a few friends over," she said, her tone dry.

Bree nodded once. "Sensible decision."

CHAPTER TWENTY-FIVE

ZACK GRIPPED THE STEERING wheel and tried not to look at Bree too often. He was failing, miserably, but with her nose buried in a book, he hoped she hadn't noticed.

He focused on the road ahead and swallowed. As soon as the invitation had left his mouth, he'd regretted it. *Everything's going to be fine.* He had to believe that. If he didn't, he should turn the car around right now. *It's fine. Nothing to worry about.*

Even though he'd asked her to come, he hadn't expected her to agree. He wanted his mom to meet Bree. He knew they'd connect. **B**oth shared the same sense of humor, the same zest for life.

Having Bree beside him now lightened his heart and made his breathing easier.

She'd changed into blue jeans and a yellow knit top that showed a tantalizing amount of collarbone. His eyes drifted to her, then to the road. She'd taken off her sandals, her bare feet braced against the glove-box. It didn't look comfortable to him, but she hadn't moved since assuming the perch.

She turned a page in her book.

He cleared his throat. "So I see you managed to brave the library."

She tipped the book toward her so she could peruse the cover, complete with a shirtless blue alien sporting large pectoral muscles. "I called Larissa and got Nora's schedule for the week. Picked up a few yesterday morning."

She reopened the book and started reading again.

"Any good?"

Shutting the book, she twisted to see him better. "I don't know. I keep being interrupted."

"Oh, sorry, I was just—"

Bree laughed. "You're such an easy mark. I'm messing with you. Yeah, it's good. Earth just developed a new technology allowing space travel to distant galaxies. They come across this dying species who need new genetic material to survive. So, you know, men and women volunteer for the opportunity of a lifetime to shag an alien."

He glanced at her, trying to figure out if she was messing with him. Her expression remained completely serious. "Would you do it?"

"Volunteer to be an alien's bride?"

He nodded.

"Tough question, because it's so highly implausible, but I guess I wouldn't make an impulse decision sending me to another planet. I'd probably want the man or woman to hang out on Earth and date me for a while, you know?"

"Makes sense."

"Yeah, too much sense, because that is *not* how the book is playing out at all."

"I'm kind of afraid to ask."

"You probably should be." She grinned and waited.

He relaxed into his seat, her renewed mischievous mood calming him. "So how is the book playing out?"

"Well." She took a deep breath. "The main character is in trouble, like, a lot of trouble with the law and debt holders and stuff, so she sneaks aboard the vessel they use for the hoop jumps—that's the way they space travel—and stows away, but of course she's found by the head commander dude, and he's not sure what to do with her, because she doesn't want to go back to Earth, and he can't keep her on the planet for no good reason since new genetic material is such a high commodity. So, you know, hilarity ensues."

"Hilarity?"

"Sex. Hot alien sex to be exact."

"Right."

"Do you want me to read some aloud so you can get the gist of it?"

"Um," he was about to refuse when he noticed her laughing eyes. She expected him to say no. "I'd love that," he said instead.

The widening of her smile made his heart speed up. She thumbed backward in the book and stopped at a page at about the third mark.

"Okay, so he found her in the cargo hold, and when they land on his planet, he takes her to his place. Now," she held up her hand, "before you think the alien dude—Xerrex is his name—"

"Sounds like a photocopier."

She continued like he hadn't interrupted. "—wasn't being honorable, he didn't want the local authorities to put her in prison because it could mean disaster for her. Who knows where she would have ended up and with whom? So to 'protect' her—" She put air quotes around the word, one hand not really making the quote quite right because she still held the book. "—he takes her home. Oh, and her name is Farrah. Okay, here we go."

She spread the pages wide across her thighs and read:

Farrah paced inside the small space of the room, panic threatening to engulf her. All she'd wanted to do was escape. All she'd wanted to do was be safe. This wasn't safe. It was far, far from it.

"Okay, wait a sec, I'm going to skip ahead here." Bree turned the page. "This is a better spot."

"Why do you think I brought you here?"

"I don't know." Farrah's chest heaved under her thin, white T-shirt. *"I don't think I want to know."*

"I did it to protect you, vermish."

"Just to interrupt here, *'vermish'* means 'loved one,' but we don't find that out until later. So it's actually rather sweet. Okay, I'll try not to stop again. I can see you're enthralled."

Zack swallowed his chuckle and nodded, keeping his eyes on the road.

He pulled her to his chest, her breasts flattening against his hard muscles. Shivers of awareness rippled through her abdomen and legs. Her breath caught in her throat. No human man had ever made her feel this way, and her body became greedy for more.

The flash in his eyes told her he knew she liked it. Her body betrayed her.

"God, I hate it when my body betrays me. I'm like, 'Fuck off body, I'm the boss.' Anyway..."

Xerrex's hands caressed her hips, creating a heat at the core of her being. A furnace of fire burned between her legs with an intensity that terrified her.

"She should be terrified because I think that's called syphilis or crabs or something."

Zack snorted. He was starting to think taking Bree to a movie wouldn't be a good idea. She would probably give commentary during the entire thing. No, taking Bree to a movie wouldn't be a good idea—it would be a great one.

She kept reading.

His lips caressed the hollow of her throat. Farrah shivered, desire licking up her body. She needed him to touch her, to not leave one inch ignored. She wanted his lips everywhere.

Xerrex's fingers skimmed her ribs, leaving a trail of lava in their wake. He slid her shirt over her head, exposing her bare breasts to his gaze. His eyes drank her in, greedy for more. With the heat flowing through her body, she didn't have the urge to cover up. She wasn't embarrassed. She wanted more.

He brushed his knuckles under the tender flesh of her breasts. Farrah groaned. What was it about him that drove her to this height of desire? How could he make her feel this way with such a simple touch?

He thumbed her nipples, and Farrah gasped.

Bree set the book in her lap. "You know what? I think I'm done reading for now."

"Why? It was getting good." He shifted in his seat.

"I've already read this bit. I know it gets good, but I've never read a sex scene out loud before, and reading it to you was making me ridiculously horny, so I think I should stop there before I call you Xerrex and ask you to pull over for a quickie."

A snort and a chuckle issued from him at the same time. "Uh—" He didn't know how to respond. His gaze cut to her, then back to the road.

For a long moment she stared at him, her cheeks pink, her bottom lip caught between her teeth.

Maybe he should pull over?

He guessed he didn't respond fast enough. Bree lifted her book, turned to the page she'd been on, and rested it against her knees. Out of the corner of his eye, her toes wiggled on the dashboard. He was positive his car had never been happier.

Not wanting to interrupt her again, he let her read, but a restlessness that had nothing to do with a country drive settled into his bones. He took in the familiar scenery, trying to focus on which crops had been planted already, which rundown barns were on their way to falling over. When those faded into the distance, he concentrated on the growl of the motor as they traveled at sixty miles per hour.

After a long while, Bree closed her book and let it slide into her lap. "You've only mentioned your mother."

He cleared his throat around the sudden tightness there. "My dad passed away quite a few years ago," he supplied after a moment. He kept his eyes on the road.

"I'm sorry." Her voice had gone soft. "I shouldn't have pried."

He shrugged. "It was a long time ago."

"Doesn't make it any easier."

"No."

Silence enveloped the car. He wished he could regain their earlier levity. He didn't want Bree to be sad for him. He'd had enough sadness in his life, strangeness, enough of the supernatural.

And he loved that Bree wasn't any of those things. He loved her quirks. He loved her humor. He loved the way he felt when he was around her and loved to see the sparkle in her eyes when she teased him. He loved her exuberance for life and how she knew so much about so many different things. He loved—

Zack stopped his train of thought, his fingers tightening on the steering wheel. He had to stop thinking that way before he started "loving" the way she wore her shoes, and the way she walked—he knew he already did.

Bree hadn't opened her book again, instead staring out the window. "My father has been gone most of my life," she said quietly.

"Did he pass away?" he prompted when she didn't say more.

"No. My mother kicked him out when my sister and I were young. He only came back once in a while when he needed money." She gave him a mirthless smile. "He was a gambler and worse. I once watched him con five dollars off a kid with a lemonade stand. My mom had to call the cops on him more than once to keep him away."

"I'm sorry."

"It was a long time ago." She looked out the window.

"Doesn't make it any easier."

"No," she agreed.

He saw her reflection in the window, her eyes downcast.

"You said your twin was different than you. What about you is the same?"

She let out a quick bark of laughter. "Nothing." Then she shook her head. "That's not true. We have the same color eyes." She blinked at him, then said, "Other than that, we're nothing alike. We don't look alike, or talk alike, or even think alike. Bianca is skinny and smart and motivated. She owns a house and is finishing up her surgical residency at a fancy hospital in California."

"That's pretty cool," he said, not knowing what else to say.

"I guess." She stared straight ahead. "She followed in my mother's footsteps."

"Your mom's a surgeon?"

"Yep." She didn't sound pleased. "Bianca is very much like my mother, in looks and everything. While I've been told I'm exactly like my father." She turned to the window, and he saw the hurt in her eyes in her reflection.

"Besides joking about strip poker, you don't seem like the gambling type," he said, hoping to lighten her mood.

It didn't.

"It's not the gambling, not really," she said in a flat tone. "It's the never staying in one place. The indecisiveness. The lack of direction."

Silence hung in the car as he processed her words. He didn't know where the insecurity came from, but he knew it was important to get her out of her funk.

He cleared his throat.

She continued to stare straight ahead.

"Bree."

She turned her head.

He kept his eyes on the road but looked at her too, so she knew he meant what he was about to say. "You've had so many cool experiences while I've only been out of state a handful of times. You can speak multiple languages. You've worked with a photographer, and at a TV station, and trained as a massage therapist. I've never met anyone like you."

He noticed the blush on her face, hoped it was a good sign, and made himself stop talking because he didn't want to sound like a fool.

She opened her book. A small smile played on her lips before she buried herself behind the pages. Zack relaxed into his seat.

The silence between them turned comfortable. He concentrated on the road, trying not to stare at Bree's legs.

Then after a while she asked, "Do you think your mom will like me?" Her voice wobbled.

He glanced at her and nodded with the certainty he felt. "Yeah, she'll like you."

Bree leaned her head against the seat and closed her eyes.

Zack focused on the road. Whether his mother liked Bree wasn't the problem. It was whether or not Bree would be freaked out by his mom.

CHAPTER TWENTY-SIX

GRAVEL CRUNCHED UNDER THE tires as they drove up the lane to the simple farmhouse adorned with red shutters. Bree's hand tightened on the door handle as Zack slowed to a stop, anxiety rolling in her stomach.

Dogs jumped, their tails wagging with gusto as he parked beside a beat-up half-ton. A lot of old cars sat in the yard, some up on blocks. With the lawn around the house neatly trimmed, and flowers blooming in large terracotta pots in front of the porch, it managed to look eclectic despite the automobile graveyard. She noticed a 1950s Chevy truck with a gorgeous rust patina, all its windows intact, and nearly drooled.

Zack turned off the engine. A black and brown dog bounced up, his floofy paws slapping against the driver's side window.

"That's Admiral," he explained. "Then there's Major, Captain, and Sergeant. Don't let their sizes fool you. They're all big softies."

He opened the door. A flurry of fluff attacked him. He merged into the mass and tumbled to the ground. Bree leaned forward. There had to be at least six dogs on top of him.

She opened her door quickly, not sure how she could help, but wanting to offer just the same. The sound of laughter reached her as another dog rounded her side of the car at a trot. The white and brown dog stopped a few feet away with an inquisitive tilt of his head.

"I'm not the rolling on the ground type," she said to him. *Not when it comes to dogs.* She hoped he wouldn't feed off her uncertainty and attack.

The dog cocked his head the other way, trotted closer, sniffed her crotch for a bordering-on-harassment length of time, then bounded away to rejoin his friends devouring Zack.

By the time she'd rounded to the other side of the car, Zack had regained his feet, the dogs circling and sniffing his crotch like he might have a special item hidden there. She smirked. Maybe he did.

He saw where she stared and tried to shoo the dogs away while he laughed out a stuttered, strangled sound. "They haven't seen me for a while. They miss me."

"I can see that," Bree said, biting her lip as one dog came up behind him and shoved its snout into Zack's butt.

A shrill whistle made the dogs scatter. They galloped toward the house, then pinwheeled around a woman standing on the wide veranda.

Butterflies reignited their dance in Bree's stomach. She clasped her hands tightly in front of her.

Why had she agreed to come? She'd been able to distract herself a little on the drive with something that resembled reading. She hadn't gotten very far. Maybe a page before she'd given up and glared at the book, trying not to glance at Zack too often. Trying not to stare at the way his hands gripped the steering wheel. Trying not to remember what those hands felt like in hers, how they made her feel when they touched her.

Zack grabbed her carpet bag and his duffel out of the trunk.

"I can take mine," she said, holding out her hand.

Zack passed it to her, and she forced herself to hold it like a normal human being instead of hugging it in front of her like a shield.

He was already halfway to the house before she realized she hadn't moved.

This is ridiculous. I'm a grown woman.

Despite her fears about Liller Investigations' validity, she wanted Zack's mom to like her. The realization scared her more than ghosts being real, or even the possibility of Liller Investigations being frauds. That first night Zack had slept on the couch with her, he'd said it was a "deal." That first night they'd cuddled, it had felt like the most natural thing in the world.

Maybe now she was beginning to understand what a "deal" was.

As she watched, Zack walked up the steps and enveloped his mother in a hug. A tinkling laugh trickled its way to Bree's ears, making her smile. Her feet moved forward. She let out a slow exhale. *No big deal. No big deal. No big deal.*

A big part of her wasn't believing the lie.

Then there was the bigger question. Was Zack her boyfriend? It felt too soon, too fast. But she was more comfortable with him after only a few days than she'd been with most of her boyfriends after a month. After going on trips with them. After hanging out with their closest friends.

Bree neared the stoop. The house, veranda, and trim were all painted a glossy white. The flowers bloomed, healthy. A broom leaned against the railing.

Zack's mom smiled at her, offering a shy finger-wave that melted Bree's heart. Her straight, white hair brushed her shoulders, and glasses were perched on top of her head. Age and sunshine lined her face.

She reached out, and Bree allowed her to take her hands. "I'm Celeste. It's so nice to meet you."

Warm skin contrasted with Bree's chilled fingers. It only took the brief touch for the tension in her shoulders to ease.

After a squeeze, Celeste let go of her hands. "Zack hasn't brought a girlfriend to the house in a very long time."

"We're just friends," they said at the same time.

Bree narrowed her eyes at him. He squinted back.

Celeste laughed. "Well, whatever you are, it's nice to meet you. Zack said you're working on one of Grace's projects."

"Yep. It's been... interesting." Bree could see the family resemblance between Celeste and Grace, where Zack didn't look like either of them except for having the same hair color as his sister. *He must take after his father.* Just like her.

Zack reached forward and touched her elbow. "You okay?"

Bree shook off the melancholy. "Totally." She smiled at Celeste. "Thank you so much for having me. I know it was last minute."

She waved the comment away. "When it's family, nothing is last minute. It's just life."

Warmth spread through Bree's chest at the inviting remark.

Celeste turned toward the door. "Come on in and make yourself at home."

The sun sank behind the house as Zack's mom opened the squeaky screen door, blanketing the farmyard in evening's golden glow. Dogs swirled around their legs trying to get in, Zack and Celeste trying to keep them out. A couple of the smaller ones snuck through. When Celeste yelled after them, they darted through the doggy door at the back of the kitchen.

Bree surveyed the living room to the right. A well-used leather couch took up the far wall, family photos covering the entire wall above. A mahogany piano stood in the corner, the top stacked with music books to the point of toppling. Floral drapes framed the large front window, and with it wedged open, the curtains billowed every few seconds.

Zack took her bag and set it near his at the bottom of the steps that led upstairs.

"I was told not to make a fuss," Celeste said over her shoulder, walking into the kitchen. The lino-covered floor creaked beneath her feet. "So I ate with Albert a little while ago, but I made you some plates."

She gestured to the fridge once Bree followed her.

Who's Albert? Zack hadn't mentioned anyone else living with his mother. Bree scanned around for another person, a hired hand to help with the yard maybe, but didn't see anyone. She opened her mouth to ask when Zack cut in.

"Thanks, Mom." He leaned in close to give his mother a peck on the cheek. "You're the best."

"Well, I know that." She smiled. "But it's nice to hear once in a while. Why don't you two eat up, then you can show Bree around, including all your favorite hide and seek spots if you want to have a round later."

"Mom—" Zack began, his face reddening.

"I love a good round of hide and seek," Bree said.

"Who doesn't?" Celeste chuckled, then made her way to the back door. "I'm going out to water the plants. There's lasagna in the fridge. You know how the microwave works." She took off moccasins and slid on rubber clogs. "Boy, that sounded rude." She pushed open the screen door and smiled over her shoulder. "There's cake too. That should make up for it." The door banged shut behind her.

Perplexed and charmed, Bree could only smile after the sweet, odd woman.

CHAPTER TWENTY-SEVEN

WITH THE SUN DETERMINED to kiss the horizon through the kitchen window, Zack rinsed his plate in the sink and passed it to Bree, who had taken it upon herself to load the dishwasher.

"Your mom is a good cook," she said after standing all the cutlery in the proper slots. "She'd give Inaya a run for her money in the lasagna department, and that's saying something."

Zack reached under the sink and grabbed the box of detergent. "Yeah?"

"Oh yeah," she said, taking the box and pouring the powder into the rectangular slot. "They could have a lasagna-off and charge tickets. It would be a vicious but delicious battle." She shut the dishwasher door with a soft thud. "So are you going to show me all your good hiding spots or what?"

He grinned. "Can't show you them all."

A pressure started in his chest before his mom's voice drifted through the open window above the sink.

"No. I didn't know she would be so pretty." There was a pause. "Of course I'm going to be nice to her. She seems like a very nice girl. It's about time he decided to get serious with someone." Another pause. "I know that. I'm just saying—" Another pause. "Well it's his business, isn't it?"

Bree's eyes had gone round. "She's talking about me. She's talking about you and me. She's called someone and is talking about me."

Zack's heart pounded. "It's only because she likes you." He grabbed her hand and guided her to the front door, away from his mom's chatter.

As soon as they stepped outside, dogs immediately swarmed them. Captain took a special interest in Bree. Zack wouldn't have said she didn't like dogs, but she probably hadn't grown up around them. She patted them and tried to get their noses out of her crotch, but she didn't get down on their level or have that natural camaraderie a dog owner had for dogs in general.

He side-eyed Bree, trying to gauge how much his mother had freaked her out. The pink of embarrassment had ebbed from her cheeks, but she appeared preoccupied. Not that he could blame her. If their positions were reversed, he'd probably be even more mortified.

So there'd already been a hiccup. Nothing to worry about, right? Didn't mean the whole visit would be a disaster.

The sky turned pink and purple as the sun sank lower. Zack headed across the yard, away from where his mother was watering the flowers. Bree kept pace beside him, her every other step a half-skip. The pressure eased in his chest with each step away from the house.

One by one, the dogs got bored with their walk and headed to more exciting ventures, like chasing rodents and trying to catch butterflies. Only Captain remained, trotting adoringly beside Bree, his gaze fixed on her face.

I know the feeling, bud. I know the feeling.

They neared the dilapidated buildings of the old part of the farm. A shed, a small barn, and a chicken coop, all in dark wood, leaned at angles that put the Tower of Pisa to shame. There should probably be hazard signs around them, but no one had bothered.

A bounce had returned in Bree's step. "I love old buildings," she breathed, trotting closer with Captain bounding beside her. She poked her head into the chicken coop. "Doesn't look very sturdy."

Captain gave a bark and dashed away from them into the tall grass at the edge of the property.

"It isn't," Zack replied, leaning against a forgotten fence post. "But it'll probably be here after we're long gone. I don't think it's moved much in the time I've been alive."

Her toes poked over the threshold.

"It's probably best not to go inside, just in case," he said. "Bugs and spiders in there too."

"I'm not scared of spiders." She huffed a breath out of her nose, but didn't go any further. "Worked as an assistant to an entomologist once, right before I moved to Wickwood. Kind of takes the scary out of bugs when you're stabbing pins into dead ones to hang on the wall." She brushed her hair out of her face. "He didn't go out of his way to kill them, mind you. We found the specimens already dead in the wild, then put them under glass."

"You've led a charmed life."

She flashed him a brilliant smile, and he sucked in a quick breath. "I like to think so," she said, her eyes merry.

Zack was glad whatever melancholy had seduced her in the car had vanished.

She surveyed the coop from the doorway. He straightened from the fence post and joined her. It hadn't changed at all in the past years. Along the back, the roost ran against the wall, the poop deck beneath, and the boxes for the hens to lay their eggs below that. Old straw littered the floor and benches.

"This is one of your hiding spots, isn't it?" she asked, gripping the rough wood of the doorway, eyes focused inside.

"How can you tell?"

She shrugged. "I would come here to hide if I needed to. Even if my parents said it was unsafe." She turned her eyes to him. "Especially if my mom said not to, because then she wouldn't look for me here knowing I listened to her rules, right?"

"Basically," he responded, keeping his voice level. They were more alike than he'd realized. "What were you hiding from?"

Her smile fell a bit. "Responsibility? Reality?" She shook her head. "But we weren't talking about me."

"We weren't?" He leaned closer.

One shoulder shrugged, her top shifting to reveal more skin. "It was only a hypothetical thought."

He reached up and touched the ends of her black hair. So soft. He could drown in her eyes forever. She licked her lips and leaned toward him, her gaze fixed on his mouth.

A dog barked. Bree blinked and pulled away. Zack had the urge to take hold of her and kiss those perfect lips, but Captain ran up to them, shoving himself between their legs.

Zack stepped back. "Want to see more of the farm?"

She tucked her hair behind her ears, cheeks pink. "Absolutely."

Taking her hand because he needed to touch her, he was gratified when she returned the squeeze of his fingers. He toured her along the treeline, showed her where they'd built a treehouse which had collapsed a couple of years ago. Then he showed her where he and Grace used to play tag, explained his mom had sold the farmland years ago and only owned the farmhouse and surrounding yard. Captain trotted ahead of them, pouncing on grasshoppers in their path.

The sky turned dark red by the time they neared the house. Dogs who had left them to their walk trotted up to say hello again. Captain chased the others away like he claimed Bree for his own.

His mom's voice floated toward them. Zack tensed at the sound and the returning pressure in his chest.

"I know he said they were just friends—"

His eyes darted to Bree. Hopefully, it looked like his mom was talking to her flowers. Bree's head tilted to the side, a frown pinched between her brows.

"Don't say that," his mom said, focusing her hose on the next plant. "She's way too young for you, and I don't think Zack would appreciate it at all."

"Um," Bree began, blinking fast.

Shit. Why couldn't this trip have been one of the painless ones? He took hold of Bree's hand and veered away from the house toward the creek. "This way," he said a little too brightly. "I've got one last place to show you."

CHAPTER TWENTY-EIGHT

B REE GLANCED BEHIND HER, then at Zack. He tugged gently on her hand as he stared straight ahead, avoiding her gaze. Celeste's quiet voice followed them as they passed a long, brown barn.

Should she broach the topic of his mother talking to herself? Celeste hadn't been holding a phone to her ear and hadn't been wearing wireless earbuds. *It's none of my business. If he's not worried, then I shouldn't be worried. Right?*

Uncertainty rippled through Bree as she focused on where they were headed, off the gravel path and over clumped grass.

His hand warm around hers, Zack led her through a thicket. With the remaining light of the day, they came upon a creek running the length of the property. A delightful gurgle and splash echoed off the surrounding trees.

Zack tugged her hand again, urging her forward.

She squeezed it tight.

With every step they took, more tension eased from Zack's shoulders. The light of twilight revealed a dock with a canoe up on the shore beside it—the same dock on the social media profile she'd thought belonged to him.

Wind brushed her cheeks as they stepped onto the creaking wooden planks, the quiet of their footsteps turning hollow beneath them. Her hand secure in his, he led her to the end of the dock, then let out a long exhale.

She'd never seen him so calm before. Even when he was in his childhood home conversing with his mother, he hadn't been this relaxed. It was like he'd shed a cloak of gloom and only Zack, the man, remained. Her stomach flipped.

"This is my favorite place on the entire farm," he said quietly. "I used to swim here every day when I was younger."

She peered over the edge of the dock. In the low light, rocks glinted from the bottom of the creek bed. "This is where you got the scar on your head, isn't it?"

"Yeah." He jerked his chin downriver. "There's a big opening over there that's great for diving. It's shallower here since the creek has gone down in the past few years."

Ever mindful of her hand in his, Bree accepted the warmth he gave her with his presence, his nearness. She thought of everything he'd shown her today and couldn't have been happier she'd agreed to come.

Spending time with Zack proved more fun, more unexpected than she'd imagined. The more time she spent with him, the more she wanted him. She shivered.

"Are you cold?"

"No, I—"

Dropping her hand, he moved behind her, and his arms enveloped hers. An involuntary, satisfied breath slid from her. She leaned against him, his chest supporting her spine and his arms like a cocoon.

Zack rested his chin on her shoulder and she inhaled deeply, his familiar scent mixing with the fresh air. The gurgle of the creek below and the rising moon behind the trees created a mood so perfect, a band of emotion wrapped tighter around her chest than his arms. She inhaled a quick, jagged breath.

"You okay?" Zack asked, leaning forward to see her better. "Maybe we should head in?"

She wanted to shout *no!* The thought of leaving the tranquility of the moment made her heart pound in a panicky rhythm. *What's happening to me?*

Trying to push the illogical feeling aside, she nodded and forced herself to turn away from the view.

She met Zack's hooded gaze. Heat flared through her body at his expression. What was going on inside his head? She resisted the urge to fidget.

When had her nervousness started? When he'd shown her the treehouse and she could imagine a little Zack scampering up the homemade wooden ladder? When she could imagine him running through the tall grass, racing away from his sister when they played tag? When she could imagine him as a boy hiding in the chicken coop, even when his mom had told him not to go inside? Thinking of him hiding there because he didn't want to deal with his father's death? Knowing if she'd been there with him, she would have sat beside him in the dirt and held him tight until his demons went away?

She couldn't pinpoint one exact moment, but an itch lived in her body, a strange irritation she couldn't exactly name and wasn't sure she wanted to even if she could.

She needed to retreat, to gather her thoughts, to regain her equilibrium, and blurted the first thing that came to mind. "Dessert time?"

His mouth curled up on one side. "Yeah. Of course." He kept his arm wrapped around her shoulders as they walked up the dock.

With the yard lights on, the house, brown barn, rows of cars, and the vegetable garden were all illuminated. Everything looked to be in its right place, like it had been there a hundred years.

She heard Celeste puttering around in the kitchen before they arrived at the back door. The screen door squealed when they pushed it open.

"Oh good, you're back," Celeste said as she closed the dishwasher door, empty now. "I'm headed to bed since I was up early, but I've left out some cake for you two. Zack, you'll have to show Bree the guest room. Everything's set up." Hefting a stack of plates in two hands, she slid them into the cupboard and closed the door.

A baking pan sat in the middle of the kitchen table, covered in chocolate icing. Bree's stomach rumbled.

"And tomorrow," Celeste went on, "you two can tell me all about the ghosts you've found on this latest job." She moved toward the stairs.

Bree twisted her hands together and thought of the footage they'd seen in the office, the person with a sheet over their head. Zack hadn't had any answers for her and she needed them. Logic would dictate that someone was playing a prank, maybe the Rivets, maybe someone else, but that only explained one part of the story. Because what the hell had happened to them in the house if ghosts weren't real?

"I don't know if I believe in ghosts," Bree said quietly, if only to convince herself.

The air in the kitchen stilled. Bree lifted her head. Celeste's face had gone pale as she stared at her son. "You haven't—?"

Zack cut her off by shaking his head.

Celeste smoothed her hair, her hands shaky. "Well, I didn't expect that." Her disturbed, somewhat hurt, expression stabbed Bree right through the heart.

"Expect what?" she asked, glancing between mother and son. Zack's grimace didn't give her any answers.

Celeste offered her a tight smile. "You kids eat some cake and don't stay up too late. Night." She turned and headed up the creaky steps to the second floor.

"Good night," Bree called after her, unsure of what had upset Celeste. A glance at Zack wasn't any help. He'd gotten out two plates and a knife to cut the cake.

Confused, but not wanting to press, Bree moved closer to the table. "I'm guessing this isn't carrot cake with raisins," she said to lighten the mood.

Zack gave her a half-smile. "No, it probably isn't. My mom knows how to bake right—raisin free." He cut a big slice of chocolate cake and slid it onto a plate, then placed it in front of her along with a fork.

Unable to resist, Bree sat down, took a bite, and groaned. "Chocolate zucchini cake," she said around her mouthful. "One of my favorites."

"Mine too." Zack settled into the chair beside her with his own piece.

After eating half her cake, she set down her fork. "I'm not sure what I said to your mom to make her upset."

He straightened, gave her a glance, then shook his head. "She wasn't upset with you. She was upset with me."

"Why?"

His gaze fixed on his fork, he said, "We're a different sort of family. She would have expected I'd have disclosed all the—" he made a circle with his fork, "—differences before I brought you here. That's all."

She touched his hand so he would look at her. When he met her eyes, she said, "We're all a bit different."

"Not like this." The words came out strained.

In the next moment, he dropped his fork, stood, and walked to the sink to stare out the window.

Bree stood too. She didn't know what to do. She said she wouldn't push him and she wouldn't. When she realized she had wrapped her hands around her middle, she forced them to her sides.

Zack turned around. "I'll take you up to the guest room."

She nodded and leaned over to pick up her plate.

"I'll come back down and clean up everything."

Bree snorted at his assumption. "I'm not leaving this here in case someone thinks I'm done with it. Too delicious to waste." She licked off her fork, grabbed a napkin from the table, and held the plate protectively close to her chest.

His eyes sparkled once more. "My mom will be happy you like it."

"Oh, she knows it's good. Just like I know my carrot cake kicks ass."

His chuckle warmed her as he led the way up the stairs.

The guest room at the top of the stairs was small, but cute. Cornflower blue curtains bracketed the window. An antique dresser stood beside the door, and a matching nightstand flanked the double bed. On the right, a half bath with flowered wallpaper and a pedestal sink was a welcome sight. Bree always loved having her own bathroom to spread out her stuff. She set her carpet bag on the upholstered bench at the foot of the bed, and her half-eaten piece of cake on the nightstand.

"So, uh, yeah," Zack said at the doorway, running a hand through his hair. "Here it is." He gestured to the room in its entirety.

"I can see that." Bree smiled, glad he was back to his usual awkward self and that they'd left the tension downstairs.

His eyes scanned the room, every corner of it. "And it looks all safe and sound and empty." When she frowned at him, he gave a strained chuckle. "Okay. Right. So I'll leave you to it." He stepped back.

"Zack," she said softly, and he stopped. She walked toward him, her eyes fixed on his face. His throat flushed as she leaned forward and placed a kiss on the corner of his mouth. Heat curled in her stomach, but she forced herself to step away. "Thank you for everything."

"Oh. Yes. That's fine. Okay. Got to clean up now. Talk to you soon. Bye." Turning on his heel, he fled the room.

She smiled as she walked to her bag to dig out her toiletries and pajamas.

Once her teeth were brushed and she'd changed, Bree lay in the middle of the bed with her blue alien book. She'd thought to read a couple of chapters, but couldn't concentrate. She took one more bite of her cake, then realized she wasn't hungry enough for it. Rising from the bed, she strode across the room and set it on the dresser to take down in the morning.

Restless, she walked to the window and opened it. The creek gurgled, lyrical and relaxing. Did Zack know how lucky he was to have grown up in such a place, differences or not?

Bree sighed, leaning her cheek against the window frame while she listened to the nighttime sounds. When her eyelids started to droop, she moved away from the window and peeled back the covers, tucking herself under the patchwork quilt, then turned off the lamp.

The sound of the creek kept the roar of the pines away. It only took moments before she drifted off to sleep.

The sound of running water woke her.

Bree's eyes flew open.

It wasn't a drip from the faucet, or the gurgle of the creek. It sounded like the tap in the half-bath had been turned on full blast.

She sat up straight, her spine rigid. Was someone in her room? She squinted at the clock on the side table—12:12 a.m.

"Zack?" she called out softly. No answer. "Zack is that you?" she asked a little louder. Still no answer. "Celeste?" She gripped the top of the quilt. The running water continued uninterrupted.

Reluctance infusing every limb, she slid from beneath the covers and padded barefoot over the soft carpet toward the bathroom. A sudden chill swept through the room. She glanced at the open window, wishing she'd closed it earlier.

Rubbing her arms to warm them, she closed the gap between her and the partially opened door. Her heart rate sped up, pounding in her ears. With a shaky hand, she reached inside to flick on the light.

The tiny room brightened, making her squint. From her angle, she couldn't see the sink. She flattened her palm against the dark oak of the door and it squealed as it opened further. The bathroom remained empty, but the tap was turned on all the way, water gushing from the faucet to pour straight down the drain.

Bree stepped inside. Unsettling goosebumps broke across her skin. With a trembling hand, she grasped the tap, turning it until the water stopped.

Her breaths echoed in her head, ragged. Why was she so scared? It was only a malfunctioning tap. One she had to put effort into shutting off because of its age.

One that wouldn't have accidentally turned on by itself.

Someone must have been in her room. Either Zack or Celeste had come in, turned on the tap, and left before she'd woken up.

But why would they do that? What purpose would they have? To scare her?

While Bree stared at the offending fixture trying to figure it out, it squeaked.

She jumped back. The squeak turned into movement as the tap turned itself on—first a trickle, then it eased into the fully open position from moments ago. The movement was slow, deliberate, nothing accidental about it.

As fast as it had turned on, it went off again. Her stomach leaped into her throat. Bree gripped the door frame, needing to touch something solid. Was she dreaming? Was this a hallucination?

Just when she'd decided to go to bed and tell herself none of this had happened, the faucet turned on again. Then off. Then on. It kept going and going.

Frantic, she backed away, her eyes fixed on the bathroom, afraid to look away. Her elbow slammed into something hard. *Thud.* A cry of alarm ripped from her throat as she spun around, but it was only the dresser, her plate of cake knocked to the floor. Black crumbs lay everywhere, the cake landing icing-side down on the carpet. The water sounds from the bathroom stopped, and when she turned to look, it felt like something, or *someone*, brushed past her.

Bree screamed. She slapped her hand over her mouth, mortified. *What am I doing? What is happening?*

A door opened out in the hall; footsteps came closer. A knock. She jumped.

"Bree, are you okay?" Zack's voice came through the door loud and clear.

"Um." Bree glanced at the bathroom. It remained quiet. "I'm not sure." She stepped over the fallen cake and unlocked the door to open it wide.

Zack stood there, concern in his golden eyes, shirtless, pajama pants riding low on his hips—and looking about as delicious as anyone could in the middle of the night.

Seeing him calmed her. Her heart rate slowed. Her breathing evened out, and she unclenched her fists at her sides.

With the calm came an awareness she couldn't ignore. The wide expanse of bare chest drew her eyes, her mouth going dry.

His eyes took in her face, his lips parting, then scanned lower, warming her body.

She glanced down at herself and couldn't say she'd dressed particularly sexy, just her normal pajama top and shorts, but the way he stared at her made her feel sexy.

His gaze resettled on her face, the heat in his eyes unmistakable. Her nipples hardened beneath the thin material.

"Are you okay?" he asked again, his voice rough. His question brought her mind back to where it had been before he arrived.

She glanced over her shoulder, then met his eyes. "Can you tell me more about those differences you referred to earlier?"

His eyes lost some of their heat and became guarded. "What happened?"

Bree swallowed. "This seems really silly." She cleared her throat. "But the water in the bathroom turned on, then it turned off, and then on and off and on and off and it kept going and it seriously freaked me out, and I was trying to get away, and I bumped into the cake and it fell all over the floor and I'll clean it up right now." She glanced down at the spill and froze.

A footprint sat square in the middle of the mess. Not a barefoot like hers. She glanced at Zack's feet. Not a barefoot like his. No, this was a boot print. A work boot. She knew what they looked like because she'd had to wear steel-toed boots for a job site once, and they left a very distinct kind of print, not like a sneaker or a loafer or any other casual style of shoe.

Blood rushed to her head, making her woozy. She reached out to grab the corner of the dresser and missed. Zack shot forward and put his arm around her, keeping her from falling. He guided her to the bed and set her on the edge.

She stood up immediately. "I need to get out of here."

Rubbing a hand over his face, Zack stood too. "Yeah. Okay. I'll get dressed and take you back to the city."

"No. I mean, I need to get out of this room." Bree zipped across the floor, over the cake, and out the door.

She stopped dead in the hallway. Zack's footsteps padded up behind her. "My room's the second one on the left."

Without waiting for another invitation, Bree dashed forward and darted through the open door. Blue tones decorated the room, and it had an en suite half bath like hers. A lit lamp illuminated the nightstand and the double bed beside it.

Before she could voice any of the hundred questions tumbling through her head, Bree closed the door to the bathroom. Hard. Then she set to pacing near the end of the bed, the corner of her thumb in her teeth as she tried to work everything out in her mind.

The water had turned on. Then it turned off. It hadn't happened by accident. Then there was the footprint. The cake was fresh. There hadn't been anyone else in the room.

Anyone she could *see*.

Bree spun around and faced Zack, who hadn't moved from his open door. "Who's Albert? Your mom had been talking about Albert. Then she'd been talking *to* someone. Who is he?"

Zack ran his hand through his hair, closed the door, and walked over to sit on his bed. The springs groaned under his weight.

"Albert is my dad." A sigh shuddered through his body.

Her heart skipped a beat. "You said your father died."

Zack nodded, his eyes pensive. "He did. When I was thirteen."

Bree swallowed. "Your mother ate with him tonight. She said so. She said she ate with Albert earlier."

Leaning forward, Zack rested his elbows on his knees and studied his hands. "She did."

When he didn't explain further, Bree took a step toward him. "Zack," she pleaded, needing him to say it. She needed him to confirm the conclusions her heart had already made, but her mind wouldn't accept.

He lifted his head and met her gaze, his eyes filled with an emotion she'd never seen from him before. Maybe it was fear. Maybe it was dread. It pulled at her chest, making her heart ache.

He nodded once, as if coming to a decision, and without looking away said, "My mom can see and talk to ghosts, and my father's has been lingering on this farm for over fifteen years."

CHAPTER TWENTY-NINE

B REE STOPPED PACING, HER fingers turning to ice. Deep down she'd known, but hearing the words aloud froze her whole body.

Zack stared at her with resigned eyes, like he steeled himself against what she'd say next.

His dad was a ghost.

A ghost who was messing with her.

He'd *haunted* her.

"Why would he do that?" she blurted. "Why would your ghost dad be playing with my taps and scaring the shit out of me?"

"I—" He stopped, then swallowed. "I'm not sure?"

"Is that a question?"

He shrugged. "He has the ability to influence objects, but I'm not sure why he went to your room." His eyes widened a fraction, then he hung his head, staring at his hands. "Maybe to play a joke on you," he mumbled.

She inhaled sharply and his head snapped up.

"Your dad is a ghost and he's pranking me?" Her voice shook. Why would his dad prank her? Then it hit her. "Because I said I didn't believe in ghosts?"

He lifted his hands in a helpless gesture, then let them fall in his lap.

"Is he here now?" she whispered, eyes darting around the room.

Zack closed his eyes, his face and shoulders relaxing. Then his brow puckered. After a moment, he opened his eyes. "No. We're alone."

Tension eased from her spine. She relaxed her hands and took a deep breath. His eyes scanned her from top to bottom, and despite the scare she'd just had, her skin tingled from his perusal.

She didn't know what to do with herself. A part of her wanted to rush over to him and demand that he hug her. The other part wanted to remain distant, hurt he'd kept this from her.

When he took a deep breath, she twitched, caught between the need to stay and the need to escape.

"My mom didn't know she could see ghosts until my dad died."

She couldn't tear her eyes away from his tortured expression, though he kept his gaze determinedly fixed on the floor.

"It was a surprise to her even though it ran in her family," he continued. "The days after his death were extremely trying, and it took her a long time to spin it positively. You'd think having your spouse dead, but not gone, would be a comfort, but it's not. At least, not at first."

While she processed the information, she stayed in the middle of the room, not retreating and not moving closer.

"How did he die?" she asked quietly, not wanting him to stop talking.

"He was working underneath a car, but the jack hadn't been placed properly."

Her stomach dropped to the floor. "Oh, god."

"He was alone at the house at the time, and the car crushed him."

She wanted him to stop right there, could see the pain it caused him to explain, but he kept talking. Maybe he needed to get it out, to let her share the weight of it.

"I found him when I came home after school."

Her feet propelled her to the bed. It squeaked when she sat down beside him and her bare shoulder touched his.

"Grace usually came home at the same time as me, but that day she went over to a friend's house. I called for an ambulance, but it was too late. He'd been dead for hours. Mom found out by following the ambulance up the drive." He inhaled through his nose and she grabbed his hand, their fingers linking. "I can say, without a doubt, it was the worst day of my life."

Eyes filling with tears, she rested her cheek against his shoulder. "I'm so sorry, Zack."

"It's okay. It was a long time ago."

She lifted her head, and he met her gaze for the first time since he had started his story. "It's not okay. It's not okay for a thirteen-year-old boy to have to deal with that. I can't imagine what you went through—what you've been going through every day since. You're a very strong person."

He brushed her cheek with his fingers. A sizzle of electricity shot through her jaw to settle in her chest. He leaned forward and brushed his lips across hers. Just once.

When he pulled away, apology swirled in his eyes. "I'm sorry, I—"

She held up her finger to silence him. "I'm mad. I'm seriously pissed, actually. You brought me here and didn't explain anything. You knew your father had the capacity to mess around with me—"

"I honestly didn't think—"

She raised her hand to stop him again, needing to get this out. "But that doesn't make me want you any less. And I do want you. I want you bad, Zack Liller." Speaking the truth aloud felt like a relief, and the resulting heat in his eyes told her he liked it. "I've been good about it, but I don't think I can be good anymore, because you're sitting here, open and honest, and its such a big turn on that all I want to do is get as close as possible."

His bare shoulder froze against hers during her declaration. Bree searched his face, her chest tight from the desire she saw there. Hunger. Yearning. How could he look at her like that? Like he was starved? Like he needed her like he needed his next breath?

She lifted her hand and cradled his face, palm cupping his cheek. His lips parted and she took advantage, grazing her thumb across his bottom lip. His breath tickled her skin, warming her.

Her eyes were drawn to his hairline. He inhaled sharply as she brushed his hair away from his forehead. Her fingertips stroked his scar. To think he could have died way back then and she would never have met him.

"So close," she murmured, her stomach flip-flopping.

With a small shake of his head, he took her hand in his and placed it on her thigh. Shivers ran through her legs at the light brush of his fingers on her skin. Lips parting, he cupped her cheek like she'd done, and brushed his thumb over the corner of her mouth.

She couldn't resist sweeping out her tongue to lick him.

Startled, his hand froze on her lips. She smiled at that, opened her mouth, and gently bit him.

He sucked in a breath and the sound hit her low. Such a little sound to have such an effect on her. Grasping his wrist, she captured his thumb in her mouth, her tongue toying with the sensitive flesh over and over again. Savoring the stain of pink across his cheeks, she released it with a *pop*.

He watched her with hooded eyes while she turned his hand over and inhaled the scent of his palm. Heat coiled inside her at the softness of his skin, the strength lying just below the surface. What would these hands feel like against her? Trailing the tip of her tongue from his wrist to the end of his finger, she watched his eyes darken, his focus never wavering.

She lowered his hand, fingers wrapped around the pulse at his wrist, holding firm. "I never knew mint and salt tasted so good together." Her voice cracked.

He snapped out of his trance. Cupping her jaw, he kissed her boldly, stealing her breath, his tongue sweeping in to explore. His taste exploded across her taste buds, toothpaste and chocolate.

She dug her fingers into the corded muscles of his shoulders, then pulled him closer. She wanted to melt into him. His arms came around her, and she purred her approval in the back of her throat. Breasts flattened against his chest; the thin material of her top did nothing to conceal the hardening of her nipples. He groaned, ran his hands down her back, settled them on her hips, and squeezed.

Until now she'd been good, showed restraint, but she didn't care anymore and that both frightened and exhilarated her. She'd never needed someone this much before.

The thought startled her. Her head reared back. Zack's lips glistened as he focused on her face. She sank into his eyes, drowning, knowing if she went any further she was going to lose herself to this. To them. She felt it everywhere in her body. In her heart. She'd only known him for a few days, but she could feel how it would be different with him.

And they were in his childhood home, sitting on a bedspread with moons and stars on it. "I don't suppose you have paper-thin walls and your mother sleeps next door?"

"Two rooms over," he said, his eyes never leaving hers, "and she sleeps like the dead."

Bree froze.

"So to speak," he added, hesitating. "My dad's gone too, and he's not the peeping type."

Good enough. She dove back into the kiss, leaving all her reservations behind. Nothing mattered but the two of them. She only wanted to focus on the moment, on Zack.

Her fingers dug into his hair, and her tongue stroked his. The heat between them built. His hands gripped her hips, urging her closer. Her nerves tingled where their skin touched.

She ran her fingers down his arms, scratching his flesh, following the path of goosebumps. With his tongue in her mouth, she suckled him, scraping her teeth lightly against his taste buds when she drew back.

When they broke apart, both of their chests heaved from lack of air. Her hands found his at her hips, interlacing their fingers. Leaving all hesitation behind, she pushed him back to lie on the bed, her body tingling at the heat in his eyes.

Knees on either side of his hips, she placed his hands above his head and held him there, captured. She wasn't planning on letting him go anytime soon.

His body strained toward her, a flush crawling up his neck. She buried her face in his throat and inhaled deeply. She couldn't get enough of his scent. Settling herself atop his straining cock, her lips skimmed to his ear. She bit him lightly, then moved downward, kissing a path to the center of his chest.

She inhaled again. His scent just got better the further she traveled. When her stomach rubbed his length, he hissed. She smiled against him, then kissed lower and lower, taking his hands with her until she wedged them at his hips.

Face hovering above his navel, she met his eyes. "I want to taste you."

His throat bobbed up and down in a swallow.

"All of you."

Keeping hold of his hands, she bit the tie of his pajama pants and pulled. The knot slid loose. Holding his gaze, she bit the elastic and guided it down enough for his cock to spring free.

Hot. Seriously hot. She took in his thickness, his heaving chest, the anticipation in his eyes—moisture gathered between her legs. He was so hard, his cock lay flat against his abdomen. With a smile of appreciation, she licked him from base to tip, watching his reaction.

He bucked off the bed and groaned.

She smiled wider and licked him again, taking the whole of him into her mouth. He closed his eyes and moaned. With each of his reactions, she got more turned on. Every time he gasped, she wanted to make him groan. Every time he groaned, she wanted to make him moan.

His silky length slid in and out of her mouth, the salt of his skin coating her tongue. She swirled her tongue around the tip, lapping up his flavor. When he opened his eyes again, she took him as far as she could.

He gasped, his fingers squeezing hers tightly.

She backed off, then took him all the way again.

He swallowed. "Bree," he said, his voice a croak of emotion.

"Mmm hmm," she said, her mouth wrapped around him.

"I need—" He stopped speaking when she took him in all the way. His eyes rolled back in his head.

She loved the power she had over him, the pleasure she was giving him. When she released him, his cock slapped against his stomach.

"What do you need?" She twirled her tongue around his tip where it lay glistening against his abdomen.

He cleared his throat. "I need to touch you."

Yes! She needed that too. "But I'm not done tasting you yet."

"If you taste me anymore, you're going to get a mouthful."

She grinned and grazed her bottom lip along his sensitive skin. "Maybe I like that." And she would like it. A lot. She wanted to taste *all* of him.

"Maybe it's my turn to taste," he rasped.

Her core clenched, more than ready to be tasted. More than ready for him. With one last, long lick, she released his fingers and crawled up his body until she stretched out beside him to press her palm against his sternum. "What would you like to—"

He rolled abruptly, cutting off her question. Heavy thighs covered hers. Warm fingers captured her hands above her head.

Her heart raced at the way he took control. She liked this side of him, this need to take charge. His cock poked out of his pants, rubbing her hip, and she squirmed restlessly against him.

The material of her top rucked up from the movement and his bare chest rubbed against the skin of her stomach, creating goosebumps. He pressed his face into her throat and inhaled deep like she'd done. The skin of her nape pebbled pleasantly under his soft breath.

"You're so beautiful," he whispered, kissing a path down her jaw and throat.

A wave of heat flushed through her body. Every touch, every brush of his mouth, every word left her feeling cherished.

She swallowed against the emotion building in her chest.

Keeping her hands above her head, he shifted down her body until he could bite the hem of her top. She watched him, avid, as he pulled it upward. His stubble scraped against her flesh, making her shiver. When the fabric tugged tight, she lifted her spine away from the bed.

Her breasts sprang free of the stretchy material. Cool air brushed her puckered nipples, the expression in his eyes heating her skin. He brushed his cheek along the outside of her right breast. She gasped at the sensation of his stubble scraping against such sensitive flesh. He smiled, then repeated the movement on her other breast. Tingles sizzled down her ribcage to her belly, then lower.

Hovering above her, he let his hot breath caress the skin around her nipple, but didn't touch her with his mouth. His tongue darted out and licked her lightly. Another gasp passed her lips.

"Zack," she begged, her body twitching. He was toying with her and quickly driving her to the brink.

His hot gaze keeping her captive, he opened his mouth and took her straining nipple inside. They moaned together. Need stabbed between her legs. Electricity sizzled where the flat of his tongue pressed against her; he worshiped the area around her nipple, then backed off with light flicks. Short breaths escaped her lips and she arched her back, wanting more.

He shifted his focus to her other breast, giving it the same attention as the first. She had to get closer, to feel all of him. She shimmied her legs free of his thighs and wrapped them around his waist.

He rocked into her, his hardness pressing through the material of her shorts, then buried his face between her breasts and inhaled.

"Zack," she said again, her tone edged with want. She burned from the inside out while his hands held hers immobile.

He lifted his head. A slow, sexy smile spread across his face and her heart flipped in her chest.

Holding her gaze, he migrated down her body, marking his path with light kisses, keeping hold of her fingers like she'd done. She spread her knees, allowing him to move between them. He paused, and his breath teased her through the thin material of her sleep shorts.

"Oh god," she whispered.

It felt too good. She dropped her knees farther in invitation. She knew she must be drenched. The heat of his mouth, the light sensation of his lips—it would not take much for her to go over the edge.

He laved the exposed skin of her inner thigh with his tongue, right into the crease, then paused at the top of her thigh.

"Slip and Slide?" he asked, looking up at her, his voice thick.

She nodded.

He caressed the scar's ridge with the tip of his tongue. Sparks shot through her legs, making her hiss. His tongue journeyed back toward her heat. Keeping her hands steady beside her, he skimmed the dampening material with his lips.

She moaned and lifted her hips. He pressed harder the second time and she gasped.

His nose at her center, he inhaled, then hummed in appreciation. Fire rippled through her veins. She needed more.

"Please," she begged.

He looked up at her, his eyes filled with desire, then let go of her fingers. Reflexively, she gripped the bedding beneath her, needing to ground herself. He skimmed his hands over her hips, then downward, taking her shorts along with him. Licking her lips, she lifted her hips to help, then settled back on the bed. Cool air spread between her widespread legs.

Hungry eyes roamed over her exposed center, taking her in. Her heart pounded in her chest at the pure longing reflected there.

Leaning forward, he licked up and down the crease of her thigh, heating her with his breath when he changed sides. She gasped. Electricity spiraled up her spine. She let go of the bedding and sank her fingers into his hair.

He settled himself more comfortably, gripped her behind her knees, and pushed her thighs back. Entirely open, her heart thudded hard in her chest. Her belly tightened with vulnerable yearning.

When he licked her, an ache exploded inside her, needing to be filled. His tongue twirled her bud with light, perfect touches. A ragged moan escaped her. *So good.* Her breaths came out hard and fast as he pushed her to the edge, his tongue taking her higher and higher. Her fingers clenched against his scalp.

He toured back down, probing her entrance with his tongue. In and out he stroked, the movement both too much and not enough. Leisurely licks followed insistent laps. He paid close attention to every part of her, leaving nothing hidden, and she didn't know if she'd ever felt so thoroughly *owned* in her life.

His path took him back to her clit. Every flick of his tongue pushed her further down the road to release. Then he sucked her clit into his mouth.

She gasped. "You didn't let me make you come," she panted, her words almost gibberish. Heat and pleasure swam in her head.

"The joy of multiple orgasms." She felt him grin against her before resuming his task.

When he released her one leg, she wrapped it around his shoulder. In the next moment, fingers slid inside. She cried out and arched off the bed. Her eyes closed. Light sparked behind her eyelids.

In and out his fingers thrust, and she answered with the movement of her hips. The things his tongue was doing to her, the sensation of his mouth suckling her, his fingers pressed deep inside her—she kept climbing, reaching for the endpoint.

When she opened her eyes, met his sparkling, flame-filled ones above the curls of her mound, the last of her sanity slipped through her fingers.

A million light bulbs shattered inside her brain. Her fingernails dug into his scalp. Wonder exploded through her along with the sparks, almost too much. Her climax tightened her whole body, his head squeezed between her thighs.

She'd never lost herself while having sex—not like what was happening right now.

He didn't let go, kept licking every tremor from her body with dedication. He didn't stop until she tugged on his hair.

Lifting his head, he grinned at her, his lips and chin dewy from her juices. Her heart rate had calmed some, but with that look, it kicked up against her ribs.

"Come here," she said, her voice hoarse.

CHAPTER THIRTY

Z ACK'S BREATH CAUGHT IN his throat at the hunger in her eyes. Flushed from head to toe, wisps of damp hair glued themselves to her cheeks and temples. An ache spread through his chest at the sight.

She'd opened herself up to him in every way imaginable, given of herself, and still with that look he knew she wanted to give more.

He wanted to give her everything.

Heart in his throat, he crawled toward her, knees on either side of her hips. Her lips parted, and she took his face in her hands, kissed him, her scent transferring from him to her.

"I need all of you," she whispered, her petal-soft lips still pressed against his.

His muscles twitched. He needed her too. More than he could admit right now. Hopping off the bed, he shucked off his bottoms. As soon as his knee hit the bedspread, she rolled, taking him with her until she was on top, his hands pinned beside his shoulders, their fingers interlaced. Her heat surrounded the base of his cock.

"Your shirt," he whispered. Even the thin barrier was too much between them.

Keeping his gaze, she let go of his hands and straightened, lifting her pajama top over her head, then tossing it to the floor.

He took her in, so feminine and uninhibited. A goddess incarnate put on earth to tempt him.

"Perfect," he murmured.

A flush traveled up her throat. Keeping eye contact, she bit her lip and ground her hips into his. Wet heat framed his cock exquisitely. He hissed, jerking upward, straining for more.

She rotated her hips again. He groaned. His fingers kneaded the flesh of her thighs, encouraging her movements, but holding her in place. Too much of this motion and he'd be spilling before he'd had a chance to be inside her. This was something worth savoring, every second with her precious.

What would he give to have a hundred moments with her like this? A thousand? He knew deep in his soul that tonight would never be enough.

What if tonight was all she wanted?

His chest squeezed as she lightly brushed his ribs upwards, then over his pectorals to thumb his nipples, longing stamped across her face.

He couldn't think about tomorrow, not right now when he needed to worship her like she deserved—not scare her off with the truth of his feelings. Gaze captured with his own, he took her hand, turned it over, and pressed his lips to her palm.

Her body stilled. Her breath hitched. Then she leaned forward and kissed him, her tongue demanding. Her hand migrated between them, fingers gripping his cock.

"Ah shit, Bree," he gasped, his lips pressed against hers.

"You like that?" she asked, breathless.

He nodded, pumping into her hand.

"You might like it even more if you have a condom in the bedside table."

He froze, panic clawing through his chest. "Uh, I don't think I do."

Fingers spasmed around him. "What about in your wallet?" she asked, her voice edged.

"Yes! My wallet." Thankfully one of them was still level-headed. "There's one in my wallet."

She lifted her leg, allowing him to roll free.

Where had he left his wallet? He rushed to his duffel bag on the floor next to the nightstand. Dirty underwear, a change of clothes. No wallet.

Limbs twitchy, he opened the top drawer of the dresser. Not there. Where would it be? He spied his jeans hanging over the back of the chair, snatched them up, and found his wallet in the back pocket, like it always was. The tension in his chest eased.

When he turned toward Bree, she lay on her side, her head in her hand, watching him. He paused a moment just to stare at her in all her naked glory: the curve of her hips, the feminine swell of her belly, the way her breasts hung heavy like fruit ready to be tasted. His heart thudded hard in his chest.

He stalked toward her.

Lips pursed, she asked, "So, you mean to tell me that when you invited me here, you didn't pack a whole box of condoms in your luggage expecting something?"

The question caught him off guard. He stopped mid-step, his erection bobbing against his stomach. "Uh, no." Because he was an idiot.

"That's so hot," she murmured.

Maybe not an idiot, then. He cleared his throat. "I'm afraid I have some bad news."

"What?" she asked, sitting up a bit.

"I only have the one."

A beat of silence. "Shit."

"I know," he agreed, nodding gravely. "We're going to have to make this last."

"There goes my plan to go hard and fast the first time, then take it slow for the next three."

His cock twitched, enjoying the visuals the statement created. He swallowed around the emotion building in his throat. "What about—" His voice came out a squeak. She smiled. He tried again. "What about taking it slow to start, then finishing off hard and fast?"

She pointed at him like he'd just gotten the correct answer in charades. "I like the way you think." Then she crooked her finger.

He jumped onto the bed, the mattress springs groaning. The air between them had cooled, but heated anew when she pushed him to lie back. Her lips claimed his. Her fingers stroked the muscles of his chest. She shifted down until she straddled him, accessing his cock, then plucked the packet from his fingers.

"Are you—?" He stopped speaking when she opened the wrapper with her teeth. *So sexy.* Everything she did turned the temperature to maximum. Even the way her lips quirked to the side as she rolled the latex slowly down his length.

Gripping him, she shifted her body forward until her heat hovered above him, her face filling his vision. She bit her bottom lip as she lowered herself an inch, guiding him into her silky depths. *Fuck me.* It was the best thing he'd ever felt.

Her breath caught. He couldn't look away from her eyes, how they widened, how they watched his face.

With just the tip of him inside her, she let go and braced her hands against his shoulders. He lifted his hips and she sank down another inch, eyes flaring. *Fucking hell.* How could anything feel this good? She flexed around him, sending sparks through his ass and legs.

When he took her face in his hands and lifted his head to kiss her, she sank down on him another inch. They both moaned. She licked his bottom lip and went further.

Every inch connected them more. It wasn't just physical. It was everything. His heart pounded hard in his chest, threatening to break free.

When she leaned back, seating herself fully, his entire body trembled. "Oh, fuck," he whispered. She felt amazing. Warm and tight and perfect.

She clenched her muscles around his length. He hissed his pleasure.

With a wicked grin, she captured his wrists and forced them over his head again, nipples brushing his chest. Lips seeking his, she moved, lifting her hips, then sliding down. The kiss was wet and wild, tongues invading then retreating. Every flex and shift of her around him was more pleasure than he thought he could bear.

Heat built between them. She tipped her hips, rocking and squeezing. *Heaven and bliss.* His hands pinned above his head, he gladly surrendered to her pace.

She broke the kiss, her lips rosy, her voice rough. "I don't think I'm going to be able to take this slow after all." She increased her speed, grinding her hips into his. "You feel too damn good."

Every time he bottomed out inside her, electricity exploded in his brain. "You're telling me," he ground out, his fingers squeezing hers, hips flexing up into her hot core.

He met her stroke for stroke, giving himself over to the glide of their bodies. She buried her face in his throat. Releasing her fingers, he wrapped his arms around her, holding her close. Hot skin, sweat, and her sweet and tangy scent surrounded them. He absorbed everything and wanted more.

She licked his neck, nipped him, then straightened. Her hair stuck to the sweat on her shoulders as she rocked. Biting fingernails gripped his chest. He held her hips tight, keeping the pace, increasing it. Pleasure shot through his limbs, tingling everywhere.

Closing her eyes, she rode him, her head tipped back. The loss of her gaze speared through him. One hand still on her hip, he took the other and searched where they were joined, thumbing her clit lightly.

"Yes," she gasped, eyes popping open. "Just like that." Her irises sparkled like diamonds.

The motion of her hips became frantic. Pressure built in his balls. He dug his heels into the bed, fucking into her, getting more leverage.

So close. But he wanted her to come first, wanted to see her expression again when she lost control. Throat and cheeks pink, a moaning sound began deep in her chest and emerged through parted lips.

Her legs clenched. Her body twitched. Shudders swept through her entire body, squeezing him tight. *Beautiful.* Her lips parted in a heated sigh.

"Bree," he groaned, his tone full of wonder he couldn't contain.

Gripping both hips, he increased his tempo. She opened her eyes, and the tenderness there sent him to the brink. She rocked with him, giving him what he needed, and leaned forward until her face was buried in his throat.

He thrust deep.

She nipped at his earlobe and squeezed his cock inside her. *Fuck.* So good. The thought became a fragment as his whole body strained. He came so hard he saw stars behind his eyelids.

Aftershocks jerked his body up into hers. They turned into trembles and his fingers flexed against her hips, trying to ground himself.

Gulping breaths echoed in his ears as Bree's lips pressed against his lobe. His heart beat hard inside his ribs. The roar of his orgasm faded, leaving him blissed out and jelly-limbed.

Long minutes passed before she rolled off him. Zack wanted to protest, to squeeze her tight, to keep her there until the morning light broke over the horizon, but he loosened his hold. His cock bobbed against his stomach, and he already missed the heat of her.

She lay beside him, shoulder to shoulder in the narrow bed. They stared at the ceiling while his mind kept repeating the same thing over and over again: *It's never been like this before.*

As the rasp of their breath mellowed into a whisper, he turned his head and found her watching him. A wide smile broke across her face. He couldn't stop his own.

"Hi," he whispered, hearing the reverence in his voice.

"Hey there."

How was it possible for everything to be this perfect? She was here, with him, and nothing could feel more right. His fingers searched for hers beside him. She squeezed his hand.

How could he give back to her what she'd just given him? She'd given him a part of herself. He could feel the importance of that and wanted to show her what she meant to him.

His eyes flicked to the time glowing red on the nightstand behind her. He sat up and she did too, her eyebrows raised to her hairline at the urgency of it.

"Come with me," he said, jumping out of bed, his body still tingling from his orgasm.

"Where?" she asked, not moving to join him.

"Trust me."

She narrowed her eyes at him. "I'm naked."

"You're free to stay that way if you like," he said, yanking on his jeans. "Or you could get dressed. Up to you, but I'd love for you to come with me." He held out his hand and hoped she'd take it.

She hesitated another moment before allowing him to help her to her feet. He couldn't take his eyes away as she tugged on her pajamas.

"Where are we going?" she asked, straightening.

He only held out his hand again.

When she took it, he whisked her from the bedroom, down the stairs, then slid his feet into some slides by the back door. Once she slipped on flip flops his mother had left there, he ushered her out into the nighttime air.

Gently tugging on her hand, they crossed the yard toward the thicket. It was warmer than he'd expected. Or maybe he was still heated from their lovemaking.

Crickets chirped and grasshoppers jumped out of their way as he led her to the creek. The gurgle grew louder and louder until the hollow sound of the dock echoed beneath their feet.

"Are you cold?" he asked, turning her to face him.

She shook her head, but wrapped her arms around her middle anyway. "Why are we out here?"

Was she cold, but trying to tough it out? She looked cold. "Just a sec." He dashed to the shed down by the canoes, and returned a minute later with wool blankets. "Here." He wrapped one around her shoulders and set the other on the dock.

"Thanks." She scanned the shadows around them. "Back to my initial question." Her tone was more curious than annoyed.

"Wait for it," he said, his eyes never leaving her face.

A single light hovered near the bank and her eyes tracked its movements. Another one joined it. The two lights circled each other, then crossed the water in a zig-zag pattern. Two more appeared in the distance.

"Fireflies," she murmured. "I've never seen them in person before."

The awe in her voice had him stepping behind her, wrapping his arms around her shoulders. She leaned into him. His lips drifted a hair's breadth away from her neck.

They stayed quiet as more fireflies joined their friends, the splash and bubble of the creek adding to the atmosphere. He'd always loved coming here at night, watching the fireflies, trying to catch one. He'd never shared them with anyone, not even Grace.

Having Bree out here with him felt right, like he'd been waiting to share this moment with her. He closed his eyes and brushed his lips against her neck. She sighed.

They stayed that way and watched until the last of the lights had gone out.

"This place reminds me of my grandma's cabin," Bree said quietly into the dark.

Zack held still, feeling the weight of her words, waiting for her to say more.

"It was on a lake and I remember always loving it there. I'd kind of forgotten all about it because I haven't been there since just after she died." The hush of the creek surrounded them when she paused. Then she continued, "She used to call me Little Bee, and my sister Big Bee because Bianca was born five minutes before me."

She reached up to her face, and his heart lurched when he realized she wiped a tear. His arms squeezed her in comfort, but he didn't want to move, or break the spell, in case she wanted to continue her story.

"I think." She hesitated. "I think I remember her visiting me after she died, in the woods behind her cabin. There was a bee, and lilies, and these dancing butterflies, and this roaring wind through the trees, and I remember that I thought she was there with me." She let out a shaky breath. "It was a magical moment, and I ran back to tell my mom and sister." She paused. "They didn't believe me, and I haven't thought about it for a very, very long time."

His arms held her close. "I believe you. Your grandmother was there. I've seen it so many times where loved ones return to say goodbye before they travel to the other side. Kids are especially sensitive to it."

She leaned her head back against his shoulders, her body sagging against him. "Thank you," she whispered.

He squeezed her again and let the stillness of the night embrace them as they listened to the swish of water lap against the shoreline.

Bree shivered.

"Do you want to go back inside and get some sleep?" he asked, rubbing her arms up and down.

"Maybe," she said, but didn't move from her place in his arms.

He knew he wouldn't be able to get to sleep tonight. Not without depleting every limb of energy.

She made a sound of protest when he stepped away from her and quickly stripped off his jeans. In the moonlight, he saw her eyes widen when she took in his nude form.

"What...?" She didn't finish the question.

He stepped past her, flashed a smile, and dove headfirst into the pitch-black creek.

The icy water surrounded him, stealing his breath until he leveled it out with practice. He surfaced, gulping a mouthful of fresh air. With lazy strokes he returned to the dock and peered up at her, treading water.

Bree wrapped the blanket tighter around herself. "I thought the water was shallow here."

He heard the concern in her voice and was warmed by it. "It is," he replied, dipping his mouth and nose below the water line, then coming back out. "But it drops off pretty deep right where I jumped."

"I suppose you should know." Kicking off the flip flops to the side, she folded her legs beneath her, and sat on the edge of the dock.

Moonlight highlighted the curves of her face. He lifted himself out enough to rest his elbows beside her, the air tickling his wet flesh, creating goosebumps.

"Aren't you cold?" she whispered.

"Nah." He shrugged, droplets of water running down his arms to fall onto the deck. He'd get used to it in a few minutes.

"The water has to be freezing."

"Want to come in?"

A stilted laugh burst from her mouth. "I don't like cold water." She poked a bare foot out of the blanket and touched the tip of her toe in the water. A sharp inhale broke past her lips. "You've got to be kidding me."

He laughed. He loved the droll look she gave him. "Guess I'm used to it."

"I take it you swim here a lot?"

"When I was younger, any chance I got. Now? Only any time I come out. Which isn't all that much." He knew he should remedy the situation, knew he should face it head-on. It only hurt both his mother and him when he avoided the farm.

"How come?" she whispered.

He shrugged. "It's hard. Hard to be here with—" He stopped and ran his hand over his wet head. "You know everything about my dad and mom, and I still find it difficult to talk about this."

She stiffened, then nodded. "I understand. You haven't known me all that long."

"That's not it," he said, knowing he was making a mess of things. "I haven't been able to tell someone—" He hesitated, remembering how Amy had left right after he'd told her, how much that had hurt, and she'd only been a co-worker. "I haven't been able to be honest with someone I've cared about, ever. You're the first person I've wanted to open up to. I learned a long time ago that people who know the truth usually don't believe me or use it against me."

"Who's used it against you?" She sat up straight, fire in her eyes. "Point them out and I'll make them sorry."

Such loyalty. "Thanks." He suppressed a smile. "I'll let you know if it comes to that." He reached over and touched her knee. The warmth of her skin traveled right into his chest. He looked into her eyes. "I'm going to swim for a bit. You should probably go inside and get some sleep."

"Don't you need sleep?" she asked, her voice breathless.

"I'm used to being up nights. I often need to do something in the middle of the night to get back to sleep."

"Like swim?"

"Or run. Or," he moved his finger along her skin, "other things."

"Okay."

"Okay what?"

"I don't know."

He grinned. "I like it when you're incoherent." He pushed off the dock into a backstroke, heading down the creek away from her.

As soon as he got into the rhythm of his front stroke, the world faded away. There was nothing left but him and the water.

And Bree. She was there too, fluttering around in his brain, her smile, her laugh. The pleasure they'd just shared with each other. It gave him extra energy to have her there.

He knew after a while she'd go inside. What would be the point of watching someone do lap after lap? He didn't look toward the dock because he didn't want to see it empty.

On his hundredth lap, the clouds began to lighten, their deep indigo color turning to gray, then white, and he headed for the dock. As soon as his eyes surfaced, they locked onto her. His heart beat harder in his chest, nothing to do with the repetitive exercise.

"You stayed," he said when he drew near.

She stood, legs unsteady, and grabbed the blanket he had left on the dock, opening it up for him.

He pushed himself up. Water cascaded off his body, splashing on the wooden planks.

She wrapped the blanket around him, then her arms, squeezing tight.

It felt too good to have her close, to have her taking care of him. "Thanks," he said, his voice rough.

When she made to pull away, he tucked the blanket under his armpits to hold it tight, and took hold of her elbows to guide her toward him.

Her eyes never left his face. Just as the sun broke over the horizon, he kissed her, his lips cold from the water, hers warm, a wool blanket between them.

He poured every emotion he was feeling into the kiss, everything tender and passionate and truthful. It swept him away to somewhere else, somewhere where nothing existed but the two of them.

A place where nothing *mattered* except the two of them.

When he broke the kiss, her gaze burned. He swallowed. "You know what I was thinking about the whole time I swam?"

Her bottom lip caught between her teeth, she shook her head.

"You. I couldn't think of anything except you."

Before she could protest, he swept her off her feet and carried her to the house, his bare ass greeting the morning sun as his blanket fell to the ground.

CHAPTER THIRTY-ONE

BREE SQUINTED AT THE dull sunlight filtering through Zack's bedroom window. She lay alone in bed, the dent in his pillow prominent enough for her to press her palm into—cold. It wasn't so long ago they'd come back inside, the sun rising.

The overcast day made it hard to tell the time, but it didn't feel late. Bree rolled over to check the alarm clock. Ten o'clock.

How long had Zack been up?

She flopped onto her back, arms outspread. Once again she'd slept solidly in Zack's arms. Had he slept at all? When they'd returned to the house after his swim, they'd both stayed awake for some time, busy making each other orgasm with their mouths. Her cheeks heated thinking about it.

This is getting serious. She knew it. She felt it. Everything about Zack was different from any guy before him.

Bree threw off the covers, found her pajamas twisted in the sheets at her feet, and shoved them on. All her belongings were in the guest bedroom. She poked her head out into the hallway. Quiet. She dashed down the hallway, then stopped dead at the open door to the guest room.

The mess of cake had been cleaned up. She could see Zack doing that for her, but what caught her eye was the perfectly made bed, complete with hospital corners. Zack didn't seem like the hospital corner type. It had to have been Celeste.

Zack's mom had seen the open door, the unmade bed, and she'd come in and made it.

Bree's face flamed. She didn't know why it bothered her that Zack's mom knew they'd slept together. Maybe because she'd insisted they were just friends?

Friends who knew each other's bodies more than "just friends" usually did.

She paused at the bathroom door, not wanting to go in. The fact that a ghost had been in there messing with her wasn't her favorite thought, even with the sun up. She snatched her toothbrush and toothpaste off the edge of the sink, grabbed her overnight bag from beside the dresser, and ran down the hall to the main bathroom.

She slammed the door behind her, clutching her bag to her chest. Why was she so scared? *It's not like ghosts can't walk through walls. He could come into this bathroom any time he wanted.*

The thought did not comfort her. Bree had the fastest, most modest shower in the history of showers.

Dressed in jeans and a T-shirt, and all packed to go, she made her way downstairs. She set her bag next to the bottom step. The mouth-watering scent of bacon and Celeste's voice lured her toward the kitchen.

Face flushed, Bree paused at the threshold. Celeste stood alone in the kitchen at the sink, her back to Bree.

"It wasn't nice, Albert. You know better than that."

Bree's stomach clenched.

Celeste set a scrubbed carrot on the towel beside her.

"I don't care if your feelings were hurt or not. It wasn't nice."

Another carrot on the towel.

"What?" Celeste straightened and whipped around. Seeing Bree standing there, her face broke into a smile. "Good morning."

"Morning." Bree stayed rooted to the spot, jittery, nervous, energy in every limb. "If I'm interrupting, I can come back later."

"No, no. You definitely aren't." Celeste wiped her hands on the dishtowel by her hip and pulled out a seat at the table. "Coffee? I have some bacon in the oven and can whip you up some eggs."

When Bree didn't move, Celeste glanced at the sink, then at Bree. "I was going to apologize for what happened last night, but I think someone else has something to say." She stared at a spot next to the sink.

Fingernails digging into her palms, Bree forced herself to stand still instead of running out the front door.

Silence filled the kitchen, then Celeste looked at Bree. "Albert says he's sorry he acted like a jackass. He was upset no one had introduced him properly yet, and that time of night is often when he's the strongest. It wasn't a good way to make a first impression. He'll stay out of your way for the rest of your visit." She turned fully to the sink. "Of course I added you were a jackass. You were. Would you like me to use another word instead?" She waited a moment. "Fine. He says to say he was sorry for being rude and doesn't want you to think of him as being a jackass. He wants to start over and tell you that you're a lovely girl, too good for our son—which isn't true in my opinion," Celeste interjected, hand to her chest. "And he hopes you'll forgive him."

Bree stood still, eyes darting between Celeste and the vacant space beside her. "Um. Okay." She scanned the empty half of the kitchen. "You're forgiven, but I'd appreciate it if he never scares the crap out of me again."

"Done!" Celeste said, clapping her hands together and drawing her attention. "Now have a seat and I'll cook you up some breakfast." She poured a cup of coffee from the brewer and set it on the table with cream and sugar.

Coffee drawing her, Bree stepped more fully into the kitchen and hesitantly walked toward the table. She kept her eyes on the sink, wary, and her hip bumped the table. She stopped, but didn't sit.

A carton of eggs in hand from the fridge, Celeste saw where she stared, paused, and sent her an apologetic smile. "He's gone now. Said he'd give us some privacy."

"Oh. Okay." Bree gripped the back of the chair.

Celeste set the eggs on the counter and came to stand in front of her. "I'm really sorry about last night. I'm going to be honest with you, Albert has his good days and his bad days. Being non-corporeal, and around the people he loves and not able to truly interact with them, it can be... hard." She ran a hand quickly through her white hair, so like Zack it snapped Bree out of her unease. "He feels guilty about being here. Thinks he should have moved on by now. Not all of the dead become ghosts, you know."

Bree loosened her grip on the chair. "I don't understand."

When Celeste turned away and moved to the counter to grab the carton of eggs, Bree finally had the nerve to sit.

"Well, let's see." Celeste took one egg and cracked it into a bowl. "Not that I'm an expert or anything, but I think ghosts hang around when there's unfinished business. When something has to be completed or figured out before their souls are able to rest. How do you like your eggs?"

Shaking her head at the quick change in topic, Bree's thoughts drifted to the Granwin House, wondering what unfinished business might linger there. "Whatever's easiest is fine. Scrambled?"

Celeste glanced over her shoulder, one eyebrow raised, so like Grace, Bree had to smile. "Whatever's easiest? It's eggs. Unless you're ordering a quiche, everything's easy."

The no-nonsense tone reminded Bree of her grandma. "Sunny side up, then," she said, smiling wider. "Thanks."

With a nod, Celeste grabbed a pan out of the cupboard beside the stove. After seeing it pre-heating on the burner, she grabbed a loaf of bread out of the breadbox beside the fridge. From the look of it, it was homemade. Bree's stomach rumbled.

Once the eggs were sizzling and thick slices of bread were in the toaster, Bree finally worked up the courage to ask, "If you don't mind me prying, what's Albert's unfinished business?"

Celeste turned away from the stove, a plastic spatula in hand. "That's a good question. I figured he would've moved on when the kids were grown, but as you can see, he's still here." Celeste turned to the stove. "Maybe it's when they're both married and settled. Maybe it's if I fall in love again—which, I'll tell you, and I've told Albert a hundred times, is not happening." She smiled over her shoulder. "Or maybe it's when we eventually sell the house. Or maybe when I die and can join him." She shrugged. "Who knows?"

A hard knot had settled in the bottom of Bree's stomach. Celeste went back to paying attention to the eggs in the pan, and after a minute, slid them onto a flowered plate she'd taken from the cupboard. Buttered toast came next, then she opened the door to the oven.

"How much bacon do you want?"

"How much you got?" Bree returned.

Her eyes crinkled with laughter. "A woman after my own heart." With the spatula, she scooped a healthy amount and shoveled it onto the plate. "There's more where that came from," she said, setting the loaded plate and a knife and fork in front of Bree. "I always make extra for BLTs later."

"This is plenty. Thank you."

"You're quite welcome. I've always loved to cook. It's nice to be able to do it for others once in a while." A shadow of hurt passed over her eyes before she turned away to rinse out the pan.

Bree stared at her plate, the knot remaining in her stomach. "Zack said he doesn't come home as much as he should."

"No, he doesn't," she answered quickly, returning to the carrots in the sink. "I don't blame him, honestly. It's hard for him to be around non-corporeal energies for any length of time. It's what makes him good at his job. It's also what keeps him away from people. I know he's not an easy person to get to know."

Bree frowned, not sure she agreed.

Celeste cleared her throat. "You'd better eat those eggs before they get cold."

Appetite waning, but not wanting Celeste's hard work to go to waste, Bree cut into her eggs, quickly dipping her toast into the yolk when it began to run. After a couple of bites, her appetite returned in full force.

"Do you know where Zack went?" she asked after swallowing.

"I think he's out in the yard, tinkering with his car. It's one of the things he and his dad had in common, a love of old cars. As you see, I have quite the collection. Most are Albert's, but Zack has added a few too. I guess if it keeps him coming back, I don't mind them in the yard. They've been there a long time." Her voice quieted, and the only sounds in the kitchen were the brush strokes against the carrots and an occasional splash of water.

Bree managed to eat her entire plate with no problem. After her last swallow of coffee, she stood. "I'll put these in the dishwasher," she said, carrying them to the counter.

"Oh, no you don't." She grabbed them from Bree before she could protest. "You go find Zack and enjoy what's left of the morning."

"Thank you." Bree felt weird for not helping out, but turned toward the back door. "And thank you for letting me stay here."

"It was my pleasure, my dear. My pleasure."

With a final nod, Bree pushed open the door and stepped into the warm morning air. She exhaled, lightened by being outside, and headed toward the old cars on the opposite side of the house.

She found Zack under the hood of his Impala. He wore a snug black T-shirt and his jeans that hugged his ass as he reached forward. Bree's stomach tightened. She knew what he looked like bare. She knew what he felt like. Knew how he tasted.

Her whole body hummed in memory. She wanted more of him, and not just physically.

Realizing she'd stopped walking, she forced her feet forward. The morning after a night of sex had never made her shy before, had never made her hesitate and rethink everything. Sex was sex.

But with Zack, she was starting to believe that wasn't true.

CHAPTER THIRTY-TWO

Z ACK HEARD THE CRUNCH of gravel under Bree's feet before he saw her. He kept his eyes on the engine in front of him, a rag in one hand, the other gripping the edge of the grill. After the night they'd shared, he wanted to spin around and grab hold of her and kiss her senseless. He wanted to bury his face into her neck and breathe everything about her inside him, to keep her there forever.

Because after everything his father had done, she'd stayed. She hadn't made him take her to the city.

Instead, he'd had one of the best nights of his life, if not *the* best night of his life. He inhaled deep. Bree was becoming important to him, and he didn't want to mess it up or scare her off. If his ghost of a father couldn't scare her off, what were the chances his feelings would?

"Hey," she said, coming up beside him.

"Hey." He straightened and finally looked at her.

With her fresh face and black hair a stark contrast to her pale skin, she was a vision. His fingers twitched, longing to touch her, but he held himself back.

"How long have you been up?" Bree leaned her hip against the bumper.

"A while." He set his rag on the edge of the car frame.

He hadn't actually slept. After they'd satisfied each other a second time, then a third, she'd laid in his arms and he'd watched her sleep. Her even breaths and the hypnotic rise and fall of her chest had calmed him.

When he'd heard his mom get up and putter around in the kitchen, he'd reluctantly left Bree to her tranquil slumber, but he'd wanted to stay. He'd wanted to snuggle with her the whole day. So why hadn't he?

"Changing the air filter?" she asked after the silence stretched between them.

He turned to see her better. "How did you know that?"

"The old one is right there," she replied, pointing to the used one in the dirt beside him.

"Right. Of course." An obvious catch.

"Looks like your battery could use a scrub, but your engine is pretty pristine. You must clean it often."

He crossed his arms over his chest. "Yeah," he drawled. "I clean it pretty regularly. Let me guess..." His thought trailed off.

"I worked at a mechanic's shop once. I mostly answered the phones, but one of the guys took me under his wing and taught me a few things. He said if I could learn to do easy maintenance myself, I could save a lot of money." She jerked her chin toward the package sitting next to his rag. "Changing the spark plugs too?"

He smiled. "You know you're something else, right?"

"Is that a good thing or a bad thing?" She squinted at him.

His heart thumped hard against his ribs. "It's a fantastic thing."

"Did you want me to help with anything? I can assist with an oil change too."

He felt a smile spreading across his face. "Not only would I love for you to help me change my oil the next time I need one, but I wouldn't want anyone else at my side the next time I'm in a haunted house."

She glanced away, a flush gracing her cheeks. He crossed his arms over his chest and tried not to notice the way her T-shirt hugged her frame, the way her jeans molded to her legs. "So how is it that someone who knows so much about cars needs a new muffler?"

Her blush brightened. "After this contract is done, I'll have enough money to fix it."

"I could fix it for you."

She crossed her arms over her chest, mimicking him. "I'll be able to fix it once the contract is finished."

He wasn't going to press the issue. He turned away and concentrated on wiping down the engine—the parts he'd already cleaned.

"Is that a '68 Mustang Cobra over there?" she asked, her attention caught by the rusted old beast three cars down from them.

"Yeah," he replied, straightening. "It's at the top of my list of remakes."

"It's a beauty. What color are you going to paint it?"

Straightening, he stood shoulder to shoulder with her to stare at the vehicle. He'd had an idea of the color since he'd bought the car five years ago from an old junker two towns over. "You tell me." *Please don't be pink.*

She walked closer to get a better look. The original color was white, with a black racing stripe down the center, but the car had been so neglected, it would need to be repainted no matter what, giving the option of changing the color.

Tapping her chin, she said, "My first instinct was cherry red, but the more I stare at it, the more I think a metallic blue would suit it, like somewhere between baby blue and electric blue."

His shoulders relaxed. "That would be a great color." And not so far off from the navy he'd been considering. "Racing stripe?"

Her lips twisted, considering. "Maybe. I'd need to see the blue first." She smiled at him. "I love old cars. Your Impala is definitely fun to ride in."

"My mom says it vibrates nice."

"Oh, my god." She slapped him on the shoulder. "Don't tell me that."

He laughed, enjoying catching her off guard. "Let me make it for you."

Her smile froze on her face. "What?"

"Let me make you the car."

"Zack, I don't—"

He shrugged off her protest. "It won't be overnight. It usually takes me a while because I don't get out here very often, but if I'm making it for someone, it will motivate me." While he'd tried to explain, her face went lax.

The lightness in his chest morphed into worry. He'd messed up. Pressuring her had been the last thing he wanted, and now she was about to freak out. He braced himself, waiting for her to end everything.

"Why did you bring me here, Zack?" A frown pinched her brows together.

He ran his hand through his hair, agitated, because he'd been asking himself the same thing ever since his dad played a prank on her. "I wanted you to have a chance to clear your head. Get away from the case." That was what he kept telling himself.

"You took me from the city where I was scared by a haunted house, but safe in the city, and you brought me to a farm with a ghost. How was that a good idea?"

"He's not here all the time." He looked away, noting the way a light wind rustled through the trees. Then he realized he was avoiding her perceptive gaze and forced himself to meet her eyes. "I guess, maybe..." He took a deep breath and forced himself to be truthful. "If he were here, then it would force my hand."

And it had. But he hadn't known his dad would take it so far. Maybe on the way back, if there had been odd occurrences, he would have broken it to her gently.

Deep down, though, he *had* wanted to tell her. He just hadn't known how to broach the subject.

Zack cleared his throat. "There was a chance he wouldn't have been around. Sometimes it's weeks before he returns."

Her eyebrows lifted. "Where does he go?"

He shrugged. "I've never asked."

"Why not?"

For a moment he thought about not answering, then went with the truth. "Because he's dead."

Bree inhaled sharply. "Please explain."

Zack almost ran his hand through his hair again, then stopped himself. "There's something everyone else gets to do after a loved one dies that I haven't been able to do, that none of my family has been able to do: move on. Other people get to grieve. It hurts. I get it. It fucking hurts. But they get to go on with their lives, do the things that make them happy without death hanging over them all the time."

Her throat worked up and down. "And some of those people would kill to tell their loved ones they love them one more time," she whispered.

"Don't judge me, Bree." He knew it sounded harsh, but wouldn't take it back. "It's physically painful for me to be around spirits."

Silence landed heavy between them. "Then why do you do what you do?" she asked, her face stricken.

So many answers to that question, and none of them would tell the whole story. "Because I'm good at it."

"Just because you're good at something doesn't mean you should do it." She took a deep breath. "Your sister is okay with putting you through hell every time you take a job?"

He looked away, toward the house and his mother coming out to water more flowers. "It's gotten worse over the years as I get more sensitive. Grace doesn't know how bad it is."

"That's why you had a bloody nose? The headaches?"

Eyes focused on his mom, he nodded. She chattered away, talking to someone no one else could see, but whom Zack could feel. He'd taught himself techniques, ways to protect himself, but it took concentration and wasn't as second-nature as he would have liked.

Bree drew his gaze when she said, "Your dad turned on the taps to the sink. He made a footprint in cake, and I've realized that the flour thing would've worked, by the way, so I don't know why you all were so against it." She took a breath. "The ghosts at the Granwin House could lock the doors. Do all spirits do these kind of things? Why haven't I seen a ghost in every apartment I've lived in?"

He felt a smile at the corner of his mouth. "The flour thing sometimes works, but the evidence can be faked and disputed so easily we never use it." He shrugged. "I've seen some spirits move things while others seem unable to do so."

"You see them, then? Talk to them?"

Zack shook his head. "That's my mother's gift. Or curse, depending on how you look at it." He hesitated, then said, "I called them hunches, but I feel it in my body. A type of pressure. Like when you're too deep underwater."

"When we were in the attic, you kept staring into the corner. What did you see?"

"I didn't see anything, but I felt a pull. Like someone wanted me to come near them. The closer I got, the more pressure I felt." He turned to her then. "Having you close helped. It gave me strength."

The flush returned to her cheeks. Her lips parted. "Zack..." Her voice trailed off, and before he could think twice about it, he leaned close and kissed her.

CHAPTER THIRTY-THREE

BREE'S HEART POUNDED IN her ears. His hand on her jaw, Zack's lips brushed hers over and over again, stealing her breath.

The scent of motor oil and his minty fragrance engulfed her. The memory of their night together threaded through her body, and she gripped the lapels of his leather jacket tight in her hands.

How could a simple kiss do such amazing things to her? Every time he touched her, it felt like the first time she'd ever been touched. Every time she learned more about Zack, she fell deeper into something she didn't fully understand. Every time he showed her his true nature, how kind and gentle he was, her stomach twisted into knots while her breaths shortened.

Whatever they'd created between them, she didn't want it to end. She knew that deep within her soul.

He broke the kiss, his eyes cautious. "Look, Bree, this doesn't have to be a big deal—"

She cut him off. "Yeah, okay." She tugged on his jacket for a quick kiss. "No big deal today." Another kiss. "No big deal tomorrow." Just one more. "Or the next." Okay, one more, but this was for sure the last one.

"We'll just take it one day at a time and figure out what kind of deal it is."

Staring into his golden eyes, she waited, her hands gripping his jacket so tightly they ached.

Zack blinked, then a slow smile spread over his face, lighting him from the inside. His arms wrapped around her in a grip so crushing, she felt it all the way to her toes.

His next kiss consumed her, took her to another place, and shook her with its intensity. She felt everything: his want, his need, his joy. Moisture pricked the back of her eyeballs.

When he stepped back, she forced her fingers to let go of his jacket, to not yank him back for more—stopped herself from asking him to take her back to his room.

"Right, yeah," he said, running a shaky hand through his hair. "It's a deal, and we'll be totally cool about it, and everything will just go forward, nothing to worry about. Piece of cake." He busied himself with finishing the wipe-down of his engine and gathered up the used rags.

Bree's mouth quirked, her body still humming as she watched his jerky movements. Maybe they both needed to focus on something else for a while.

She cleared her throat after he finished the majority of his clean up. "So what do you think about Liller Investigations getting some good press?" She rushed on when he opened his mouth. "My friend, Inaya, who you met, she works for the newspaper. She's writing an article about paranormal investigating."

Crouched by his toolbox, Zack froze, his hand on the lid, his smile falling. Everything quieted around them. He closed the lid, the click of the clasp echoing.

"What kind of article?" No emotion lived in his tone.

The contented warmth that had wrapped itself around her chest turned icy. "I'm not sure." She let out a nervous laugh. "It's about the Granwin House and it depends on how everything works out."

He stood slowly and turned to her. "Bree, please tell me you aren't helping her with the article."

She shifted, then shrugged. After this new ground they'd just broken together, she needed to be truthful. "I guess I'm her unofficial source. Or official one, I don't know. It was my idea to write the article in the first place, before I knew you guys. Before the night at the Granwin House."

Fingers twitching at his sides, his eyes widened. "I don't suppose you read through the whole contract you signed?" His throat bobbed when he swallowed. "The one Grace gave you?"

"Um..." Her cheeks heated. "I skimmed it." *The first page, anyway.*

He let out one long, slow breath, then inhaled deeply. "There's a clause in it stating you can't talk to the media about a current investigation. It voids the contract. You get nothing."

Blood rushed through her ears in a roar; her heart pounded in her temples.

"I get nothing?" She wasn't even sure she had asked the question. She couldn't hear her own voice.

When Zack nodded once, she knew she'd said it aloud.

I'm going to be evicted.

"Any dialog with the media needs to go through Grace. It's all in the contract."

She heard the words, but they were muffled. Her stomach flipped over.

"What can I do?" she whispered, hoping he had the answer, the solution that would fix this.

"I'll talk to Grace." His words came out fast. "I'll talk to her and make sure she doesn't drag you through the mud, make you pay the biggest penalty. But your job?" He let out a heavy breath, looking toward the house for a moment. "I don't think I can save that. I'm sorry."

Bree pressed her lips together, swallowing against the bile climbing her throat, and willed herself not to cry. Why did she always have to ruin everything? The one time she decided to take a real chance on a guy and she fucked everything up.

"What does this mean for us?" Her voice wavered and she cursed herself for it. She was made of stronger stuff than this, but the shaking in her hands told a different story.

"I don't know. I just—" Zack let the hood of his car fall. *Thump.* "I just need time to think, to work this through." He picked up his toolbox, then the box of rags with the dirty filter sticking out of the top. "I'll give her a call and..."

The way he didn't finish that sentence confirmed her worst fears. There was no easy way out. Grace was his sister. He'd side with family. Bree had seen how close they were. She was the one who'd messed up, after all.

Zack adjusted the box of rags under his arm, opened his mouth like he was about to say something more, then strode toward the garage, his gait swift.

Bree fisted her hands, but the pain in her chest grew while the world around her spun. The urge to run, to pack up everything in her apartment and never look back, overwhelmed her. But that thought opened a nauseous pit in her stomach.

A crow cawed, catching her gaze. The bird flew from one tree to the next, the branch bobbing under its weight. Then a bee crossed her vision, fat and fuzzy, on its way to its hive heavy with pollen.

She couldn't do it. Not this time. Inaya was here. Zack was here. She liked Wickwood a lot more than she thought she would. She couldn't just run.

With a deep breath, she steeled her spine. She might have messed up, but she wasn't defeated. She'd fix this. Somehow.

Phone to his ear, Zack exited the garage, not even looking her way as he jogged to the house, tense. Bree's feet moved toward him, his urgency pulling her. *Something's wrong.* More than just her fuckup.

When she opened the back door, she heard his voice, low and earnest. The sick knot in the bottom of her stomach shifted into a nervous throb.

"What exactly happened to her?" he asked, his hand running through his hair.

Silence filled the kitchen as he waited for the response. "What kind of injuries?" He listened for a moment, his focus away from her.

"Shit," he muttered after a minute. "How is she doing now?" He nodded, saw Bree standing in the doorway, then turned away. "Who have you called?" He leaned against the kitchen sink, his back mostly to her. "Is Roman available?" More waiting. "Yeah, you're right. Okay." He fiddled with the dishcloth hanging on the bar of the stove. "Good idea." He glanced at Bree quickly, then away. "I'm still at Mom's, but need to stop in town before I come out. Probably three hours. That okay?" He nodded. "Yeah, see you then. Be safe." He lowered his phone and touched the screen to end the call.

He stared at his cell for long seconds before turning to her. "We've got to go. I need to head back to Granwin House."

She wrapped her arms around her waist. "What's happened?"

He ran his hand over his face. "Rory's been hurt. Scratched or something while she slept. She's okay, but scared. I'm not sure if it was us being there that made the situation escalate or not, but the Rivets don't want the ghosts in the house anymore. We're going to try and get rid of them."

She squeezed herself tighter. "Is that safe?"

"We'll have help." He walked through to the foyer. "I see you're packed," he said, gesturing to her overnight bag. "I'll let my mom know we're leaving, and we'll head out."

"Did you tell Grace about the article?" Her question stopped him on the bottom stair.

He let out a hefty sigh. "Not yet. Didn't get a chance before I found out about Rory."

She stepped toward him. "Then I can come and help."

He looked away and shook his head. "I can't let you do that. I'm sorry." Taking the stairs two at a time, he left her to stare after him.

He doesn't want my help. That's how much of a screw-up she was. Not even fit to have around. She'd probably do more harm than good.

A shiver raced up her spine and scalp at the thought of them battling hostile ghosts. How did they go about doing that, anyway? She wasn't sure she wanted to know.

Bree stood in the same spot when Zack came back down. He reached for her carpet bag, snapping her out of her numb state.

"I can carry it."

"Okay." He continued on, haste in his steps, and pushed through the screen door to step out onto the porch. It closed with a solid bang, the echo of it reverberating through her body long after they'd left the farm.

CHAPTER THIRTY-FOUR

THE DRIVE HOME REMAINED silent. Bree crossed her arms over her chest and stared out the window, not really seeing the scenery. Beside her, Zack didn't say much. He concentrated on the road, his hands tight on the steering wheel, his speed edging over the limit.

Why did she have to come up with the idea for the article in the first place? Sure, at the start of this whole thing she was one hundred percent sure that ghosts weren't real. And yes, her blog followers would love a story like this, especially with all of her screwups on her first day. But that wasn't the real reason she'd initially wanted Inaya to write the story for the newspaper.

No. It really had to do with her dad.

He was a crook through and through. He always had been and always would be. She knew that. She believed that. He'd left when she was six years old, but even then she'd seen his handiwork time and again. Every outing to a store, or a restaurant, or the market. Deceit was a fundamental part of his nature.

Exposing the liars and cheats who crossed her path had always been a way to draw a line in the sand, to say to the world she was nothing like her dad, no matter how much she looked like him.

This time it had backfired. Bad. She'd ruined everything. Her stomach clenched, making her swallow against the taste of bile.

Okay, she'd messed up, so what? She hadn't thought ghost hunting would be her calling, so it wasn't the loss of the job that had her feeling so sick inside.

It was this chance she had with Zack. She'd wrecked it, maybe irrevocably. How would he be able to trust her after this? How would she be able to trust herself?

The scenery changed from open fields to the sprawling houses at the edge of town. The tension in her chest only increased.

When the Impala rumbled to a stop in front of her building, she sat there, not wanting to get out.

"I wish—" She pressed her lips together, not knowing how to finish the sentence. She wished for so many things. That she'd read the contract. That she hadn't thought of the stupid article in the first place. That she'd trusted him from the beginning.

Her eyes lifted to his. Regret and disappointment echoed back at her. His Adam's apple bobbed up and down.

"I have to go, Bree."

She grabbed the door handle. "Right." She still didn't want to leave. *How do I fix this?* She swallowed, not knowing what else to say, not having anything else to say. "Stay safe, okay?"

"Yeah. Will do."

She opened the door and grabbed her carpet bag out of the backseat. He gave her one nod. After she closed the door, he pulled away from the curb. The nausea in the pit of her stomach didn't fade as she lost sight of him, the Impala turning the corner.

She stared and stared down the street, thinking he would come back. He didn't.

A car horn honked, snapping her out of her daze. Refocusing on her surroundings, she went inside and trudged up the steps to her apartment. Her feet felt as if she were wearing cement shoes.

When she turned the door handle, it clicked open, unlocked. She let out a sigh. *Inaya is here.*

Her friend rushed toward her, eyes wide, her hand gripping her phone. "Bree, I was just about to call you—"

"I messed everything up again," Bree said at the same time, the tears starting as soon as she dropped her carpet bag at her feet.

Inaya stopped in front of her. "What happened?"

"Everything was great, perfect. We'd come to an understanding, we were going to figure out what a deal was, then I told him about your article." She gripped Inaya's shoulders. "I voided my contract talking to you about it. I lost my job. I can't pay my rent. I'm going to get evicted. Worst of all, I fucked up everything with Zack. He hates me now." The last sentence bubbled out between ragged exhales.

Warm arms wrapped around her, making her cry harder. She squeezed her friend tight, burying her face in her shoulder. Wrenching sobs emerged from deep within Bree's belly, ones she couldn't stop. Ones where it hurt just to breathe.

Inaya's hands ran up and down her back, calming her, and after a while the sobs subsided into hiccups.

"Okay," Inaya said against the top of her head. "Let's take this one issue at a time." She stepped away and reached for the box on the counter beside the fridge. "One tissue at a time," she added, handing it to her.

Bree wiped her face as Inaya led her to the kitchen stool. "Start with telling me about how you can't pay your rent and you're going to get evicted."

Bree stood and retrieved the eviction notice out of the side table by the front door. With a deep breath, she passed it to her.

"Oh, Bree." Inaya scanned the notice, lifting it closer to her face. "Why didn't you tell me about this sooner?"

"Because I don't need a babysitter." She sniffed, retaking her seat.

"Sometimes we all need a friend. I could've helped out."

"I thought I had everything under control, but without the money from the contract, I—" She lifted her hands then let them drop. "—don't have everything under control."

"Tell me about the contract. How did you break it?"

"There's a clause that says I can't talk to the media about an ongoing investigation. Everything has to go through Grace." She stared at her hands. "I messed up big. Zack didn't even want me on the job site."

"*I* don't want you on the job site."

Bree's head shot up. "What?"

"That's what I was trying to tell you when you walked in. You can't go back there. Ever. I forbid it."

Bree tipped her head to the side. "You forbid it?" *What is going on?*

"It's that *Sheely's Misery* story. Seriously, you can't ever go back there. Promise me."

Frowning, Bree went back to her bag and dug out her phone. It wasn't like Inaya to freak out over nothing. "I didn't get a chance to read it yet." She went to the shared folder and found where Inaya had put the *Haunted* issues.

Inaya's concerned gaze pressed against her as Bree found the one titled *Sheely's Misery* by Allen Skinner, and opened it.

This is a true story. Anyone who grew up near the town of Maybrook would know the story of Sheely House. But have any of you stayed a night in that wretched place? I have, and I can tell you now, my friend lost his life there, and I barely escaped with mine.

Swallowing hard, Bree's weak legs gave out and she leaned her butt against the stool, feet braced against the floor. Inaya wrapped her arms around herself.

Bree kept reading. The author hadn't believed the stories, but they were hosting guests at Sheely House and his goal was to put the rumors to shame. His friend had laughed at him for taking on such a trivial challenge, but had come along anyway.

I woke up in the middle of the night, my stomach burning...

I couldn't move...

A knife slicing through my skin...

Blood ran down my body to pool on the sheets...

The phone jiggled in Bree's shaking hand as she continued to read his descriptions of what had happened to him. His friend in the next room kept screaming, but he couldn't move or go help.

The screams stopped so abruptly, I knew there was no way for him to be alive.

He described more, visions of the past, of the atrocities that had happened there, experiments. With each revelation, the evil gripping him tightened its hold. Bree's breath caught in her throat.

Then I saw her. An apparition at the door. A woman in a nightgown. She pointed at me, her mouth fixed in a scream. As quickly as the torture began, it stopped, my body and voice released from their prison. I knew she had saved me, this woman in white.

Bree read the last line, her aching fingers clenched on the edges of her phone.

I say this to you, Dear Reader, even to the most courageous of you: stay clear of Sheely House and the evil misery dwelling there.

Bree blinked and met Inaya's eyes. "I've got to warn them." She closed the document and pressed Zack's name in her contacts. While the phone rang, Inaya read the eviction notice again.

The phone kept ringing until his voicemail picked up. Listening to him say, "Leave a message," had her heart pounding in her chest.

"Hey, Zack," she said after the beep. "I have something important to talk to you about. It's about that *Sheely's Misery* story. It's really bad.

Phone me back." She ended the call and looked at Inaya, a new sort of panic blooming in her chest. "He didn't answer. I'll text him too."

"What about Grace?"

"Good idea." Bree called Grace's number, but there was no answer. "Straight to voicemail," she said when the message started. "Hey, Grace. It's Bree. I don't think you guys should go back into that house. Call me and I can explain better. Thanks."

She lowered the phone. Maybe they weren't answering because they didn't want to talk to her. Maybe Zack had already told Grace about the contract. Maybe they wouldn't check messages until it was too late.

She shot to her feet and grabbed her carpet bag off the floor. "I really need to warn them."

"You can't go back there."

Bree rushed to her bedroom and Inaya followed, the eviction notice still in her hand.

"I mean it," she said as Bree dumped out the bag on her bed.

"Rory was hurt last night."

A sharp inhale. "Oh, no." Inaya's hand flew to her mouth. "Like this man?"

"I don't know," Bree said as she threw items into her carpet bag.

Dropping her hand, Inaya rubbed the sides of her arms and shivered. "Poor kid. I hope she's okay." After a minute of watching Bree shove things into her bag and change her clothes, she lifted the eviction notice. "It says here your rent is in arrears."

Bree let out a huff. "I paid Mr. Constable this month's rent when Theo gave me my paycheck, but I've basically used all of it up now. I might have forty bucks left." A charitable number, but it seemed unimportant now. What was important was warning Zack and the others. Their lives were at stake.

"I can loan you the money, Bree. I know you'll pay me back."

"I hate borrowing money," she muttered, zipping up the carpet bag.

Inaya squeezed her shoulder. "I know, but sometimes we don't need to do this adulting stuff on our own."

Her head snapped up. "That's what Zack said." She pressed her lips together.

"Aw, hon, come here." Inaya pulled her into a hug. "If he's as good a guy as I think he is, you'll be able to work it out."

Bree let Inaya's words calm her, but her mind kept going back to the article. How would she be able to work it out if he ended up dissected?

"I don't want you to go back there," Inaya said against her temple.

Squaring her shoulders, Bree pulled away. "And I really, really, need to warn them. They don't know what they're up against." She swung her bag over her arm. "I'll drive there and tell them, then we can board up the house, call it a day, and get on with our lives." She nodded once, hoping that was all true.

Inaya's frown didn't lessen as she followed her to the door. She stopped Bree briefly with a hand on her arm. "You stay safe."

"I'll be safe because I'll be with Zack." As soon as she said the words, she knew them to be true.

CHAPTER THIRTY-FIVE

A s soon as Zack turned the corner, out of sight of Bree's apartment, he pulled over and shut off the ignition. *How can I fix this?* He gripped the steering wheel and stared straight ahead, not seeing anything in front of him.

It hurt to see the turmoil in her eyes, the self-deprecation, the uncertainty. He'd wanted to grab hold of her, to squeeze her to him and tell her that everything was going to be okay—but he just wasn't sure it was going to be.

There was no way Grace would overlook this. It was spelled out clearly in the contract for a reason.

He needed time to figure it all out, to clear his mind so a solution would present itself.

His phone buzzed. Grace. He read the text.

Stella is on edge about this one.

The job. He had to concentrate on the job. Tomorrow he could meet with Bree and tell her how much he cared. That even if his sister fired her, it didn't change the way he felt. Hell, he could help her find a job if she wanted.

The urge to turn the car around, to talk to her right now and assure her this hadn't changed anything between them overwhelmed him. He wasn't going to let their newfound relationship slip through his fingers.

He reached for the key, then stopped when his phone buzzed a second time. Grace again.

Hurry.

Talking to Bree would take more than five minutes. He owed her that.

He had a ghost to catch. He still had to pick up his gear from home. Not needing any more distractions until the job was done, he turned off his cell phone and tossed it onto the seat beside him.

A knock at his window caused him to jump. Lucas Martinez stood on the other side, his eyebrows pinched together. Zack rolled down his window. "Hi."

"Hey, Zack. Is everything okay?"

"Yeah. Everything's fine. Just peachy. How's everything with you?" When Lucas didn't respond, only stared at him, Zack followed up with, "Why do you ask?"

"Because you're in a no parking zone."

Zack peered through his windshield at the signage on the sidewalk. Yep. There it was. He sat in a tow-away zone. An $80 fine tow-away zone in front of the library. He looked up at Lucas. "Sorry, I'll—"

"I'm afraid I'm going to have to give you a ticket."

"You serious?"

Lucas slapped the top of the car with a whoop. "No, man. I'm totally messing with you." As Zack exhaled a sigh of relief, Lucas leaned his hip against the side of the car and crossed his arms over his chest. "What's up? You're obviously distracted."

Zack slumped, not sure where to begin.

"It's Bree isn't it?"

He sat up straight as an arrow.

Lucas whistled. "You went and fell in love with her, didn't you?"

The question hit him so hard in his chest, his breastbone stung. Zack's grip tightened on the wheel. *Fell in love?* A grin split over his face—one he couldn't stop.

"That's great, man! Happy for you two. Knew I sensed something happening between you the other day." He shook his head, a smile pursing his lips. "She never looked at me the way she looked at you."

The underlying meaning of those words wasn't lost on him. "You guys were…?"

"Yeah," Lucas answered. "We dated a couple of times, but it was all she wanted, and that's fine. It was fun while it lasted." He shrugged. "I'm glad she's found someone. She deserves to be happy. So do you." He straightened away from the car. "I'll let you go."

He double-tapped the top of the car and stepped away. Then he paused. "Maybe we should grab a beer sometime."

Zack peered up at him and raised his eyebrows. "You want to hang out?"

Lucas glanced down the street. "Most of my high school friends moved away. Don't really hang out with people in this town, but you've always been a good guy. Going for a beer is better than going home and watching TV with only my dog for company every night."

Zack got it then. He'd lost touch with the few people he'd been friends with in high school too, and it was harder to make friends as an adult. Easier to get sucked into social media and your own personal space, and close out the world. He'd gotten a taste of how it could be different with Bree. It might be even harder to make friends as a cop than it was for a paranormal investigator.

"Yeah, I'd like that." He reached over to his glove box and pulled out a business card. "Give me a call."

"Cool." Lucas flashed him a smile and stepped away. "Now move your car before I give you a ticket." Hands in his pockets, he whistled on the way to his police cruiser where it was parked behind Zack's.

Taking a deep breath, Zack started his car and merged into traffic. He loved Bree.

He sat with that truth, letting it settle, and it felt like the perfect fit.

This morning, when he'd forced himself to leave his bed with her sleeping so soundly next to him, he'd acknowledged she was the vibrant light he needed in his life. Everything was always dark, dreary, and serious. She made it all disappear.

It didn't matter that she'd messed up the contract, and as soon as this job was over, he'd find her and tell her everything that tumbled around in his head and heart.

It would definitely take more than five minutes.

He drove to the other side of town, retrieved his gear, and headed toward Maybrook.

When he pulled into the long gravel drive to the Granwin House, he saw the work van right off, then the cherry red Miata beside it: Stella's car. He felt good about her being here. With Roman, their resident demonologist, out of the country, Stella was the best at recognizing and removing malicious entities.

Sam lifted equipment out of the van, and Grace stood a few feet away, her phone to her ear. She nodded to him, then turned to the side as she spoke into her cell, a frown pinching her brow.

He was ready to get this over with. The faster they finished, the faster he could get back to Bree. *In and out.* Not that a person should rush a cleansing, but they'd never encountered a problem they hadn't been able to solve. If they finished before it got too late, he could call her tonight.

Eagerness in his limbs, he gripped the door handle and stepped out. Stella rushed out of the house, gave him a wave, and stopped to lift a box off the porch before hurrying back inside. His long strides closed the gap between him and the van.

Grace lowered her phone and tucked it into her blazer pocket. "Stella's saying there's more than one energy pattern here."

Zack nodded. Nothing they couldn't handle.

He knew he should tell her about Bree, the article, and the voided contract. He didn't. It would just get in the way of the investigation at this point. Tomorrow would be soon enough.

Grace squinted at the house, her hand blocking the sun, and glanced at his car. "I thought you'd bring Bree. Is she coming on her own?"

"No," he said. "She'll be sitting this one out."

From Grace's expression, he knew he wasn't fooling her. "You'll need to explain to me what's going on sooner or later."

He nodded because he knew Grace wouldn't accept anything less.

"I'm ready to start," Stella called from the top step.

"We'll need more time to set up," Grace answered back, then shook her head. "So impatient, these witches. You'd think they'd understand the concept of recording evidence." She frowned at him. "You ready for this?"

"Born for it."

She clucked her tongue at him.

"How's Rory doing?" he asked, the kid's safety his top priority.

"I just got off the phone with Fletcher." Her frown deepened. "I'd thought she was scratched, but actually she'd been cut. Straight incisions on her abdomen. He sent me a photo."

Zack's chest tightened at the thought of something harming that little girl. They needed to be diligent here so she'd stay safe.

"It's weird," Grace continued. "I sent the image to Roman and he said he'd never seen a demon make such precision cuts before. He thinks we must be working with something else."

Not a demon, but a malicious spirit. Or something else entirely?

Grace's phone rang. "I'm going to get you to set up the perimeter cameras," she said as she pulled out her cell. "We're just finishing the ones on the ground floor now. Probably take about forty-five?"

He nodded. "I can set up a few in that time."

"Good. Meet you back here." She touched her phone to take the call. "Grace Liller."

He jogged the rest of the way to the van. Sam had gone inside with his last batch of cameras, and Zack grabbed the perimeter equipment in the duffel bag.

They'd found good angles on their initial trek around the property, and he headed straight for the edge of the treeline, taking a fraction of the time they had that first day.

The energy of the cemetery pressed in on him more than it had a few days ago. For good measure, he set up an extra camera nearby. The small drop of blood that ran from his nose should have worried him, but he swiped it with a tissue and continued on to the last tripod site before heading back to the house.

Halfway there, the familiar sound of a car needing a new muffler echoed up the lane. His heart pounded in his chest.

She shouldn't be here, but he was so glad to see her, he didn't care.

Grace walked towards Bree's car.

Why had she come when he'd told her not to?

He froze in place. *Oh no.* Maybe she meant to tell Grace about the broken contract herself.

Dread sweeping through his chest, he jogged toward them.

CHAPTER THIRTY-SIX

B REE TURNED OFF HER engine. Relief mixed with her nerves. The paranormal team hadn't gone inside yet. Grace took a call, her phone pressed to her ear. Sam unloaded gear from the van. And an unfamiliar blonde woman stood on the porch, staring straight up at the house's tallest peak.

Zack wasn't anywhere to be seen, but she'd parked beside his car.

A swallow lodged in her throat as she stared at Grace. Not only did she need to warn them about the evil living in the house, but she needed to face Grace about the broken contract, needed to apologize. She knew she was about to be fired, expected it, but it didn't make it hurt any less.

She should be used to it by now, but she wasn't.

Steeling her spine, Bree got out of her car. Telling them about the *Haunted* story was more important than her pride.

Grace lowered her phone and strode toward her car. As she drew near, Bree noticed Zack rushing toward them from the edge of the treeline.

He looked good. Like, really good. Like, the edible kind of good. *You saw him a couple of hours ago.* Didn't matter. He still looked edible.

"So you decided to show up," Grace said, her blazer unbuttoned, revealing a powder blue dress shirt.

Needing to get this out before she lost her nerve, Bree stopped in front of her. "I'm sorry about Inaya. It was entirely my fault."

Grace blinked. "Who's Inaya?"

Tension reverberated through Bree's body. "My friend Inaya."

"Okay." Grace dragged out the word, her brow pinched.

Zack didn't tell her about the newspaper article. Why didn't Zack tell her about the article? *Because he cares about you and didn't want your contract to be voided.*

Warmth spread through her chest. That was why he was looking so panicked as he raced toward them.

Lips pressed together, Bree willed herself not to spill everything.

"What about your friend?" Grace asked, her head tilted to the side.

Bree's eyes cut to Zack as he neared, his breaths short. "Um. Never mind. That's not really why I'm here. I came to warn you."

Grace straightened and placed her hands on her hips. "Warn us about what?"

"There was a story about this house, one in a pulp magazine. It detailed how a person was tortured, his friend killed when they stayed here years ago."

They both stared at her, deadpan, like her words didn't even register.

Didn't they believe her? She wasn't sure what was going on in their heads. Grace's eyes narrowed on her, and Zack opened his mouth to say something, then stopped himself.

And the blonde up at the house seemed engaged in conversation with the front door.

Finally, Grace said, "Pulp magazines are fiction. We've handled a lot of paranormal cases. I'm sure we'll be fine. We're always careful."

"It might be connected to what happened with Rory." Now she had their attention. Bree slipped her phone out of her back pocket. "I'll just show it to you."

She found the story and passed her phone to Grace.

Grace's eyes skimmed the story, Zack reading over her shoulder. Unable to stand still, Bree paced a short path in front of them. Their faces changed from relaxed to concerned to disturbed. As they neared the end, Zack's face flushed.

Swallowing, Grace passed the phone back. "Thank you for tracking this down. And you're right, it's important. Rory's cuts were thin and straight, like from a knife, similar to the victim in the story. They weren't the gouged marks we'd expect from demonic activity."

Bree inhaled sharply.

"She's okay," Grace reassured her. "Scared, but okay. The cuts will heal."

"But will she?" Bree asked. Had Rory had the same kind of visions this man had?

"That I can't answer." Grace looked toward the house, then back at her. "Everything's almost all set up. We'll work together, we'll take every precaution, and get this house fixed for the Rivets."

The way she was so emphatic about it, Bree believed her.

The phone in Grace's blazer pocket rang. She took it out and looked at the screen. "I've got to take this. Excuse me." She walked away toward the van, leaving Bree alone with Zack.

A strained silence fell between them. Bree wanted to hug him, the urge so overwhelming that her fingers twitched on her phone. He was well and whole. She'd arrived in time.

Bree let out a long breath. "You didn't tell her about the breach of contract."

Zack stared at her, his eyes searching her face. Her toes curled in her shoes with the need to be closer.

He shook his head. "I was going to wait until after we're done with the house. We need to concentrate, and bringing something like that into the mix isn't a good idea."

With a nod, Bree broke his gaze to stare at his feet. Good old combat boots.

"What are you doing here, Bree?"

Her head snapped up to meet his eyes, and she nervously plucked at the bottom of her T-shirt. "I needed to tell you about the story."

"You could have phoned."

"I tried. You didn't answer. Neither did Grace. I didn't have Sam's number."

His hand went to his back pocket. "I forgot I'd turned it off." The intensity of his gaze made her squirm. "So you decided to come out all this way and tell us?"

She nodded. "It was important." *Wasn't it?*

His eyes bored into hers.

Why was he looking at her like that? Her cheeks burned, her heart pounding a heavy rhythm. "I also wanted to see you." She swallowed. "And fix this mess I made with the contract."

Zack looked away, and she was able to gulp a deep breath.

"Like I said," he murmured, his eyes meeting hers again. "The contract can wait." He stepped closer until his boots almost touched hers. "Coming all the way out here, telling us about the story, it means a lot." He took her hand in his and shivers ran up her arm to her scalp.

Bree nodded, her throat too tight to make words.

"Do you want to stay and help?" he asked.

He was giving her another chance. She cleared her throat and squeezed his fingers. "Inaya told me not to come back here, said it wasn't safe." He nodded like he understood that, so she rushed on. "But I want to help if I can."

His mouth curled into a half-smile, his fingers lacing through hers. Was he going to kiss her? She didn't care if they had an audience if it meant his lips against hers.

A sound from the house made her turn her head. The blonde paced back and forth on the porch, saying something repeatedly, like a chant.

"That's our resident witch," Zack said, following her gaze.

He'd mentioned a witch before, when they'd been waiting for their hot dogs by the river. It felt like so long ago, but it had only been a handful of days.

She didn't look like a witch to Bree. The red sports car had to be hers, and she wore a pink knitted top and white skinny jeans, something Bree would have attributed to a college student—or an outfit Bree might have worn while working at Theo's.

Does it matter what a witch wears? She can dress however she wants.

Bree glanced down at herself. She had on a similar outfit to the one she'd worn here before, black jeans and a band T-shirt. She touched the ends of her black hair. "I've never met a witch before."

"She's a good witch. Nothing to be scared of." His tone held humor. "She doesn't hex nice people. Just the ones who piss her off."

Was he making fun of her? She gave his fingers a sharp tug. "I'm not scared."

After a moment of Zack staring at her and Bree trying not to fidget, he said, "I can introduce you."

It was only last night that she'd been haunted, only last night that she had admitted to herself ghosts were real. Now there were witches in the world too. She wasn't sure if she could handle meeting a witch.

Of course I can handle meeting a witch.

If the woman over there was a good witch, did that mean there were bad ones too? Did she have a cauldron, eye of newt, and all that? Could she fly, turn people into toads? *I really hope not, or I might be in trouble...*

Bree squared her shoulders and interlaced her fingers with his. "I'd love to be introduced."

As they neared the steps, the witch straightened away from the door. "Whoa, there's a serious energy shift happening." She spun around, her eyes fastening on the two of them.

Foot on the bottom step, Bree hesitated.

The witch stared at Zack, then at Bree, then at Zack. "Wow, this energy between the two of you is intense. Intensely good! You guys should go off and have babies or something."

"Uh..." *Right this second?* Bree's cheeks warmed, not sure what was happening. A similar flush crept up Zack's throat.

That wasn't a spell, was it? She didn't have the power to influence with her words alone, did she?

"I'm sorry if I'm disturbing you. I can leave," Bree offered, not knowing what else to say.

"No way! Don't you dare. This is the first time Zack's energy has been this positive since I met him. I mean it's mixed with a lot of heavy shit too, but there's extreme light now."

Zack's flush deepened.

Lips parting, warmth bloomed in Bree's chest. What did that all mean? Could the witch really know that from their energy? Bree wouldn't have believed it possible a week ago, but after everything that had happened in the past few days, she wouldn't rule anything out. She didn't feel the intense need to procreate—well, no more so than last night—so she didn't think the witch's words had influenced her. She supposed she was safe enough.

"I'm Bree, by the way." She remained on the bottom step.

"Cool. Cool. I'm Stella. Look, guys, I'm going to need to step away for a bit and clear my head. I'll talk to Grace, then take another walk to the cemetery."

Bree made room for her to pass as she bounced down the steps, her blonde ponytail flopping against her shoulder. The witch headed toward the van.

Zack put his hands in his pockets and rocked on his heels. "Well, that was decidedly Stella."

Bree clasped her hands together. "She seems nice."

"She is." He ran his hand through his hair, and Bree had the sudden urge to run both her hands in there too.

A witch-induced impulse? She didn't think so, just Zack's natural magnetism.

His eyes moved beyond her, and Bree turned to find Sam and Grace striding toward the house.

"I told Stella to take ten minutes," Grace said, looking between the two of them. "So you have ridiculous, arcing, electric energy between you two?" She raised an eyebrow.

"Is that what she said?" Bree asked, her voice squeaking.

Sam grinned as he moved by her up to the front door.

She glanced at Zack, who was trying his hardest not to look at his sister. Bree was pretty sure the banister wasn't that interesting.

"Right," Grace said, grabbing their attention. "I'm not sure how this is going to affect her read of the house, but she's gotten used to Sam and I, so I'm sure after a time she'll be able to get a handle on you two." She tipped her head to the side.

After a second, Bree cleared her throat. "Did she say you and Sam have ridiculous, arcing energy too?"

Grace squinted at her. "No." With a glance at Zack, she nodded. "Let's catch some ghosts."

The comment jarred Bree, and she peered up at the house. Sunlight highlighted its intricate design, making it appear harmless, but after everything, she knew it was anything but.

Warm fingers squeezed hers. Zack's eyes held confidence, bolstering her. If he were here, she could face anything. She gave him one nod, and they started up the steps together.

Her phone buzzed in her back pocket. She took it out and saw Inaya's picture. Did her friend have some sort of sixth sense and know she was about to step into the house?

"Is it okay if I take this?" she asked Grace up on the landing.

Her boss nodded once. "You have the same ten as Stella."

"Thanks." Reluctantly, Bree let go of Zack's fingers to take the call. He continued on, and she watched until he sent a small smile over his shoulder, then disappeared through the door.

Heart fluttering in her chest, she touched the circle on her phone and held it up to her ear. "What's up?"

"Bree." Inaya's voice held an edge she'd never heard before. "I'm so sorry."

Her hand tightened on the phone. "What happened?"

"I called Brian to tell him I wasn't doing the article anymore. I couldn't do it, Bree, even if your contract was already broken. I couldn't hurt you that way, so I called him to tell him I'd write a different story."

Bree's chest squeezed. This should be good news. Why did Inaya sound so devastated? Bree held her breath.

"That's when he told me he'd been writing his own article." A heavy exhale on the other end of the line. "Bree, he went into my work computer and stole all my notes. He said his brother had been ripped off by the Lillers. He even went into our shared folder because I had it bookmarked and took all your notes."

"Oh, no." A black fog hazed the edges of her vision.

"I know. I'm so sorry." A shuddered breath reverberated across the line. "He fashioned his article after the first version we were going to write, the stuff about the ghost hunters being frauds." She paused, and Bree's heart pounded hard in her chest. "It's going to be printed in tomorrow's newspaper. The front page."

"What?" Her fingers turned to ice. "How do we stop this?"

"We can't. Monday's edition has already gone to the printer. It's already being printed. Right at this moment. We can't stop it. I'm so sorry."

"There's nothing we can do?" Every part of her ached in horror. Why was this happening? She'd thought maybe she could make things work. "There's got to be something." She couldn't give up now.

"Short of breaking the law and sabotaging the printing press, I don't think so." Inaya's sigh could have pushed a person over. "I'm so furious I quit. I can't believe Brian went into my stuff without my permission. I can't work for someone like that."

"You love your job." It was all she could think to say when the world spun around her. Zack. Grace. Sam. Tears threatened to spill. They would loathe her after this. *All my fault.* It had been her idea from the start. If she hadn't told Inaya about it, none of this would be happening.

"I'll find another," Inaya said through the haze of her thoughts. "You always get a new job pretty quick, and there's more than one newspaper in town." Inaya exhaled loudly over the phone. "I'm so sorry, Bree. I know you must hate me right now."

She took a ragged breath, her throat feeling like someone had taken sandpaper to it. "I don't hate you, but I do kinda hate your boss."

"And Douglas. The asshole."

"Who?" She sniffed.

"Douglas. Brian's brother. I saw the new version of the article. The stuff he's quoted to have said is horrible. I guess I should be glad Brian didn't credit me for it."

Douglas. The man from the train bridge. *What a disaster.*

A burning ache settled into Bree's chest. She stared at the front door of Granwin House and thought of all the people inside who would never speak to her again.

Zack would never forgive her for this.

CHAPTER THIRTY-SEVEN

As Sam placed the last camera in the corner, Zack helped Grace check the microphones. Stella had already set up a circular table in the middle, the rest of the furniture pushed up against the walls.

She kept her setup simple, as always. No bells or pendulum. No parlor tricks of any kind, only a bowl of sage and oil in the center of the table surrounded by five white candles.

Despite what lay ahead for them and the ominous short story about the house, Zack's mind was entirely preoccupied with Bree. She'd come here on her own to warn them. She cared about him enough to do that, even though she was terrified of this place. He couldn't stop the elation inside him at the meaning behind it.

He'd wanted to take her in his arms and hold her close as soon as he'd seen her. She looked good, a delicious kind of good that made him remember everything they'd done together the night before, made him think about everything he still wanted to do.

They had time. *No rush.* The way she'd responded to him taking her hand in his, the way her cheeks had flushed with pleasure—they were on the same page. Like they'd planned this morning, they could figure out what kind of deal this was together. He looked forward to every second of it.

The contract stuff didn't matter. So she'd messed up. Didn't everyone mess up once in a while? They'd work through it.

The back door banged shut, and hurried footsteps headed toward them. Stella rounded the corner, stopping just inside the door.

"I'm ready. I felt some really positive energy near the gravesite. We should ride that wave and start as soon as possible." Her eyes skimmed over them. "Where's Bree?"

"She's taking a call," Grace said, walking toward the table.

"Okay. Let's all get settled, and she can join us when she's done." Stella glanced over her shoulder at the front door. "Hopefully, that isn't too long."

She scurried to the far side of the table and sat in the chair, her back to the windows. "I'll have Sam beside me here," she gestured to the next seat, "then Grace, and you're beside her, Zack."

That meant Bree would be between him and Stella, and with Stella reading Bree's energy so high already, he didn't know if it was a good idea. He also understood Stella liked to make a triangle between Grace and him to balance their energy.

Stella hadn't ever failed them; he trusted her decisions. While everyone got settled around the table, she lit the five candles with a lighter from her pocket. Zack placed his hands flat against its surface.

The front door squealed open, and he straightened in his chair.

"Oh good," Stella murmured, placing her hands on the table.

As soon as Bree rounded the corner, Zack knew something was wrong. He jumped to his feet, startling the others. He could tell her shift in mood from her posture, her stricken expression, and the way her rounded eyes found his, lips pressed together.

"I'm sorry I've kept you waiting," she said, her voice shaky as she hurried to the empty spot.

"We haven't been waiting long," he reassured her as they sat, wanting to say something else, to take her aside and ask her what had happened during her phone call.

Bree clasped her hands in her lap and studied the spot on the table right in front of her.

The way Stella stared at Bree made him even edgier.

After about a minute of Bree avoiding everyone's gaze, including his own, she finally focused on Stella.

The witch's face had gone pale. "I think," she hesitated, her voice small. "I think we should probably get started."

Grace shot him a look, and he couldn't ease his frown. This wasn't like Stella. Something had shaken both her and Bree. Contacting spirits directly wasn't something you wanted to do with bad energy flying around the participants. What was going on?

Before he could suggest stepping away from this for a minute, Stella spoke.

"I've been sensing two separate energies here. A positive one from the cemetery, and a negative one from the house." She didn't announce this to anyone in particular, her eyes fixed over his right shoulder to a space near the doorway. "I'm sensing support from the cemetery energy. I don't want to lose that support by delaying further. I'll open with a blessing." She gestured for everyone to join hands.

Bree's hand was icy cold in his, and as soon as Bree touched Stella, the witch winced.

Grace's eyes flicked to him again. He didn't know what was going on either, but Stella would stop if she needed to. He shook his head once.

After a long stare, Grace focused her attention back on Stella, and they waited for her to begin her blessing.

Stella opened her mouth, then closed it again, giving a small shake of her head. With a nod, she started again:

In this moment, it's strength we need find
to inspire a healthier and happier mind.
We call to the Goddess for guide and support
so that we can grow strong instead of falling short.
With our arms open, honest and wide
we wish to welcome a harmonious guide
to keep us centered, at peace with love
and in balance with Divine light from above.

She lifted one of the candles and lit the bundled leaves in the bowl in the center of the table. The scent of sage and burning oil lifted high, enveloping them.

Smoke of air and fire of Earth
cleanse and bless this home and hearth.
Drive away all harm and fear.
Only good may enter here.
Only good may enter here.
Only good may enter here.
So mote it be.

A gust of wind swirled around the room. Bree gasped, her fingers tightening on his.

Pressure built in his chest, making him take a slow, deep breath through his teeth. The spirit must be very close for such an instant effect on him. He resisted the urge to touch his nose and make sure it wasn't bleeding.

Across the table, Sam stared at him, his brow pinched. Grace's fingers tightened on her husband's, but she kept her gaze glued to Stella.

The wind around them calmed, and Zack watched Stella, her eyes closed, as she read the energy she'd summoned. Everyone remained quiet as her face contorted into a grimace.

She gasped, then let go of Bree's hand. Everyone else dropped hands too.

"I'm sorry," Stella murmured, opening her eyes. "There's too much going on in this room for me to get an accurate reading." She stared at Bree, who'd fixed her gaze to the tabletop, her lip caught between her teeth. "It feels like there are dozens of spirits here," Stella went on, "but that doesn't make sense to me. I didn't feel them earlier. I must be getting crossed signals or something."

"What would you have us do?" Grace asked, her gaze steady. "You're the one in charge here. Tell us what you need."

Stella hesitated, her gaze passing over Bree's bent head to him. "I only need three for the ritual. I might get a better read if there were less people for this session."

An uncomfortable silence followed her statement.

Grace touched his hand. "You never got a chance to check out the basement last time you were here. Why don't you two have a tour of the space and let us know if you find anything?"

He gave her one slow nod, then turned to Stella. "How long do you think you'll need?"

"Thirty or forty minutes maybe?" She scratched the bridge of her nose. "Once I can figure out who we're dealing with, then we can all work together to do the cleanse."

"I'm sorry I ruin everything all the time," Bree whispered, then abruptly pushed her chair back.

Before she could stand, Stella grabbed her forearm, her eyes vacant and unfocused.

*Moon of finest silver wane
take away bad luck and pain.
As you fade into the night
bring new hope back in sight.*

Bree froze, her jaw slack.

In a state of shock, Zack just stared, because he didn't know what to do. He'd never seen Stella force a spell on someone before. Eventually Bree turned her head, her panicked eyes meeting his.

"Stella?" he asked.

His sister looked just as staggered as he felt. Beside her, Sam's wide eyes were glued to the pair.

Just as Zack reached out to separate them, Stella let go. Bree shot to her feet and backed away, almost tripping over her chair in the process.

"I'll just," she took two more steps back, "I'll just wait out here." Bree headed straight out of the room.

His gaze swept over everyone present, noting the lack of color in Stella's face, then chased after Bree. He caught up with her at the front door.

"Hey, are you okay?" He took her hand in his and turned her toward him. "Did she hurt you?"

With a squeeze of his fingers, Bree shook her head. "She just startled me, that's all." Eyes wide, her throat bobbed in a swallow.

Zack scanned her features, her face as pale as Stella's moments ago. "I can understand if you want to leave." Taking a deep breath, he added, "But I need to stay."

She pressed her lips together, her eyes lowering. "I think I was causing problems in there."

"We won't go back into the sitting room. We'll check out the basement like Grace asked."

She nodded, but wouldn't meet his gaze.

With one last squeeze of her fingers, Zack picked up the duffel bag from beside the front door. "Can I put you in charge of the camera again?" he asked, pulling it out. Hopefully, a specific task would focus her. "You took such good shots last time."

That earned him a flick of her eyes and a quirk of her lips. "Sure," she said, her hand outstretched.

He grabbed a flashlight, notebook, and the EMF meter before heading to the basement door beside the kitchen. Following at a slow pace, she hung the camera around her neck.

Maybe this wasn't a good idea. Maybe he should send her home right now. But if she went home, that's exactly where he would want to be. Call him selfish, but he wanted Bree close. Whatever was bugging her right now, he needed to get to the bottom of it so he could help.

He gripped the antique doorknob. "You ready?"

Gaze focused on him, she gave him a firm nod.

That's my girl.

He opened the door and switched on the light. Rickety steps led down into the dimness. A wide plank floor stretched from wall to wall of the low-ceilinged room. Boxes and plastic storage tubs skirted the edge, leaving the middle part clear for walking. A furnace and water heater dominated the left side.

As soon as Zack stepped onto the floorboards, an inescapable feeling of dread saturated his every muscle. Never had he felt an all-consuming negativity in such a sudden way.

"There's some seriously heavy shit down here." His voice wobbled, surprising him.

Bree stepped closer. "Where's it coming from?"

He let go of his instincts to shield himself for a moment, allowing the energy to penetrate his mind. The flood of foreboding that washed over him had him breathing fast and hard. He stared into Bree's eyes. "Everywhere."

Her anxious face paled even more.

He wanted to reassure her, but the words wouldn't come. "Let's take some shots," he said instead and moved away from the stairs to the discolored floorboards on the other side of the water heater.

"Water damage," he said, mostly to himself, remembering what Fletcher had said about the old water heater leaking everywhere.

Bree came up beside him. "What water damage?" The *click click* of the shutter echoed around them.

"There," he said, pointing ahead of them. It was hard to miss.

Behind the camera, she frowned. "I don't see any water damage." She took a picture in the direction where he pointed, then examined the screen to see what came up. Her frown deepened.

Coming up behind her, he viewed the captured image. They were consistently colored planks, no damage in the picture, but when he looked to where he'd seen the damage, it was still there, a dark water stain taking up a good portion of the floor's surface, then trickling to the outer wall of the basement. He looked at the image on the camera. Nothing.

"I see it, but it's not in the photo."

She met his gaze over her shoulder, eyes filled with concern. "Maybe it has to do with one of your hunches?"

"Maybe," he allowed as he walked past her. "But it's never happened before. I always just sense things, not *see* them."

He stopped when the toes of his boots touched the edge of the stain. A spike of pain stabbed him in his lower abdomen, and he hissed out a breath.

"What is it?" Bree asked, hurrying toward him.

Extending his arm, he stopped her from getting any closer. "The energy in here," he said through clenched teeth, the pain increasing with each passing second. "It's not good. Not like anything we experienced above this floor. And it's getting worse."

A wet sensation made him reach up to his face. His fingers came away from his nose, dotted with blood.

Bree grabbed his arm. "Then we need to leave."

"We're not done yet," he replied, panting.

"It's hurting you!" She yanked his arm to get him to move. "Oh, god," she gasped, her eyes trained on his stomach.

Zack looked down and lifted his jacket away from his body. A line of red cut straight across his abdomen, blood trickling out.

"We need to get out of here," Bree said, her voice high-pitched and panicked. "We need to get you help." She backed away, her hand tight on his wrist.

The pain moved up into his scalp, through his eyeballs, and blurred his vision.

Bree spoke again, but her voice sounded far away, further away than it should have been, because he could feel her icy hand on him. Or was it him who was cold?

A pounding sound in his head made him turn. Bree's face filled his vision, her eyes wide with concern and fear. Her lips moved, but he couldn't hear her. She might have said "Grace" but he wasn't sure. Keeping hold of his hand, she backed away.

He couldn't go with her. He wasn't sure why, but he couldn't, not yet. He pulled his hand from her grip.

The pain in his stomach lessened, and the strumming in his head dissipated a fraction. He took a step toward Bree.

The world groaned. She must have heard it too because she looked at his feet. Staring at the floorboards, Zack shifted his weight to his right foot.

Another deep groan. His head snapped up. Bree reached for him.

Then she disappeared as the floor swallowed him whole.

CHAPTER THIRTY-EIGHT

"Zack!" Bree screamed.

The wooden planks beneath him impossibly shattered into a hundred splinters, his body plunging straight down.

She tried to reach for him, to catch his hand in hers, but she wasn't fast enough. Down he went into the dark, the wood floor disintegrating.

Frantic feet thumped on the floor above. The others must have heard her scream, and the horrendous noise of the shattering floor. She shouted for Grace again.

Her entire body shaking, Bree bent on her hands and knees and peered over the edge of the person-sized hole.

"Zack!" she yelled, not seeing him in the dark. "Flashlight. Flashlight."

Turning, she found it close by and snatched it in her trembling hand. The wide beam cut a path through the dim hole.

"Oh my god. Zack!"

A full story below her, he lay on his back, arms spread wide, eyes closed, blood coming out of his nose. A smear of red covered his stomach.

Shoes stormed down the stairs.

"Call 911!" she shouted, turning slightly. "Zack's fallen."

Grace headed toward her, phone already in hand, her eyes wide, and face pale. "What happened?" She punched numbers into her phone and held it up to her ear. Sam rushed right behind her, and Stella paused at the bottom of the staircase.

"I don't know." Bree's breaths came out in short, panicked bursts. "It's like the whole floor exploded. It doesn't make sense. Not when it happened. Not right now. He just fell straight down." She stared down into the hole, hating how still Zack lay. "He's bleeding. He was being cut right before my eyes. He's not moving. We need a ladder." Blood pounded in her ears.

"We need an ambulance," Grace said into the phone, feet edging closer to the gap in the floor. "And gear to get someone out of a twenty-foot hole." She relayed the address while she strode back to Stella, then passed her the phone. "Stay on the line with them."

Sam knelt and took the flashlight from Bree. She barely felt it leave her freezing fingers. Then he lifted his arm, stopping Grace from getting too close. "Don't want you to fall in there too."

She knelt beside him, and they inched their way to the edge. Sam aimed the beam down the hole.

Grace inhaled sharply. "Zack!" she called down. He didn't respond.

Cheeks growing damp, Bree wrapped her arms around herself, feeling utterly helpless. The image of Zack lying so still, bleeding, burned her brain, though she was too far away from the edge to see him now.

Was he dead? He'd fallen so far down, the space like an old cellar with its dirt floor. Broken planks had partially covered him, other white shapes poking through the hard-packed floor.

White shapes?

Dread settled into the pit of her stomach to mix with the fear and anguish at seeing Zack hurt. What was down there with him?

Sam and Grace discussed how best to get to him. Bree heard snippets of the conversation, but couldn't fully focus. There'd been a ladder at the back of the house; Sam went off to find it. Stella remained near the steps, her face ashen as she told them an ambulance was on its way.

I need to see him. Bree needed to see what was down there with him, what her brain told her.

Grace yelled down to Zack, trying to wake him up. Bree scooted closer.

Eyes wide with apprehension, Grace met her gaze and said, "He's breathing. I can see his chest rising and falling."

He's alive. He's alive. He's alive. Bree's heart pounded in time with the mantra.

"There's so much evil energy here," Stella whispered behind them, a stair creaking under her feet like she retreated.

Bree leaned forward so she could see better and tried not to panic when she saw an increased amount of blood on Zack's stomach. She swallowed the bile welling up in her throat and pointed at the round, white object near Zack's feet, next to broken boards.

"What's that?" Her voice shook.

"What?" Grace asked, as she turned her head to watch Sam coming in with a ladder.

"That white thing." Bree grabbed Grace's hand, the one holding the flashlight, and pointed it in the right direction.

Grace leaned forward a bit more. "It looks like a skull."

"And that?" Bree asked, directing the flashlight farther along. "And that?" A little farther.

Grace swept the flashlight along the length of the dirt floor. "Bones. Lots and lots of bones."

"The spirits are restless," Stella whispered, and Bree turned.

The witch had backed up two steps, and gazed vacantly ahead, the phone dangling forgotten in her hand.

"Is she okay?" Bree asked, turning to Grace.

"Most likely." She swept the flashlight back and forth over the bones, finding more in the corners. Her voice might be calm, but Bree saw the anguish in her eyes. "We can't worry about her right now. She's not the one who's bleeding."

A *clang* and a *thump* made Bree turn her head. A metal ladder preceded Sam down the stairs, his route taking him carefully past where Stella stood frozen. He'd tucked a wad of white towels under his arm, and tossed them beside Grace before lowering the ladder down the hole. More wood dislodged off the sides, raining downward, as he carefully set the legs beside Zack's unconscious form.

Bree reached for the top rung, wanting to be the first one down there to help, but Grace stopped her, a hand on her shoulder. "Sam's a volunteer medic."

An unreasonable denial sat on the tip of Bree's tongue, but when she noted Sam's determined expression, she resettled on her knees. Grace patted her shoulder before she let go, holding the ladder for extra stability.

The rungs squeaked and the ladder bobbed as Sam cautiously descended. He grabbed the towels before descending farther.

"Hurry," Bree encouraged, scared Zack had lost too much blood, that he'd been impaled by a piece of wood and was dying on her while she watched.

"He's going as fast as he can," Grace said, her voice soft.

It seemed to take a lifetime for Sam to arrive at the dirt floor. Skirting the debris, he bent on one knee and placed his fingers against Zack's throat. "It's strong," he called to them.

Bree sagged in relief and might have fallen against the ladder if Grace hadn't put her hand on Bree's shoulder, giving her a reassuring squeeze. Solid and comforting, Bree leaned into her.

"Where's he bleeding from?" Grace called down when Sam lifted the fabric of Zack's shirt.

"Cuts on his abdomen—scalpel cuts like Rory's." He examined Zack's body without overly touching him. "Doesn't look like he's bleeding anywhere else, but I don't want to move him in case there's a spinal injury." He pressed the towels to Zack's stomach. "I'll stop the bleeding as best I can while we wait. Looks like he had a bloody nose too, but it has stopped."

"It hurts him, you know." Bree pulled her eyes away from Sam's movements to connect with Grace's gaze. "Being around the ghosts makes his nose bleed. Gives him headaches." Grace's lips parted. "I probably shouldn't be telling you. I mean, I should tell you, but Zack wouldn't want me telling you because if he did, he would have told you himself, wouldn't he?"

Grace's wide eyes softened in understanding. Her lips parted like she would speak, when a whispering voice interrupted.

"Too much screaming."

They turned to see Stella. Halfway up the steps now, the witch dug the heel of one hand into the side of her head. "They want to sleep. They've been screaming for so long." She turned and scrambled up the steps, footsteps echoing hollowly behind her.

Bree's heart ratcheted its pounding up a notch. She and Grace stared at each other, their breathing noisy between them.

"We'll figure out that part later," Grace said, her face pale. "Let's worry about Zack right now."

When Bree heard the ambulance coming up the drive, she shot to her feet. "I'll get them."

It was about time she could do something. Sitting there helplessly, not being able to do anything, watching him bleed—it was too much. She ran up the steps and found Stella directing the paramedics to the house, one of them carrying an orange spinal board.

"This way," Bree said, becoming frantic at the sight of the board. What would happen if Zack had an irreversible back injury? *I'd help him through it.* What if he couldn't walk ever again? *It wouldn't matter. It wouldn't change the way I feel about him. Nothing would.* Not after seeing him in that hole and thinking him dead.

Bree guided the paramedics to the basement door. They went ahead of her, their boots thumping down the steps. She followed, and Grace stepped away from the hole, allowing them access.

Minutes passed as they discussed the best way to get Zack out of the hole safely—some of the longest minutes of Bree's life. She just wanted him out of there as fast as possible. Because he was bleeding with hundreds of bones, human bones. He was hurt, and Bree didn't know how to help.

Why had none of her jobs ever included basic medical training? Why hadn't she taken the job at the daycare where first-aid had been one of the requirements, or the temp position at the veterinarian's office? Why couldn't she be as amazing as her sister, a surgical intern. Frustration bubbled up, nearly choking her.

It seemed like an hour, but probably wasn't close to that, when they took Zack out of the hole secured to the spinal board. Bree couldn't hold her tears as she followed the paramedics upstairs and to the rear of the ambulance, where they transferred him to a stretcher.

She and Grace tried to climb into the ambulance at the same time, but the paramedic waved them away. "I can only take one. Who's coming?"

Grace was family. She wasn't. Bree stepped back. "You go," she said to Grace, even though the words killed her to say.

Grace stared at her, lips parted, color rushing to her cheeks. She gave Bree a quick hug, then pushed her up into the back of the ambulance, whispering in her ear, "You take care of my brother for me."

Bree couldn't look away from Grace's face as she grabbed Zack's hand, and the paramedic closed the door, sealing them in.

CHAPTER THIRTY-NINE

BREE PACED A GROOVE in the floor of the waiting room, every seat taken around her. Arms wrapped tight around her middle, she squeezed the air out of her lungs. Restlessness and fear infused her every limb. Even if there'd been a chair available, she wouldn't have been able to sit still.

The ambulance ride had taken so long. They'd bandaged Zack's cuts, checked his head for damage, hooked him up to fluids, and checked his vital signs while she'd clutched his hand. They'd said he'd need surgery because of the depth of the cuts along his stomach—deep enough to graze internal organs. She'd stared at his face and willed him to wake up and give her his adorable smile.

He hadn't opened his eyes once.

What occurred at the house seemed impossible, even though she stood right there when it happened. The wooden floor had shattered like it was glass, Zack falling straight down. She'd seen some strange things over the past few days, but her mind wouldn't accept that one.

Her stomach twisted again. *Please let him be okay.* She'd seen his cut as it happened, a straight line of red emerging out of nowhere. There had to have been someone there, someone she couldn't see who held a knife—a ghost.

That entire house was a menace. No one should live there ever again. It needed a wrecking ball, then the remains burned to a crisp.

Bree let out a slow exhale. Who was to say that would help? Ghosts were probably immune to wrecking balls and fire.

They needed to get rid of those ghosts, but Bree didn't want anyone returning, putting themselves in harm's way. How had Stella been planning to remove them? Was it dangerous? She wanted to know a lot more about the process and ghosts in general, since both were such a big part of Zack's life.

Her arm still tingled where the witch had grabbed her. She ignored it, focusing instead on the number of tiles on the floor from wall to wall, and how the crowd in the emergency waiting room diminished as the minutes ticked on.

An hour later, Grace and Sam rushed in, faces pale, to find Bree still pacing.

"How is he?" Grace asked.

"He's in surgery, that's all I know. They won't tell me anything more because I'm not family." Bree looked away, not wanting to see the pain in Grace's eyes. "You should've been the one to come with him."

"Nonsense." She squeezed Bree's elbow. "You needed to be here, and now we're all here, so it doesn't matter." She glanced around. "I'll track someone down and find out what's happening."

Bree swallowed around the hard knot in her throat. She'd had too much time to think while she'd paced, her mind dwelling on the worst-case scenario. There was so much she needed to say to Zack. If only she could have the chance.

And there was something she needed to confess to Grace.

Sam leaned toward her and bumped her shoulder with his own. "He's going to be okay. He's a healthy guy. His heart is strong. If anyone can walk away from a fall like that, it's Zack."

Bree nodded, not knowing how else to respond. "What took you two so long to get here?"

Letting out a shaky breath, Sam lifted his hands in a helpless gesture. "We couldn't leave Stella in the house like that. She'd opened herself up to the spirits there and couldn't walk away without hurting herself. We had to wait until she was safe."

From his earnest expression, Bree believed him. She was about to ask how a witch made themselves safe when Grace returned, her face pinched in a frown.

"Well, no one around here knows what's going on. They might've taken him to the surgical ward. I guess we'll have to wait." She started on the path Bree had paced only moments earlier, ignoring the glances of the others in the waiting room.

Minute by minute, the waiting room emptied. Sam took up two chairs, trying to get comfortable. Bree kept walking, not wanting to stop and let the panic take over. Grace did the same on the other side of the middle row of chairs.

When only the three of them remained in the room, Grace spun on her heel with wide eyes and said to Bree, "Distract me. I don't think I can handle thinking the worst anymore."

"I voided our contract." Bree's heart leaped into her throat as soon as the words were out. A twisted knot formed in her stomach beside the one that had settled there since Zack's fall.

Grace's eyes narrowed. "How?"

She swallowed, nerves scratching at her throat. "When I began working for you guys, I thought you were a big scam, and my friend Inaya works for one of the papers in town."

Grace's whole body tensed. Sam's feet hit the floor with a bang.

Bolstering her courage, Bree clasped her hands together in front of her. "We started working on a story together, but then we scrapped the whole idea when I found out how legit you are." She stopped and took a deep breath, not wanting to continue, but knowing she had to.

"There's more to this confession, isn't there?" Grace asked, her eyes regretful.

Bree nodded, her courage waning because what was about to happen was so terrible. "Her boss took the article and is going to print it anyway. Actually, he stole it, changed it, and is putting his name on it. His brother is the same Douglas guy who got mad at Zack and me on the train bridge."

"Douglas Walsh?"

"That's him. He's interviewed in the article, and I guess it's horrid. It's going to be the front page of tomorrow's paper." She squeezed her hands together. "I'm so sorry."

Grace and Sam exchanged a loaded glance, then he gave his wife a head wobble like he considered something.

Bree's gaze bounced between the two of them, wondering if Grace was about to murder her with her husband's blessing.

"Grace, I want to fix this."

Eyes narrowing, she crossed her arms over her chest. "How do you propose to do that?"

Before Bree could answer, the double doors at the end of the waiting room opened, and a doctor and nurse strode toward them. "Are any of you Zack Liller's family?"

Dread puddled in Bree's stomach.

"We all are," Grace said without missing a beat.

An echoing warmth spread through Bree's chest.

"I have good news. Mr. Liller is going to be okay. We were worried about a spinal injury, but his scans have come back clear. The wounds on his stomach have been stitched. Some of them were extremely close to hitting vital organs." He looked at all of them in turn. "We're going to need an accounting of what happened to him for our records, and we need to know if the police should be involved. But I'm happy to say he'll be making a full recovery."

Bree's chest tightened so much at the words that she thought her heart would explode. *A full recovery.* "Can we see him?"

"He's in recovery right now, but as soon as he's moved to a room, you'll be able to see him. Someone will come and get you." With a nod, the doctor and nurse left.

Grace gave Bree's shoulder a squeeze.

Aware that she was crying uncontrollably, Bree nodded, staring at the floor. Then Grace's arms were around her, squeezing her tight. Grace was crying too. A second later, Sam's arms came around them both and she caught his reassuring, but watery, gaze over his wife's shoulder.

"He's going to be okay," Grace said into her hair.

Bree nodded, because that's all her throat would allow her to do. *He's going to be okay.*

CHAPTER FORTY

T HE POUNDING IN ZACK'S head had to be a jackhammer. A jackhammer right beside his bed. It could be the only explanation for how badly it hurt.

He braved cracking open one eye. His eyelids were glued down, but with effort he managed to open them a smidgen. The beginnings of dawn peeked through beige vertical blinds. He wasn't at home in bed, but in a hospital room.

A hospital room? He closed his eyes again.

A vision of Bree's face, frightened, screaming, filled his mind. He'd fallen in the Granwin House. He'd fallen and now he lay in a hospital bed.

He tried to sit up, but something pulled at his arm and stomach. He hissed out a breath. A rustling noise rippled beside the bed.

"Oh, Zack. Oh, my god. Don't move. You'll hurt yourself." Bree's voice reassured him, even with her high-pitched and frantic tone. He sank back into the pillow.

Cool fingers touched his arm, the one without the tubes coming out, then grazed his forehead. He opened his eyes to see her press the button at the side of the bed. The back rose, humming a monotone tune.

A tear in the corner of Bree's eye was quickly wiped away, but he saw it. With the bed adjusted, she gave him a wobbly smile, kissed him on his cheek, and whispered in his ear, "I'm so glad you're okay." She sat on the chair beside the bed, but kept her hand on his arm.

Again his abdomen tugged when he shifted. He touched his stomach and felt a bandage under the blue and white hospital gown. He frowned, his eyes meeting Bree's.

"You were cut. Like Rory."

He opened his mouth to ask more questions when the door opened. Grace and Sam came in. His big sister wore a stern but worried expression. Sam's was a mix of concern and humor.

"You gave us quite a scare there," Sam said, his tone mocking, but the relief in his expression told Zack it wasn't a joke.

He tried to speak, but only croaked. In a flash of movement out of his peripheral vision, Bree poured a cupful of water from the plastic pitcher beside the bed, inserted a straw, then held it to his lips.

The cool liquid soothed his throat. "What happened?" he rasped.

"What do you remember?" Grace asked, her eyes scanning between him and Bree.

Leaning his head back, Zack closed his eyes. What did he remember?

"We went into the basement." He paused as the images came to him one by one, disjointed. "There was a lot of negative pull coming at me I couldn't shake." He cleared his throat, wanting to sound more normal. "I saw this stain on the floor that wasn't there. Then the floor sort of collapsed under me." He opened his eyes. "That's it. That's all I remember."

Bree shook her head.

"That isn't what happened?" He was sure he'd gotten it right.

"I was yelling at you to leave, to come with me, and it was like you couldn't hear me. Like you couldn't speak. You were in this trance. I don't know how long, but it felt like a long time. Then there was this loud cracking sound. I tried to get you to move, but you wouldn't. Then the floor cracked again. That's when you fell and found all those bones."

"Bones?" He looked at Grace for confirmation.

Her face turned grim. "You stumbled on a mass grave. We stayed with Stella while Bree came with you here. She was able to isolate some of the spirits and speak with them. We don't have all their stories yet, but she said there are probably a couple dozen spirits in the basement needing rest."

"What about the negative energy she talked about?" Bree asked, her voice hesitant.

"There's still a malicious entity there, but once the others have a resting place, she'll be able to deal with it better."

Bree shivered, and he moved his arm so she knew he wanted to hold her hand. They linked fingers.

Grace blinked at their joined hands, then spoke to Bree. "About our Douglas problem—"

"What Douglas problem?" Zack interrupted, his eyes darting between the two of them.

"The one where Bree unintentionally ratted us out to the Walsh family and they're going to print a defamation article about us tomorrow." She glanced at her watch. "I mean today, since it's four in the morning."

His head whipped toward Bree.

"Inaya's boss, Douglas's brother, stole her notes and changed the article. It's going on the front page." She studied their joined hands, her cheeks pink. "I don't have the words to express how horrible I feel about it." She lifted her eyes to him. "You guys don't deserve to have bad press for the good work you do."

"I wouldn't be so sure about that article being printed," Grace said. Both he and Bree swung their heads in her direction. Sam smirked at them.

"What?" Zack asked, wondering why they weren't more furious over Bree's mistake.

"I made a few phone calls," Sam said. "Asked a few pointed questions about state slander laws. Got some interesting answers." He shrugged as if it wasn't a huge deal.

Bree's fingers tightened on Zack's arm, then relaxed. "What aren't you telling us?" she asked.

Sam grinned at her. "I was a solicitor in another life."

"A solicitor?"

Almost smiling, Grace leaned toward him. "That's what those fancy British people call an attorney."

"You're a lawyer?" Bree asked him.

"Was. In the UK," Sam confirmed with a nod of his head. "Haven't taken the bar here, but I've thought about it a few times. What I do have are connections, and those connections are reaching out to your friend's paper as we speak." His smile widened. "If that paper hits the streets today, we've got ourselves a very solid lawsuit."

"So that's why you wanted Inaya's number," Bree said, her mood lightening. "I have to admit I was worried." For the first time since he woke up, Bree's body relaxed. "A lawsuit," she repeated, "because they'd be publishing unsubstantiated lies."

The almost-smile on Grace's face turned into a smug grin. "Your friend Inaya was very helpful and gave us a copy of the article. We'll be able to disprove most of what's in there in a court of law. Plus," she paused dramatically, "we have recordings of Douglas trying to sabotage our investigation at Granwin House."

Understanding her implication, Zack let out a laugh. It hurt like hell and he ended up hissing instead. He clenched his teeth, hand on his stomach while Bree ran a soothing hand up and down his arm. "He was the one running around with a sheet over his head."

"Yeah," Grace confirmed. "One of the cameras on the perimeter recorded him getting out of his car and putting on the sheet. Complete with his license plate number. I'm pretty sure the article will never see the light of day."

"I'm so glad," Bree said quietly.

The subdued response gave him pause. Where was the old Bree who said everything on her mind with no filter? He examined her closely for the first time since he'd awakened. It was like an entity lived heavy on her shoulders.

He glanced at his sister and brother-in-law. "Can you give us a minute?"

"Take all the time you want." Grace leaned forward and gave his other hand a squeeze before standing. "I'm going home to get some sleep."

Sam gave him a gentle slap on the shoulder.

On their way out, Grace paused at the door and turned to meet his gaze. "When you're feeling up to it, we're going to have a discussion about how our business affects you physically." Her eyes scanned to Bree quickly before she stepped into the hallway.

Sam gave them a salute and followed, closing the door gently behind them.

Alone, Zack turned his body as much as he could with the pull of his stitches, and captured Bree's gaze. "Tell me what's wrong."

A red tinge splashed cheekbones. She sucked in a ragged breath. "I thought I'd lost you. I saw you fall and saw your body on that dirt floor, and I thought you were dead."

He tried to reach for her, but she shook her head. "I need to tell you something." Her spine straightened.

Zack leaned back in the hospital bed, nervous for what she would say next.

She exhaled slowly, her eyes on her hands. "When I went to the Granwin House, I knew I had to tell you about the *Haunted* story, but

I also needed to tell you that I think this is bigger than just a deal. This thing between us, I think it's a *big* deal."

His heart pounded in his chest.

She took a deep breath. "When you fell, when I thought you were dead, I realized being uncertain about the big deal was way less scary than the thought that I might never be with you again. Or see your smile again. Or laugh with you again. Or hold you again." Her breath hitched.

She lifted her gaze and tears threatened to spill.

He reached out to her, his stitches twinging, but he ignored them.

She took his hand, her grip tight. "I've never loved a man before. I don't know if I'm going to do it right. Or wrong. And it hurts. Right here." She touched her sternum. "But losing you would hurt more. I want to be with you, and I hope you care about me enough that you'll forgive me if I mess up." She let out a harsh laugh. "*When* I mess up."

While he was afraid to exhale and wreck the moment, a smile lifted the corner of her mouth. She went on, "I've never met anyone like you, and I don't know if I'm going to be able to be with you the way you deserve, but I sure as hell want to try."

The tightness around his heart eased. Exhaling, he closed his eyes for a moment, relishing the feeling of being complete.

"Oh, Bree," he murmured.

When he opened his eyes, her grip on his hand tightened, her expression concerned. He squeezed her fingers. "I've never met anyone like you. You're amazing. I want you in my life so much."

A tear slipped down her cheek.

"Now come here and give me a kiss, because I don't think I can reach your lips, and you're way too far away."

She sent him one of the most brilliant smiles he'd ever seen and leaned toward him. With their hands still joined, he tugged, throwing her off balance, so she flopped beside him on the narrow bed. He hissed when her elbow made contact with his side.

"I don't want to hurt you!" Horrified eyes pleaded with him even as she nestled closer, her length snuggled against his.

"You won't." He hugged her tightly. The twinge of stitches was nothing compared to how good she felt, how they fit together.

Bree lifted her face and kissed him on the chin.

Head bending, Zack kissed her tears away. Everything in the room faded. Nothing mattered but the two of them.

CHAPTER FORTY-ONE

A FEW WEEKS LATER...

BREE REACHED FOR THE two coffees, the Saturday issue of the Daily Times tucked under her arm. "Thanks, Fran." She inhaled the scent of Costa Rican Dark deep into her chest.

Fran smiled at her. "Anytime, sugar. You know we always love to see you." She shifted her focus to the next customer.

Bree gave Theo a wave through the round window to the kitchen, and he lifted his hand in return. The new girl, up to her elbows in dough, looked like she fit in perfectly.

That's good. Theo needs someone reliable.

Not that Bree wasn't reliable. She just wasn't a good fit for a bakery. A shudder went through her as she remembered waking up before the sun to get here on time—not that she ever got here on time.

After fixing her two white cups with cream and sugar from the side cart, Bree found a free table near the window. Excitement bubbled through her stomach as she set the coffees down, the paper beside them. She perched on the edge of the seat, toes tapping on the tile floor to watch out the window, eyes scanning the people on the sidewalk in search of Zack.

Her phone buzzed in her tote bag, and she pulled it out. Bianca. She answered without waiting for it to ring a second time.

"Hey, Big Bee," she said, taking a sip of her coffee.

"Hey, Little Bee," Bianca replied, a smile in her voice. "Did I catch you at a bad time?"

"Not at all. Just waiting for Zack."

"When am I going to meet this amazing Zack you're always talking about?"

Bree grinned. "Well, I'm bringing him to the wedding, so..."

"But that's months away."

The pretend whine in Bianca's voice made Bree laugh. "I'm going to try and convince him to do a video call with us the next time we have a wedding meeting."

Bianca groaned. "Great. Scare him off with Mom's bridezilla act."

"She seemed fine last week." Her mom had been guarding her words, but normal.

"She's driving me bananas. I made a joke they should elope in the Caribbean and save us all the trouble, and she nearly bit my head off."

That sounded like the mom Bree knew.

"She kept saying she had to have it at the cabin so Grandma would be there."

Bree's chest squeezed. "I want Grandma there too."

"I do too, but she's taking it to the next level in micromanaging. Come back so you can take some of this heat."

"Not a chance. I've got important things to do here." And she did, but she also didn't want to leave her twin high and dry. "I wasn't going to tell you until I was sure, but I've been thinking about visiting earlier than the wedding. Maybe in a couple of weeks."

A squeal had Bree holding her phone away from her ear.

"I'm so excited. Jessica asks about you all the time. Mom will be so pleased."

Bree's grip tightened on the phone. "Will she, though?"

"Yes." Bianca's answer was immediate. "Yes, she will. She wants to make amends. I've told you that."

"Hearing it and believing it are two different things."

"I know. I know. But it's true." There was a pause and a shifting of movement. "I'm going to call Mom right now and tell her. Remember our video call on Monday night."

"I will."

"Okay. Talk to you soon. Love you."

"Love you, too." Bree hung up and stared at the phone for a minute.

Baby steps. It was all she could hope for with her mom, progress, despite the old wounds surfacing.

She took another sip of her coffee and spread the paper out flat on the table. The front-page headline read: *Ghost Hunters Tell All* by Inaya Badie.

They'd accomplished a lot over the past few weeks. At Bree's suggestion, Grace worked with Inaya on the article to give Liller Investigations good PR. The paranormal investigator had been resistant at first, but with Inaya's great interview skills, she'd been able to win Grace over. Not only had the Daily Times liked the article, they also offered Inaya a full-time position with one of their news columns.

After three sessions at the Granwin House with Stella, they were able to get to the reasons for the haunting. Bree absently rubbed her arm where the witch had grabbed her. She hadn't come to terms with the unsolicited spell, but she had to admit, since Stella had touched her, Bree's luck had definitely turned around.

Stella had wanted her name to remain out of the paper, but Bree gave an account of her first (and last) ghost hunting experience as a skeptical witness. She opened the next page and skimmed the last few paragraphs.

Devastated by the death of his wife and son, Matthew Sheely was driven mad in his attempt to cure tuberculosis...

...Seven of Sheely's victims have already been laid to rest, the others still waiting for family members to claim the remains. With the help of a local medium, each of the deceased has been named, solving cold cases from over a hundred years ago...

...With Sheely's ghost removed from the premises, and wards placed to protect the inhabitants, only the ghost of his wife, Isabelle, remains to protect those who reside there.

For those who want an otherworldly experience, the Granwin House will be open for business as a bed and breakfast next month.

Bree straightened when a familiar gait outside the window caught her eye. Zack stepped around a woman, and when he saw Bree through the window, he smiled.

She couldn't help but grin. He did that to her, made her chest feel like it was about to explode with joy.

The door tinkled, and he headed straight for her with a Daily Times tucked under his arm. He leaned over for a kiss. The contact warmed her cheeks and made her heart beat faster. She'd seen him yesterday and still didn't want the kiss to end.

When he pulled away, his eyes told her he was as reluctant as she was.

"What do you think of the article?" she asked as soon as he sat across from her.

He picked up his coffee and blew on it, his eyes twinkling over the rim. "Love it. I know Grace acted like she was digging in her heels, but I think she actually had fun with it." He leaned forward. "And I know you said you had a surprise for me, but I have a surprise for you first."

She straightened. "Really? What?"

"The Rivets are back in their house."

"That's great news," Bree said, but her worry for the family must have shown.

He linked their fingers. "I know there's one ghost left, and you're concerned for Rory, but I was there last night. Sheely is gone and the others are being put to rest. Even Rory likes Isabelle. Sheely's wife loves the house so much, she's never wanted to leave. The Lady in White they call her, and she's been nothing but kind. The bed and breakfast is booking up fast."

That allowed her to smile. "As long as Rory is happy."

"She is. She says hi, by the way. We compared scars." He waggled his eyebrows.

She chuckled. "I bet she has even more of a crush on you than ever." She gave his fingers a squeeze. "I'm so glad everything has been settled there." And she really was. Thinking about Rory, anyone, living in that house had given her literal nightmares.

Zack took a sip of his coffee. "What's your surprise?"

Nervous butterflies came to life in her stomach. "Did you read the whole paper or just the one article?"

His brows puckered. "Just the article."

She let go of his hand and tapped his paper. "Turn to page four."

Interest in his eyes, he did as she asked, opening the paper wide. She moved their coffees to make room. The Daily Times covered the entire small table, the scent of ink and newsprint overriding the aromatic coffee smells for a moment.

Zack's eyes scanned the page until he found the right article. His eyes widened, he glanced up at her. "You wrote this?"

She nodded, nervous, her cheeks heating. He leaned forward to read the article, his mouth curving up into a smile. When he laughed, Bree's shoulders relaxed. He laughed again, and she took another sip of coffee. By the time he finished the article, he rubbed a tear from the corner of his eye.

"That is so good, Bree. So funny. You didn't tell me you used to work for a children's party planner, and you definitely didn't tell me you were writing for the paper."

She shrugged, trying not to show him how much she relished the praise. "You know I super appreciated that Grace paid me despite voiding my contract. It took a lot of stress off my shoulders. Her only condition was that I didn't write about it anywhere else except for Inaya's paper, and I thought that fair.

"When I worked with Inaya on the article, I met her new boss. We got talking, and she looked up my blog and hired me the next day. It was what Inaya and I took in school together, journalism, before I bailed. This story," she said, tapping the paper, "happened quite a while ago, and I have plenty more where that came from. They're also going to send me all over the state to try new and strange jobs I've never done before so I can write about them."

Zack's face had lit up during her explanation. "Tell me more about it."

"It'll be great. I just have to do these jobs as best I can, which will probably be horrible sometimes, and funny a lot of the time. Then I have deadlines for articles, and I can do that. I know I can do that. Writing about this stuff is actually my very favorite thing to do. So this job is perfect. And," she took a deep breath. "I'm going to take journalism night classes so I can finish my degree."

"Wow, Bree, that's amazing. Perfect for you." His eyes shone as he grabbed her hand and gave it a squeeze. "You'll do great. I have absolute belief in you."

Bree's heart thumped hard at the trust in his eyes.

With one last squeeze, he dropped her hand and folded up the paper. "So did you actually tackle the rest of those boxes last night, or did you and Inaya watch a movie?"

"Movies. Two of them. Back to back rom-coms. It was great. The boxes can wait."

She and Inaya had gotten a new place together and had moved in last weekend. Bree kept telling herself she'd get to those last boxes, but they were still stacked by her bedroom door. She grinned. "We're going to have a housewarming next weekend." She squinted at him. "You might be on the guest list."

"Nice," he said with smiling eyes.

The flutter in her stomach became almost violent. "There's something else."

"Okay," he said, voice wary.

Her nervousness increased tenfold. "I'm thinking of going to California in a couple weeks."

A shadow passed over his features.

Bree rushed on. "I'm going to visit my sister and mom and give Bianca some relief with the whole wedding planning thing." She took a deep breath. "Want to come with me?"

He blinked. "You want me to meet your family?"

The flat tone of his voice made her bulldoze ahead. "I know you don't like to travel, but it's not for very long, and honestly, I want you to meet them. I know it's soon and you probably don't want to because, you know, family drama and stuff, but—"

Zack stopped her by covering her hand with his own. "It's not that I don't like to travel. It's that I've never had someone as awesome and sweet and funny as you to go with. What's the fun of traveling if you have to do it on your own?"

She sat up straight, hope blossoming in her chest. "So you'll come with me?"

"I'd absolutely, positively, love to come with you. Grace and Sam are going to the UK next month, and since we don't have any jobs lined up until after that, I'm one hundred percent free. I'd love to meet your family." He gave her hand a squeeze. "I'd be honored to meet your family."

Her smile was probably maniacal, but she couldn't stop it. She jumped up, lunged around the tiny table, and hugged him to her chest. "Oh my god, I'm so happy you said that." She buried her face in his neck. "I love you so much."

The words came out of her in a whoosh. She'd never said them before, even though she'd known she loved him since he'd been in the hospital, since even before that if she was being honest with herself. She jerked away, needing to see Zack's reaction.

His expression lit up the whole coffee shop. Cupping her face in his hands, his eyes filled with mischief as he came in close. "Marry me," he whispered.

Bree's heart stuttered in her chest. "We've only known each other for a few weeks."

"I know what I see when I look at you." His eyes said *forever*.

So did she. Her heart raced. "I'm only twenty-seven. That's way too young to get married."

He grinned. "Then marry me when you're thirty."

"Okay," she agreed with a nod. "Sounds reasonable."

His resulting smile dazzled her and made every one of her limbs turn to mush. He took her lips, gently at first, then insistent. She held on tight as she basked in the moment, then inhaled deeply, the scent of rosemary and mint filling her head.

Within Zack's embrace, she knew she was exactly where she was supposed to be.

Had he just proposed marriage? That had not been something he'd planned, but it slipped from his mouth like the most natural thing in the world.

And had Bree just agreed?

With his mind whirling, he broke the kiss to stare into Bree's grey eyes. He knew he wore a goofy smile, but couldn't stop it. Bree's face echoed his joy and his heart beat hard in his chest. The people around them were staring, but he didn't care.

Her phone buzzed. Zack stepped away to gather his wits while she checked her screen.

"It's the reminder I set for myself for Selma's show," she said, her grin still in place.

Zack glanced at the time on the wall. "We're going to be late if we don't leave now."

"Then let's go!" On a laugh, she gathered up their coffee cups and shoved the two newspapers in her tote.

He'd parked his Impala down the street, and in no time they were headed to the edge of town. Rain clouds formed in the distance and looked to be moving in their direction, the heat of the summer air turning muggy.

Had he made a mistake in asking her to marry him? Probably. It was way too soon for him to ask that sort of question. But he couldn't take it back now. *Wouldn't* take it back.

Edgy silence drifted between them. He kept sneaking peeks at her to gauge her mood.

Finally, Bree said, "So I've been thinking about what you asked me."

He swallowed. "Yeah, you're right. It's too soon." He didn't want to push her away.

She shook her head. "Nah, I think it's about time."

His eyebrows shot up. "Really?" It was not what he'd been expecting. They'd only been dating a few weeks.

Then he noticed the twinkle in her eye. "We're not talking about the same thing are we?"

The corner of her mouth lifted. "I was talking about the Mustang Cobra. What were you talking about?"

"The Mustang..." His heart picked up tempo. He'd asked her again just last week when they were changing out her muffler, and she'd frozen up about it. Now she wanted him to make the car for her. "Yeah, that's what I was talking about."

Her smile widened.

"It's going to take a while," he added.

"Maybe three years?"

"Yeah, that's about right." She wasn't scared off. She wasn't going anywhere. A surge of adrenaline had his fingers tightening on the steering wheel.

"Great! That'll give me enough time to pick out the right shade of blue."

He laughed, a feel-good laugh right from his belly. Again he glanced at Bree. She attempted to look casual, but she practically vibrated with excitement.

Zack flipped his signal to turn off the highway. The Powerhouse Theater was an old power station renovated with the preforming arts in mind. It gave low-budget performances a cost-effective alternative to the larger, fancier theaters in town.

After parking in the gravel lot full of a couple dozen vehicles, Bree and Zack made their way hand in hand through the narrow hallway. Recently whitewashed, it smelled of paint. The door at the end of the hallway opened into a warehouse space.

Familiar pressure pressed on his chest as soon as he walked through the doorway. His hand tightened on Bree's for a moment, and she snapped her gaze to his.

Someone called her name and grabbed Bree's attention. Inaya waved at them, and they climbed the bleachers to the top row where they'd been saved seats. Grace, Sam, and his mom were there too. They'd had to purchase two more tickets from Selma, but she'd been more than happy to oblige.

His mom grinned at Bree. "Albert and I are so excited for this."

Bree's eyebrows shot up. "Albert's here?" She glanced at him.

He nodded once. His dad was definitely in the building.

When Bree looked at Grace, his sister rolled her eyes.

"He is here," his mom said, patting Bree's hand. "And he doesn't get out much, so this is exciting for him."

"I'm sure none of us have any idea why watching women prance around on stage would be exciting for him," Grace said with a bland expression.

Beside her, Inaya snorted.

Zack had to cough behind his hand to cover up the laughter.

Sam wasn't doing much better.

His mom sighed. "All of you are the worst." She patted Bree's hand again. "Except you, of course."

A hopeful expression crossed Bree's face as she straightened, but after a shake of Grace's head, she slouched back down.

The teasing camaraderie had Zack's chest warming. Despite everything, Bree and his sister had come to terms with each other. Bree often took her jokes too far, and Grace rarely showed her humor when she should, but they'd achieved common ground enough for them to enjoy each other's company. Most of the time.

The lights dimmed, and the people still standing found spots on the bleachers. After everything quieted, a spotlight lit the center of the stage.

Selma posed in a circle of light wearing a top hat, fishnet stockings, a black bodysuit, and of course the go-go boots. The woman was fit. Fingers on her top hat, Selma tipped her chin down, a cane tucked under her armpit. Music played, a classic and modern mix, with a heavy beat filling the theater. Anticipation built around them.

Then she began to sing.

Zack couldn't believe the talent. Her rich voice filled the warehouse, weaving magic around them.

After the first mesmerizing minutes, Bree leaned close to him. "Did you know?"

He shook his head, eyes glued to the stage as the other dancers joined Selma on stage, everyone in a line. He did not know Selma was this gifted, but Bree probably guessed after their meeting.

It was like a Broadway show, but all the twenty-somethings in the chorus line were replaced by those of the golden age.

"Amazing," Bree breathed.

She'd whispered the comment, but Zack heard her. He leaned in closer. "You're amazing."

She turned her head, the lights from the stage creating patterns on her cheeks. She took his hand and held on tightly.

He kissed her, a brush of his lips against hers, and his heart hammered in his chest. Nothing ever felt so right as it did when she was next to him.

When she turned to watch the show, resting her head on his shoulder, his arm came around her, bringing her closer.

Hip to hip, shoulder to shoulder, he knew he was exactly where he was supposed to be.

EPILOGUE

THAT SAME NIGHT...

HANDS CLENCHED AROUND THE steering wheel of her Miata, Stella drove toward Wickwood, dust billowing out behind her from the gravel road.

She swiped at the tear she'd been trying to hold in, kept telling herself Nana seemed happy and unbothered she'd been displaced from her home two months ago to live at Cedar Ridge. Her grandmother had smiled when Stella arrived, asked her to stay for tea, and asked after Loki and Aubrey.

Knuckles white, Stella sniffed and took the next turn a little too fast. Gravel bounced against her undercarriage in a clatter and sprayed into the ditch.

She hated seeing Nana in an institution. She'd raised Stella like a daughter, always vivacious and free-spirited. This disease was taking her away piece by piece. Cedar Ridge might be one of the better homes in the area, but Stella needed to get her out of there before Nana lost herself completely.

What good was being a witch if she couldn't save those she loved?

With storm clouds gathering above the city, Stella turned onto the main highway. The glow of Wickwood brightened the underside of tempestuous clouds. As she neared the edge of town, the tension in her shoulders eased. Each mile closer, her grip loosened on the steering wheel.

But even as the soothing energy of her hometown calmed her, it did little to ease her worries. On top of everything, three of her clients dropped her this morning, all in a row, canceling their website development contracts. She had more clients, but it would cut into her bottom line.

At least she'd finished everything at the Granwin House on a high note. She'd completed her final cleanse and ward on the house two days ago. Only positive energy remained on the property.

Stella slowed her speed as the houses on the edge of Wickwood took up both sides of the road, then slowed again and turned left, heading toward old downtown.

Aubrey would be waiting. They liked to have drinks at Bitters Tavern a couple nights a week if they could, and today her best friend of seven years mentioned having a surprise for her.

Usually, Stella liked surprises, but after the day she'd had, she didn't know if she could handle it.

Two blocks away from the bar, all the instruments on Stella's dashboard blinked.

"What the?" She held her breath, waiting for something worse to happen. When everything seemed fine, she exhaled and kept driving.

One block away from the bar, the whole dashboard went black. The engine sputtered, *puht, puht, puht,* then died completely. Silence pulsed around her.

"Shit." Shoulder checking to make sure the next lane was clear, she thankfully had enough momentum to pull over. Unease coiled in her stomach as she rolled to a stop in a parking spot and shifted into park.

One foot on the gas, the other on the brake, she turned the key.

"Come on, Bessie." Nothing. The engine wouldn't even turn over. She tried again. *Completely dead.*

Shoulders suddenly heavy, she rested her forehead on the steering wheel and let out a shuddering breath. Now she'd have another bill, probably something substantial with the way her luck was going. Would this week ever end? At least she stalled near the bar. She could call for a tow, and since they lived together, she could catch a ride home with Aubrey.

Inhaling deeply, Stella grabbed her purse from the passenger seat, opened the door, and stepped out into the muggy evening air. The second after she slammed her door, an unusual presence pressed against her energy, something nearby.

Stella spun around, searching, eyes scanning up and down the street.

It wasn't that late; some stores were open and a few shoppers walked the block while cars drove slowly by. But no one looked out of place. No one stared at her or paid her any attention.

The feeling that someone watched her slowly dissipated, but unease solidified in her chest.

Taking a deep, settling breath, she locked her car, tucked her purse under her armpit, and crossed the street toward the bar. Her pace clipped, she strode along the edge of the sidewalk, careful not to brush too close to anyone's energy.

A crack of thunder echoed overhead. She flinched, and the people around her dashed for shelter. A moment later, the heavens opened. Stella ran the rest of the way, the rain soaking through her clothing in less than a minute.

Sneakers sloshing, she pushed open the door to Bitters. As soon as she stepped over the threshold, the energy of the people inside punched her in the gut, sweeping away the remaining unease she'd felt earlier.

She sucked in a breath, closed her eyes, and whispered the quick dampening spell Nana had taught her when she was little. Breathing in and out three times, she opened her eyes again, and the vibrations dulled to a manageable level—except for one particular energy vibration coming from the bar.

Sensual and sweet, its hot flavor settled on her tongue. She'd never experienced such a compelling combination before. Her feet carried her toward it before she realized, her eyes scanning the crowd in search of its origin.

"Stella!" Aubrey's voice rang out toward her from the far corner.

Stella stopped and blinked. Already halfway to the bar, she forced herself to turn around and walk in the opposite direction. With one last glance over her shoulder, she wove through the patrons standing at the tall tables in the middle of the room.

"Sorry I'm late," she said, patting the water out of her wavy blonde hair and sliding into the booth. Aubrey had already ordered her a lager, and Stella took a healthy swig before adding, "I visited Nana before I came."

"How is she?" Aubrey asked, concern furrowing her brow as she played with the straw in her cola.

Aubrey's ghost, Finn, was here too, hovering at her side, his energy a light shimmer that Stella had grown used to over the years. He'd been hanging around her friend since before they'd met in college.

"Okay, I guess," Stella replied with a shrug. "I just hate seeing her there, you know?"

Aubrey reached over and gave her hand a squeeze. "I know." She let go and tucked a strand of her chin-length brown hair behind her ear. "We'll figure out something better for her."

Though she nodded, Stella saw no solution. None of her problems were going to magically disappear. That wasn't the way the world worked.

The energy from near the bar renewed its pull on her. She glanced over, but only saw the bartender and a couple of guys with their backs to her.

"Happy birthday!" Aubrey said, recapturing her attention. Her friend pulled out a small package wrapped in silver paper and a bow, and placed it in front of her. Grinning, she said, "I know it's a little early, and this doesn't change our plans for your actual birthday in a couple of weeks, but I just had to give it to you now."

Before she could touch it, Stella felt the lure of the thing inside, its positive energy calling to her.

"What is it?" she asked, her fingers twitching to snatch it.

"Open it up and see."

Tentatively, she reached for the box and ran her fingers along the edge, expecting something to happen. The box remained the same, but continued to pulse positivity.

"Come on," Aubrey urged. "Why are you being so weird? Open it."

Stella picked up the package, turned it over, then with one last quick glance at Aubrey, she tore the silver paper to reveal a small, square jewelry box inside. Eyebrows raised, she lifted the lid.

Resting in a layer of white fuzz, a necklace lay curled in on itself. An iridescent sphere, a stone polished to a gloss, hung on an antique silver chain. Flicking her eyes to Aubrey's excited smile, Stella touched the pendant.

She sucked in a breath. For a moment, the positive energy exuding from the necklace overpowered the alluring vibration coming from the bar. Many objects had energy signatures, but not usually this strong. She lifted it out of the box, and her hand shook from the intensity of it.

"Where did you get this?" she asked, making no attempt to stop herself from looping over her head.

"A man came into the store the other day and sold it with a bunch of other stuff. It had your name written all over it. I couldn't fathom selling it to someone else." Aubrey let out a sigh. "I knew it would look perfect on you."

The weight of the pendant nestled itself against her heart. She closed her eyes and inhaled deeply. This close to her, the energy warmed her whole body. She'd never been in contact with such an object before. Where had it come from?

"Do you like it?"

Stella opened her eyes to find Aubrey frowning at her. "Love it. It's beautiful and unique." She smiled.

"Oh, good. For a second there, I thought it made you uncomfortable or something." Aubrey took a sip of her cola, eyes watching her over the rim of her glass.

With the new energy of the necklace lapping at her, the dampening spell Stella cast when she entered the bar waned. And that meant the vibe coming from the direction of the bar intensified. She took a gulp of her beer.

What was going on with her? She glanced at the bar to see what or who caused the vibration. Nothing had changed. Cole, the bartender, chatted with two guys sitting on stools.

Cole had never given off this type of energy before, so it couldn't be him. It had to be coming from one of the other guys.

"What are you staring at?"

Stella's attention snapped back to her friend. "Nothing. Just distracted. My car broke down a block away from here, and I need to get a tow and a mechanic." She touched the pendant, her fingers tingling. "But this is positively lovely. A thoughtful gift brightening my day. Thank you." She took another sip of her beer.

"Sucks about the car. I thought Bessie would outlive us all. Remember when we went camping that one time and we thought she was dying in the middle of nowhere, but we had just forgotten to get gas? That was hilarious."

"Ha. Hilarious. Yeah, right. We were sure laughing at the time." Actually, it had been terrifying, but they were lucky enough to phone a gas station in the next town, and a teenager drove a jerry can out to them. They'd been able to continue on to the national park without any further hiccups.

Had she run out of gas today? She'd just filled up, so that didn't make sense.

"How was work?" Stella asked, not wanting to dwell too much on her dead car.

Aubrey let out a long breath. "Business was pretty slow. I keep waiting for it to pick up. I know I'm not the only antique store in town, but I know mine's the nicest. I'm waiting for the rest of the city to notice." She twirled her straw.

Her antique store *was* the nicest in town. Filled with light, everything Aubrey touched resonated with love and caring. Every time Stella walked into the store, she wanted to buy something, and it wasn't just because Aubrey was her friend. She had an excellent eye for antiques.

Stella touched the pendant at her heart, another testament to her friend's good taste. "How about I stop by and do another blessing? Maybe a prosperity spell and a good luck spell too."

Aubrey smiled, her shoulders relaxing. "That would be great."

Stella stole another glance at the bar. Where was that delicious vibration coming from? She couldn't focus on anything else. And the titillating energy combined with the one hanging around her neck made her nerves twitch. She needed to get to the bottom of this.

"Want another drink?" she asked Aubrey without looking at her. "I want another drink." She hopped out of the booth, her sneakers still damp and squishy from the rain.

"You could flag down the waitress." Aubrey's voice followed her to the bar. "And you've barely touched your first beer."

Stella wouldn't have been able to stop her feet if she'd tried. With her new necklace propelling her forward, she followed the energy wake right to the end of the bar and stopped behind the man on the left like she hit a physical wall.

The energy came off him so thick it was almost visible. Broad shoulders narrowed into trim hips. He must work out regularly if the muscles in his arms were any indication. His head was angled slightly, allowing her to see that his short dark hair migrated into a line of scruff along his jawline, highlighting the strong ridge of his chin. Dense vibrations came off him, washing over her in waves, making it hard to breathe.

Why? She stepped closer, their bodies almost touching; his body heat complemented his vibrations. Why was his energy so potent?

She closed her eyes and inhaled. A citrusy spice filled her head. Was it his laundry detergent? Cologne? How could her body be on fire after five seconds of standing next to him?

"What are you doing?"

Her eyes flew open. "What?" she asked, blinking over and over again to clear her vision.

He'd turned his body toward her, his brows lowered over copper eyes. "Are you smelling me?"

If she'd thought his energy potent from behind, it was nothing compared to the full force of his gaze. Sun-kissed skin and high cheekbones framed his perceptive gaze, while his rough stubble gave him a slightly rugged appearance. He'd rolled up his dark green button-up shirt past his elbows, revealing corded forearms that made her mouth water.

The middle-aged guy beside him peeked around his shoulder, one eyebrow raised.

She should probably say something. "Um..." She turned to Cole, who stared at her with his head tipped to the side. "A lager and a cola, please," she blurted.

Cole straightened, nodded, and got to work fixing her drinks.

Stella let out a breath, hoping that was the end of the awkwardness created solely by her not thinking through a random trip to the bar.

"So, *were* you smelling me?"

And her hopes were dashed.

She flicked her gaze up to the stranger's face. His eyes twinkled at her, and she couldn't help but smile at her foolishness.

"That would be silly, wouldn't it?" she said, trying to strike a casual pose against the empty stool beside him despite the fact she *had* been smelling him.

"Lucas," he said, sticking out his hand.

She stared at his fingers, strong and sure. What would it be like to touch a man who gave off such remarkable energy? After hesitating so long he began to drop his hand, Stella abruptly grabbed it.

Lightning shot up her arm so fast it was like he hid a hand buzzer in his palm. His face changed from smiling to serious in under a second, and she knew she wasn't doing any better.

They dropped hands at the same time. Her heart pounded hard and fast in her throat, her eyes locked with his. What the hell?

Cole set the drinks on the bar top, clearing his throat to grab her attention.

"Thanks," she said, knowing he'd put it on her tab.

She grabbed the drinks and tried her best to ignore the man beside her, whose energy still made her buzz. How was he doing it? How was he making every nerve ending tingle?

Trying to keep her cool, she gave him one nod and turned back to her table.

"I didn't get your name," Lucas said, stalling her.

She glanced over her shoulder, taking in his facial features one more time. "Stella," she replied, attempting to keep her voice even.

His copper eyes glowed their pleasure.

She continued to the booth where Aubrey waited, her friend's eyebrows raised under her bangs.

"What was that all about?" she asked when Stella slid her drink to her.

She barely restrained herself from taking another peek at Lucas over her shoulder. Had he watched her as she walked back to the table? It felt like he had.

"Oh, yeah. He's definitely watching you," Aubrey confirmed without her needing to ask.

She felt his eyes on her. *This is nonsense.* She needed to get herself under control. Stella closed her eyes and redid the dampening spell. When she opened them, she could breathe easier. "Tell me when he stops looking."

"Sure," Aubrey said, taking a sip from her new drink. "Are you going to tell me what happened there?"

Stella didn't know where to begin and shook her head. "Maybe tomorrow when I can think everything through with a clear head." She took a swig of her new beer, abandoning the old one. "You were supposed to tell me when he stopped looking."

"He hasn't stopped looking yet."

Throat working, she swallowed hard. She had to see for herself. A glance over her shoulder revealed that sure enough, Lucas watched her, a frown wrinkling his brow—which transformed into an easy smile the second her eyes met his.

She whipped her head back toward Aubrey. This was too much. Her dampening spell weakened at an alarming rate. Lucas's energy and the energy of the pendant around her neck competed for her attention, and every other energy vibration from every other person in the bar pulled and slapped at her in a way that made the hairs on the back of her neck stand on end.

"I might be ready to head home." She took a deep breath. "I've had enough of people for the night."

"Sure. No problem." Aubrey frowned but knew her well enough not to force her to stay in a crowded room. "Want to call a tow truck for your car?"

A long breath escaped Stella. She'd already forgotten and didn't really want to deal with it right now. She wanted to go home, have a salt bath to cleanse herself from everyone's energy, and go to bed. "I'll call one in the morning."

The next time a waitress came by, they paid their tab and headed out. As they neared the doors, Stella couldn't resist one last look over her shoulder.

Lucas still watched her, his smile creating a dimple in his right cheek. Her stomach flipped tiny somersaults inside her. She turned away quickly. When they stepped into the night air, she inhaled a deep breath, glad to see the rain had stopped.

Renewed tension crawled across Stella's shoulder. She might have left the competing energies of the people inside the bar, but the unease she'd felt earlier returned. Was someone waiting for her outside? Watching her?

She scanned the sidewalk up and down, but the rainstorm had chased everyone away, leaving the street empty. Cars driving up the street splashed in the puddles left by the shower.

Aubrey sent her a glance. "Where did Bessie die?"

"This way," Stella said, cocking her head to the right. "Where did you park?"

"Same way," came her quick reply.

As they walked side by side, Stella's unease slowly unfurled, and once her car was in sight, she squinted at it.

The lights were on. But everything had been dead when she left it.

She stopped in her tracks, her heart leaping in her throat, when she realized the car purred softly, the motor running.

"I thought you said your car died," Aubrey said, pausing beside her.

"It did."

"It looks like it's alive now."

"It does." Stella kept walking toward it.

It wasn't an apparition. It looked as if her car had fixed itself. She stood there staring at it for long minutes. "I don't understand this." The key wasn't even in the ignition. It was in her purse.

"What's there to understand? Now you don't have to call a tow truck and now you won't have a repair bill to pay."

Stella blinked. "I guess." But could she trust Bessie after this? Maybe it would be a good idea to get a mechanic to check it over anyway. Maybe Zack would take a look? She knew he was handy with cars.

"Okay, I'll follow you home just in case it acts up again," Aubrey said, jogging to her blue Civic farther down the street.

"Good thinking," Stella agreed, unlocking her door. The car kept running, purring, like it normally did. Was her baby turning into a high-maintenance vehicle because of its age?

Sinking into the comfort of her bucket seat, she closed the door and put her key in the ignition just to be safe.

This had been one weird day. And she was used to weird days, so that said a lot. She touched the pendant at her heart, liking the zing it gave her fingertips.

She closed her eyes and exhaled one slow breath. *Things are going to be okay, even if I should consider renaming Bessie to Veronica.*

Thank You for Reading!

If you liked GHOST OF GAMBLE, I would absolutely love it if you would leave a review at your favorite retailer.

Not ready for this story to end?
The Wickwood Chronicles continue in
GHOST OF AN ENCHANTMENT.
https://books2read.com/u/mZ2ZRe

Do you want to find out how it all began?
Read Grace and Sam's story, GHOST OF A BEGINNING,
for free when you sign up for my reader updates!
https://dl.bookfunnel.com/v5bvza013c

All of J.E.'s books can be found at:
https://books2read.com/jemcdonald

GHOST OF A GAMBLE PLAYLIST

These are the songs I listened to while writing this book.

1. Sure by Smerz (Okey)

2. Infin Path by Neggy Gemmy (Bad Boy)

3. Higher Ground-pluko Remix by ODESZA, Naomi Wild, pluko (Higher Ground Remix)

4. Floating (feat. Khalid) by Alina Baraz, Khalid(The Color Of You)

5. Fallin by Alina Baraz (The Color Of You)

6. GOODMORNING, Goodbye by FRENSHIP (GOODMORNING, Goodbye)

7. Lucy by Still Woozy, ODIE (Lucy)

8. jump by gabriel black, Sofi de la Torre (jump)

9. Pretty Thing by Dizzy (Pretty Thing)

10. At Least The Sky Is Blue (Johnny Jewel's Moody Midnight Remix) by Ssion, Johnny Jewel, Ariel Pink (At Least The Sky Is Blue Remix)

11. Alkaline by Thandie (Alkaline)

12. Let Slide – Blue Motel Remix by Kauf, Blue Motel(Let Slide Blue Motel Remix)

13. How Can He Be by Matty (How Can He Be)

14. High by Alina Baraz (The Color Of You)

15. France (Grands Boulevards) by Yumi Zouma (France Grand Boulevards)

16. On The Low by Tove Styrke (On The Low)

17. Whispering Wind (B-Sides) by Moby (Play &Play: The B Sides)

18. Inside by Moby (Play & Play: The B Sides)

19. Same Old Song (S.O.S Part I) by Two Feet (Same Old Song S.O.S Part I)

20. Sheet Forts ft. OmenXIII (prod. Oil color) by VELVETEARS, OmenXIII (Hikikomori)

21. Apocalypse by Cigarettes After Sex (Cigarettes After Sex)

22. indie film lovers by Onyx Deimos, kerri (indie film lovers)

23. A River (Jabs Remix) by J. Views (401.1)

24. Blood and Bones by TRACE (Blood and Bones)

25. Gold (JNTHN STEIN) by Cabu, JNTHN STEIN, Akacia(Gold Remixes)

26. Romanticise by Chela (Majestic Casual – Chapter 2)

27. Groundswell by Methyl Ethyl (Everything is Forgotten)

28. Dreaming by Yomaez, Water Park (Dreaming)

29. My Body by lemin. (My Body)

30. Cut Them Loose by Maths Time Joy, Ayelle (Sunset Motel)

31. Falling Into Me by Let's Eat Grandma (Falling Into Me)

32. Bite The Hand by Julien Baker, Phoebe Bridgers, Lucy Dacus, boy genius (Bite The Hand)

33. Sour Breath by Julien Baker

34. Hymn by Rhye (Hymn)

35. Runnin by EREZ (Runnin)

36. Too Much – LEISURE Remix by Tora, LEISURE (Too Much LEISURE Remix)

37. Runaway by Sasha Alex Sloan

38. Take It All by Helena Deland

39. Forever's Gone by DRAMA (Gallows)

40. Touch by Ghostly Kisses (Touch)

41. Ghost by The Acid (Liminal)

42. Crush by Cigarettes After Sex (Crush)

43. Too Much by Tora (Take A Rest)

44. Vale by Maribou State (Kingdoms in Colour)

ACKNOWLEDGEMENTS

There are so many people to thank who helped me get where I am today. Without you, this book wouldn't have happened.

First, thank you to my editor, Heather. If you hadn't forgiven me for accidentally ambushing you in New York, and you hadn't believed in Bree, then none of this would have happened. Thank you for your patience with a newbie, and for all your hard work to whip this manuscript into shape.

Thank you to my community of authors who've had my back throughout the thick and thin of it. This publishing thing is a wild ride, and I'm so appreciative of you all hanging onto the "oh shit" handle right along with me.

Thank you to my beta readers for this book, Bevin, Caryn, and Melodie. Without your insights, this story would not be what it is today. You are my front line of defense and I appreciate every one of you so much.

Thank you to my local writing group. We're small but feisty, and I love hanging out with all. (You know who you are!) I was so lucky to have found such a supportive group of people eight years ago. You all are the best.

Thank you to my ARC team, and the book reviewers, and bloggers who took a chance on this book. I appreciate every review so much. Thank you!

Thank you to Jessica and her lovely team at Pages of Passion bookstore in Saskatoon. Your support for indie authors and enthusiasm for romance is beautiful to see. I wish you all the success in the world.

Without the cheerleading efforts of my whole family, I wouldn't have made it this far. A BIG thank you to my mom who helps me out with the day to day, giving me extra time to write. And without you leaving

Harlequins in the bathroom when I was younger, I'm not sure I would have discovered my love for romance at such an early age. My dad is my number one fan, and declared me a bestseller before I'd sold my first book. Thanks, Dad, for your belief in me.

And thank you to my three girls for being such great little people. Your limitless energy and imagination will always be a source of inspiration. And if you're reading this before you're thirty, then put the book down because there's swearing and sex in it.

Lastly, thank you to my husband, Marcel, to whom this book is dedicated. You make time for me to write whenever I need it, and that's so damn sexy it probably counts as foreplay. Thank you for being such a great father, a supportive husband, and my best friend since our first date.

More Works by J.E. McDonald

https://books2read.com/jemcdonald

WICKWOOD CHRONICLES

Ghost of a Gamble
Ghost of an Enchantment
Ghost of a Summoning
Edge of a Shadow, Part One
Edge of a Shadow, Part Two
Ghost of a Beginning (Prequel)

GOLDENLACH RIDGE SHIFTERS

Captive Wilderness
Caged Fury
Conquered Betrayal

BLUESHIFT

Star-Crossed Captive
Star-Born Anomaly
Star-Cursed Odyssey (Prequel)

About The Author

J.E. McDonald was born and raised in Saskatchewan, Canada, The Land of the Living Skies. As a child, she was either searching the clouds for identifiable shapes, or star-gazing way past her bedtime. She's an anti-morning person who wakes up at 5am to write. Needless to say, coffee is a morning requirement. She cut her teeth watching Star Trek, James Bond movies, and reading the Harlequin novels her mother left in the bathroom—which resulted in an extremely skewed sense of sex education by age eleven. All of these factors contribute to her love of writing paranormal romance with humor, mystery, and lots of spice. J.E. resides in Saskatchewan with her husband and three daughters.

www.jemcdonald.net
Facebook: /JEMcDonaldAuthor
Instagram: /jemcdonaldsk
TikTok: @jemcdonaldsk
Threads: @jemcdonaldsk

www.ingramcontent.com/pod-product-compliance
Lightning Source LLC
Chambersburg PA
CBHW021755190726

48290CB00005B/1281